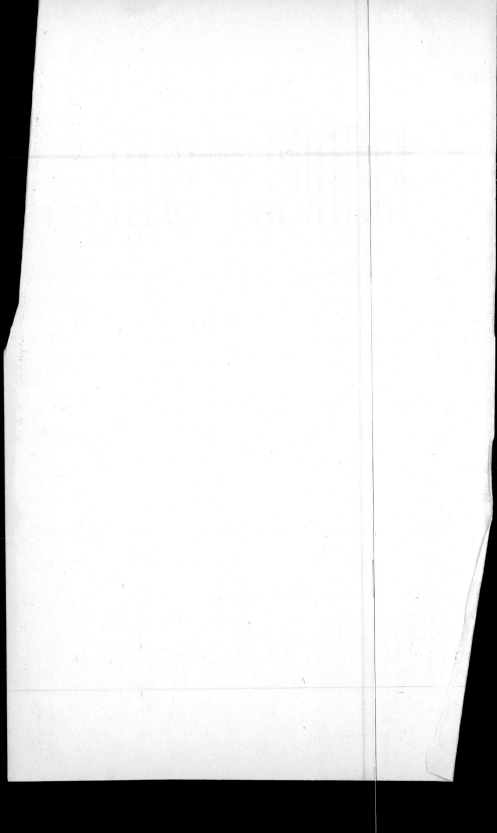

NOTHING BUT THE RENT

NOTHING BUT THE RENT

SHARON MITCHELL

A DUTTON BOOK

DUTTON
Published by the Penguin Group
Penguin Putnam Inc., 375 Hudson Street, New York, New York 10014, U.S.A.
Penguin Books Ltd, 27 Wrights Lane, London W8 5TZ, England
Penguin Books Australia Ltd, Ringwood, Victoria, Australia
Penguin Books Canada Ltd, 10 Alcorn Avenue, Toronto, Ontario, Canada M4V 3B2
Penguin Books (N.Z.) Ltd, 182–190 Wairau Road, Auckland 10, New Zealand

Penguin Books Ltd, Registered Offices:
Harmondsworth, Middlesex, England

First published by Dutton, an imprint of Dutton Signet,
a member of Penguin Putnam Inc.

 REGISTERED TRADEMARK—MARCA REGISTRADA

ISBN 0-525-94306-4

Printed in the United States of America
Set in Sabon
Designed by Leonard Telesca

PUBLISHER'S NOTE
This is a work of fiction. Names, characters, places, and incidents either are the product
of the author's imagination or are used fictitiously, and any resemblance to actual persons,
living or dead, events, or locales is entirely coincidental.

*This book is dedicated
To my friend, Frances King, who has touched my life
in a million and one ways—all of them good.*

ACKNOWLEDGMENTS

A big thank-you to my funny, crazy, inspirational, and wise friends: Michelle Reeves, Donna Brock, Karen Johnson, Erica Markum, and Kim Ewing.

To my friends at Boston University, thanks for the encouragement and reviews of the early drafts of this novel.

Lora and Allen Cornelius, thanks for knowing how to keep a secret.

To Francine Brooks, thanks for taking care of Luc while I was taking care of business.

Sharon Friedman, you are a wonderful agent, who really nurtured me through this process. Your efforts on my behalf are greatly appreciated and will not soon be forgotten.

Finally, thanks to my mother, Mrs. Bertha Mitchell. Mama, it was your love, support, and belief in a better life for me that made everything possible. You are truly amazing.

PART ONE

Always a Bridesmaid

Chapter

1

Monique's black Jetta raced along on I-94. Shortly after they crossed the Mississippi River, nostalgia and anticipation kicked in. On Gayle's right, the sun reflected off the windows of the gleaming skyscrapers in downtown Minneapolis. Wanting to take it all in, Gayle tried to turn toward the window, but the shoulder harness kept her plastered against her seat. She tugged on the strap to loosen its pressure across her chest, then continued with her appraisal of the city.

Gayle had never spent a lot of time in Minneapolis, but she was pretty sure that most of the towering glass-and-concrete buildings hadn't been there during her student days. Had it really been eight years since she'd graduated from college and last set foot in Minnesota? Why had it taken Angie's wedding to bring her back? She'd always loved the "Mini-Apple."

Gayle touched her friend's bare arm. "Monique, isn't this exciting?"

Before answering, Monique honked her horn at a Chevy Blazer that had cut in front of her without signaling. "Which part? Trying to outrun a tornado yesterday, or having those brats keep me up all night? Or, perhaps the uncontrollable thrill that will wash over me when I see Angie's obnoxious family again?"

"Oh, come on, Monique. It isn't as bad as all that," Gayle said.

Still, she'd asked herself the same question. With less than a hundred black students at their alma mater, it was next to impossible not to know every one, but Gayle hadn't realized Angie felt so close to them until she'd asked them to be in her wedding. Unlike Monique, Gayle felt honored to be one of Angie's bridesmaids.

Monique said, "I don't know why I let y'all talk me into investing time and money in someone who hasn't bothered to pick up the phone in three years."

Monique was not singing that old song again! Gayle, Roxanne, and Cynthia had spent weeks convincing her that the wedding would be like a reunion for them. Cynthia and Roxanne hadn't understood Monique's negative attitude, but Gayle had. Angie and Monique used to be roommates, and though she would never have admitted it, Monique had been hurt when Angie hadn't made much of an effort to stay in touch.

Gayle knew all too well that good friends were hard to come by. That's why she had been ecstatic when Monique had accepted a job as a prosecutor in Cleveland after finishing law school at Case Western Reserve. Not only did Gayle have a close girlfriend nearby, she had somewhere to go every once in a while when she needed a break from her family.

Monique put up a fuss whenever things didn't go her way, but eventually she saw the sense of things. Just as she had about the wedding. In the end, she'd realized that having the four of them in the same place and at the same time was an opportunity that shouldn't be missed.

They'd driven from Ohio together, and so far Monique had been in top form. When she wasn't complaining about how slow everyone else was going, Monique entertained her with stories of the criminals she dealt with. Gayle didn't know if she should laugh or be scared by some of her tales. She definitely didn't like the idea of Monique owning a gun for protection.

Then, just as they reached Madison, Wisconsin, the thunderstorm Monique had been driving in for most of the day was upgraded to a tornado warning. They spent the night at a Holiday Inn with other refugees of the storm. Unfortunately, a lot of those folks had what Monique referred to as "demonic children."

"I'm sorry the kids kept you up last night."

"What are you apologizing for?" Monique asked. "They weren't your bad-ass kids screaming and running up and down the halls all night."

Gayle shut up. Monique seemed determined to hold on to her foul mood. She had offered several times to help with the driving, but Monique had turned her down every time. Gayle was kind of glad, because the only thing worse than Monique's aggressive driving was having her as a backseat driver.

Gayle looked over Monique's perfect profile. Her long black hair had been slicked back and fashioned into a ponytail with a gold barrette. Try as she might, Monique couldn't entirely blow-dry out its natural wave. Dressed in cutoff jeans and a tank T-shirt, Monique had no idea how drop-dead gorgeous she was. But when men panted over her long, golden limbs, it only seemed to piss her off.

Gayle glanced down at her own chocolate-colored legs. They were long enough but just a little on the chunky side, in her opinion. She could only wish she had Monique's problem. Was there really such a thing as too much positive attention from men? she wondered.

"Well, your troubles will soon be over. Look," Gayle said, pointing, "there's Lake Harriet. We're almost there."

"Thank God." Soon Monique got off the highway and turned onto West Fiftieth Street. "First thing I'm gonna do when we get there is take a nap." Near the end of the block, she slowed the car down to a crawl. "It's been years . . . but I'm pretty sure it's the last house up there on the left."

Roxanne's car was parked in the driveway of a gray and white Cape Cod. "Pull in behind Roxanne," Gayle said.

"OK, but could you at least wait for me to put it in park before you hop out of the car? Who would take care of your poor sick mother if something happened to you?"

The smile disappeared from Gayle's face. "Don't joke about my mother's health."

"SORRY!"

Gayle moved away from the car and slowly walked over to the stairs leading to the front porch. She already felt guilty about leaving her mother alone with only her irresponsible kid brother to look after her. Monique was trying to be funny, but she really could be insensitive at times. She had a lot to learn about family responsibility.

Roxanne came out the front door of the house, petite and curvy as ever.

"Hey, y'all," she called out.

"Hey, yourself, Shorty," Monique replied.

Roxanne bounded down the steps and wrapped her arms around Monique. "Who you calling Shorty, Goliath?"

Gayle laughed when Monique quickly stepped out of Roxanne's embrace as if she had an infectious disease. "Where's my hug?" Gayle said.

"For you, a hug and a kiss," Roxanne said, briefly placing her lips against Gayle's cheek. Then she had to rub off the lipstick mark she'd left. She looked from Monique to Gayle. "Damn, y'all look good."

"Well, Monique always looks good, but you need to get your prescription checked," Gayle said. "Look at me. I'm all sweaty and my shorts are stuck to my butt and everything."

Roxanne put her hands on her hips, then swiveled them. "Child, please, you know my motto. If you got it, flaunt it." She threw back her head and laughed. Roxanne's joyous laughter was like a tonic. Gayle's own natural reserve generally started to thaw within minutes of being around her.

Gayle's eyes were full of love and admiration as she took in her friend. Roxanne's tie-dyed T-shirt was tight-fitting and had a streak of powder blue in it that matched the blue in her shorts. Her arms and legs were toned yet womanly-looking at the same time. She wasn't really pretty. Her skin wasn't smooth, and she had a little space between her two front teeth. But she had something that appealed to everybody, and not just Gayle. It was her energy. Her zest for life drew people to her. Men, kids, even animals were attracted to Roxanne.

Monique looked Roxanne over herself, then said, "You look

all right, but you ain't all that. And I see you still got those twigs in your hair."

"Dreads, not twigs."

"Whatever. You still look like Medusa's kid sister to me." Monique walked to the rear of the car and popped the trunk.

As she reached for a suitcase, Roxanne said, "I wouldn't do that if I were you."

Monique looked up, puzzled. "Wouldn't do what?"

"Take your suitcases out."

"Why not?"

"We gotta pick Cynthia up from the airport."

"You mean she's not already here?"

"Oh, she's here all right. She just called. Says she's been at the airport for an hour. Angie forgot to get someone to pick her up, and she can't do it herself. She still has to get her dress beaded, and then she has to stop by the florist's to make sure enough corsages will be made."

"Well, I'm sorry she's got problems. But you and Gayle can fetch Cyn. I'm taking a nap."

Roxanne shook her head. "I don't think so. First of all, it's a zoo in there—wall-to-wall relatives, and we know how much you love Angie's family. Secondly, we ain't staying here. We're staying with one of Angie's aunts."

Monique slammed the trunk down. Directing accusing eyes at Gayle, she said, "I knew I should have stayed my ass in Cleveland."

Gayle pushed Cynthia's Louis Vuitton garment bag away from her face. It kept shifting from its place on the hook above the car door. She was also finding the backseat of Monique's car a lot less spacious than it was up front. "Monique, would you turn on the air? It's getting a little hot back here."

"The air is on. It's not my fault Cyn packed enough for an around-the-world cruise. It's her shit that's blocking all the air."

Cynthia, who was touching up her makeup, paused. Her blue eyes showed surprise. "What? I barely brought enough for three days. I have something to wear each day, and then after my evening shower I need something to change into. I can't put the same funky clothes back on, can I?"

Monique was already frowning as Cynthia droned on. ". . . Then I brought a couple of outfits in case we go clubbing, but those are just party dresses. They hardly take up any room at all. Of course, I needed a dress for the rehearsal dinner and a nice pantsuit to wear back on the plane. . . ." She sucked in her pale cheeks and then swiped blush across each one. " 'Cause, girl, you never know who you might meet on a plane."

"What's that trunk sitting on your lap?" Monique asked.

Cynthia took one more look in the mirror, then closed her compact. She patted the pink case perched on her knees. "What, this little old thing? This is just my cosmetic case."

"Give me a break," Monique scoffed. "Except for that ugly bridesmaid's dress, everything I brought for the weekend could probably fit in that case."

Cynthia laughed and reached around to pat her garment bag. "That's the ugliest thing I brought. Plus, those black dresses will be drawing some serious heat."

Monique nodded her head. "Now you're talking sense. I told Gayle one of us is going to pass out."

Cynthia said, tracing her lips in coral, "What was Angie thinking? Black bridesmaids' dresses in the summer, for God's sake!"

From the backseat, Roxanne said, "Now, y'all, we gotta be nice to Angie. This wedding is stressing her to the max. I only talked to her for a few minutes, but she was in a panic. A couple of the groomsmen canceled at the last minute."

Cynthia snapped open the locks and deposited the compact and lipstick in the case. She had to stuff down its contents several times before it would close properly. "How rude! It's a wedding, not a housewarming party. You don't just cancel, especially when you're in the wedding."

Monique said, "You know, I think I might be able to help Angie out."

Gayle turned toward her. "How?"

"Well, if she has too many bridesmaids, I'd be more than

willing to bow out. I could get a hotel room. Better yet, I could skip the wedding altogether. Y'all could stop by after the wedding and we could chill. Maybe go shopping, meet for dinner, have a few drinks, party a little later on?"

Gayle stared at her in amazement. Monique meant every word she had just said.

Cynthia placed a hand against her heart and snapped her neck back. "No way," she said. "A lot of people from school will be in town. What if someone spots us gallivanting around Minneapolis? How are we going to explain why Monique's in town but not at the wedding?"

"OK, I'll do it. I wouldn't want to ruin *your* good reputation by not being in Angie's funky old wedding," Monique said. "But that dress has got to go. It's made of some kind of acetate material, has puffed long sleeves and a big bow across the butt. We're going to look like Cinderella's ugly stepsisters—"

Gayle and Roxanne laughed from in back.

"Angie must by crazy. It's the middle of August; a time of year when the humidity and those famous mutant Minnesota mosquitoes are at their worst."

Cynthia put her hands over her ears. "Stop, Monique! You're scaring me."

"Look at it this way," Gayle said, laughing. "Although the long sleeves ain't going to help you with the heat, they might deter the mosquitoes."

Cynthia said, "I just hope Angie appreciates all the sacrifice we're going to for her. I mean, really, I sat at that stupid airport for two hours."

"You could have taken a cab," Monique pointed out.

"Yeah, I could have, but by the time I figured out Angie had forgotten all about me and called to let her know I was here, Roxanne said she'd come pick me up."

"Oh really?" Monique said, arching an eyebrow. "Roxanne, how come this is the first I heard about *you* volunteering to pick up Cyn?"

Roxanne shrugged her shoulders. "I could have driven, but then I'd have to listen to you giving directions all the way there and back. Thought I'd skip the aggravation."

"Well, just so you know, I ain't no chauffeur," Monique said.

"Monique, you act like you're the only one who has things to do," Roxanne said. "Have you forgotten that after I drive back to St. Louis on Sunday, I gotta fly to Boston, find a new place to live, then I got to pick my shit up and move clear across the country? Girl, please. I figured a fifteen-minute drive to the airport wasn't gonna kill you."

Tired of fighting with it, Gayle took the garment bag off the hook and draped it across her lap. Meanwhile, Monique continued to argue with Roxanne. "If it was only fifteen minutes . . ."

Gayle smiled. It was just like old times.

Chapter

2

Cynthia trudged along, her larger suitcase bumping against her knee. And her shoulder was starting to hurt. The duplex that Angie's aunt lived in didn't have a driveway, so Monique had to park halfway down the block. Even with Roxanne carrying one of her bags, she still had a heavy load.

Actually, she'd told her friends a little white lie about packing only the bare necessities. But it wasn't her fault. She'd been stuck at the office late every night this week. With only a couple of hours to pack, she'd been forced to fill her suitcase with anything she thought she might need. Maybe she *had* thrown in a couple extra outfits that she probably wouldn't wear. But she had no choice. Lately, she could never tell if she'd like how something looked on her until she actually tried it on, and she simply hadn't had the time.

Cynthia also barely had time to take in her current surroundings. For an old lady, Angie's aunt was moving at a pretty good clip as she led them to their rooms. From the little she did see of the house, dreary was the word that came to mind. No, make that old and dreary. The furniture looked like it had been bought decades ago. It wasn't raggedy, just old and outdated. Nobody put slipcovers on their furniture anymore. The place smelled of mothballs. And why didn't the woman turn on a light or two? Was she trying to save on the electric bill? At the very least, she could pull up a window shade and let some sunshine in.

No, she was *not* happy about this. It wasn't like she was expecting the Ritz-Carlton, but a little ambiance would have been nice.

They followed gray-haired Aunt Louise—she insisted that they call her that—down a narrow hallway. "You girls will be staying in this here room," Angie's aunt said. She flicked on the light switch as she entered the bedroom.

It was a tight fit to get all five of them into the tiny space. A small homemade lace doily covered a nightstand that separated two twin-size beds. It was hard to tell with all of them packed into the room, but Cynthia really didn't see any other furniture unless the small window fan that was pushing out warm air counted.

Cynthia didn't bother to mask her horrified expression. If she hadn't been tired of lugging her bags all over town, she might have taken up Monique's earlier suggestion that they get a hotel room somewhere.

Aunt Louise reached into her apron pocket and brought out a key. "This is to the front door so you can let yourselves in and out."

Gayle took the key and thanked her.

Aunt Louise folded her arms over her huge bosom and shook her head. "Don't thank me. I'm doing this for my niece. Normally, I put the chain on the door at nine, but I'll leave it off until ten this weekend. I know you girls will probably be out late."

"Ten is late?" Cynthia mouthed behind the old lady's back.

"Now I'm going to finish watching my program. Make yourselves at home. . . . But I don't want no sinning going on under my roof, because this is a good Christian home."

"Yes, ma'am," Gayle said.

Aunt Louise firmly closed the door on her way out.

Monique immediately plopped down on the bed, her long legs dangling over the edge. "Damn," she said. "There goes our plan for nonstop partying. I could kill Angie for sticking us with this religious nut."

"Not a religious nut," Gayle teased, sitting down beside her. "A good Christian!"

"Like we couldn't figure that out," Roxanne said. "Did you see all those open Bibles? I think I even saw one when we passed by the bathroom."

Cynthia was still standing in the middle of the room, surrounded by a mountain of suitcases. The matching lime green sleeveless vest and pants she wore were a little tight across the middle and in the hips and were more than a little wrinkled from a day of traveling.

"What's the matter, Cyn? You look like you're in shock. Not going to be able to stand a fundamentalist Christian for a few days?" Gayle asked.

Cynthia shook her head. She took just one step before stumbling over one of her bags. "No, girl, that ain't it. You know, I go to church every Sunday. Not just on Easter and Christmas like some people," she said, giving Monique a pointed look. She kicked the bags out of her way and sat on the other bed. It groaned and creaked in protest. "It's this room. How are we all supposed to *survive* in this room? And it doesn't even have air-conditioning."

"Cyn, it might come as a shock to you, but not everyone has air-conditioning. My parents' house doesn't have air-conditioning, and we all manage just fine," Gayle said.

Cynthia picked up a Bible from the nightstand and opened it up. "Proverbs," she said, and started fanning her face with it. "I'm going to melt up in here."

Roxanne sighed. "What are you, milk chocolate?"

"More like white chocolate," Monique said from her prone position.

Cynthia didn't know why Monique was always teasing her about her light complexion when she was only a few shades darker herself. "Go ahead, laugh if you want. But when I get overheated I throw up. We'll see how funny it is then," Cynthia said. She undid the button on her pants and eased the zipper down, then began fanning down there.

"Damn, Cyn," Roxanne said, "I know Aunt Louise told us to make ourselves at home, but really . . . don't nobody want to see you fanning your stuff. And with a Bible, too. Isn't that blasphemous?"

"I'm hot and these pants are a little too tight. I think they shrank the last time I took them to the dry cleaners."

Monique rolled over and then eyed Cynthia's fleshy stomach pressing against the zipper of her pants. "Yeah, it must have been the dry cleaners."

"What are you trying to say?" Cynthia said. It was fine for Monique to talk. Not everyone was blessed with natural thinness. Monique might try putting herself in someone else's shoes every once in a while. She didn't work nine to five like Monique did. Cynthia's public relations job demanded a lot of her time. She didn't always get to eat or exercise properly.

Gayle cut in before an argument got started. "She's not trying to say anything. I say we unpack our stuff and freshen up before Angie gets here with her fiancé."

"OK." Cynthia put the Bible back on the nightstand. "But I still don't know how we are supposed to sleep in here. It's too damn hot. And those beds are too small for two people to fit in them."

Gayle said, "Floor or bed, I don't care as long as I have a clear path to the bathroom."

Without consulting her friends, Cynthia claimed one of the beds for herself.

Monique turned to Roxanne. "I'll flip you for the other bed." Like magic, a quarter appeared, but Monique lost. "Two out of three?" she said.

"No way."

"But I've been driving since yesterday," Monique said.

"Like I haven't? How do you think I got here from St. Louis? By flapping my wings?"

Having no comeback, Monique said, "So, what do you think Angie's fiancé will be like?"

Cynthia stopped unbuttoning her vest. "Child, I can't even imagine. Angie can be so obnoxious. It's probably some little nerdy guy she can boss around."

"Angie's not that bad," Gayle said. "You make her sound like a dominatrix."

"Now, I didn't say she was gonna beat that man with whips and chains. But Angie is big, broad-shouldered, and stocky.

She has that booming voice, and worst of all, she is always laughing at stuff that ain't funny. That laugh of hers sounds like a bullhorn," Cynthia said.

The vest had come off. Cynthia frowned at the red stretch marks along her sides—maybe laser surgery would help—and the roll or two of extra skin at her waistline. She quickly draped the vest over her lower belly.

Gayle said, "Angie is all right. Can you name one mean thing she's ever done to you?"

While Cynthia thought about that, Monique said, "We never said she was mean. But she is irritating. Angie insists on debating subjects that she knows nothing about. Then she gets pissed if you didn't see things her way."

"Yeah," Roxanne said. "I don't know how the two of you managed to live together for a whole year, considering how neither one of you can stand being wrong."

Gayle and Cynthia laughed.

Monique rolled her eyes at Roxanne. "Like I was saying, when Angie wasn't debating, she was talking about her precious family. And we've all met her mother and her Neanderthal brothers on more than one occasion. For the life of me, I don't know what there is to brag about—"

"Shush!" Gayle said. She walked over to the door and peeked out. There was no one there, so she closed it again. "I thought I heard something."

"I'm sure Aunt Louise is in the kitchen watching a gospel show and frying up some chicken," Monique said dryly. "Don't worry. She doesn't seem interested in being anywhere near us."

Gayle came back over to the bed. "Still, y'all better watch your mouth. She is Angie's family, remember."

Suddenly, Cynthia's eyes lit up. "Talk a little louder, Monique. Maybe Aunt Louise will hear you and kick us out. A nice spacious, air-conditioned hotel room may be in our future after all."

"I need a cigarette," Monique said. "Do you think Aunt Louise would mind?"

"Yes!" her friends all said in unison.

Despite Gayle's warning, Cynthia continued to speculate about Angie and her fiancé. "OK, just tell me this. What kind of name is Arnel? Sounds pretty ghetto to me. And I'm sorry, but can anyone explain how someone on the wrong side of mediocre can find a husband, hell, a steady boyfriend, before any of us? Mark my words, the man is a nerd, blind, or both."

A half hour later, Cynthia thought she would drop dead on the spot when Angie showed up with a man who was extremely attractive in both personality and appearance. All four of them barely responded to the enthusiastic hugs and kisses Angie bestowed upon them. They were too busy staring at Arnel. Dressed in a pair of cowboy boots, tight-fitting jeans, and a cotton shirt with the sleeves ripped off, this guy was nowhere close to being a nerd.

Without taking her eyes off him, Cynthia sat down on the couch, almost crushing Roxanne, who quickly scooted over to make room for her. Arnel sat down in the chair across from them and rested his hands on his knees.

"I want to thank you for coming all this way. I'm sure you have very busy lives. But I just want you to know it really means a lot to Angie," he said.

"No thanks necessary," Gayle quickly assured him.

"I drove through a tornado to get here," Monique said. It was a statement that could be interpreted several ways.

Arnel smiled at Monique, his light brown eyes crinkling at the corners. "From what Angie's told me about your driving, the tornado had more to be afraid of than you did."

While the others laughed, Cynthia stared at Arnel's teeth. They were almost too perfect. Somebody had spent a pretty penny on braces.

"Uh-oh, now I'm scared," Roxanne said. "What else has Angie been telling you about us?"

"Nothing but good things," Arnel said as he played with one of Angie's hands—she was sitting on the edge of his chair. "Wait, there was that time she asked one of you—I think it was you, Roxanne—to trim her hair."

Roxanne groaned, then covered her face in her hands. "What can I say? The scissors slipped. . . ."

"Four inches?" he asked. "That's a whole lot of slipping."

Anyone listening to him make jokes and tease them would have assumed that he'd known them for years. He even managed to charm Aunt Louise by talking about singing in his church choir. All the while, he held Angie's hand and kept giving her affectionate smiles as she reminisced about their college days.

Cynthia, who was sitting next to Gayle, said under her breath, "She's remembering a hell of a lot more good times than I do. Must be those rose-colored glasses she was always wearing."

Gayle smiled, and through her teeth said, "Be nice."

Cynthia wanted to be nice. Staring at the man went against all the good manners her mother had instilled in her. But she couldn't figure out what he saw in Angie that was so appealing. How had this happened? Where the hell had Angie, of all people, come up with this wonderful man? Would it be a crime if she grabbed Angie by the throat and shook her until she explained how she had managed to pull this off?

Cynthia caught herself. She couldn't be the only one among her friends feeling this way. They were probably just better at hiding their jealousy. Monique, though, was examining Arnel like he was a lab specimen. Cynthia knew she was trying to detect some personality flaw. But except for being head over heels in love with Angie, the man seemed perfectly normal. Maybe he'd use the wrong fork or slurp his food at dinner. A girl had to have hope. . . .

Arnel continued to be the perfect gentleman through dinner. Cynthia was grateful for the interruption when the doorbell rang. It gave her time to choke down a couple of bites of food. She'd been too absorbed with Arnel's every gesture to bother with eating.

The best man and his girlfriend were joining them for dessert. When Aunt Louise ushered them into the room, Arnel got up from the table to hug his friend—a manly hug that was more of a back-thumping than an embrace but warmer and more affectionate than a handshake.

After kissing his friend's girlfriend on the cheek, Arnel introduced them, "This is Keith, my oldest homie, and this is his girlfriend, Vicki." Everyone said their hellos and Angie offered Keith her seat so that he could sit across from Arnel.

Gayle picked up the nearest empty dish. "Aunt Louise, let me help you clear the table and wash the dishes."

Aunt Louise took the plate out of Gayle's hands. "I don't want nobody messing around in my kitchen, putting everything in the wrong place." She loudly began stacking plates herself. Off toward the kitchen she marched, the tails of her apron strings dangling against her wide behind.

An awkward silence followed.

Angie said, "You have to excuse my aunt. She's not used to having so many people in the house at once."

"I bet," Cynthia muttered under her breath.

"Let's eat dessert in the sitting room," Angie said.

Angie volunteered to enter the sanctuary of Aunt Louise's kitchen to help bring in the dessert. The rest of them moved into the sitting room. Its well-kept furniture was probably older than all of them. The green paisley upholstery of the sofa and love seat had started to fade a little, but the plastic slipcovers had undoubtedly helped slow down the aging process. The room was dimly lit by two old-fashioned brass lamps with white lampshades that had also been covered in plastic to keep the dust off. A framed picture of Jesus with his hands clasped in prayer and his eyes aimed heavenward was illuminated by a small built-in light. Cynthia felt like she'd stumbled into some kind of early seventies time warp. Maybe she would get Aunt Louise a subscription to *Better Homes and Gardens* as a thank-you present.

Angie and Aunt Louise came in with dessert. Lucky for them, Aunt Louise's sourness didn't extend to her cooking. During dinner, Cynthia's envy had robbed her of her appetite. She hadn't been able to fully appreciate the smothered pork chops, cabbage, corn on the cob, and corn bread. But the sight of the hot peach cobbler topped off with vanilla ice cream had all their mouths watering.

Conversation halted. All that could be heard was the sound of silverware touching china as they concentrated on polishing off the delicious dessert.

Cynthia had tried to strike up a conversation with Keith's girlfriend while the men were talking. But it was difficult to get a read on Vicki because she hadn't said much. She seemed content to listen to Keith tell childhood stories about him beating up various people.

Vicki was sporting this huge diamond on her left-hand ring finger, which she was more than happy to hold out for them to inspect. It must have cost a fortune because when Cynthia, who knew a little bit about jewelry, sized it up, what little color she did have drained out of her face.

No one protested when Angie suggested they call it a night.

They had barely closed the bedroom door when Cynthia started venting all the thoughts she'd kept under wraps all evening. "Vicki shows up with a big rock on her finger, plus a man, yet not one of us could round up an escort for this wedding," she complained.

Monique was convinced that Keith was a shady character. "What does he need a cell phone for? He works in Phoenix, Arizona! And how much are they paying shoe salesmen these days that he can afford a rock like the one Vicki was wearing? And he seemed to know an awful lot about the law. In my experience, the only people well versed in law are lawyers and criminals."

Cynthia didn't care how Keith made his money. At least he thought enough of Vicki to buy her that gorgeous ring. And then there was Arnel. He was so captivated by Angie—of all people—he hadn't been able to keep his hands to himself. She wondered, Can a person literally die of envy? If so, I don't think I'm going to make it through the weekend.

Chapter

3

They heard Mrs. Cooke exclaim, "Angie, why did I bother spending all that money on Jenny Craig if you gonna turn right back around and regain the weight?"

"But, Ma, the dress fits perfectly," Angie said.

"Perfectly? Only because the dressmaker had to let it out. You looked so beautiful before. Now look at you. Who wants to see an overweight bride?"

Monique drummed her fingers along the armrest of Angie's mother's couch. She was tired and not at all prepared for a day of family disputes. "Why do people have to show their behinds during major life events like weddings, divorces, graduations, and funerals?"

Roxanne, who was flipping through one of the Cooke family photo albums, said, "You'd think Mrs. Cooke would cut her some slack with company in the house. And the wedding's less than twenty-four hours away. Besides, anybody who knows Angie knows she is big-boned. Why should she look any different on her wedding day?"

Actually, Angie looked like she could play defensive tackle for the Minnesota Vikings, but Monique decided not to point that out.

Angie said something to her mother, but Monique couldn't make it out. They were in the living room and the other conversation was taking place in the downstairs bedroom.

Monique looked at her watch. It was ridiculous that they'd been sitting here for almost a half hour.

"How embarrassing for Angie," Cynthia said, showing compassion for someone other than herself for the first time since arriving in Minneapolis. "I can't imagine my mother acting like that. Especially not on the day before my wedding."

"Me either," Roxanne said.

"Well, I can imagine it. My mother is always sticking her two cents in," Monique said. "But I wouldn't just stand there and take it like Angie. I'd tell her where she could go."

Gloria tried her damnedest to run Monique's life, but she wasn't having it. Her mother's tentacles were far-reaching, but even they couldn't stretch from Houston to Cleveland. Despite the thousand or so miles that separated them, Gloria had tried to use her "connections" in Cleveland to make sure that Monique was mixing with the "right crowd." And thank God for the genius who created Caller ID. The device had spared her from being pressured to attend countless receptions, banquets, and fund-raisers. If Angie was smart, she'd buy herself one, or better yet, she should get as far away from her mother's constant criticism as she possibly could.

Mrs. Cooke was the first to emerge from the back bedroom. She was a big woman, tall and stout, no waistline to speak of—a box body. Angie would look just like her in twenty years.

Indifferent to what they might or might not have overheard, she walked over to the bar and poured herself a rum and coke. She took a huge swallow and said, "I really wanted this to be a family wedding. Angie has plenty of relatives to stand up for her. I don't know what possessed her to bring in a bunch of strangers."

Monique immediately decided that Aunt Louise had to be a relative on the mother's side. The rudeness and bitchiness was hereditary. She also had to bite her tongue to keep from setting the record straight. Angie begged *them* to be in her wedding, not the other way around. It's not like they were dying to wear an ugly dress and spend money they didn't have to finance this trip.

Mrs. Cooke took another gulp. The polyester caftan she was wearing swished as she walked over to where they were sitting. She looked each of them in the eye, then asked them what they thought of Arnel.

Gayle quickly said, "Arnel seems very nice. He's friendly and he really seems to love Angie—"

"Love?" Mrs. Cooke snorted. "Love?" she repeated. "What's love got to do with it?" She started to pace about the room. "So Arnel *loves* my daughter," she said, emphasizing the word "loves." "My Angie could have done a lot better than that boy."

If Monique bit her tongue any harder, she'd chop it in two. What planet was the woman living on? From where she was sitting, Angie was the lucky one.

"I didn't sacrifice, scrimp, and save to send her to college so that she could marry some computer programmer at an insurance company."

Had the woman forgotten that Angie was an employee at the same worthless company? Monique wondered.

"What kind of future does he have?" she asked. "He'll still be making the same money ten years from now." She finished off her drink but kept the empty glass in her hand. "No, Angie should have held out for somebody better than Arnel," she said bitterly. "Love?" she muttered to herself as she left the room. "That's a laugh." Soon they could hear drawers being opened, then slammed in the kitchen.

No one said a word. Monique felt like they'd just been roughed up by a first-rate boxer. What had they gotten themselves into? First, the woman insults them; then she shares her distorted version of the truth.

Gayle glanced a couple of times in the direction of the bedroom door. Monique wondered how long it would take before she went in to check on Angie. But Angie came out of the room before Gayle got the chance.

From the salty streaks on her cheeks, it was obvious she'd been crying. She sat on the couch, hugged a pillow, and started crying again. Monique looked on in disgust; the girl really ought to pull herself together. So her mother had called her fat. It probably wasn't the first time and probably wouldn't be the last. Angie had always been so thick-skinned around them, and Monique knew for a fact that during some of their heated arguments, she'd called Angie worse names than "fat."

Gayle moved closer to her, and Angie let go of the pillow and started crying on her shoulder.

"The wedding is a mess. My mom hates every decision I've made. One of my aunts is mad at me because I picked the little girl next door to be the flower girl instead of my cousin . . . but YaKida is twelve. She's got breasts and everything. She's too old be a flower girl. Right?"

Gayle nodded her head in agreement and made soothing noises. Eventually, Angie stopped crying and only gave an occasional hiccup or two.

While Angie was carrying on, Monique had walked over to the bar and poured herself a gin and tonic. "Want one?" she asked.

Gayle shook her head. Her eyes implored Monique to come over and say something to comfort Angie. Monique looked away, then added a little more gin to her glass. She was sure Angie didn't want to know what she thought of the whole situation.

In between hiccups, Angie said, "Then two of my groomsmen canceled at the last minute—well, not exactly canceled. One was a friend of Arnel's who lives in Denver, and the other was his brother out in San Diego. The wedding was only a week away, and they never sent a check to rent the tuxes. Finally, I made Arnel call them." Angie sat up. Seeing the wet patch on Gayle's shirt, she said, "Sorry. . . ."

"It'll dry," Gayle said.

Yeah, buddy, Monique thought as she eyed the wet patch. It would dry all right—and leave a big fat salt stain.

". . . That's when they told him they weren't going to be able to make the wedding. . . ." Angie's story ended in a wail.

Irritated, Monique frowned, then reached for her drink. "Angie, please don't start bawling again," she said.

Angie sniffed. "I . . . I can't help it. This week has really sucked. I only had a few days to find replacements. Two of my cousins said they'd do it, but they're mad at me for not asking them in the first place. So they told me I have to pay for their tuxes. Then today my mother all but called me a fat cow."

Gayle patted Angie's shoulder and told her, "Arnel is a great guy. If he's happy with the way you look, then there isn't a problem. The most important thing is that the two of you are happy with each other, and if other people don't like it, that's just too darn bad."

Cynthia chimed in, "That's right. Men like women with a little meat on their bones. At least that's what my mama's always told me."

Angie hiccuped and nodded her head.

Mrs. Cooke came back into the room at that point. Completely ignoring Angie, she said, "Y'all drove here from Louise's, right?"

Monique nodded, wondering where this was leading.

"Good. I need you to run some errands for me. I'd do them myself, but if I let Angie take care of the details around here, this wedding is going to go down in flames like a marshmallow at a bonfire."

Apparently, she had decided that if she had to tolerate their unwelcome presence, the least they could do was make themselves useful. Roxanne, Monique, and Cynthia found themselves running all over town to pick up relatives at the airport, grocery-shop, and stop by the drugstore to buy aspirin and a pair of queen-size No Nonsense panty hose. Gayle was left behind to make sure Angie survived her mother's "helpful" behavior.

By the time they'd finished their errands and come back to get Gayle, they were hot and sweaty. They wanted to stop by Aunt Louise's to shower and change out of their sticky clothes, but Angie said there wasn't time. So, funky and all, they headed over to the church for the rehearsal.

The rest of the wedding party met them there. Monique thought it was strange that they had never met or even heard of Celeste, the maid of honor. When they were in school, they usually talked about good friends back home, but none of them could recall Angie talking about a friend named Celeste. And besides, they had stayed at Angie's a few times since she lived right in the Twin Cities, and they had never met anybody named Celeste.

When Monique thought about it, the only *friends* Angie ever talked about were relatives. Her two hulking brothers, the shortest one being six two, her cousins, and Keith made up the rest of the bridal party. Then there was the ring bearer and the controversial choice for flower girl.

The rehearsal itself was pretty quick, except for one skirmish with the church's wedding coordinator. She insisted that Angie use a stand-in to walk down the aisle for her because it was bad luck to do otherwise. Angie wanted to do it herself and told the woman she didn't know what she was talking about.

Standing in the rear of the church behind the last row of pews, Cynthia said to Monique, "Angie must reserve her antagonistic side for non-family members only."

Both Roxanne and Gayle begged Angie to let the woman do her job.

Angie finally relented.

With the rehearsal over, again they wanted to shower and change, but Mrs. Cooke said they had to be at the restaurant for the rehearsal dinner by seven-thirty and it was almost seven now. Angie assured them that sundresses and shorts would be fine. Rather than give them directions, Mrs. Cooke insisted that they follow her to the restaurant.

Monique drove. Since Angie hadn't even given them the name of the restaurant, they were left at her mother's mercy. "Do you think this woman is deriving sadistic pleasure out of taking us all over east Jesus before she feeds us?"

"I'm starving!" Roxanne complained.

Coming from anyone else, the complaint might have meant something. But Roxanne was always hungry. Monique ignored her and focused on keeping up with Mrs. Cooke. The woman was zooming through yellow lights almost as if she wanted to lose them.

After about forty-five minutes, Mrs. Cooke finally pulled up to a hamburger joint. Clearly, they were lost.

Monique got out of the car to see what the problem was. A few minutes later, she climbed back into the driver's seat.

"Well?" Roxanne said.

"Well," Monique said, "this is it."

Cynthia was confused. "What do you mean, this is it?"

"I mean, this is where the rehearsal dinner is."

Cynthia stuck her head between the driver's and front passenger seats. "You've got to be kidding," she said.

"Do you see me cracking a smile?" Monique said. "Let's go."

It was Monique's bad luck to be seated next to Cynthia during the meal. She had to listen to her every complaint about the no-frills rehearsal dinner. And when she thought no one was looking—but Monique was—Cynthia spit her hamburger into a paper napkin.

"Yuck! What is this mystery meat?" Cynthia suspiciously inspected her greasy red plastic cup before taking a sip of Coke. "We had to drive all over town for this?"

As words like "déclassé" and "proper wedding etiquette" tumbled from Cynthia's affronted lips, Monique was struck by the irony. Cyn's "bougie" attitude would have made her the perfect daughter for her own mother. As one of Houston's premier hostesses, Gloria would rather have lost her coveted position as president of the Women's Guild than set foot in a place like this. Monique, on the other hand, could care less about where the rehearsal dinner was held. As long as she didn't see any roaches or rats strolling around like they owned the place, she was fine.

Just imagining her mother's appalled expression at the insane suggestion of having a rehearsal dinner at a hamburger joint brought the first smile Monique had been able to muster all day. She took another bite of her sandwich and chased it with a bit of ginger ale. A cold beer would have been better, but Monique didn't mind. Suddenly, the food had started to taste a lot better.

Doing her rounds as hostess, Angie stopped near their end

of the table. She smiled down at them. "Are we having fun yet?"

A vision of Gloria dropping into a dead faint at her feet as the members of her wedding party dressed in designer clothes made their selections at an all-you-can-eat salad bar flashed into Monique's mind. She blinked, then looked at Angie. "What?"

"I said, are you having fun yet?"

A wicked grin split Monique's face. "Tons of fun," she said.

Chapter
4

Cynthia threw the curling iron on the counter in disgust. The strand of hair she was working on was just as straight as it had been five minutes ago. "This is crazy. It's hot as hell in here. Why did Angie invite two hundred guests to a church that only seats about a hundred and fifty?"

The rest of the wedding party was waiting for them in the vestibule. Roxanne hoped Cyn was not about to throw one of her tantrums. And they were always over the smallest things. "It'll be all right," Roxanne said. "Wedding ceremonies don't last that long." At least, she was hoping that would be the case today. She had felt air-conditioning when they'd first come in, but then the church had started to fill.

Roxanne snatched the comb out of Cynthia's hand. "You look beautiful, now come on." She pulled Cynthia into the hallway before she found yet something else about her appearance to fuss with. Before taking her place next to one of Angie's brothers, Roxanne took a quick peek at the guests through the doors they were about to enter. People were fanning themselves with hymnbooks and dabbing at sweat and melting makeup with Kleenex.

The music started, and then the procession started. Walking down the aisle was a trial. Arm in arm with her escort, Roxanne found the heat from their bodies, not to mention the heat generated by the long-sleeved black dress, unbearable. Roxanne strained to keep a smile on her face as she felt sweat dripping from Angie's brother Paul onto her bare skin. A drop ran down to settle in her cleavage, and her skin crawled.

Roxanne was a few paces behind Cynthia. She prayed Cyn's dress would make it through the ceremony. She hadn't tried it on until they were in the changing room of the church. First, it looked like they weren't going to be able to get the zipper all the way up. But a combination of Cyn sucking in her stomach and Gayle and Monique holding the edges of the fabric together had helped as Roxanne eased the zipper up.

Then she had to break up a spat that Monique started when she implied that Cyn had deliberately sent in measurements that were smaller than her actual size. Cyn, of course, began to defend her good name, until Roxanne had reminded them both that they were in the Lord's house and that was no place for getting ugly. But Cyn had to get in the last word. She blamed the problem on Angie's incompetent seamstress.

Once the dress was on, they discovered that it was three inches too long. And no one seemed to have a needle and thread. Finally, Roxanne had run out to her car and come back with a roll of masking tape. Good thing they were in a church, because only an act of God was keeping both Cyn's hem and Roxanne from falling down!

Roxanne was bone tired. Not even trying to keep the attention of thirty or so adolescents had this kind of effect on her. If anything, teaching energized her. At least teenagers were supposed to be sulky and oppositional. What excuse did Cyn and Monique have? she wondered.

Roxanne breathed a sigh of relief when Cyn's dress made it to the altar intact.

Arnel was looking extremely handsome in an all-white tux with a black cummerbund and bow tie and a red rose in his lapel. Roxanne hoped her own groom—if she ever found a groom—would look so at peace with himself on his wedding day.

Once members of the wedding party had all assembled at the altar, they, along with the rest of the guests, waited for the bride to make her entrance. Finally, the wedding march began, and the two double doors in back were opened again.

Angie looked beautiful, the best Roxanne had ever seen her. She wore a short-sleeved white satin dress with a plunging V neckline and a string of pearls that emphasized her breasts and drew attention away from her boxy waistline. The veil had a lace headband and did not cover her face, which was good because she was positively glowing. She was carrying a bouquet made up of white and red roses.

Roxanne loved weddings. They brought family, old friends, and sometimes even old enemies together. Like Angie's parents. They were divorced, and after having experienced Mrs. Cooke's acid tongue, she could easily see why. But whatever animosity existed between her parents was temporarily put aside for today, and Mr. Cooke was giving Angie away.

Her parents might not still be married, but Angie should count herself lucky. At least she knew where her father was and that he cared. Roxanne and her sisters all had different fathers. Her mother had paraded a succession of "uncles" through their home, sometimes for a few months, sometimes for a couple of years. One day her mother's boyfriend would be daddy or uncle, and the next day he'd be gone for good.

Roxanne's eyes turned once again to the bride and her father. Mr. Cooke walked slowly, pride shining in his eyes. As they neared the first row of pews, Angie's step faltered and she swayed as if she might faint. Witnessing this, guests gave a collective gasp. Angie leaned on her father's arm for support, smiled weakly at him, then righted herself and continued her walk down the aisle.

Roxanne's most fervent wish came true. The wedding service was over in less than twenty minutes.

By the time they got to the reception hall, they *all* were swooning—more from hunger than anything else. Like most receptions, this one was running late.

Roxanne sat at their table, resting her knuckles under her chin. "What's the holdup?"

Gayle said, "The food isn't going to be served until everyone in the bridal party has arrived. That's a problem because the maid of honor seems to have disappeared somewhere between the church and the reception hall."

"But I'm starving," Roxanne whined.

Cynthia carefully eased herself into a chair next to Roxanne. "What's new? You're always hungry."

"You don't look like you've missed too many meals yourself, Cyn."

"Are you calling me fat?"

"You said that, not me. But I'm not the one who has to sit with my legs stretched out in front to keep my dress from ripping apart," Roxanne said with a smile.

"Like I told Monique, the woman got my measurements wrong." Cyn took a small mirror out of her purse. She traced a finger along her cheek. "I am not fat. I am pleasingly plump. A little curvy, that's all."

"Yeah, more curves than a mountainside," Roxanne said.

Cyn threw the mirror back in her purse and closed it with a snap. "I'm going to freshen up my makeup." She stalked off to the bathroom.

Gayle said, "Roxanne, why do you and Monique keep teasing Cyn about her weight? It hurts her feelings."

Roxanne was genuinely surprised. "Really?"

"Yes, really. So be nice to her when she comes back."

"I will." Roxanne looked down at her own curves. She wasn't exactly skinny herself, and the big black bow splayed across her butt wasn't helping. Cyn had to know she was only kidding.

Gayle knew Roxanne didn't mean any harm. "You know, I'm hungry, too. But we're luckier than everybody else here. At least we have a reserved table."

There was no assigned seating. The other guests had to scramble to get a table because, as at the church, more people had been invited than there was room for. People competed for tables like it was a game of musical chairs.

Cynthia came back from the bathroom. She sat down next to Roxanne. "You know, most of the people here are older relatives and their kids," she mused aloud. "There is hardly anyone from school here. I don't even see many people close to Angie's age." Cynthia shook her head. "No wonder she wanted us to be in the wedding. Four years at college and no real friends to show for it."

There was no trace of her earlier anger. It always amazed Roxanne how Cyn got over things so quickly. She was definitely not one to hold a grudge. Roxanne decided not to apologize since Cyn didn't seem upset anymore.

Monique returned from the bar with two drinks in her hand. "If y'all want a free drink, you better get over there now. I overheard Mrs. Cooke telling the bartender to run up a fifty-dollar tab and after that to start charging people."

"A fifty-dollar tab?" Cynthia said. "You know, *I* could have put this wedding together better than this." She reached for one of the drinks.

Monique pulled the glasses out of Cynthia's reach and shook her head. "Uh-uh, get your own. These two are mine."

Celeste, the maid of honor, and her date showed up an hour and a half late. Her hair was messed up, her lipstick gone, and her dress wrinkled. She gave them all a slightly defiant smile and flounced off to the ladies' room without a word to say for herself. When she returned, she looked a lot less like she'd been getting busy in the backseat of a car, and the reception finally started.

Angie's father made the customary toast to the happiness of the new bride and groom with one little oversight. The only people with a glass of champagne were Angie and Arnel. Nobody else had been served champagne, but Monique took a swig out of each of her glasses when the toast was given.

After the toast, a buffet consisting mostly of cold cuts and unidentifiable substances on fancy crackers was served.

Cynthia said, "It's after five. I can't believe they aren't serving a sit-down dinner."

"I ain't ate nothing all day." Roxanne took a bite out of her egg salad sandwich. "This is better than nothing."

In between posing for numerous pictures, Arnel and Angie found time to cut the cake. The bridesmaids stood in a long line with everyone else to get some. When they finally got to the table, the caterer cut a very thin piece that she then halved to make two servings.

Cynthia turned her nose up at the minuscule portion and handed the plate back to the caterer. "May I have a *slice* of cake?" she said.

The caterer got all flustered and tried to explain that with several guests still to be served, she was cutting small slices because she didn't want to run out. Just then a round of applause came from the banquet room.

Roxanne pulled on Cynthia's arm before she could jump all down the caterer's throat about the cake. "Let's see what's going on," she said.

Cynthia allowed herself to be dragged along, but not before snatching her plate of cake out of the caterer's hand and picking up a fork from the table.

The wedding guests were standing, many of them were smiling and laughing, but Roxanne couldn't see what all the fuss was about. Sometimes it really sucked to be so short. The DJ was playing an old Temptations song. They finally found an open spot in the circle of people who were encouraging a couple as they glided across the dance floor.

Roxanne couldn't believe her eyes. Mrs. Cooke and her ex-husband were twirling around the dance floor. With her high heels on, she was a couple of inches taller than him, and even though she was taking the lead half the time, they were in perfect sync with each other. Everybody else had moved out of the way and given them the floor. The brand of slow dancing they were doing was old-school. Roxanne had never mastered all that twisting of the hands and arms and could never remember to turn when she was supposed to. A regular old slow grind would have to do for her. But Mr. and Mrs. Cooke looked good together.

"Isn't it romantic? Maybe we got us a love connection going on here. Wouldn't it be a trip if Angie's parents got back together?" Roxanne said.

Monique had materialized next to her. "It's only a dance," she reminded her. "I'm pretty sure the Cookes didn't break up due to stylistic differences on the dance floor."

Not taking her eyes off the couple, Roxanne said, "But look at them. Look at how perfectly matched their timing is. If they can be this in tune with one another after a divorce, surely they could have—" She broke off as Mr. Cooke wrapped his arm around as much of Mrs. Cooke's sequin-clad body as he could and leaned her back for a low dip.

A deep-throated howl of pain erupted from Mrs. Cooke. She frantically clutched her dance partner's shoulder, causing Mr. Cooke to lose his balance, and they both tumbled to the floor with a thud.

"Oh, Lord! Oh, my Lord. My back!" Mrs. Cooke cried from somewhere underneath her ex-husband, who was staring down into her face.

The music continued to play, but the crowd, first stunned into silence, rushed forward to offer assistance. From somewhere in the throng, Mrs. Cooke yelled, "Get off of me, you fool."

Monique turned to Roxanne, one eyebrow raised. "And you were saying?"

Roxanne could see the laughter Monique was struggling to keep in. But she had better not laugh because that would set her off, too. She would have turned to Gayle, but Gayle had been one of the first to hurry over to help the Cookes. Where was Cyn?

Then she spotted her. Cynthia had pulled up a chair, stretched her legs out—still worried about her dress, no doubt—and was calmly eating her cake and watching the action. She looked happy.

Mrs. Cooke had to be taken home to get her muscle relaxants. Apparently, the trick back was not a new phenomenon. Then they had to calm Angie down and see to it that she and her new husband got to the airport. No one knew where the honeymoon was. Arnel had wanted to surprise her.

By the time they got to Aunt Louise's place later that night, they had abandoned their plans to go to a jazz club. No one was in the mood. Instead, they raided Aunt Louise's refrigerator and hoped she wouldn't discover it until after they were long gone. After their hunger had been satisfied, they returned to their little home away from home.

Monique removed the fan from the window of the small room, then lit up a cigarette. Before Gayle had a chance to object, Monique turned her back to them and stuck her head out of the window. It was a wasted gesture. The smoke wafted back into the room.

Cynthia held the ends of her dress together as Gayle unzipped her. "I don't know about y'all, but I can't wait to get back home," she said. "My hair is a mess. I ain't stopped sweating since I got here. The humidity in Tampa can't hold a candle to this. Even the prospect of getting back to work looks inviting."

She stepped out of the dress and left it on the floor. Gayle picked it up, folded it, and put it on top of one of Cynthia's cases. "I'm in no rush to get back to work. But I do need to get back home. I don't like leaving my mama alone for so long—"

A sound that was a cross between a snort and cough came from the vicinity of the window.

Roxanne said, "Monique, you OK?"

"Yeah . . . just breathing in the lovely Minnesota night air." Monique carefully ducked her head under the window and tossed out her cigarette.

"I hope you put that cigarette out before you threw it away," Gayle said.

"Yes, Mom, I did."

"I'm tired," Cynthia said, "Can y'all hurry up and get undressed? I can't sleep with the light on."

Gayle had already undressed and made her little pallet on the floor.

"This is our last night together," Roxanne said. "Don't y'all want to stay up and talk?"

Roxanne got her answer. Monique put out the light.

Roxanne sighed, then turned over on her stomach. Despite her exhaustion, she was too excited to sleep. A whole new world was opening up for her. She had worked full-time and attended school part-time for three and a half years to get her master's degree. Now she was finally done. The traditional belief was that you went East for education, South for relaxation, and West for excitement. Roxanne couldn't remember what one went North for and she didn't really care. She was going to see if she could turn that saying on its head. Having lived in St. Louis most of her life, she'd had plenty of education and more than enough relaxation. Now it was time for some excitement, and she was headed for the East Coast.

With her new job and the move coming up, this wedding couldn't have happened at a worse time, but she hadn't wanted to miss out on spending time with her friends. It had been hectic, even crazy, at times, but she was glad she'd come. Who knew when all four of them would get to spend this much time together again?

Smiling into the darkness, Roxanne hugged her pillow. She was so happy.

PART TWO

Running in Circles

Chapter
5

As Gayle stood waiting for the elevator, she took off her red leather gloves and rubbed her hands together. Their normal color was streaked with white and red lines. She didn't know why she even bothered to wear gloves. They did absolutely no good.

Four years of Minnesota winters had made her very susceptible to frostbite. Nowadays, just picking up a glass with ice in it made her fingers go numb.

She wanted to stick her hands under her armpits to thaw them out, but that was a little hard to do with her heavy winter coat on. Besides, with her luck, the president of the bank would step out of the elevator at just that moment. Instead, she cupped them to her mouth, hoping to warm them that way. Despite having Thinsulate lining in her boots, her feet were like blocks of ice. I really need to get my circulation checked out, she thought.

Columbus had been hit with six inches of snow overnight. The bus had crawled along High Street from Clintonville to downtown. Not only did the bus get to her stop late, a ride that normally took twenty minutes had taken over forty this morning.

Looking at the Seiko watch Monique had given her for Christmas two years ago, Gayle saw that it was eight-fifteen. She sighed. Other bank employees were also gathered around the elevator, but this gave her little comfort. She liked to be in the office by seven-thirty sharp.

In less than two years, she had worked her way up from an entry-level position to client services manager and now supervised a staff of eight people. She was very conscious of being the only black manager in her unit, of not having an M.B.A., and of being a woman in a male-dominated environment. She knew she was scrutinized in a way her peers weren't. That's why she made it a point to be the first to arrive and the last to leave the office.

Everyone's eyes were fixed on the arrow and seemed to be willing the elevator to get to the first floor. For that reason alone, its descent was excruciatingly slow.

When the elevator finally arrived, people hurried past Gayle. She made a space for herself but had to lean against someone's chest to prevent the door from closing on her. Every time someone wanted to get off at a lower floor, she had to step out of the elevator to let them pass. Gayle was ready to strangle someone by the time she got off on the eighth floor.

The operations department took up a city block, and it was quite a hike to her desk, which was in the far right corner of the floor. Gayle started taking off her coat, scarf, and hat as soon as she stepped off the elevator. She walked quickly past the rows and rows of desks where purchasing and sales clerks were already studying computer printouts to make sure that buys and sells were matching up.

Gayle's "office" was a tiny cubicle that had just enough room for her desk and three chairs. A computer took up a large portion of the desk. A small fern hanging from one of the walls was the only personal touch.

She just couldn't bring herself to make her office more comfortable. She hadn't planned on being in it this long. When she'd first started working at the bank, she saw it as temporary. A way to save a little money before she enrolled in graduate school. Then her mother got sick. Working here all day and then taking care of her mother and the house was like having two full-time jobs. Where was she going to find time for school? Maybe it would be different once her brother, Buddy, left for college.

Gayle threw her outerwear on the chair across from her desk.

The partitioned walls of her office were about two feet higher than those of the clerical and entry-level administrative staff offices. This supposedly afforded her greater privacy. But anybody could hear what was going on in her office without even trying. If she really needed to talk to someone privately, she usually used one of the conference rooms.

She was wearing a tailored double-breasted navy blue suit with a white silk blouse. She placed her leather briefcase on the desk and reached over to open the bottom right-hand desk drawer. It contained several pairs of shoes. After searching for a few moments, she retrieved a pair of three-inch navy blue Aigner pumps. She pushed her boots under her desk and put on the pumps. Now she was in full business uniform.

Gayle glanced at her watch again. It was almost eight-thirty. She opened up the briefcase and took out copies of the *Wall Street Journal* and the *New York Times*. The workday didn't start until she had skimmed both papers. She didn't want to be the last to know about some major shake-up in the world of high finance.

Gayle cursed under her breath. "Damn, I'm not going to have time to finish reading these." She picked up various slips of paper on her desk. Underneath her briefcase she found what she was looking for.

She groaned when she saw her schedule. She had totally forgotten that she had to train the new girl today. Plus, it was time for distribution checks to go out, and she had to start working on performance evaluations, too. But first things first. She really needed to get some coffee.

Several of her coworkers greeted her as she made her way to the kitchen. Normally, she would have stopped to chat, but not today. She gave everyone a smile but didn't deviate from her goal of getting a caffeine fix. Inside the tiny kitchen, with only a microwave, a full-size refrigerator, and an industrial-size coffeemaker, she found two carafes sitting on the coffeemaker's hot plates. Being late had one advantage. For once somebody else had been forced to make the coffee.

On her way back to her office, Jillian, one of the assistant vice presidents, stopped her in the hall. She was loaded down with manila folders and had two pencils sticking out of her curly red hair. Gayle liked Jillian. She was in her early forties but had more energy and sparkle than most of the clones around here who were half her age.

"Gayle, a bunch of us are going to happy hour after work. You want to come?"

"I don't think I can. I'm really swamped today. I'll probably be working late." Gayle was not a bar person in general, and she certainly wasn't going to spend her free time hanging out in one with a bunch of people from work. What would she have to say to them once they had finished talking about the weather, sports, and the stock market?

"Can't it wait? You know what they say about all work and no play. . . ."

"If I don't start my evaluations today, I'll have to come in over the weekend," Gayle said. "Maybe some other time."

Jillian smiled. "Now, where have I heard that before? You're going to make me think you don't like us if you keep turning us down."

Was there a law that said she had to socialize with her co-workers? It wasn't about liking or disliking them. Gayle just wasn't into hanging out with people she had very little in common with. It wasn't a good use of her time. It should be enough that she went to the company picnics and played in the corporate softball league every spring?

Jillian lost her grip on the files. Gayle caught one before it fell. "Thanks," Jillian said, tucking one of the pencils deeper into her thick curls. "So, when *are* you going to come partying with us?"

"When this bank stops working my fingers to the bone," Gayle said. *I wish she would stop pressuring me.* "Jillian, I'll catch you later. I really have a ton to do."

Coffee cup in hand, Gayle stuck her head in the new trainee's cubicle. "Everything going OK?" she asked.

Suzanne, a fresh-faced Ohio University business grad, nodded her blond head.

"Great," Gayle said between sips of coffee. "I'll be over in ten minutes to show you how to do monthly distributions."

Back in her cubbyhole, Gayle listened to her voice mail. She frowned at one in particular. Fred had left yet another message calling in sick. This was the fourth time this month. She had been putting off talking to him about his absences. Fred was a nice guy, and when he did show up for work, he generally did a good job. It would be a shame if she had to fire him.

There were two more messages from clients who hadn't received their distribution checks. Gayle made a note to herself to trace them.

Her nails clicked against the keyboard as she quickly logged on to her computer. Nine new e-mail messages, four of them from Angie. Didn't that girl ever do any work? Gayle regretted giving Angie her e-mail address because now she was subject to daily, detailed reports of Angie's wedded bliss.

Not that she wasn't happy for her. But with each New Year's Eve spent alone watching *Dick Clark's Rockin' Eve*, Gayle was feeling more and more convinced that life, especially a love life, had passed her by. Almost thirty years old and nothing to occupy her time except work and family responsibilities.

Her prospects in her teens and early twenties hadn't been any better. There couldn't have been more than about twenty to twenty-five black males on campus. But after she had eliminated those who were only interested in white women, the geeks and nerds, and those who were confused about their sexual orientation—and she didn't need that headache—that left about seven available men. Included in that batch were guys who liked Gayle as a friend but who preferred to date women who were either incredibly immature or with whom they had absolutely nothing in common. All men wanted from her was a shoulder to cry on. Apparently, this wasn't the stuff girlfriends were made of.

As for white men, Gayle had no burning desire to date them. But she might have if one of them had ever asked her. She honestly didn't believe that most white guys even viewed the black women on campus as female. Except for a few, who were looking for "the black experience," the majority of them steered clear. It didn't matter. Most of the guys at the school were so white-bread and clueless they really couldn't hang.

Gayle jerked her thoughts back to the present. Besides Angie's messages, there was one from her friend Kenny. If Angie wanted to brag about married life, surely Kenny was e-mailing to complain about it. Ever since college, he'd only seen Gayle as a sympathetic ear. If he thought she was so wonderful, why had he dated every woman on campus but her? She didn't want to deal with Kenny right now. In fact, all the messages could wait. She needed to get back to Suzanne.

Even though Suzanne looked like a Barbie doll, she was actually pretty sharp. It didn't take long for her to learn the procedures for sending out dividend checks, and for that Gayle was grateful.

Gayle taught her how to make fifty random inspections of the five thousand or so checks being sent out to make sure that they were quality-controlled. Once she was confident Suzanne could handle things on her own, Gayle left her to it.

She checked her watch again. Only ten-thirty. She could spend the rest of the morning reviewing accounts on the computer to verify that they were not overdrawn and to check for out-of-balances. She hadn't looked at them in a couple of days, and there was nothing worse than a pissed-off client whose subscription or redemption had not been processed within the five-day trade deadline.

As she sat hunched over the computer for the next two hours, periodically one of her staff would come in with an account-fee summary that needed her signature before it could be sent off to the comptroller's office. She was searching for a record of the dividend checks for the clients who'd left the phone messages when yet another shadow fell across her desk. Thinking someone else needed her to sign something, she automatically reached for her pen. When papers weren't immediately shoved under her nose, Gayle looked up to see what the problem was.

To her surprise, Reggie, one of the accountants from downstairs, was leaning against the front partition with his arms folded across his chest. Reggie was tall and lean with a tennis player's build. Dressed in a blue oxford shirt and royal blue Dockers, despite the tie, he was looking pretty casual for a bank employee. He wasn't classically handsome, but he had nice regular features. He also had a great sense of humor. And it didn't hurt that he was the only black man Gayle had met at the bank who wasn't a security guard or janitor.

Reggie had been with the company for about six months. He had moved from D.C. to take the job. Being one of the few black professionals at the place, he and Gayle would sometimes have lunch together.

Reggie shook his head. "Every time I see you, you've got your eyes glued to that computer screen. Those numbers must be fascinating. The least you could do is stop by and visit me sometimes, instead of hiding those pretty legs behind that desk."

Gayle felt her face grow warm. Thank God she was too dark for him to see she was blushing. She was so flustered, she didn't know what to say.

But then Reggie was always making silly comments. No point reading too much into them. She wished she could figure out what his deal was, because he was making her knees shake.

"I guess some of us have work to do, Reggie. It's a good thing the accounting department doesn't rely exclusively on you, because the bank would be in sad, sad shape. You're never at your desk."

"Could it be that I'm super-efficient, which frees me up to talk to my favorite black manager?"

He was full of such crap. Gayle said, "I'm the only black manager. And a very busy one at that. What do you want?"

"Nothing. I haven't seen you in a while. So, I thought I'd

drop by and say hi. Did you miss me? I hope you haven't replaced me with another guy during my long absence. I know how fickle you women can be."

It was times like this that Gayle wished she'd never gone to school in godforsaken rural Minnesota. It had totally retarded her social development. There had been very little opportunity to develop flirting skills.

Gayle was really envious of those women who could toss out great comeback lines without effort. Rather than risk saying something stupid or not funny, she usually said nothing at all. She would always think of what to say long after the situation was over, then would spend the rest of the day kicking herself for not having said it.

She replied seriously but not necessarily truthfully. "It's only been a week since I last saw you. I didn't have time to miss you."

"Thanks, you really know how to make a guy feel special. But I'll forgive you. How about some lunch? I'll even pay, to show you what a great guy I am."

Gayle really wanted to go, but she knew it was impossible. She had too much stuff to get through today. Well, maybe she could squeeze it in. She looked at her to-do list and then at the adorable pleading look in Reggie's eyes.

He put his hands together as if he were praying she'd say yes. Gayle looked at the list again. Then she said, "Reggie, I really can't get away today. I'm barely going to have time to order in a sandwich. But I could do it on Monday."

"Aw, I really wanted to talk with you today. Hey, why don't we get together for dinner tonight? Have you been to that new restaurant in German Village?"

Gayle was in shock. Was he asking her out on a date? No, he couldn't be.

"Well, cutie. Do we have a date or what? Should I be offended by how long it's taking you to answer?"

"Huh? I guess I could go out ... but not tonight. I promised my mother I'd take her grocery shopping."

"OK, mom outranks the lowly accountant. So how about Friday?"

Gayle smiled. They were talking in circles. "I already told you that I can't have lunch with you today."

"I meant *next* Friday, and for dinner, not lunch," Reggie corrected her. "Dinner is better than lunch. More intimate, don't you think?"

Intimate? Reggie wants to get intimate with me? Why?

"This time I'm taking your silence as a yes," he said with a smile. "How about eight o'clock reservations? I say we dress up. Make sure you wear something to show off those legs."

Gayle bowed her head. *Please stop talking about my fat legs.*

"I'll pick you up at seven-thirty. You live in Clintonville, right? That's just a hop, skip, and a jump from Worthington," he said. "I'm going to be out of town on business for most of next week, so why don't you give me your address now?"

For an easygoing guy, Reggie wasn't wasting any time. Gayle was being blown toward this date like a leaf in a strong wind. She was slightly breathless as she wrote out her address on the back of one of her business cards. As an afterthought, she added her home phone number. She didn't want him getting lost. As she handed the card to him, she couldn't resist mentioning a few neighborhood landmarks like the Kentucky Fried Chicken on the corner of her street or the Big Bear Supermarket, which was a block over, just to make extra sure he found the place. She hoped she didn't sound too desperate.

Reggie glanced at the card, then stuck it in one of his pants pockets. "Don't worry, I'll be there with bells on." He smiled broadly. "This is great! I'm glad you said yes. See you later." He breezed out of her office just as quickly as he had come in.

Gayle's mind was racing. I can't believe he asked me out. I don't know what to wear. I should call Monique or Cynthia. They're the fashion queens. . . . But I can't. Monique was visiting her parents and Cyn was at work. She forced herself to calm down. After all, she had a week to plan for this date.

She sighed. I should have just gone to lunch with him. Now I'm probably going to spend a week worrying about nothing.

She couldn't remember the last time she'd been on a date.

She rarely spent any time with men outside of work. All of her close friends were women. The few male friends she'd had in college had long since disappeared except for an occasional call for advice or an invitation to a wedding.

Gayle often fluctuated between thinking either there was something seriously wrong with her or there was something seriously wrong with men. She'd have liked to believe men were the ones with the problem. Either way, sitting home night after night had done nothing for her self-confidence.

Gayle picked up her pen and stacked the papers on her desk. She silently scolded herself. Get a grip, Gayle. You've got work to do.

She stared at the blank performance-evaluation forms. This was a part of her job she really disliked. She had no problem telling people when they were doing well, but unfortunately some people did better than others. There was always at least one person who would be angry and hurt because a colleague got a raise and he didn't. And somehow it never failed that the one person who felt slighted was the pushy type that came storming into her office demanding an explanation.

She took the cap off the pen and picked up the form. Oh, well, this is what I'm being paid for. . . .

Several hours and two cups of coffee later, a three o'clock meeting gave Gayle a much-needed break from the evaluations. On her way to the conference room, she ducked into the ladies' room. She hadn't been to the bathroom all day. It had to be a personal record. Her girlfriends would be impressed. They claimed she ran to the bathroom all the time.

When Gayle took a seat in the conference room, the eight other section managers were already there.

The trainer said, "Good afternoon. Today's management training session is 'Cultural Sensitivity in the Workplace.' "

She groaned inwardly.

All of the other people in the room were white except for José, who was in computer operations. She wondered how hard it was to be culturally sensitive toward nonexistent people. Then again, maybe that made being sensitive easy. You couldn't offend someone who wasn't there.

The trainer, a middle-aged white man, started his presentation with examples of comments white people make and what people of color really hear. He described a situation in which a white manager "praises" a black employee by saying, "Wow, I'm surprised. You really did a good job on that project. Your family and friends back home must be really proud of you." Then he asked the group what they thought of this statement.

Marcie from Purchasing raised her hand. "I don't see anything wrong with it. The person did a good job, and the supervisor let him or her know it."

José and Gayle exchanged self-pitying looks. What are we doing here?

"Anybody else have a different interpretation of the situation?" the trainer asked, looking expectantly at Gayle.

She suddenly found the legal pad in front of her incredibly fascinating. For once she decided not to be accommodating. They could at least *attempt* to figure things out for themselves.

After all, she wouldn't have gotten this far in life without learning something about them. All she had to do was turn on the television or open any magazine. Learning about white people was a piece of cake. So how come the only thing most whites know about blacks comes from sports, entertainment, and crime reports?

When she was at college, people constantly inundated her with stupid questions and comments. Why do you put curlers in your hair every night? I can't believe you only wash your hair once a week! Must be nice to get a free ride through college. Wow! I can't believe how articulate you are. Other black people must have a hard time understanding you. Why are you stressing about getting a job? Being black gives you an advantage over everybody. Why do all the black people sit together in the dining hall? Isn't that separatist?

The trainer tried prompting the group. "While it's true the supervisor complimented the worker, what other message did she give by saying 'I'm surprised' or by mentioning family and friends?"

Gayle made doodles on her legal pad. Why couldn't *they* learn through experience and observation like black people did instead of having to be spoon-fed everything? We'd never get away with saying half the stupid stuff they did. But if you let on in any way that it bugged you, then you're being overly sensitive or militant.

After the trainer's question, the silence stretched uncomfortably.

Then Rick, a relatively new manager, spoke up. "Well, I suppose the supervisor also implied that even though the employee did well, she didn't really expect him to, and that him doing well was unusual for people from his background."

"Exactly! Exactly!" the trainer said. "The manager is also making assumptions about the type of background the person comes from. So you see, the compliment is lost in all the little attacks and stereotyping that's going on."

Congratulations, Sherlock.

Almost immediately, Gayle felt ashamed of herself. Rick was cool. She didn't know what had gotten into her today. Maybe it was all the snow. Or maybe she was tired of people being rewarded for doing things she considered to be basic common sense. If she approached one of her white employees and said, "I'm really pleased and surprised that you're able to take orders from me. It must be difficult for a white person to give up power like that," and tried to convince everyone she was just paying the employee a compliment, they'd look at her like she was crazy.

The trainer went on talking about how to interact in ways that weren't culturally offensive, but Gayle wasn't interested. She was thinking about what she'd wear on her date with Reggie. Now, that was something that required *real* problem-solving.

Chapter
6

Roxanne waved a hand near the edges of the windowsill, and the blanket slipped off her shoulders. She watched it land on the hardwood floor, then abandoned it. Instead, she waved her hand again, tilting her head to examine the window more closely.

There, she felt it again. The draft that had made it impossible for her to stay warm during the latest cold snap was definitely coming from this bedroom window. She went into the living room-cum-dining room of her one-bedroom apartment to fetch a chair. It scraped across the bare floor on her way back, reminding Roxanne that she still hadn't bought any throw rugs or curtains since moving to Boston last fall.

She put her chair at a safe distance away from the radiator. The little sucker's constant hissing and popping had long ago confirmed that lack of heat was not the problem. Once in the chair, she still had to stand on her tiptoes to reach the top of the window. The coldness became more pronounced. She gently yanked on the yellowed shade, which had long ago lost its pull string. She cursed profusely when the rod popped out of place and landed in a dusty heap on her blanket. She'd just washed it.

With the shade gone, Roxanne saw the problem. Icicles had started to form around an inch-wide jagged gap at the top of the window. "No wonder I've been freezing my ass off!" she said. "The window's broken." She jumped off the chair and picked up the phone by the bed. She hit the redial button.

It rang two times, then the answering machine came on. "Hi, this is Bob. I'm not in right now, but if you leave a message, your call will be promptly returned." A long series of beeps followed.

Roxanne hung up and sat on the edge of the bed. No point in leaving a message. She had been leaving Bob messages since Tuesday. He was obviously operating under a different definition of "promptness."

She swung her legs onto the bed and leaned back. Suddenly, her head smacked against the wall. "Ouch!" She rubbed the place where her head had made contact. Roxanne hadn't bought a headboard yet, either, or a dresser or a whole lot of other things that would have made her apartment seem more like a home. Boston was turning out to be more expensive then she had originally thought.

When she'd moved, she hadn't known she would be lowering her standard of living. She was actually starting to miss the graduate student apartment where she had lived in St. Louis while working on her master's in education. At least it had come furnished.

"Damn, it's cold in here." Two pairs of wool socks and a sweat suit weren't helping at all. Roxanne crawled to the end of the bed. Reaching down, she grabbed for the blanket she'd left on the floor, but couldn't. She sighed, then tumbled off the bed.

Might as well put the window shade back up while I'm at it, she thought. Given the paper-thin walls, I already have no privacy, but there's no need to encourage Peeping Toms. To think I actually thought these old brownstone buildings were quaint when I first got here. But I really only had a few days to look for a place, she reminded herself.

In her apartment search, Roxanne had quickly learned that while the exteriors of the buildings in the Allston-Brighton area were generally well maintained, especially those on major streets like Commonwealth Avenue and Washington Street, the interiors were a different story. Some of the apartments had walls that were so dingy and smudged it was difficult to tell the original color of the paint underneath. She had hiked up fifth-floor walk-ups and had seen cramped, claustrophobic basement apartments with steel bars on all the windows. And the rents were outrageous!

Just 'cause I looked at a few hellholes, I let myself be fooled by a new coat of paint on the walls and hardwood floors, she thought, mad at herself. I wonder if there is some government office where I can lodge a complaint. I was robbed!

She hadn't noticed the unlit stairwell or the grime that clung to the hallway walls or the overpowering aroma of a variety of foreign foods and spices that slipped under every door, every crack, crevice, or open window before she signed the lease on her place. She was also the last to know that Allston-Brighton was basically a ghetto for Boston University and Boston College students who wanted to avoid their universities' attempts to monitor their sexual, alcoholic, and antisocial behavior.

Boston had a lot to offer, you just had to pay for the privilege. Roxanne's life was very full. She joined several social service agencies, mostly geared toward youths. Most of the other volunteers she met were in business or were just neighborhood folk who wanted to help. They seemed surprised that after teaching all day, Roxanne was still willing to spend more time around kids.

For her it was a joy, not a burden. She knew she couldn't save the world, but she knew how important it was for kids to have just one person there to encourage, to take an interest, to tell them that there was more beyond the six or seven blocks that was their world. To know that someone had faith that they could succeed not only in those six or seven blocks but anywhere. That's what her Grandma Reynolds had done for her, and Roxanne wanted to be that person for other children.

No, Boston wasn't so bad. Like any place, it was what you made of it, and Roxanne was going to try to make a life here.

A movement on the sidewalk below caught her eye. Bob,

her building super, was out front walking his mangy, pot-bellied bulldog. Roxanne started to open the window to at-tract his attention, then thought better of it. She quickly threw on her house slippers, the only shoes in sight, grabbed her keys, and ran out of the apartment.

When she got downstairs, he was gone. One side of her street led to Comm Ave. At the other end, a marker separated Allston-Brighton from the tree-lined streets of Brookline, a posh suburb. She thought she saw Bob turn down one of the Brookline streets and took off after him.

She found him at a nearby playground. His dog had his leg hunched up, relieving himself.

"Bob," she called from a few feet away. "Bob," she re-peated. The shaggy, dark-haired man gave no sign of having heard her. She knew it was him. No one else could have had that aging-rock musician look and such a homely dog. Rox-anne continued walking toward him.

Years of playing in loud bands must have damaged his hearing. Maybe that's why he never answers his phone or his door, even when I know he's in there.

She touched his leather-clad back and he turned around.

"Oh, hiya, Roxanne."

"Hiya, Bob." Roxanne took a step away from the bulldog, which was nuzzling her leg. "Bob, did you get my messages?"

Bob scratched his unshaven chin. "Messages?"

Was there an echo? "Yes. I have a broken window, and it's letting cold air in." The dog was sniffing her leg again. Rox-anne decided to let him as long as he didn't start humping it.

"Are you sure it's broken?"

"A big hunk of it is missing. That sounds broken to me." Bob was really working her last nerve. "I need you to fix it."

"OK. Sure," he said. Bob bent down to pet Bill.

Roxanne waited. Bob kept stroking his dog. "When?"

He looked up. "Huh?"

"*When* are you going to fix my window?"

"Soon."

"Good." Roxanne turned to walk away.

"Uh, Roxanne . . ." She turned back around. "You might

want to put a sock in the hole and maybe tape some plastic up. . . ."

"Why?" He'd better get his grungy behind over and fix that window, or else she was calling the management company.

". . . And Roxanne, would you leave a key above the door? Just in case you're not there when I come by. I can't seem to find the master keys."

When Roxanne stuck her key in the door, a voice from behind called her name. She turned around and smiled. It was Mohammed, one of her neighbors. "Hi, Mo. What's up?"

"Do you have . . . map?" he said in his halting English.

Mohammed was from the Sudan. There were so many guys coming in and out of the apartment across the hall, Roxanne couldn't figure out just how many people lived there. She'd met Mohammed a few weeks ago. "A map of Boston?"

He nodded.

Roxanne pushed open the door. "Yes, I have one. Come on in."

The phone was ringing. "Let me get this. Have a seat, Mo," she said, gesturing to the only piece of furniture in the room, a used sleeper sofa she'd picked up at a rental furniture warehouse.

Roxanne ran to the bedroom and dove for the phone before the answering machine picked up. "Hello?"

"Hi, Roxanne. It's Kathy."

Kathy was another one of the volunteers at the Roxbury tutoring program Roxanne was involved in. They both worked with elementary-age kids once a week.

"I ain't speaking to you," Roxanne said.

"Why not?"

"Because of that man you fixed me up with."

"Cameron? What did he do?" Kathy's voice got louder. "Did he get fresh?"

"Calm down. He didn't do anything. He was fine. But what made you think I'd be attracted to someone who wears more jewelry than I do?" Cameron had shown up at the restaurant with rings on every finger except his thumbs and more gold chains around his neck than Mr. T.

Kathy laughed. "Oh, that. But he was nice, wasn't he?"

"He was very nice. Just not my type."

"Well, I was just trying to help you out, girlfriend. You said you ain't had a man in so long, you thought it was going to dry up. What did you call it? This dry spell you're going through?"

"The Drought and the Pestilence." Roxanne couldn't understand it. She'd never had any problem getting a date. But since moving to Boston, she hadn't met anyone. Kathy, bless her heart, kept trying to set her up, but it wasn't working. "Thanks for thinking of me, but don't do me any more favors."

"Well, all right," Kathy said, pretending to be offended. "I just called to remind you that you're supposed to go to happy hour with me on Tuesday."

"Do I have to?" Roxanne had been to a couple of them before, and it really wasn't her kind of thing. The typical scenario was a bunch of well-dressed black people standing around sipping overpriced drinks and speaking only to people they already knew. Although she thought of herself as someone with social skills, conversations with this crowd usually died a quick death once they found out she was not in business or law and had never vacationed on Martha's Vineyard, a symbol of status among the nouveau middle class.

"C'mon, Roxanne, you know, I'm trying to do a little networking. I need a job. But I hate to go to functions like this by myself."

Roxanne could never turn down a friend in need. "OK, OK. But I can't talk now, one of my neighbors is in the living room. What time do I have to be there?"

"Meet you at the Pru at five-thirty." Kathy hung up.

When Roxanne walked into the living room, Mohammed was still standing where she had left him. He was cute, had an interesting face. High cheekbones, all planes and angles. But, boy, was he tall, and rail-thin, too. Roxanne smiled at him. If the loose-fitting tunic and sandals didn't give away his

African roots, surely his hair would have. He wore his Afro three or four inches longer than the typical African-American male. "Mo, I told you to make yourself at home."

"No, no," he said. "Do not wish to trouble you."

Smiling, Roxanne gave him a little shove toward the couch. "Sit down. Give me a minute to find the map." She was still learning the city herself, so she had all kinds of maps. She bent over the neatly stacked piles of books and folders next to the dining room table. A bookcase, she told herself, that's the next thing on my list. Soon as I get a little money. She found the map.

As she handed it to Mohammed, she said, "So, what do you need a map for?"

"I have new job."

"That's great. Are you trying to find it on the map?"

"No, I need map for job. I am cabdriver."

Roxanne laughed. "How can you be a cabdriver? You don't even know the city. You just moved here two weeks ago!"

Mohammed was on his feet again and headed to the door. "This is why I need map."

"Oh," Roxanne said. "Well, you can keep that one."

"Thank you, Roxanne."

She shut the door behind him, then sat on the couch with a bemused look on her face. Hmm, if getting a job as a cabbie is that easy, maybe I should try a little moonlighting. Lord knows I could use the money.

Her musing was interrupted by a knock at the door. Maybe Mohammed needed something else. Roxanne peered through the peephole. A man she didn't recognize was standing there. "Yes?" she said through the closed door.

The man leaned closer to the peephole as if that would help him see her better. "I am Azzedine, Mohammed's friend."

"Just a minute," Roxanne said, unlocking the door. He probably wanted to use the phone. The guys across the hall didn't have one.

She let him in and held out her hand. "Hi, I'm Roxanne." He shook her hand and came farther into the room. He didn't say anything, just looked around.

"Why you live here by yourself?"

Roxanne had heard that question before. The fellows across the way didn't understand the concept of living alone, especially a woman living alone. She said, "Am I supposed to be living with someone? I have no family in Boston."

She looked Azzedine over again. He was kind of cute. Not as tall as Mo, but he had a nice set of teeth when he talked, which apparently was not often. He continued to stand silently in the middle of her living room, surveying its meager contents. "Azzedine, did you need to use the phone or something?" she asked.

He shook his head.

"Then what can I do for you?"

"I would like it very much if you had sex with me."

"What!" Roxanne's eyes just about popped out of their sockets.

He frowned and seemed taken aback by her tone of voice. "I would like—"

"Azzedine, I know what you would like, but you don't walk up to a woman and ask her to have sex with you."

"But you are an American woman."

Lord, she thought she'd heard just about every line a man could use to get a woman into bed. But this was a first. "I know. I know. But that doesn't mean I'll have sex with every man that asks me." Roxanne's hand was already on the doorknob. "Azzedine, you gots to go. I'm going to take a hot shower. And I suggest you take a cold one."

"A shower?" he said as he backed out the door, clearly not understanding the need for one under these circumstances.

Roxanne closed the door and threw herself on the couch. She covered her face with a pillow and pressed hard.

The Drought and the Pestilence had surely descended upon her.

Chapter

7

Dear God,

I pray for everybody else most of the time. So I'm hoping that you'll forgive me for focusing on myself just this once.

Lord, I need a man. OK, maybe I don't "need" a man, but I know I'd be a lot happier with one than without one. I'm tired of going places by myself or with my girlfriends. I'm tired of eating leftovers that last an entire week because I've got no one to share a meal with. I want to have children, Lord. When I was in high school, my health teacher told me I had the perfect body for giving birth. Well, Lord, I am willing and able. But I can't get pregnant by myself. Besides, kids are better off with a mother and father who want and love them.

I've tried to be a good person. I work hard. I respect my parents and I try not to hurt anybody. I know that I'm not perfect. Sometimes, I hold envy in my heart. But Lord, it just doesn't seem fair that I should end up alone in this world. I know it's not for me to judge others, but Lord, I've never done anything criminal. I've worked for everything I have. As you already know, Lord, I'm not exactly a virgin, but there are a lot of women out there who give it away to just about anybody that asks . . . and to some who weren't asking. They might as well tie a mattress to their backs. I'm not like that, Lord, and when

I do let a man worship at the temple, you better believe I use some protection, because I don't want to bring any children into this world without a husband.

Like I said before, I've tried to be a good friend and a loving person. Lord, if I'm not doing something right, could you please send me a sign, because I've given this a lot a thought and I can't figure out what I've done to deserve this loneliness.

In Jesus' name, Amen.

Cynthia raised her head and opened her eyes. She felt better. That little chat with God was long overdue. No doubt her mother had had numerous conversations with God on the same subject. But the Lord helps those who help themselves, and Cynthia thought it was time she put a pitch in on her own behalf.

With sweat popping off his forehead and his long black robe almost touching the ground, Reverend Solomon stepped down from the pulpit. He began pacing up and down the aisle as if his greater proximity to the congregation would make it easier for them to hear his message. He paused in mid-sentence, wiped the sweat with a damp handkerchief, and shook hands with a few people.

"I said . . . it's amazing what God can do, if you just ask him. God is amazing, if you just pray." He nodded his head, almost trance-like, talking more to himself than to his congregation.

"Amen. Praise be the Glory! Speak the truth, Rev," her fellow worshippers said. Cynthia silently hoped Reverend Solomon knew what he was talking about.

For their final selection, the choir underlined his message by singing "Jesus Is on the Main Line, Tell Him What You Want." After they were done, the minister raised his arms, signaling the start of the benediction. The congregation stood up, and at two o'clock the morning service at Shiloh Baptist Church had reached an end.

Cynthia had attended Shiloh for only a few weeks but had

already become familiar with some of its customs. So when the service was over, she turned to shake hands with the people next to her.

Sister Davis smiled at her with snuff-stained teeth from underneath the brim of her white Sunday-go-to-meeting hat. "You sho' nuff was moved by the spirit today, Sister Johnson." The middle-aged woman had befriended Cynthia the very first time she'd come to Shiloh. Now she had taken to saving Cynthia a seat next to her.

Cynthia said, "What do you mean?"

"You sho' nuff was clutching that Bible," she said, pointing to the small leather-bound Bible Cynthia brought to church every Sunday. "Not everybody prays while the preacher is preaching, but you was praying something fierce." Her brown eyes questioned Cynthia. "I sho' hope your prayers get answered."

"Me, too," Cynthia said. "Me, too."

Sister Davis smiled back, her curiosity still not satisfied. "I hope you're staying for the after-service refreshments."

Cynthia wanted to get home. Four hours in church was more than enough time to do her business with God. "Well, I don't think so—"

Her arm was firmly grasped by Sister Davis' gloved hand. "But you have to come. That way I can introduce you to some more people. Ain't that right, Brother Colby?"

A man who had been passing by their pew stopped. He was kind of husky, but Cynthia thought he hid it well in his double-breasted suit. And he was tall, well over six feet. He looked like he had played sports at some point in his life. Probably football.

He smiled at her and said, "Of course, Sister Davis. Whatever you say is right."

The daisies on Sister Davis' hat shook when she nodded in agreement. "Brother Colby, I got to talk to the Rev about the Poor Saints' offering. People were kind of stingy this week when the plate was passed around. Take Sister Johnson downstairs and introduce her around."

He made a sweeping gesture with his hand, inviting Cynthia to step into the aisle. "No problem. I was headed that way." As they walked toward the back of the church, he said, "This is the first time I've seen you here."

"Oh, I've been here a few times before. I've only lived in Tampa for two years," she said with a smile. "I'm still searching for the right church." One with fine young brothers like yourself in it would suit me to a T.

But that wasn't her only reason for going to church. Cynthia's mother was a preacher's kid, and she'd instilled the same sense of religious commitment in her daughter. You didn't just attend church, you were supposed to be a part of it. Her mother had been director of the choir and president of the ladies' auxiliary. Cynthia herself had been Sunday-school Bible-fact champ four years in a row and always had a key role in the Christmas and Easter plays. Then there was Bible study and Bible camp in the summer. Her parents weren't fundamentalists but thought it was important she be familiar with the word of God.

Her college years were the worst time for Cynthia. After hearing some university-trained theologian talk about her metaphysical relationship with God instead of the Resurrection one Easter Sunday, Cynthia had started skipping church altogether. There weren't a whole lot of down-home Baptist churches to turn to in the small Minnesota town, either.

In the past few years, though, she was slowly reacquainting herself with the enjoyment she used to experience as a churchgoer. She still wasn't sure about the religious part, but church definitely gave her a sense of belonging, a sense of community. Maybe it was the music or the heartfelt, unapologetic, blatantly emotional praise of God or the people or a combination of all three. It seemed like church was the only place she got to think without interruption. Like today, after praying she felt calmer, more at peace.

About half of the people from the morning service were milling around in the basement. She liked Shiloh. With less than a hundred people present on any given Sunday, it had a homey feel to it. A place where you could meet people. Cynthia assumed the food was to her left because a large group of people had gathered around two tables. There were considerably fewer men than women and children. Most of the men were dressed in dark suits, blue or black, and hung together in small circles. A few had mistakenly thought they would look good in purple or green suits. They had to be single because no self-respecting woman would let her man out of the house looking like that, Cynthia decided.

Brother Colby said, "Can I get you something to eat or drink?"

At least he had manners. Some men would have made a beeline for the food and left her to fend for herself. "Brother Colby, what's your first name? Mine is Cynthia."

Her hand was swallowed up in his large one. "Pleased to meet you, Cynthia. I'm John." Cynthia snuck a peek at his other hand. Good news. He wasn't wearing a ring. Suddenly, Cynthia wished there was a mirror nearby. She wanted to check her makeup.

"Well, John, I'm not very hungry. But I'd love something to drink. Water would be fine."

"No problem. I'll get it." Cynthia admired his broad back as he walked away. So big . . . and so accommodating, too. She liked a man who was willing to wait on a woman a little.

Cynthia fished her lipstick out of her purse and used the shiny brass top from it as a mirror as she reapplied the color. She rubbed her lips together. That would have to do for now. John was headed back this way with a styrofoam cup in his hand.

"Here you go," he said.

"Thanks," she said, accepting the cup. "You really don't have to stay with me," she lied. "I'm sure there are other people you'd rather be talking to."

He shook his head. "Don't sell yourself short. It's always nice to met a fresh face. I already know everybody here."

Encouraged by his words, Cynthia took a step closer to him. Just then she caught the eye of a young woman who was bouncing a toddler on her hip a few feet away. Cynthia smiled at her. The woman rolled her eyes and walked away.

Humph . . . I guess everybody's not as friendly as Brother Colby. But Cynthia didn't much care. She had plenty of female friends. "So, John, what do people do for fun in Tampa?" She wasn't just making polite conversation. She really wanted to know. Tampa just wasn't doing it for her. Once you'd been to the beach, done Busch Gardens, and driven to Epcot Center, you'd pretty much covered the Tampa Bay area.

While John was telling her about the local nightlife, Cynthia noticed that the woman with the baby had reappeared and was pointing at them. The woman standing next to her was probably a relative. They both had the same doe-like eyes, slender elongated trunks, and tiny waists. Maybe I know her from somewhere. But nothing came to mind, so Cynthia turned her attention back to John.

She was laughing at something he'd said and lightly touching his arm when the two women joined them. The older of the two glanced at Cynthia's hand where it rested on John's jacket and then at John. The young woman with the baby gave her a hostile stare.

John put an arm around the older woman's shoulders, effectively ridding himself of Cynthia's hand. "LaVonne! Hey, honey, I want you to meet Cynthia. She's new to the church."

LaVonne put her arm around John's waist and pulled him closer to her. She looked Cynthia up and down. "Yes, I thought you might be new."

"Cynthia, this is my fiancée, LaVonne, and her little sister, Aneta. And that bad boy"—he playfully shadowboxed with the toddler—"is Tyree, my soon-to-be-nephew."

Fiancée? Cynthia forced herself to smile and held out her hand. "Pleased to meet you." Neither woman showed signs of reciprocating the gesture. So Cynthia tried to nonchalantly let her hand drop by her side.

John seemed oblivious to the hostility in the air. "Sister Davis asked me to bring her down here and make her feel welcome. Cynthia here is trying to find a church to join."

LaVonne said, "So, have you found what you were looking for here at Shiloh Baptist?"

Cynthia was no dummy. The woman was trying to be smart. The nasty attitude was uncalled for. How was she supposed to know John was her man? It wasn't like he was wearing a sign. And if she was this insecure, then she shouldn't have let him out of her sight. "I'm not sure. John was just taking me under his wing when y'all showed up." Two could play this game.

"I'm sure he was. John's like that. He's got a big heart. Man's never met a stray dog he could turn away." It was said just a little too sweetly. Surprised, John looked down at La-Vonne. "Well, if this isn't the right church for you, just let me know. Tampa's got plenty of churches. I'd be glad to make sure you find another one."

John looked from Cynthia's face, which had turned bright red, to his fiancée. LaVonne's serene expression belied the nails that were digging a hole in his side where she held him around the waist. "Well," he said, "we got a few people to talk to before we leave. Nice meeting you, Cyn"— LaVonne gave him an arch look—"I mean, Sister Johnson." LaVonne's firm hand guided him away.

Cynthia was left with Aneta and Tyree, who lunged for the string of pearls around her neck. Cynthia knew her face was red, she could feel it. Smiling at Tyree, she said, "He's cute. How old is he?"

Aneta pulled the baby's hand away from Cynthia. "Cut the bullshit. Go find your own man, 'ho," Aneta hissed, careful to keep her voice low so people around them wouldn't hear.

Too stunned to reply, Cynthia watched her walk off.

"Sister Johnson, did Brother Colby just up and leave you?" Sister Davis didn't wait for an answer. "And I told that boy to keep an eye out for you. Never mind," she said, linking her arm through Cynthia's. Sister Davis led her over to the buffet table. "Are you hungry?"

Cynthia replayed the exchange with LaVonne and Aneta in her head. She'd been dissed in the house of the Lord. Her earlier sense of peace had vanished. Even the church had failed to provide sanctuary.

Sister Davis was waiting for an answer.

Was she hungry? She certainly felt empty inside. "Yes," Cynthia said. "I'm starving. I'll have some of that chicken and dressing, some greens, maybe a slice of ham . . . that coconut cake looks good, too." By the time she'd sat down to eat, Cynthia had filled two plates.

Chapter

8

After the applause died down, Gloria, Monique's mother, broke through the crowd and rushed forward to hug her two sons. Beaming proudly, she grabbed their hands and, standing between them, raised their arms high in the air before lowering them in a bow. They were an attractive trio. Her brothers, handsome and self-assured, standing next to their willowy, beautiful mother, who was decked out in a silver-and-black-sequined suit.

Monique thought it only fitting that her mother share the limelight. After all, Jarrod and Maurice were the product of her years of hard work and indoctrination. Of course, they had flawlessly performed a violin and flute duet for their parents' fortieth wedding anniversary. So what if they'd only had a day and a half to practice, they were the naturally gifted children in the family.

Monique had not been asked to perform for the occasion, but that was hardly surprising. Though she had spent several years dutifully plucking out pieces on the piano, to everyone's disappointment—except her own—she was no musical genius like her brothers. Monique remembered watching her mother's pained smile from the front row as she sat through one of her innumerable horrendous recitals. While Monique gamely played a rendition of a Scott Joplin ragtime tune, hesitating and striking the wrong keys in ways that probably had the composer turning over in his grave, her mother pasted on a smile under the brim of her colorful straw hat and continually twisted her gloves in her hands.

Monique was convinced that during those moments her mother was wondering if this talentless child could really be hers. After a performance, on the way home in the car, her mother would sometimes accuse Monique of not applying herself just to torture her. It was no big mystery why Monique was hovering on the edge of the crowd in the back of her parents' living room rather than standing up front with her brothers.

The musical portion of the show over, the crowd parted a bit and she noticed her father, who was now standing at his wife's side, stifle a yawn. His gray eyes, which were always tired, seemed even more so tonight. It was only ten o'clock, but her father wasn't as young as he used to be. Every time she came home there seemed to be more signs that her father was getting old, slowing down. He caught her staring and gave her a weary smile and a wink. Their secret wink. She missed him, missed visiting his study, which always smelled of aftershave and cherry pipe tobacco, missed talking to him while mesmerized by his pale hands as he cleaned his pipe—the pale skin inherited from octoroon grandmothers on both sides.

Her father winked at her again and she winked back. He was just as bored with this party as she was. There was a time when she wished she could have endured it good-naturedly like him. But she had found that she couldn't. Still, her mother had been wrong about her. It wasn't that Monique had deliberately tried to piss her off. It wasn't her fault if she had no interest in the piano, or ballet, or the Jack and Jill Club. She had tried to muster up some enthusiasm for that stuff. In fact, she used to pray every night for God to make her the girl her parents wanted.

But He never did. Tired of never getting it right, Monique reached a point where she just didn't give a shit.

Watching her mother affectionately pat Maurice's cheek, Monique decided that her two brothers' brilliance should more than make up for her shortcomings. In fact—she grabbed a champagne glass off one of the caterer's trays—she wouldn't even be missed if she slipped away right now.

Uncertain about her next move, she paused to sip her drink once she reached the kitchen. Then she opened the back door and went out on the deck. She shivered as the night air chilled her bare arms. The heat from the crush of people inside had made her temporarily forget that it was still winter—even if Houston was considerably warmer than the snow and ice she'd left behind in Cleveland two days ago.

What a choice: either stay out here and freeze to death or go back in there and be bored to death. Monique was considering her options long and hard when the bright lights from her parents' enclosed pool caught her eye. They were beacons in the surrounding darkness, pulling her toward them.

As she left the deck, her heels clicked on the brick walkway that led to the pool. She touched the retractable sliding glass that encircled the pool. During the summer, the glass was removed to allow open-air swimming. Her hand closed over the door handle. *Please, God, let it be unlocked.* The door slid back and Monique was relieved that she hadn't been forced to break and enter her own parents' property. She had been willing to pick the lock if necessary. Anything to avoid mingling with her parents' fake friends.

She sat on one of the cushioned recliners for several minutes, not making a sound, not moving. After setting her glass on the ceramic tile, Monique closed her eyes and let one hand hang limply over the side of the chair, while the other massaged her throat. This was the first moment's peace she'd had since her plane had touched down, and even now she could hear her mother's voice above the din in the living room.

Her mother was an active community-service organizer and fund-raiser. When Monique was growing up, her house had been Party Central. Her mother could have won the hostess-with-the-mostest award. Her father, on the other hand, was a quiet, unassuming man. Monique figured he must really love her mother because there was no other explanation for why he put up with her. Love made people do things totally against character.

"Is this a private party or can anyone join?"

Monique's lips curled upward. She'd know that voice anywhere. Without opening her eyes, she said, "Tyson, pull up a
chair."

Tyson's family and Monique's went way back, starting from
around the time their great-grandfathers became partners in
a medical practice in the late 1800s. His was always the one
face that Monique had been genuinely glad to see at the various pretentious social functions she was often forced to attend: the inane country-club gatherings and cotillions that
drove her up the wall.

It was with him that Monique had shared her opinion of all
the high-class do-gooders. If everybody was so devoted to helping those less fortunate than themselves, instead of strutting
around in sequined evening gowns, admiring ice sculptures
and elaborate flower arrangements at some stupid fund-raiser,
why didn't they just buy clothes and food for the poor? she'd
ask him. Tyson would just smile and agree with her.

She had looked for him earlier. He must have come in late.
Now he was here and she wasn't alone.

The cushioned seat of a nearby chaise made a whoosh of
air as he accepted her invitation. Monique opened her eyes in
surprise a moment later when he threw something on her lap.
She looked down at Tyson's white dinner jacket. "Thanks,"
she mumbled as she tucked it around her shoulders. The familiar tangy scent of him enveloped her.

Tyson repositioned his chair so that he could face her directly. "I saw you sneaking out of the party, so I followed you
just to make sure you stayed out of trouble. And what happens? I find you out here half-naked. What are you trying to
do, catch pneumonia?" His brown eyes told her that he was
only teasing.

Monique shook her head. "Hardly. This is the warmest I've
been in months. And I was not 'sneaking out,' I just didn't
think my presence would be missed."

Tyson leaned over to tuck the jacket under her chin.
Monique silently accepted his ministrations. He'd always been
her caretaker—as if he couldn't help it. "That just goes to show

how wrong you can be. I was talking about the Rockets with your dad when, right in the middle of the conversation, he asked, Where's Punkin'?" Monique laughed as he tried to imitate the way her father pronounced her nickname. "Of course, the man couldn't be without his precious Punkin', so I came looking for you."

Monique smiled at him. On the low seat, his knees were almost chest level. Tyson had always been long and lanky, but it looked like he'd picked up a few needed pounds in his old age. "Well, Punkin' is fine, so you can rejoin the festivities. Besides, I thought you said it was too cold to be out here."

"Maybe for a girl. But I'm a manly man," he said, puffing out his chest. This was a joke between them. Monique had always been his equal in just about every sport. So he was always trying to find ways to prove how manly he was. He curled up his arm. "Here, check out these biceps."

Through the thin material of his dress shirt, Monique detected a small bulge. She erupted with laughter. "You call *those* biceps?"

Tyson snatched his arm away in mock injury. "Thanks a lot, Monique. You really know how to flatter a guy's ego."

"Tyson, you know I think you're the greatest thing since sliced bread. So stop fishing for compliments."

His eyes no longer teasing, he said, "I know no such thing. When was the last time we spent more than five minutes alone together?" He stared intently, waiting for her answer.

Monique shifted uncomfortably in her seat and held in a sigh. She was not liking where this conversation was headed. They'd been having such a great time. Why did Tyson have to go and get all serious on her? He was right, though. This was the first time in a long time that they'd actually been alone. She'd forgotten how much she missed joking around with him. Tyson was not one to joke, so the fact that he was so relaxed with her made their friendship special. "I don't know how long it has been, Tyson, but we're talking now. That should count for something." The last statement was more of a question. One Tyson left unanswered. He seemed to be waiting for her to say something more.

To fill the silence, Monique asked, "How is your residency going?" Tyson was doing his residency in OB/GYN at the Texas Medical Center.

"This is my last year," he said, his voice as flat as day-old beer.

"So, what are your plans once you finish?"

He shrugged his shoulders. "I'll be free to go anywhere I please. I could stay here in Texas. I like the L.A. area. University Hospital and the Cleveland Clinic have some pretty good programs. Where do you think I should go?"

Now it was her turn to shrug her shoulders. "What are you asking me for? It's your career."

"That's true, but I value your opinion." He paused briefly. "There was a time when you could get me to do anything you wanted. You probably still could."

Monique looked at him in dismay. Why couldn't Tyson leave well enough alone? What he did with his life was none of her business. Monique reached for her champagne glass. But what she really wanted was a cigarette. It seemed like ages since her last cigarette. Her mother had forbidden her to smoke during the party. "Tyson, you're a big boy now. A manly man, as you put it. So you don't need me to tell you what to do."

He sighed heavily, and in Monique's opinion impatiently, which was so unlike him. "I didn't say I *needed* your opinion. I was just interested in hearing it. How would you feel if we were living in the same city?"

"It's a free country. You can live anywhere you want." From the way his face fell, she knew she'd been too harsh. She tried to make it better. "I mean, I just don't understand why you'd want to come to Cleveland. Tyson, you've lived in Texas all of your life. You wouldn't survive the first blizzard. Do you even know what lake-effect snows are?"

"If you survived, so could I. And as for why I'd be willing to relocate to Cleveland, you know why. So stop playing dumb, it doesn't suit you."

Monique snapped to attention. Her eyes anxiously scanned his familiar features, the wide-set eyes below thick, dark brows and above unsmiling lips. A nerve twitched in his cheek. His usual mask of calm and reserve was not there. What had gotten into Tyson tonight? He was never this argumentative with her—with anyone. "Tyson, what do you want me to say?"

"If you have to ask, then forget it."

They sat in the ensuing silence, listening to the night sounds, interrupted only by the occasional tinkle of laughter or raised voice of one of the partygoers. A gaiety that seemed incongruous with the tension that radiated between them.

Tyson's chair squeaked as he stood up. "We'd better go back in. I think your mother mentioned something about opening up presents."

Monique shook her head. "No, you go. As usual, the no-good daughter forgot to bring a gift."

"It's OK. I knew you'd forget, so I bought two presents and put your name on one."

She stared up at him, not really surprised. Tyson always had her back. Even when she had returned from her first semester at college and was branded by her family as militant for her views on everything from apartheid to welfare reform, Tyson had supported her right to have an opinion. Tyson, who hated conflict, had stood up for her. "You didn't have to do that," she murmured, thinking not only about the gift but about the many unasked-for favors he'd done for her over the years.

"I know," he said, holding a hand out to her. "You need some help getting out of that chaise?"

"No. You go ahead. I want to sit out here a little longer." She sat up and removed his jacket, then held it out to him. "Thanks for the loan."

He ignored her outstretched hand. "Keep it." His eyes lingered as they roamed over her long limbs. "As pretty as you look in that dress, you need another layer to keep warm. Just put the jacket in the front closet or something when you're done."

When he turned toward the house, Monique called after him. "Tyson?"

He turned around. "Yes."

"Are we straight?" she asked, her eyes begging for reassurance.

He gave her a sad smile. "Always."

Her eyes followed him until he disappeared through the kitchen door. Tyson was the most forgiving person she knew. He'd told her everything was straight between them, that they were still friends. So why didn't she feel any better?

Her confusion propelled her out of her chair and over to the edge of the pool. She stared down into its shadowy depths. When it didn't reveal any new insights, she slipped off her shoes and she dipped a toe in. The heated water felt surprisingly warm against her skin. Within seconds, the small sea of ripples quickly subsided, leaving the surface of the water as dark and mysterious as it had been before. She still had no logical explanation for her decision to break off her engagement to Tyson all those years ago.

Sighing, she put her shoes back on and wrapped his jacket more tightly around her shoulders. His scent engulfed her as she headed back to the party feeling lonelier than she had all night.

Chapter

9

When the bus reached her stop, she jumped off and hurried down the street. Walking home from the bus stop each evening always depressed Gayle. It reminded her that she was still here.

Except for her four years at college, Clintonville was the only place she'd ever lived. She'd come home after graduation with the intention of working for a year and then applying to a business school on the East Coast—she'd always wanted to live in that part of the country—but things had just happened to keep her in Columbus.

In her neighborhood, homes that had once been symbols of pride and tangible proof of the American Dream had been bought up by absentee landlords as a way to make a quick buck without exerting much effort. She tried not to notice the benign neglect evident in the untended yards where grass and weeds grew at will; in the chipped and faded paint on the houses; in the vacant lots that spoke of the lack of interest in rebuilding; and in the driveways with their collection of junk cars. All were signs of a neighborhood in decline.

Gayle's parents were among the few people on the street who owned their own home. When her maternal grandmother had died years ago, they'd used the insurance money as a down payment to buy the house from the man they'd been renting from. Her mother had been overjoyed when the sale of the house was finalized. It didn't matter to her that what she owned was inner-city real estate. For a woman who'd come from generations of poverty, owning property was a major achievement, period.

As Gayle turned into the walkway of her parents' two-story home, her heart constricted.

Parked behind her Nissan Sentra in the driveway was her father's old dusty, dented blue Ford pickup. Why was he here? He hadn't been around for a couple of weeks, which suited Gayle just fine.

The smell of his cheap cigar assaulted Gayle's nose when she stepped through the front door. Frowning, Gayle laid her briefcase down on the plaid-cloth-covered easy chair in the living room. She slowly took off her coat, gloves, and hat. Her mother was a pack rat who collected furniture, papers, clothes, and other bric-a-brac (which she called "decorations") without giving any thought to whether things matched or if there was room for them. But Gayle had insisted that the living room remain tidy because it was the first thing people saw when they came in the house.

An expensive black leather love-seat-and-couch set took up most of the room. In stark contrast, an old-fashioned Tiffany-style lamp was set on a small modern white and black marble end table in the corner between the couch and love seat. Against one wall was a glass-and-brass shelf where her mother kept an assortment of the "treasures" such as her ceramic panther, clowns, and cherubs, a red rose encased in glass, her photos of Dr. King and the two Kennedys, and the one surviving crystal candlestick from the set Gayle had given her a few years ago.

The chain from the ceiling fan brushed Gayle's cheek as she walked over to a small rolltop desk. She began sorting through a small pile of mail. Gayle sighed and tossed the letters back on the desk: bills as usual.

She followed the muddy boot prints her father had tracked on the carpet she'd shampooed last weekend. Gayle was annoyed. She had enough to do around here without her father causing her extra work. As she neared the kitchen, she could hear voices.

"C'mon, Barbara. It don't make sense for us to be paying for two separate places. Besides, I stopped drinking. I haven't touched a drop in two weeks."

Gayle stood in the entryway between the dining room and kitchen, leaning her head against the wooden doorframe.

After almost thirty years of a less than blissful marriage, her parents had finally separated last year. Her father's ideas of family values came from the old school. As long as he held a job and brought home a paycheck, he felt he had done his job as husband and father.

They'd had to coax, beg, and at times trick him into participating in family-oriented activities, whether it be attending school functions, going to church, or going to see a movie. And when he was around, he was often in a bad mood. It was like he didn't really want to be around them. After work, he'd eat dinner and then isolate himself in his room watching TV, smoking cigarettes or a cigar, and sipping Budweiser until he dozed off.

When payday rolled around, though, he became a totally different person. He'd stop off at Marty's Corner Bar to cash his check, pay the tab he'd run up during the week, and proceed to start a new one. After a few beers, he became Mr. Congeniality. He'd be all smiles and jokes for everyone within earshot. Every stranger and stray became a "friend" whom he'd drag home with him late at night to meet his un-suspecting family. He and his newly acquired bosom buddies would stumble into the house, catching his wife with rollers in her hair or finding someone in a state of undress or the house looking like a disaster area.

He never seemed to notice everyone's embarrassment and anger as they ran for bathrobes to hide their semi-nakedness or as they tried to casually pick up any clothing, dishes, or toys that had been left lying around. With his arms draped around his "friend's" shoulders to keep from tipping over, he would attempt to make introductions but half the time couldn't remember the guy's name.

Still, Gayle would rather have dealt with that than those times when everyone would be perfectly content and at peace and he'd come home and start raising hell. Buddy might be watching TV, Gayle reading, and his wife sleeping. Yet something in what they were doing would provoke an argument. And somehow Gayle always wound up being the peacemaker. Just thinking about it caused her stomach to churn. A child shouldn't have to be the voice of reason.

As she stood in the entryway to the kitchen, a familiar tightness settled in her chest and in the pit of her stomach. Unpredictability and uncontrolled escalation were always the bywords whenever her parents were together. She took a deep breath and stepped into the room.

Her parents were seated at the kitchen table. The kitchen was a mess, as usual. Dishes were piled in the sink; the table was cluttered with the morning's newspaper; sugar and instant coffee grinds made a trail from the red plastic lazy Susan at the center of the table to the coffee mugs.

There, something caught Gayle's eye. It wasn't the chipped rim or broken-off handle of her father's mug, but the words etched on the mug in red: THE WORLD'S GREATEST DAD. She couldn't remember which one of them had spent good money on such a blatant lie.

They still hadn't seen her, and she silently observed her father. He wasn't handsome, but he had a wiry virility. He used to be an attractive man. She had inherited his coal black skin and the high cheekbones, but not his compact muscular build, developed over years of manual labor. At fifty years old, he had no gray in his hair, but the lines and loose flesh on his face, not to mention the perpetually bloodshot eyes, told of years of abuse.

Gayle's father noticed her first. He got up from the table and gave her a big hug, grinding the dust from his work overalls into her silk blouse and suit. She stood passively in his arms. His coffee breath, stale, smoke-filled clothes, and sweat-mixed-with-alcohol body odor were nauseating.

"How's my black beauty doing?" He took a step back, held her by both shoulders, and looked her over, smiling. "You looking good. My little girl is a business tycoon."

Gayle's eyes and flat voice revealed nothing. "Hi, Daddy. I'm doing OK. How about yourself?"

"I was just telling your mama here that I'm doing good. I'm just missing my two favorite girls." He looked over at his wife.

Barbara Blackman was petite and small-boned. It pained Gayle to see how loosely her old faded housecoat hung on her. Mama was still in her robe. She hadn't even bothered to get dressed today. Same thing yesterday. And she used to take such great pains to fix herself up.

The stroke had changed everything. She couldn't go back to work at the laundry. The heat and the physical exertion were too much for her. Her mother had to be missing her friends like crazy; she'd worked at the laundry for over twenty years. Gayle certainly missed hearing all the gossip. Her mother's eyes used to light up as she recounted who was sleeping with whose husband and who was pregnant for the third time in as many years. Now her mother's eyes and her light brown skin both looked colorless most days. *She's spending too much time in the house.*

Gayle leaned down to kiss her cheek. Her mother's skin was soft and smelled of Ivory soap and cocoa butter lotion.

She smiled at Gayle. "Your daddy was just telling me he stopped drinking. He's going to AA meetings and everything," she said.

"That's great, Daddy. I'm happy for you." And she meant it. But it was going to take more than a couple of AA meetings to convince her that he was "cured." Hell, he'd reeked just now when he hugged her. To be honest, though, she couldn't tell if he'd been drinking or not. He'd been a heavy drinker for so long, the alcohol seeped through his pores along with the sweat.

Her mother thought everything would be OK if her father would just stop drinking. Gayle didn't think so. Drunk or sober, Daddy's real problem was his inability to have a real relationship with people. He was fine as long as nobody needed him emotionally. He was always the life of the party, but let a problem crop up and he found the nearest bottle of alcohol to hide himself in.

Like her mother, she hoped he'd stop drinking because, among other things, she was afraid for his health. Her father hadn't had a checkup in years. The only time he'd ever seen a doctor was after he'd been hurt in one of his many car accidents. Even Uncle Dave's death from cirrhosis of the liver last year hadn't scared him into quitting. Her father didn't want to hear anything about death and dying, especially if it meant giving up the bottle or those nasty cigars and cigarettes he smoked day and night.

Gayle prayed the damage hadn't already been done. There was no way she could take care of two sick parents. And it would be difficult to dredge up sympathy for her father. He would have brought it on himself.

Gayle began clearing away some of the dishes. After dampening a towel, she wiped the table down.

Her mother said, "Gayle, I thought maybe we could do the grocery shopping tomorrow morning."

Gayle frowned and shook her head without thinking. She had planned on going to the office to finish those performance evaluations. She really wanted to clear her desk first thing Saturday morning; then she'd have the rest of the weekend to relax. "Mama . . . I was going to work tomorrow. Why can't we go tonight?"

"I told Sister Walton I'd stop by and visit her at the hospital tonight. You know she went for surgery on her back this week. Slipped and fell right outside the county courthouse last winter. She gonna have a good lawsuit." She shook her head, "All this money we paying the government, and they can't even put salt on the sidewalks."

"Well, if you ask me," her father said, "ain't nothing wrong with her back. I saw Sister Walton two Sundays ago, shouting and rolling all over the church floor filled with the Holy Ghost. Flailing around like a beached whale. Two ushers tried to help, and she liked to knock them out with them big arms of hers. And it's funny how she won't let anybody tend to her excepting Deacon Walton."

Gayle had to laugh. Her father probably wasn't lying. Sister Walton had been trying to lure Deacon Walton back ever since their divorce years and years ago, and Sister Walton *had* been given to exaggeration and hypochondria even before her accident. She chuckled again. If nothing else, her father could tell a good story.

Her mother said, "Willie, hush talking 'bout that woman like that. She really is sick. I talked to her yesterday and she was feeling real poorly." But Gayle could see the laughter lurking in her eyes as well.

"If you say so," Willie said.

Barbara rolled her eyes at her husband. Tired of his foolishness, she said, "Gayle, I told Sister Walton I'd stop by around eight. Visiting hours are over at nine. It'll be dark by then."

Her mother hadn't learned to drive until she was in her thirties. She'd always been an anxious person, and having to endure her husband's reckless driving for years hadn't helped any. It was as if her father didn't want her mother to feel more comfortable behind the wheel because he drove like a maniac or took a different route every time they had to shop or do business in an unfamiliar part of town.

Her mother also hated driving at night, and she point-blank refused to drive on the freeway. The hospital Sister Walton was in was on the other side of town, so Gayle knew better than to suggest that her mother drive herself there.

She shrugged out of her blazer. It had been a long, hard day, and spending the evening at a hospital was the last thing she wanted to do. "Mama, I'm beat. Can we do this some other time?"

Barbara's eyes clouded over. "Of course, honey. It's just that after being holed up in this house all day, I was looking forward to going out. You said I don't get out enough, remember?"

Gayle sighed. Mama had a point. It was rare that she even wanted to go anywhere besides church, and Gayle hated to disappoint her. She looked over at her father. He was going through the refrigerator as if he still lived there. "Daddy, would you do me a favor and take Mama to visit Sister Walton?"

Straightening up, Willie removed a fried chicken leg from his mouth. "I wish I could, Gayle, but I got stuff to do tonight."

Gayle opened her mouth to ask what that might be, then decided to skip it. Today was payday, and the only thing her father did on Friday nights was drink. In fact, she was surprised he was even here.

Gesturing toward her with the chicken leg, Willie said, "Gayle, you was gonna do something with yo' mama tonight anyway. Why not take her to visit Sister Walton? You wouldn't want to disappoint her, would you?"

Gayle would never disappoint her mother. He did enough of that for the both of them. She pushed away from the table. "Mama, just let me change out of my work clothes. Meanwhile, call Sister Walton and tell her we're on our way."

Chapter

10

They'd been there for almost an hour. Despite floating from one small group of well-groomed people to the next, so far Kathy's efforts had yielded zero job prospects. Roxanne wasn't sure how this networking thing worked. She'd gotten all of her jobs the old-fashioned way—through job listings. Cynthia had told her time and time again that with all of her volunteer activities, Roxanne wasn't fully exploiting her personal contacts.

Fully exploiting personal contacts? Even the phrase didn't sound right. Roxanne didn't volunteer her time so that it would look good on her resumé, or so that she could eventually hit somebody up for a job.

While Kathy worked the room, Roxanne helped herself to the food. On her third trip to the buffet table, the server seemed to recognize her yet reluctantly gave her another plate of roast beef. Roxanne wanted to tell him this was supposed to be dinner, but she didn't want to embarrass herself.

Seated again, Roxanne nursed a rum and Coke and stared out the window of the restaurant, perched atop the Prudential Center. From fifty-two stories high, the spectacular view of Cambridge and the Charles River failed to move her. Boredom had set in. She'd tough this out because Kathy had been such a good friend to her when she really needed one. But Roxanne wasn't budging from the table; she was tired of being snubbed. The ice in her drink tinkled as she swirled it with a straw.

She turned at the sound of throaty laughter. A woman around Roxanne's age, her mane of hair so long it stopped around her waist and so shiny jet black it couldn't be real, was smiling up at a man dressed in a Brooks Brothers suit. Her long, professionally glued-on and decorated nails grasped his shoulders like hawk claws clasped around the throat of its prey.

Roxanne couldn't make out what they were saying, but after the man spoke, the woman roared with laughter again. She wore a gold satin blouse, a long black leather skirt, and pumps and leaned in toward him as if mesmerized by his every word. Roxanne knew she couldn't have worn that disco outfit to work. Homegirl must have left work early so she could change clothes for this "after-work" affair.

For his part, the guy seemed a little surprised that whatever witty remark he made went over so well. Smiling, he reached into his inside breast pocket and withdrew a thin oblong object. Was that a cigar? He looked about twenty-five. Did people under the age of fifty smoke cigars? Apparently so, because now Shiny Blouse Woman was holding her hand out for one.

Roxanne shook her head. Kathy had better get a job out of all of this. Got me up in here with all these "bougie Negroes."

"Would you mind if I sat here?" A voice close to her ear made her jump.

When she turned toward the voice, the most fabulous-looking man she had ever seen was looking at her. A smile played around his lips. Well over six feet, he had a neatly trimmed mustache and a shaved head, reminding her of Michael Jordan, and he had the most penetrating brown eyes she'd ever seen. A woman could get lost in those babies.

Before she could collect herself enough to answer him, Kathy, who had taken a break from schmoozing, hastened to assure him that the empty chair was his for the taking. He eased his long body into the chair.

"My name is Marcus."

Two women dressed in power suits had been sitting at their table all along. They hadn't said two words to Roxanne and Kathy, but the minute Marcus sat down they suddenly came to life. All smiles and inviting glances, they introduced themselves.

Roxanne narrowed her eyes. The nerve of them heifers. Why don't they just hang a flashing sign around their necks that says AVAILABLE?

Not to be outdone, Kathy jumped in and asked him what he did for a living. This was the standard icebreaker among the educated set, Roxanne had learned. She wondered what they'd talk about if, God forbid, they ever met someone who was a regular working stiff.

Handsome said he was a financial analyst. "Really?" one of the other women said, flashing him a megawatt smile.

Oh, no, you don't, Roxanne thought to herself. If y'all couldn't talk to us, you sure as hell ain't gonna get to talk to him. "You and Kathy are in similar fields. She's an accountant," she said, trying to help her friend out.

He said, "Oh." This apparently didn't interest him because he turned his back to Kathy and said to Roxanne, "And what do you do?"

Roxanne had to lean away from him. Man, those eyes were like tractor beams, just pulling her in. "Who, me?" she said. "I am a teacher."

That's how it went. Every time she tried to bring up a subject they could all talk about, Marcus switched the focus back to her. Before long, he turned his chair around and straddled his powerful thighs across it. When he put his arms on the back of the chair and leaned forward, giving her his undivided attention and a whiff of whatever aftershave he was wearing, everyone and everything else in the restaurant faded away. It had been a long, long time since anyone had taken this much interest in her.

She didn't notice the faint sound of a chair being pushed away from the table.

Someone tapped her on the shoulder. "Uh, Roxanne . . . I'm going to mingle."

"Huh?" For a moment she took her eyes off Marcus. Kathy was standing next to her.

Kathy rolled her eyes and then smiled. "I said, I'm going to mingle. I'm here to network, remember?"

"Oh, yeah. Have fun," Roxanne said vaguely, her eyes already feasting on Marcus again. She wondered how his clean-shaven head would feel under her hands.

The man was fine, and with his face inches away from hers, she had to stop herself from molesting him on the spot. Roxanne bit the inside of her mouth to keep from shouting, "Take me! Take me! I'll be your love slave." It took a lot of effort to focus on his words and not on his luscious lips. Roxanne didn't care if she was indulging in reverse sexism.

He was so intense, with those deep, liquid eyes. Roxanne didn't know what to make of his complete attention to her. He wasn't acting lewd or anything. But being someone's sole focus felt weird. It reminded her of an old *Star Trek* episode where this space babe kept following Captain Kirk around like a zombie, saying, "I am here for you, James Kirk."

It was not that she thought she was a boring person, but she wasn't that damned interesting, either. She was relieved when he finally ran out of questions to ask her. It gave her a chance to get to learn something about Marcus besides the fact that he made her hot all over.

Marcus had moved to Boston less than a month ago from New York City, and like her, he complained that it was really hard to find people to hang out with. Being from the " 'hood" in Detroit, he wanted to know where the "homies" were in Boston.

At the end of the evening, Marcus produced a business card from somewhere and slipped it to her as they were shaking hands. It was a smooth move, the way he did it. Roxanne would have to remember that move just in case she ever had any business cards one day.

Roxanne thought a lot about Marcus in the days that followed. She wasn't so sure the evening would have ended as innocently as it had if she hadn't been there with Kathy. In a way, she was grateful for Kathy's presence. Her friend probably saved her from herself. After months of the Drought and the Pestilence—as ashamed as she was to admit it—Roxanne probably would have jumped Marcus' bones if he'd seemed the least bit interested. That was the real reason she waited a few days before calling him. It had been almost a year since she'd met anyone whom she felt attracted to. Roxanne didn't want to be ruled by her hormones. She wanted to take things nice and slow.

"Hi, may I speak with Marcus Slick?"

"Speaking."

"Hi, Marcus. This is Roxanne Miller. I don't know if you remember me. . . ."

"Roxanne Miller?" he repeated.

"We met at the Pru Center the other night."

"Oh, yeah. Roxanne, the teacher," he said. Relief flooded through her. "How's it going?"

"Fine. Just fine." Silence. Roxanne said nervously, "You gave me your number . . . so I thought I'd give you a call."

"Good. Good. Nice to hear from you." More silence.

Roxanne could hear computer keys clicking in the background. "Did I catch you at a bad time?"

He hesitated for moment, then said, "Well, I am at work."

Roxanne put her hands on her hips. If he didn't want her to call him at work, then he shouldn't have given her his work number. "Oh, well. I don't want to keep you from anything."

"No problem. I gotta run. Thanks for calling."

Roxanne set the phone back in its cradle. "That went well," she said with a sigh. Maybe she'd waited too long before she called him. The fire that was lit under him the other night seemed to have gone out. He didn't suggest they get together. He didn't even ask her for her phone number.

Guess I should have jumped on that when I had the chance. She laughed at her earlier presumptuousness. No need to worry about taking things nice and slow. That problem had taken care of itself.

Chapter

11

Cynthia put the last of her packages in the trunk of her Toyota Camry and slammed it shut. She settled herself in the driver's seat and turned to her favorite jazz station, hoping it would calm her down.

She couldn't believe that Pauline had let her down *again*. Last night she'd met some strange man in the club and left with him. What would have happened if Cynthia hadn't been the one with the car? Would Pauline have just expected her to find her own way home? Was she supposed to have called a cab?

Cynthia pressed down on the accelerator. She was *this* close to kicking Pauline to the curb, but since she was one of the few people at work who actually enjoyed some of the same things that Cynthia did, she didn't want to totally lose her friendship. If only Pauline was a little more reliable and not so casual about everything.

Whoever heard of coming to a club with your girlfriend but then going your separate ways once you got there and not meeting up again until closing time? Not only was it not fun, but it was probably dangerous. Cynthia was just not used to this nineties brand of female friendship. Now Pauline hadn't even bothered to show up for their planned shopping spree at Old Hyde Park Village. She was probably still shacked up with that guy.

Cynthia had sat outside that café sipping iced coffee for

close to an hour before she finally accepted the fact that Pauline was not coming. If Cynthia hadn't desperately needed to buy some clothes that actually fit, she would have left then and there. But the extra five pounds or so she must have picked up over Christmas was making maneuvering around in her old outfits decidedly uncomfortable.

And why did it have to be a nice day today? Nothing brought out mothers with baby strollers or totally lovesick, walking-hand-in-hand happy couples like warm weather and sunshine. Normally, shopping, especially when it was in a quaint outdoor setting like Old Hyde Park Village, was one of her favorite activities, but today it had been sheer torture. She didn't need to be reminded that while everybody else seemed to be with someone, even if it was just a group of friends, she was alone. She didn't need to witness fathers keeping a watchful eye on the kids as they played along the fountain in the center of the village.

Even when she'd been stuck in godforsaken Minnesota, she had never felt this lonely. At least then she'd had her girl-friends, and they had created their own little back-home community. They had their Rick James posters and Al Jarreau albums. Out of necessity, they became unlicensed hairdressers, giving one another relaxers and haircuts because nobody in the little podunk town knew how to do black hair.

They had to organize their own dances and parties because whenever bands came to the school, they played rock or some New Wave alternative crap that didn't have a beat. And if one of the white students had a private party, everyone had to get drunk first before they would have the courage to start the spastic flailing of arms and legs they called dancing. On the rare occasions when Cynthia and her friends went to one of them, they spent most of the night trying to avoid being knocked down or stepped on by the drunken dancers who kicked and spun around the floor, eyes closed, totally oblivious to other animate and inanimate objects in the room.

But she had survived all the social and cultural deprivation because she knew her confinement would end in four years. Meeting the same situation in Tampa was like a slap in the face. Cynthia had just assumed that this type of problem would disappear once she got out into the real world. But if anything, it was even worse, because, unlike in college, she didn't have a convenient group of potential friends to choose from. Instead, she had to go out and find them.

And for the first time in her life, she was having trouble finding friends, black friends. She had plenty of acquaintances from work. But she didn't have a homegirl. Somebody with whom she could communicate by just a glance or who, instead of looking confused, would understand her—not only literally but at an emotional level—if she lapsed into "black English" every once in a while.

Her hands full, she pushed open the door to her apartment with her shoulders, then reached back to extract the key. Too tired to take her new Fendi bag and her three new suits to the bedroom, Cynthia threw them on the nearest chair and kicked off her sandals. She'd been shopping all afternoon and her feet were killing her. She picked up the remote and turned on the CD player before plopping down on the couch. A mere five seconds of Luther Vandross crooning "There's Nothing Better Than Love" assaulted her ears before she pushed the skip disc button. It was like he was mocking her.

Where was the life she deserved? Where were her friends? Where were the husband and two children: one boy and one girl. She had *not* signed up for this. When she talked to her friends about it, Monique and Gayle both sympathized, but only Roxanne seemed to understand. Her situation in Boston was depressingly similar. But even Roxanne had no idea how horrible it was. Roxanne, who had never met a charitable organization she didn't love, had more opportunities to meet new people. And besides, she was friendly to anybody who paid her a little attention.

Although Cynthia thrived on going out and meeting people, it couldn't be any old body. She'd grown up in a household where well-educated but down-to-earth black people were in ready supply. She was not used to not having at least *one* interesting person around.

Cynthia sauntered over to the freezer and took out a half

pint of rum raisin ice cream. She really shouldn't be having this, she'd eaten two hot pretzels at the mall. Forget it, she could make up for it by eating less during the week. Most nights, she got home too late to cook a proper meal anyway. Cynthia opened the cutlery drawer but couldn't find a clean spoon. Sighing, she opened the dishwasher, retrieved a table-spoon, and rinsed it in hot water.

Why hadn't she been thinking about stuff like meeting people when she'd accepted the job? She hated when life's little unwritten rules snuck up on her. Why did she have to consciously think about where to live or go to school for fear that there might not be other people like her around? She should be allowed to just enjoy the pleasure of getting a job offer without having to ask a bunch of other questions that should be irrelevant. Like, were there any single, hetero-sexual, black men living in this town?

With a spoonful of ice cream in her mouth, Cynthia sat back down on the couch. She picked up a stack of circu-lars that had come in yesterday's mail. Maybe there was a sale she'd missed. But after today's little expedition, she doubted it.

A thin news magazine fell out of the pile, and Cynthia turned it over to the front side. It was one of those small weekly papers that primarily did feature stories on local events and pop culture. She idly looked at the index. It had a per-sonal ads section.

A while ago, Roxanne had jokingly suggested that Cynthia try the personal ads. She'd tried just about everything else, from going to church to being a barfly at the one and only lo-cal black nightclub in Tampa. Cynthia had told Roxanne she must be out of her mind. You never knew what kind of psy-cho you might meet like that.

Still, she opened up the personals. It wasn't like she had anything better to do.

Chapter

12

All week long Gayle had been fighting the impulse to tell her friends about her date with Reggie. Somehow, it didn't seem real to her. She had almost convinced herself that Reggie had only been kidding when he asked her out. Being a kidder was a large part of his charm. Besides, he'd been away all week. She wasn't even sure he'd remember. But Gayle had been shaken out of her denial when he called earlier in the day to confirm their plans for the evening.

By the time she got home from work, the panic she'd kept at bay all week by immersing herself in work was starting to bubble up to the surface. Without pausing to say her usual hello to her mother, she went straight to her bedroom. She quickly shed her clothes and for once didn't bother to hang them up.

As she headed for the bathroom, Gayle looked through the open door of her eighteen-year-old brother's room. That boy lived like a pig. She spotted a plate of leftover rib bones and an overturned plastic 7-Eleven Big Gulp container on the floor next to the bed, which had no linen on it. How in the world could Buddy sleep without covers? Where were his sheets?

A poster of the rapper LL Cool J in a Kangol hat, sporting a big gold chain, arms folded across his well-developed chest, and an arrogant expression on his face, hung crookedly on the wall above the bed. She could smell Buddy's Air Jordans from where she was standing in the hall.

Gayle smiled as she always did when she saw the KEEP OUT sign posted on the door. Who in their right mind would want to go in there?

Her own room was clean and orderly, with one exception. Gayle had decided long ago that making the bed up was not a productive use of time. She spent most of her time at home in bed, either sleeping, reading, watching TV, or talking on the phone.

She took a fast shower—giving the hot spots "a lick and a promise," as her mother put it. There were telltale signs that Buddy had been in the bathroom recently. Wet towels were on the floor, and his hair clippers, not to mention his clipped hairs, were on the sink. She almost tripped on a basketball as she climbed out of the shower. She forced herself to work around his mess rather than clean it up like she usually did.

Using the back of her arm to rub the fogged-up mirror, Gayle peered at herself intently. "Damn!" In her haste she'd forgotten to put on her shower cap. Great, she thought, now what am I going to do? I don't have time to curl it.

She wrapped herself in a towel and went into her room. She picked up her watch off the dresser. It was ten after seven. She hoped Reggie was the type that was fashionably late.

She crossed over to the nightstand and picked up her cordless phone. She dialed Monique's number. It rang four times before she answered.

"What took you so long? I was just about to hang up." Before Monique could speak, Gayle said, "Never mind. I need your help. I got a date and I don't know what to wear."

"A date!" Monique said.

"Yeah, a date. You know, a man, a woman, a cheap roadside motel. Oops, I'm sorry. I'm describing your dates, not a normal one. And I don't think I like that shocked tone in your voice. On occasion, I do get asked out."

Monique couldn't recall when those occasions were, but she was happy and excited for her friend. "Ooh . . . what's his name? What's he look like? How do you know him?"

"Monique, I don't have time for twenty questions. I'll fill you in later. Right now I'm standing here in my panties and bra, and he'll be here in seventeen minutes. So just help me."

"All right. Even though you're being mysterious, I'll be nice and help your ass anyway. Where y'all going?"

Gayle gave her the particulars, then she put Monique on the speakerphone while she stood in front of her closet and described its contents. She had plenty of business suits, but they seemed too formal and drab for an evening out. Despite Reggie's desire to see her legs, she was *not* going to wear a dress. It was freezing outside. They finally settled on an emerald and gold pantsuit. The jacket had a V-shaped neckline and gold buttons, and was hip length. It was tailored to emphasize one of her better features: her small waist. The pants were loose-fitting and flared at the bottom.

It took only a minute to find the right pair of shoes to go with the outfit—pumps in the perfect shade of green. And to think, after all those times people had called her obsessive, organizing her shoes by color had come in handy.

"OK, OK, we're looking good." She was breathing a little easier as she went over to the jewelry box. Just as she tilted her head to clip on a huge gold Monet hoop earring, the mirror revealed that her hair was still sticking out all over the place. She let out a cry of dismay.

"Gayle, what's wrong with you, girl?"

Gayle whined, "My hair is a mess. I don't know what to do with it. Reggie's gonna be here any minute. I look like Don King's twin sister."

Monique didn't have a solution for that. She could get away with just wearing her long hair straight down her back. She didn't have to go through the changes the average sister did. "Sorry, I can't help you. You need an expert's advice. Better call Cynthia," she said.

"Hold on a minute. I'm gonna put you on the three-way." Gayle's dash to the phone base was hampered by her efforts to run with only one shoe on. When she reached the edge of the bed, she slipped on the other shoe, then speed-dialed Cynthia's number. The phone was picked up immediately.

"Hallo, Johnson residence."

"God, did the phone even ring? And why you sounding all uppity? Who were you expecting to call? The Queen of England? Never mind, it's just me and Monique. So listen, no questions or comments. Here's the deal. I got a hot date in five minutes, and my hair looks like the Bride of Frankenstein. Tell me what to do."

Although Cynthia was dying of curiosity, she wisely took note of Gayle's panic-stricken tone. "Well, you certainly came to the right place. I'll hook you right up," she said. "Do you have any styling gel?"

"Yeah, hold on." Gayle ran down the hall to the bathroom. The gel was supposed to be on the sink. "Damn!" she muttered. "Mama's always moving my stuff."

She ran into her mother's room and spotted the gel on her mother's dresser. When she got back to her room, Monique was sharing her limited knowledge of "the date" with Cynthia.

Over their chatter Gayle shouted, "OK, I'm back. What now?"

Cynthia was instantly all business. "OK, rub some through your hair. Then brush all your hair to the center of your head like you were gonna make a ponytail. Pull your hair tight. Now make a bun and use some bobby pins to hold it in place."

Gayle did all that. "Uh-huh," she said, waiting for further instruction.

"OK, do you have any fancy barrettes or hair clips?"

Gayle replied in the affirmative.

"Monique said that you have on a green outfit with gold trim. Find a gold hair clip and attach it to hold the bun. Now use a comb to create a few whatchamacallits . . ." Pausing to search for the right word, she felt a little bit like a 911 dispatcher. "Strands, I mean, tendrils, near your ears and the back of your head."

Gayle quickly followed her instructions. Then she viewed herself in the mirror. Seeing her elegantly coiffed reflection, she cried, "I don't believe it. It's a miracle. I look great!"

"Under my gifted guidance, was there ever any doubt that you wouldn't?" Cynthia said.

Gayle could almost see Cyn's self-satisfied grin.

"Now, if you don't mind, I must return to the fascinating task of sorting my dirty clothes." Cynthia added, "Speaking of dirt, you know you got to call me and dish the dirt on this date as soon as it's over. We have to live vicariously through each other, since hell will freeze over before all of us have a Friday night date at the same time. Ciao!"

Monique was still on the other line. "I know you're running late, but don't forget to put on some makeup and some perfume. It adds to the sophistication and allure," she advised. "Have fun. I'll talk to you later."

Click.

Hmm . . . allure and sophistication. Gayle looked at the three bottles of perfume on her dresser. She didn't want to overwhelm the man. Trésor, the light scent of peaches and apricots, should do the trick.

She'd have to skip the makeup. Mascara made her eyes itch. She didn't own any blush, either. If God had wanted dark-skinned people to have red cheeks, they wouldn't have had to apply a ton of goop before anyone could see it.

She did have foundation but rarely used it. Her skin was normally even-toned and blemish-free. Besides, it was too messy. Whenever she wore it she'd find brown smudges on her clothes where she had inadvertently brushed up against her face. She wore lipstick regularly, but even then used only one shade—Fashion Fair's plum passion.

Gayle's lipstick was in her briefcase downstairs. She would put some on before she left the house. She grabbed a small gold evening bag out of the closet, checked herself in the mirror one last time, then skipped down the stairs.

It was a little after seven-thirty, but Gayle was feeling considerably calmer than she had been a little while ago. She was humming to herself when she reached the first floor. She was about go to the living room to pick up her lipstick but stopped dead in her tracks when she heard her parents' raised voices.

Her mother shrieked, "That's always been the problem. I ask you to do something for me and you won't do it."

"I didn't say I wouldn't do it, woman," her father said. "I told you I couldn't do it tonight. You always twisting my words around and you always gotta have yo' way."

"Right. Right. You come over here talking 'bout how much you changed and I ask you to do the simplest thing for me and you find some piss-poor excuse. You can help out every Tom, Dick, and Harry on the planet. But you ain't nowhere to be found when your own family needs you for something. That's why you ain't living here right now."

"I ain't living here because you such a nagging, demanding b—"

Gayle came into the room, her eyes wide and questioning. "Mama! Daddy! What's going on in here? Why y'all screaming and carrying on?"

Barbara rolled her eyes at her husband. She was so filled with fury, her entire body trembled. "Ain't nothing going on but what's always going on. I asked your sorry father to do something and as usual he won't do it. You would think I was asking him to run me a hot bath at the North Pole instead of traveling a few feet. He claims he ain't got time to check out the furnace because he has to help your Aunt Ruby put some carpet down."

"I am not claiming anything. It's the truth," her father said, banging his mug on the table.

Gayle flinched.

"Humph," her mother snorted, "you must think I was born yesterday. I just spoke with Ruby today, and she said she wasn't speaking to you because the last time you showed up at her house, you were drunk, and upset all the women at the Tupperware party she was having. Now, if you and your sister made up since this morning, I don't know nothing 'bout it . . . but I guess I could call her and find out."

Her father pushed his chair back from the table and stood up. "What is this, the fuckin' FBI? I don't have to prove nothing to you."

"That's 'cause you can't prove nothing. You's a big liar and a poor excuse of a man."

Gayle should have known this was going to happen. Every night this week, her father's truck had been parked outside when she got home from work. Everything had been too calm, too normal. He'd stay for dinner, linger to play a game of spades, then leave. But she should have known that sooner or later, her mother would ask him for something besides the pleasure of his company and the fighting would start.

Why couldn't Mama have waited one more day? Gayle had told her she'd get someone in to check the furnace this weekend. But she had to ask him. She just couldn't resist needing Daddy to act like a real husband.

"I guess you won't be satisfied until you read about your family in the newspaper. Is that what it takes—us being blown to bits in a gas explosion—before you'll pay us any attention?"

Willie pulled at his hair in an exaggerated show of frustration. "Woman, what the hell are you talking about? Stop acting like a fool!"

Somewhere above the shouting, Gayle heard the faint sound of the doorbell ringing. Oh, my God! Reggie! How long had he been out there? She hoped to God he hadn't heard all the fuss going on inside.

"Mama! Daddy! Be quiet!" she yelled. "I think my date is at the door."

"I don't give a shit who's at the door," her father said. "She started something and I intend to finish it."

"Yeah, that's your problem. The only person you care about is yourself. Look at you. Embarrassing my baby!" her mother said.

"Well, if I'm such an embarrassment to everybody, I'll leave." Her father picked up his soiled baseball cap from the table. He shoved it on his head, gave his wife a long, hostile stare, then looked at Gayle. "And you wonder why I drink?" He turned on his heel and headed for the front door.

The front door! Gayle quickly followed her father. She

came into the foyer just in time to see him muscle past Reggie without a word.

Reggie pressed himself against the wall to let her father pass and was now regarding her with raised eyebrows.

She closed her eyes for a moment, then pasted a bright smile on her face. I'll just pretend that nothing weird is happening. If he doesn't ask, I am not offering any explanations.

It would have been a lot easier to pretend everything was OK if she hadn't heard her father's truck door slam, followed by the sounds of a revved-up engine and squealing tires as he tore out of the driveway. Still smiling, she said, "Hi, Reggie. C'mon in. Here, give me your coat."

Reggie mumbled "Hi" and followed her into the living room.

"Why don't you sit down while I go let my mother know I'm leaving." She waited until Reggie sat down on the couch before she said, "She's in the kitchen, so I'll say a quick good-bye and be right back."

When she got to the kitchen, her mother was slumped over the table, her head resting on her arms. Her shoulders shook as she cried.

Gayle went over to her and put a hand on her shoulder. "Mama, are you all right?"

Without lifting her head, her mother said, "Yeah, I'm fine . . . I'm fine." Her voice broke. "Your father just gets to me sometimes."

She sat up and wiped her face with the back of her hands. She looked at Gayle through teary eyes and tried to smile. "You look real pretty, honey."

Gayle thanked her but continued scrutinizing her mother's face. "Are you sure you're all right?"

"I'm fine," her mother assured her. "I just have a sick headache from crying like a fool. I'll just get some aspirin." When she tried to stand up, though, she wobbled and clutched at the table.

Gayle grasped her mother's body to steady her. Her mother sank back into the chair. "Mama, what's the matter?"

"Nothing. I guess I stood up too fast. I'll just sit here for a minute." Then, remembering Gayle's date, she ordered,

"Girl, don't keep that man waiting like this. You go on and get out of here. Have a good time."

Gayle stood there uncertainly. Finally, she said, "Well, if you're sure you're gonna be OK. I won't be out too late. . . ."

"I told you I'm fine," her mother said. Gayle thought she sounded really weak.

"Just do me a favor and bring me my blood pressure medication from my room before you leave." Her mother slowly bowed her head until it touched the table, as if sitting upright was an excruciatingly painful thing to do.

Gayle turned to leave the kitchen. She wouldn't be going anywhere tonight.

Reggie stood up when Gayle entered the living room. Gayle felt like crying when she looked at him properly for the first time. As promised, Reggie had dressed up for the occasion. He actually had on a suit instead of his usual chinos. He had visited a barber as well. Without thinking, she said, "Reggie, you look beautiful."

Grinning, he said, "Gee, I don't think I've ever been called beautiful before."

Gayle blushed and wished she could take back the words. What a dumb thing to say to a guy. Three little words and her intention to act sophisticated had been blown out of the water.

Her eyes widened in shock when Reggie slipped a finger under her chin to lift up her bowed head. Smiling into her eyes, he said, "You clean up pretty nice yourself. Are you ready to go?"

His light touch confused her, made her hesitant to do what needed to be done. She took a couple of steps back. "Reggie . . . I . . . I can't leave my mother. She's not feeling well. I think her blood pressure is acting up." She quickly averted her eyes, not wanting to see his disappointment or, even worse, his anger.

"Is there anything I can do? Does she need to see a doctor? I'd be more than happy to drive you anywhere you need to go."

Gayle looked up, surprised at the concern in his voice.

Reggie had never even met her mother. There was no trace of insincerity in his expression. "No. No. I don't think she's that sick."

"That's good," he said, expelling a little breath. "Do you want me to stay here with you? We could order a pizza and watch a movie."

She was tempted, but she couldn't. It was awfully quiet in the kitchen. She hoped her mother was OK. She shook her head, regretfully. "No, Reggie, it's a nice thought, but I would be too worried about my mother to relax and enjoy myself."

Filled with an overwhelming need to get him out of here before he changed her mind, Gayle walked over to the front door and opened it. He had no choice but to follow behind her.

When she apologized yet again, he said, "Really, Gayle, I understand. I'll see you on Monday." He faced her once more before disappearing out the door. "I hope your mother knows how lucky she is to have such a good daughter."

Gayle simply nodded in response. After she closed the door, she stifled a sob before returning to the kitchen to check on her mother.

Chapter

13

Roxanne took stock of the people sitting at the small table in the vice principal's office. Dion Booth had his arms folded across his chest and a defiant expression on his face. Mr. Shockley, the vice principal, smoothed his tie. He was strictly in an observer role today. During her probationary period, one of the administrators always sat in on her parent-teacher conferences.

Roxanne addressed the young woman sitting across from her. With rows of finger waves gluing her hair to her scalp and three earrings in each ear, she hardly looked old enough to be the mother of a thirteen-year-old. "Mrs. Booth, Dion is a smart kid. I know he is. He gets B's on his quizzes. I don't want to flunk him, but he just hasn't been coming to class regularly."

Mrs. Booth's eyes grew larger and swung around to her son's. "What you mean? I send him to school every day."

Roxanne nodded understandingly. "I'm sure you do. But Dion has missed"—she opened her grade book and flipped a couple of pages—"he's missed eight classes in the last month."

"What?" Mrs. Booth was now giving her son a hard look. Dion sat up straighter in his chair. "I send this hardheaded Negro to school every day. Drop him off at the school door myself. I don't know nothing about him missing class. Dion, where the hell have you been? You sho' nuff ain't been in school," his mother said.

Dion dropped his eyes. "Around."

"What did you say?"

"I be around."

Mrs. Booth looked ready to snatch a knot in the boy. "Yeah, well, you can tell that to your father when he gets off work tonight."

Dion gave Roxanne a hostile glare.

"Dion, I know you're mad at me. But I couldn't just sit by and watch someone as smart as you flunk out." Although plenty of her colleagues were probably willing to do just that, she added to herself. She'd been appalled at the depth of burn-out some of the teachers were showing. In their minds, Dion would have been one less paper to grade, one less knuckle-head to discipline.

"I get B's on my tests," he muttered. "What's the fucking problem?"

Mrs. Booth whirled around and smacked him across the back. "You watch your mouth."

Roxanne said, "First of all, if you can get B's and only show up half the time, that tells me you could get A's if you were willing to apply yourself. Secondly, your final grade consists of more than just tests—participation counts, and you have a paper to do."

Dion shrugged. "How is learning about Andrew Jackson and all them other dead white guys gonna help a brother?"

"Maybe if you came to class, you would find out," Roxanne said. "In fact, maybe that could be the theme of your paper. How Andrew Jackson or some other historical figure helped a brother out or maybe even passed laws that harmed people of color. What do you think?"

He rubbed his nose and said through pursed lips, "Aw 'ight, I guess."

Roxanne smiled at him. "Good. So I will see you in class this afternoon?"

"Aw 'ight." Dion stood up. As he pushed away from the table, Roxanne noted how tall he was for his age. Then again, just about all her students towered over her. And what had possessed young boys to start wearing their hair in big fat twisted braids? she wondered. He looked like the Scarecrow from *The Wizard of Oz*, but Dion probably thought he was stylish. His beltless pants—which had to be two sizes too big—bunched around his ankles and rode dangerously low over his nonexistent hips. Dion had better get out of here before Mr. Shockley writes him up for a dress code violation on top of everything else, she thought to herself.

While he considered her proposition, Dion gave her a doubting look. "So I can say bad things about these dudes in my paper, right?"

"Only if it's true and you can back it up with facts."

"Aw 'ight."

Mr. Shockley said, "Dion, you can go back to your second-period class."

As Dion opened the door, his mother called after him, "Don't think I ain't gonna tell your daddy. Got me missing work over this foolishness."

Mrs. Booth shook hands with Roxanne and the vice principal.

"You handled that well," Mr. Shockley said after Mrs. Booth left.

Roxanne shrugged. "It helps to have concerned parents. Poor woman didn't know what Dion had been up to."

As she walked into the outer office, the receptionist called her over. "Miss Miller, I just got this message for you."

Roxanne looked at the little pink message slip. "Please call Marcus Slick," it read. An unfamiliar number was scribbled underneath.

At first the name didn't ring a bell, then Roxanne remembered him. Well, well. It took Mr. Slick a while, but he gets an A for effort. Not only had he remembered the name of the school where she worked, but he had actually taken time to track her down. Roxanne was flattered. She might just get to know Mr. Slick after all.

When she called him that evening, Marcus seemed really glad to hear from her. He kept telling her how happy he was that she had called, and invited her to go furniture shopping with him on Saturday.

It didn't sound like the most thrilling date, but Roxanne was anxious to see him again. He could have asked her to help him do his laundry and she probably would have said yes. After all, the man was fine. They agreed to meet at the Park Street stop on the Green Line the next day at ten o'clock.

When she saw him from the window of the train, even all bundled up in his winter clothes, he was looking just as fine as she remembered. And he was *working* that full-length cashmere wool coat. A tan-and-brown-plaid scarf hung around its collar. The tan fedora he was sporting would have put Indiana Jones to shame; it matched the leather gloves he was holding.

Roxanne got off the train. Marcus walked over and gave her a great big hug. Shamelessly, she held on to him a little bit longer than necessary. She couldn't help it. It wasn't every day she got to press up against such a fabulous specimen of manhood.

For a brief moment she gave into fantasy. She imagined that she and Marcus were lovers reuniting on a train platform during wartime. When Roxanne opened her eyes, though, the sight of a drunk urinating against a wall in the dimly lit station quickly brought her back to reality. I really need to stop reading those trashy romance novels, she told herself.

There were several furniture stores on Mass Ave in Cambridge, so they took the Red Line over to Central Square. Roxanne had learned early on that nearly every place in Boston was a square or a circle. As they worked their way toward Harvard Square, Roxanne learned a little about Marcus. He had played professional basketball for the New York Knicks for a year, which explained his great physique. After a career-ending injury, he had gone back to school and gotten his M.B.A. from Columbia.

My, my, my. A man with brains and brawn.

Marcus said, "Most of the guys I hung out with growing up are either dead or in jail. Both of my older brothers are doing time for drug dealing. Sports was the only thing that saved me." The sadness in his voice touched Roxanne. Instinctively wanting to comfort him, she took his hand in hers.

Roxanne noticed that he peppered his language with a lot of black slang. It was obvious that he still longed to be back with the fellas in the " 'hood." The desire not to lose sight of where you came from was something she could really identify with.

At the next furniture store, they stopped in front of a display window. Marcus stood close behind her. Even though they weren't touching and were wrapped in layers of clothing, Roxanne swore she could feel the heat emanating from him.

"Let's go in," he said. He insisted she give her opinion on the beds and couches, adding, "You should have a say in this, since you'll probably be seeing a lot of them."

That sounded promising.

He didn't buy any furniture, but Roxanne got the impression that Marcus was a man with expensive tastes who liked to weigh all his options before making a decision.

They went for a late lunch at the Border Café, a little Mexican restaurant in Harvard Square. "Roxanne, you're so easy to be with. I can't believe all the stuff I've told you about myself. I've never opened up to anyone this quickly."

He paused to scoop up some salsa on a tortilla chip, then offered it to her. Roxanne brought his hands closer to her lips and accepted the chip as if having a gorgeous man hand-feed her were an everyday occurrence. For a crazy moment she was tempted to suck away the drop of salsa that had landed on his finger. She snapped her head back before she completely lost her mind.

"I'm surprised you picked such an inexpensive place to eat." He looked around at the wooden tables and quaint Southwestern decor. "I hate to say it, but most of the women I know would have stuck me for the most expensive restaurant they could find."

"Maybe you've been hanging out with the wrong women."

"Maybe." He smiled. "Roxanne, you're so sweet, a genuinely nice person. You're not bossy and you don't talk a brother's ear off."

Little did he know that she was so quiet because she had

lost the power of speech. That had happened when he decided to sit next to her in the teeny little booth rather than across from her. The manly leg pressing against hers under the table was having a strange effect on her vocal cords.

After the meal, they took the train back to Park Street. In parting, Marcus said, "I'll be out of town most of the week. But I'll call you real soon."

He kissed her on the cheek, and Roxanne floated onto the train. It could have been a B, C, D, or E train. She hadn't bothered to look. She touched her face in wonderment where Marcus' lips had been. Not even the familiar subway stench of unwashed bodies could get to her today.

After she was sure Marcus had left on his business trip, she called Monique.

"Hello."

"Monique, it's me. Hold on for a sec." She clicked off and dialed another number. When it started ringing, she clicked back over to Monique. "Listen to this."

The whirl of an answering machine started, then Marcus' voice came over the line. "You have reached the Slick residence. No one is available to answer your call. If this is an urgent matter, please page 917-555-1066."

The brief husky, soft-spoken message sent a little shiver up Monique's spine. "Who was that?" she said.

"Isn't that the sexiest voice you've ever heard?" Roxanne said excitedly.

Monique laughed. "He did sound smooth. Leave it to you to find a 'Mr. Slick.' What's his first name—Rick?"

"No, Marcus. Girl, he is fine."

"I can see you now. Tongue practically hanging out your mouth. Subtlety is not a strength of yours."

"Child, forget subtlety. And yes, my tongue is watering. I wanna break me off a piece of that sweet potato pie. I'm telling you, he makes you wanna slap your mama."

"As you know, I always want to slap my mother. And lucky me, she's coming for a visit real soon," Monique said, sounding aggrieved.

"It'll be all right. You can do some mother-daughter bonding."

"Yeah, right," Monique said. "Have fun with your new man. And try to keep your tongue in your mouth. You don't want to catch no flies."

Roxanne hung up. *I'm hoping to catch a lot more than flies with this mouth.*

Chapter
14

Tap . . . tap . . . tap. The basketball went from the floor and back to Monique's hands as she dribbled it down the hall. Despite the fact that she was wearing an overcoat and gym clothes, a thin film of sweat covered her body, making her shiver a little. Finally, she stopped and put the ball under her arm. *Time to put on my game face.*

She turned the key in the door and pushed it open. The strains of Bach's Brandenburg Concerto No. 5 greeted her as she entered her apartment. Monique always left the radio on when she left for work, but not tuned to the classical music station. *Guess Gloria's plane got in, all right.*

A stack of letters were on the table. Monique frowned when she saw that they'd been opened. Walking over to the dining room table, she placed both her apartment keys and the ball on it.

"Monique, darling, you're home." The scent of Gloria's powdery perfume reached the room a millisecond before she did. Gloria approached her daughter with outstretched arms, then stopped short as she took in Monique's sweat-soaked exercise gear. She took another step forward, kissing the air a few inches away from Monique's face. "Sorry, darling, I would kiss you but you look absolutely disgusting."

"Hello, Mother," Monique said.

"Why would anybody want to run up and down a basketball

court? Why don't you play something more relaxing, like golf?"

Because I live in fucking Cleveland, Ohio, and it's forty-five degrees outside. Monique turned her attention back to the letters in her hand. "Mother, is there any particular reason why you've been reading my mail?"

"But, darling," Gloria said, "I didn't think you'd mind."

Monique shrugged out of her coat. She was nearly thirty years old and her mother still didn't know what she would mind. Monique stuck the coat in a nearby closet, then turned to look at her mother.

Gloria was looking well maintained as usual: tall, elegant, and a pageboy cut with not a hair out of place. Her golden skin was lightly made up. People said they looked alike. That innocent look she was perpetrating, however, didn't cut any ice with Monique. "Opening other people's mail is a federal offense, you know."

Gloria drew herself up a bit. "Really, Monique, I just wanted to make sure you were doing OK. I thought you might need some help paying your bills. I'm sure that—that job of yours doesn't pay much."

"It pays fine," Monique said, grabbing a pack of cigarettes off the coffee table.

While she searched for a match, Gloria said, "Wherever did you pick up that foul habit?"

Monique didn't say anything. Gloria had asked her the same question a million times.

Gloria answered her own question. "Probably picked it up at that left-wing college you went to. I should have made you go to school in Texas, where schools don't fill kids' heads with a lot of socialist nonsense and unladylike habits. Well, I hope you're not smoking out in public. It makes a woman look hard."

Monique almost laughed out loud. She had started smoking back in Texas—in ninth grade.

Getting no response from her daughter, Gloria said, "That reminds me, darling, I want to talk to you about something."

"What?" Monique asked. It was never a good thing when her mother wanted to talk.

Gloria said, "First I'm going to have a cocktail. Then we can have a chat." She walked over to a small open shelf between the kitchen and the dining room where Monique kept an ample liquor supply. Monique got up to help. She automatically took a martini glass out of one of the kitchen cabinets. Gloria always had one martini before dinner and one after.

"Thanks, darling," her mother said as she poured equal portions of Absolut vodka and vermouth in the glass. "Do you have any olives? Or a twist of lemon will do." Monique retrieved a jar of olives for her mother and a glass of ice for herself.

She proceeded to pour a generous amount of scotch over the ice in her highball. "So, what do you want to talk about?" She went to sit on the couch, but her mother's alarmed voice stopped her midway down.

"Monique, don't sit on the couch. You'll ruin it. You're a mess."

What the hell was this crazy woman talking about? This *is* my house. But Monique kept her cool. She moved from the couch to an antique wingback chair. Her mother had bought it for her. During her last trip to Cleveland, she'd also taken it upon herself to rearrange Monique's entire living room. If her father hadn't been there, Monique would have tossed the chair and her mother over the balcony. As Monique sat down in the chair, she thought, Maybe if I get enough sweat stains on it, I can justify buying a new one.

All business, Gloria opened a burgundy leather briefcase lying on the coffee table and took out a bunch of important-looking folders and brochures. She put on her reading glasses, which she wore suspended from a gold chain around her neck.

"How was the first day of the conference?" Monique asked politely. Her mother was in town on behalf of one of her numerous charities.

Gloria looked up from her papers and peered over the top

of them. "What? Oh, the conference is OK. I'm supposed to give my speech tomorrow. But that's not what I wanted to talk to you about." She paused, a pregnant one. "Monique, are you happy?"

"Yes."

When she offered nothing more, Gloria repeated herself. "I mean, are you really happy—living here in Cleveland and with that—that job?"

"Yes."

Her mother snatched her glasses off and picked up her martini glass. "For God's sake, Monique, you can't be happy. Working for peanuts . . . and being around criminals day in and day out. You were raised to achieve more."

Monique stubbed out her cigarette and shook another one out of the pack. "And don't I know it. Let's see. I'm supposed to play golf and tennis, not basketball. I was supposed to attend Rice or Spelman or Howard, not some small liberal arts college in Minnesota. I'm supposed to be involved in the Junior League or the Urban League or some other type of league, not Amnesty International. I was supposed to learn to play the piano, not the bongo drums . . . oh yeah, and I was supposed to be a doctor, right? Daddy is a doctor. Big brother Jarrod is a doctor, and big brother Maurice is a doctor, too. Did I forget anything, Mother?" She took a deep drag from the cigarette.

Gloria's hazel eyes pleaded with her daughter. "Monique, I didn't mean to upset you." *Then why are you hassling me with all this bullshit?* "I know I've been a little disappointed by some of your decisions. But it's only because I want the best for you."

Which means, Mother, that what I want for myself isn't good enough. Monique took a long swallow of the scotch. It didn't burn her throat at all, just warmed it. Warmed her all over.

Gloria moved to the end of the couch closest to Monique's chair. "Monique, do you remember Dr. Clemmons?"

"Yes, he went to school with Daddy at Tulane."

"That's right. Well, he was in New Orleans when your father and I were visiting your Aunt Renee at New Year's. And guess what?" Monique didn't venture a guess. Instead, she sucked on a piece of scotch-soaked ice. "He's a dean at the Wharton School!" Gloria's face flushed with excitement.

"And?" Monique said.

"And," her mother continued, her eyes shining, "I thought to myself, Wouldn't it be great if Monique went back to school and got her M.B.A.?"

Monique sighed. "Mother, I already have a degree—a law degree."

Gloria laughed dismissively. "I know, I know. But think of how much mileage you could get out of it if you had a business background as well. Making the switch to corporate law would do wonders for your career. . . ."

Monique stared at her mother. *She hasn't been listening to one word I've said.* "Gloria," she began. Her mother hated it when she called her by her first name. But this time she didn't even catch it. She was too busy outlining Monique's proposed career move.

"I talked to Dr. Clemmons, and he says having additional degrees and work experience in another field can sometimes work in a candidate's favor when they apply for business school." Gloria paused to retrieve the folders she'd been looking at earlier. "So when I got home, I sent away for some information from Harvard, Columbia, Wharton and . . . Emory. I thought, Wouldn't it be lovely if you went to Emory? Then your brother would have some family staying in town and could introduce you to the right people in Atlanta."

The ice melted on Monique's tongue. This was déjà vu. Like applying for college all over again and having her mother trying to tell her what school was best for her. Monique tried not to choke on suppressed laughter or the ice as it slid down her suddenly tight throat.

Gloria thought, Jarrod wants family living nearby? Not hardly!

Monique knew for a fact that Jarrod didn't want any family member within a thousand-mile radius of Atlanta. What? And find out about him and his boyfriend, Dr. Tim?

Monique didn't think so. But she kept her mouth shut; Jarrod's love life was his business and she had her own problems with their mother.

"Look, Gloria—"

The phone on the coffee table rang, and Gloria picked it up. "Washington-Edwards residence."

Washington-Edwards? Why is Mother answering my phone like that? Her mother claimed to be a distant relative of Booker T. Washington, so she went with a hyphenated name. The Washington name might mean something back in Houston, but it didn't mean diddly in Cleveland. Monique went by plain old Edwards.

The person on the other end was going to think they had the wrong number. Monique held her hand out for the phone, but her mother whispered, "It's your father."

Monique smiled in relief, then walked over to pour herself another drink, this time without adding extra ice. Her father was shy and soft-spoken, a soothing contrast to her mother. Monique had always liked hearing his thoughts on everything from sports to the pitfalls of running a black-owned business. It bothered him that he had to prove his competence as a physician to black patients when the same kind of testing didn't go on for similarly qualified white doctors. Monique missed him and wished she could see him more often—without Gloria around. Drink in hand, she sat back down in the chair.

"Yes, Henri. My plane got in fine, dear. I'm sorry I didn't call you sooner," Gloria said.

Monique opened her eyes.

"Henri wants to say hello, but don't stay on too long. You need to get ready."

Monique took the phone and covered the mouthpiece with her hand. "For what?"

"The concert at Severance Hall. It's one of the scheduled activities at the conference." Monique groaned. "Monique, did you forget? I'm going to change, and we can have a quick dinner on the way. The concert doesn't start until eight."

Monique dismissed her with a tired wave of her hand. "Hi, Daddy."

"Hey, Punkin'. You sound kind of down."

Monique laughed. "How could you tell? I only said two words."

"I know my little girl. What's the matter?"

"Nothing. Mother's dragging me to some classical music concert."

"My sympathies." Her father was a jazz enthusiast himself. "But it will make you a well-rounded person."

"Yeah, that's what y'all said when you made me take piano for five years, and look where that got me."

Henri laughed. "Well, no one is asking you to play tonight. All you have to do is sit and enjoy."

"I'll try." There was a momentary click. Monique said, "Mother, did you pick up?" Silence. "Mother?"

"Yes. Yes. I thought someone called my name." Because of her nearness, Gloria's voice echoed over the line.

Monique rolled her eyes. "No, Mother. No one called you." *Or was talking about you, you nosy wench.*

"Oh . . . Monique, you need to hurry. We don't want to be late." Gloria hung up. Monique could hear her moving around in the bedroom. Probably trying to decide what to wear.

"I'll let you go, Punkin'. Love you."

"Right back at you, Daddy."

After he hung up, she held the phone against her chest for a moment. If she missed nothing else about Houston, she missed her daddy. If only she could convince him to move to Cleveland. With a wistful sigh, she put the phone down and stood up. If wishing could make things come true, she'd be staying in the comfort of her own home tonight instead of hanging out with a bunch of society matrons.

During her shower and while she was getting dressed, Gloria kept issuing dire predictions that they would be late for the concert. But if anything was going to make them late, it was her mother's constant hovering. First, she'd tried to tell her what to wear from the selection of new clothes she'd brought with her—Monique didn't know why she had bothered, their tastes were not similar. Then she'd started up about business school again. Monique finally persuaded her to leave the bedroom by suggesting she fix herself another drink to calm her nerves.

Monique clipped on a pair of earrings and glanced in the mirror. Shrimp, the pale pink color, wasn't one she wore often, but the scooped-neck dress did look good on her. She took an opal-and-diamond ring out of a cherrywood jewelry box and slipped it on the third finger of her right hand. Monique held her hand up to her face and then smiled at her reflection. The ring went well with her dress. The dress was short and showed off quite a bit of her long legs. But that would be OK once she got inside. In the meantime, her coat was long enough to ward off any arctic breezes that came her way.

Monique jumped when Gloria came up behind her and gave her shoulder a little squeeze. "You look absolutely beautiful," Gloria said. Monique smiled at the compliment, but froze as her mother rambled on. "It's a good thing abortions weren't legal back when I was carrying you, because Lord knows, I didn't want to have another baby. My real estate business was just starting to take off, and I was thinking about going to graduate school. But your father was just dying to have him a little girl."

Monique's hands gripped the edge of the dresser. "I was so relieved when the doctors held you up because your father would have wanted to keep on trying until he got a girl." Gloria gave a little laugh, then picked up a nearby brush to tamp down any wayward strands. "I was very happy, too. I was getting a little tired of being the only female in a house full of men. I wanted to have somebody that reminded me of me."

She turned Monique around and held her by both shoulders. Smiling, she said, "Now, seeing how beautiful you look, I realize it was worth the eighteen hours of labor and the scars left by the C-section the doctors finally realized they had to perform. I don't even mind all the sacrifices I had to make in my career plans."

Monique stepped out of her mother's grasp. Her brief moment of pleasure had completely evaporated. "Time to go, Mother," she said, picking up a small sequined bag from the bed.

On her way to the front door, she stopped in the bathroom to grab some aspirin. The top of her scalp was tingling. She could feel a headache coming on.

Chapter

15

When the chamber music recital was over, a round of appreciative applause broke out and Gloria was jolted out of her light nap. Instantly alert, she began to scan the auditorium in search of familiar and, more important, prestigious faces among the four hundred or so concertgoers.

Watching her mother, Monique mused, Some things never change.

Back home, her mother faithfully attended the exhibits of scores of up-and-coming artists and the premieres of any Broadway shows that made a stop in Houston. She also had season tickets to the opera and the Houston Symphony Orchestra. Monique could remember standing at her mother's side at a modern art exhibit while people raved over "the passion, symmetry, and artistic precision" of a particular painting. Monique looked at it, too, but all she saw was a red rectangle set off by a white border. Her mother never noticed that she was bored out of her mind most of the time.

As she got older, Monique began to realize that her mother had two responses to these cultural events: dozing and talking. This was especially true during the Houston Grand Opera, where Gloria's eyes would usually close the minute the curtains opened. Or she would spend most of the evening craning her neck in the dimly lit theater—not to follow the action onstage but to spot fellow socialites in the crowd. Her mother's favorite part of the performance seemed to be intermission. This provided her with the opportunity to act on her true reason for coming in the first place: hobnobbing and rubbing elbows with the movers and shakers of Houston.

"That was really lovely," her mother commented as they made their way to the grand foyer of Severance Hall.

"Mother, how could you tell? You were dead to the world," Monique replied.

But Gloria wasn't listening. She was waving to someone standing by the elevator door.

"That's John Prentiss over there. He's the national chair of the substance abuse committee. I was the chair last year." She said in a conspiratorial whisper, "I'm trying to get on the conference planning committee. I know I can come up with someplace more exciting than Cleveland."

Her mother never ceased to amaze her. Gloria didn't even like half of the committee work she was doing, but she did it because it was the "right thing," the "Christian thing," or because it was "family tradition." She had been determined to instill this same sense of community spirit in her children as well.

Monique didn't have a problem with community service. She actually enjoyed participating in walks for hunger or doing canned-food drives during the holiday season. That kind of stuff was important and really made a difference in people's lives, but—

"Hello, Monique," a familiar voice said from behind her.

Monique whirled around. "Tyson!" Her voice registered her shock. "Oh, my God! What are you doing here?" She gave her former fiancé and lifelong friend a hug. Tyson was around six six, so Monique was never self-conscious about her height with him. Compared to him, she was short. Although he towered over most people physically, he was about the least intimidating person Monique knew.

Tyson smiled broadly at her. "The conference theme is 'African-American Health and Healing.' And the last time I checked, the state of Texas classified me as a healer."

Gloria said, "Tyson. This is a surprise. Imagine, the two of us being in Cleveland at the same time!"

Tyson kissed Gloria on the cheek. "Hello, Gloria."

Behind her mother's turned back, Monique gave Tyson a knowing look. Her elation had changed to anger in a matter of moments. Monique didn't believe for a minute Gloria's overdone surprise. Tyson's mother was her best friend, and they talked every day. How could she not know Tyson was going to be here? *I've been set up.*

Gloria's next words confirmed her suspicions. "Boy, am I tired." She gave an exaggerated yawn to emphasize her point. "It's been a long day. I'm dead on my feet."

"OK, Mother," Monique said. "I'll take you home."

"Don't be silly, darling," Gloria said, slapping her playfully on the arm. "Stay and talk to Tyson. I'll get Mary Beth De-Witt to take me home. Her hotel is near you. You remember Mrs. DeWitt, don't you? Her son is a law clerk for Justice Thomas."

"Mrs. DeWitt?" Monique didn't remember her, nor did she understand how her son's occupation came into it.

"There she is, darling." Before Monique could speak, Gloria darted between several people and disappeared behind one of the red marble columns in the foyer.

Monique rolled her eyes and said to Tyson, "That was about as subtle as a Mack truck."

"Now, Monique, don't be so hard on your mother. You know how Gloria is. She just wanted to surprise you."

Well, she certainly had done that. "Tyson, I'm always happy to see you. But you should have told me you were going to be here."

"Sorry."

Tyson took her hand and she instantly forgave him. She never could stay mad at him. Not when he put up with so much from her.

He said, "Let's get out of here. I could use some caffeine after sitting through that snooze fest."

"There's a café a few blocks over."

As they walked past the classical architecture of the Cleveland Museum of Art, they said very little, but they didn't have to. Silence with Tyson felt right.

Tyson was two years older than her and had always been part of her life. He'd been there for all the major firsts: her first boy-girl party, her first kiss, her first cigarette, the debutante ball. It seemed as natural as breathing that he would be her first lover.

Tyson had been really sweet. He'd made such a big production of the whole thing. He'd actually made reservations at a hotel. Doing it in the car would be too tacky, not to mention uncomfortable, he had explained. Besides which, he didn't want to disrespect her like that. And doing it at one of their parents' houses was out of the question. What if they got caught?

When it came right down to it, neither one of them knew what they were doing, but they stumbled through it anyway. Tyson was all concerned with making sure they had protection and kept telling Monique they could stop. He wouldn't do it if she didn't want him to. But Monique hadn't wanted to stop, not because of some burning passion for him but because she was curious. She wanted to know what all the fuss was about.

The earth didn't move and she didn't see stars, but it was something beyond the realm of her usual experience. Living with her family, she learned how to numb out the pain, and along with it just about any other feelings as well. Tyson would always be special to her for awakening a depth of feeling she didn't even know she possessed. She'd always be grateful to him for that, among other things.

He was constantly at her side, trying to keep her out of trouble, trying to talk her out of whatever crazy plan she'd hatched to thwart her mother. But Tyson never deserted her, no matter what. Like the time she smoked her first joint on an overnight school trip and decided she wanted to ride a cow in the middle of the night. While Monique lay sprawled against the side of a barn stoned out of her mind, Tyson was the one who tried to scrape the cow shit off her sneakers so that no one would know she'd been out in the pasture.

"This is it," Monique said. Located at the corner of a busy intersection, the small coffeehouse was shaped like a pie wedge. "You know you kept me sane, don't you?" she told Tyson.

Tyson held the door for her. "I did? How?"

"By being the one real person in a sea of phonies and social climbers. And you always saved me when I was too dumb or stubborn to save myself."

Tyson didn't say anything. They seated themselves at a small table that looked out onto the street. Not much foot traffic on a cold early spring evening. Monique ordered an espresso. Tyson was having caffè latte and biscotti.

Monique silently regarded Tyson. His right hand bore his college ring from Rice. Tyson had been educated exclusively in Texas. First Rice, and then Baylor for med school.

"I can't believe you want to be an OB/GYN," Monique said. "Don't you get tired of looking at women's stuff all day long?"

Tyson laughed. "Now, what kind of question is that to ask a heterosexual male?" He sprinkled dry vanilla in his espresso and took a sip to see how hot it was.

"Have you made any decisions about next year?" she asked.

"Not yet. I thought I'd check out a couple of the hospitals while I was here."

So he was still thinking about moving to Cleveland. Monique didn't know how she felt about that. It would be nice to have him around, but there was still this strain between them, not on the surface but it flared up whenever the conversation turned personal. Could they ever be as close as they used to be?

"Are you happy living here in the frozen tundra?" he asked.

"Yes."

Tyson took a bite out of his biscotti before going on. "I'm glad. Your mother's been worried about you. She doesn't think you're happy."

Monique slapped her hands down on the table. "My mother needs to stay her ass out of my business. Do you know, she's trying to push me to get an M.B.A.? She's out of her fucking mind!"

"Hey . . . hey . . . You don't have to get loud," Tyson said, grabbing her hand. "Don't kill the messenger, and don't curse."

"Sorry," she mumbled. "It's just that my mother hasn't been here twenty-four hours, and she's already driving me crazy."

"Monique, I know you're going to get mad at me for saying this, but I think your mother has a point."

Despite her stormy eyes, Tyson didn't back down. "Before you bite my head off, listen to what I have to say. Although I don't know why your mother is trying to get you to go back to school, I had noticed long before she said anything that you don't seem really happy. That is, when I get the chance to see you. You hardly ever come home anymore—"

At this point Monique just had to jump in. "Tyson, what are you talking about? I was just home a few weeks ago."

"Yeah, but only because it was a special occasion. How many times a year do you normally come home? Once or twice?"

"You know why I don't come home. If I could come to Houston and just see Daddy and, of course, you, then I'd be there all the time. But I can't deal with Mother constantly breathing down my neck."

Tyson let go of her hand and picked up his cup. "I'm glad you included me in the select group of people you'd want to see. I thought maybe you weren't coming home because of me."

Monique just stared at him. God, Tyson, don't do this to me. Don't make me feel more guilty than I already do.

They had dated all through high school. Just before she left for college, Monique had suggested that they date other people. Tyson hadn't liked the idea, but he'd gone along with it. He really didn't have a choice.

But whenever she came home, Tyson always seemed to be in between relationships. During the Christmas and summer breaks, they would pick up where they left off. She and Tyson had been invited to parties as a couple; she practically lived at his off-campus apartment; and he more than anyone seemed tolerant of her liberal views. He didn't always agree, but he didn't treat her like a child who was having a tantrum, either, whenever she spoke with feeling about something that was important to her.

"I see you're still wearing the ring," he said.

Her face burned. Tyson had told her she could keep the engagement ring. Monique stared at the round opal surrounded by eight small diamonds in a gold setting. It was the most beautiful thing anyone had ever given her. Tyson had looked so vulnerable, so scared while he waited for her answer after he proposed to her. When she'd said yes, the sheer joy that overcame him was something Monique would never forget. It meant a lot to her that Tyson, of all people, would go against tradition and give her something other than a diamond solitaire.

This isn't right, she told herself. *I should have insisted he take the ring back.*

"I . . . I didn't . . . I didn't know you were going to be here tonight." Monique began inching her hand back toward her side of the table.

"It's OK, Monique." He captured her hand before it disappeared out of sight. "Let me see." He held her hand and examined the ring. "It looked good on you then, and still looks good on you now."

He was smiling but she knew him. He was upset. "Tyson . . ." Monique began, "I am so, so sorry."

He released her hand. "Monique, really it's OK. My life didn't fall apart. I finished med school. And I haven't exactly been a monk. You didn't ruin me for other women. I just haven't found anybody I feel . . . I mean, I felt quite as strongly about. I've never felt for anybody the way I feel . . . felt for you," he corrected himself again. "Maybe it's because you know me like the back of your hand or because our families are so close."

Tyson seemed frustrated. Answers as to why the relationship had failed eluded him. Her parents had been ecstatic about the engagement, especially her mother. Monique had been happy, too, at first. But she got tired of *her mother* accepting congratulations from everyone who had read about the engagement in the *Houston Chronicle* and *The Defender*. It seemed like every time she got back to her apartment, there was some urgent message from her mother about the dress, the flowers, the invitations, whatever. Rather than being excited by the prospect of marriage, Monique grew irritated.

At the same time, her mother was pressuring her to move back to Houston to go to medical school, a request that had Monique questioning her mother's sanity. She had never once indicated that she had any desire to become a doctor. She had been a political science/international relations major. Law was a logical career choice. But for some reason, though, her mother seemed to think she was going to med school like the other ninety percent of her family.

As usual, Tyson knew her better than she knew herself. She tried to explain away her lack of enthusiasm. But when she had complained that it felt more like her mother's wedding than hers, Tyson suggested that they elope. Rather than jump at the chance, Monique was rendered speechless. She never imagined that straightlaced Tyson would go against the wishes of their parents. But to please her, he was willing to risk angering them. She should have been moved by his generosity and the obvious love he felt for her. It was then she was faced with the fact that she just didn't want to get married, no matter what the circumstances. Tyson might be willing to forgo the fancy wedding. However, she asked herself, would he, would they, really be able to carve out a life that was independent of what their families wanted for them, especially if they lived in Houston, which was Tyson's plan? Monique hadn't believed they could.

Tyson had been devastated. He didn't beg her to reconsider, for which Monique was very grateful, but he did not attempt to hide the tears that coursed down his cheeks. Monique had never felt so horribly guilty in her life.

She covered the ring with her other hand.

Tyson noticed her little maneuver. "Monique, it's OK. You don't have to feel guilty. It was for the best. Do you really think I would want to be married to somebody who didn't love me?"

Monique reached out to comfort him. "Tyson . . . I do love you."

"Yes . . . but not enough."

Gloria came running out of the bedroom. She was still wearing the same clothes she had had on earlier. "How did things go with you and Tyson?" she said.

Monique threw her purse down on the sofa. "I thought you were 'dead on your feet,' Mother."

"Oh, I couldn't sleep. Did you and Tyson have a good time after I left?"

"I always have a good time with Tyson. He's a great guy."

"Oh, Monique, Tyson is just the kind of man I would have picked for you. He comes from a good family, has impeccable manners, and he has a great future ahead of him in medicine. The two of you looked so perfect together tonight. Maybe after all these years the Washington-Edwards and Foster families will finally be blood relatives!"

Monique wearily sat down on the couch and picked up her cigarettes.

When she had called off the wedding, her mother had acted as if Monique had stuck a knife through her heart rather than Tyson's. Gloria was more concerned about how the most important decision Monique had ever made affected her—ruined *her* plans, embarrassed *her*—than she was about her daughter's happiness and emotional well-being.

That's what this has been all about. Gloria has never gotten over her fantasies about me and Tyson. "Mother, when are you going to get it through your thick skull that I am not fucking Lady Di and Tyson is not goddamn Prince Charles. Besides, have you been paying attention to how that little fairy tale ended?"

Grabbing the back of the armchair for support, Gloria said, "Monique, I do not appreciate you talking to me in that tone of voice. I just want you to be happy. Why can't you see that you and Tyson are made for each other? What's wrong with him? Why won't you even consider marrying him?"

"First of all, Tyson isn't asking me to marry him. You're still living in the past. Secondly, why do I have to get married? A wedding certificate is just a piece of paper. Besides, Tyson and I have been doing what married people do since I was sixteen years old." Monique took wicked pleasure in seeing her mother's appalled face when the implication of what she was saying sank in.

"Monique!"

Monique blew a puff of smoke in her mother's direction. "If you don't like what I'm saying, then don't pull any more stunts like tonight. Don't ask me personal questions, and in general, stay out of my business."

"I can't believe you're talking to me like this." Gloria picked up the phone. "I'm going to call Mary Beth DeWitt's hotel. Maybe I can stay with her tonight."

Monique laughed. "And have her think that you're unwelcome in your own daughter's home? I don't think so, Mother."

There was a long pause before Gloria hung up the phone. "Fine, then I'll sleep on the couch."

Monique was so tired of this. "You can have the bed, Mother. Stop being such a drama queen."

Her voice quivering, Gloria said, "I'll take the couch."

Monique stood up. "Fine. Suit yourself. I'm going to bed."

Chapter

16

She spoke to Marcus on the phone every day, sometimes twice a day, but that wasn't enough for Roxanne. She hadn't seen Marcus face-to-face since the day they'd gone shopping. Marcus was bent on moving up in his firm. Being new, he felt he had a lot to prove and spent long hours at work. Sometimes, she felt like she was in a long-distance relationship.

But not tonight. Roxanne smiled to herself as she placed a pink candle in a sterling silver holder. She'd finally gotten him to take a break by tempting him with a home-cooked meal.

Roxanne had grown up watching her grandmother at work in the kitchen. Her Grandma Reynolds could take a wrinkled-up old chicken and turn out something scrumptious. It was almost magical. Now, as an adult, Roxanne liked to whip up her own magic. She loved shopping for bargains on crockery and dinnerware. The salespeople at Williams-Sonoma and Crate & Barrel knew her by name.

Roxanne covered the small round table located near the kitchen with a pink linen cloth. She placed her best china, a turquoise and pink design with gold trim and a white center, as well as her good silver—the ones that matched—on the table. Roxanne rearranged the flowers she'd bought from a vendor at Copley. Not wanting them to wilt from the heat generated by her cooking, she cracked open a window.

When Roxanne ran out of things to do, she took a seat on

the couch and turned on the TV. According to the running clock on the Prevue guide, it was eight-fifteen and twenty-nine seconds. Marcus was late. She hoped he hadn't gotten lost. He'd never been to her place before.

At eight-seventeen, the buzzer rang. Roxanne walked over to the door and pressed a button on the box next to it to let Marcus in. At least she hoped it was him. The speaker on the security system had been broken since day one.

She ran into the bathroom to check herself. She had her contacts in tonight instead of the wire-rimmed glasses she wore when teaching. Good, no stains on her clothes from cooking. The jeans and blue silk blouse ought to be all right for a casual dinner at home, she told herself.

Moments later, there was a light tap on the door.

She smiled when she saw him. Damn, he looked fine.

"Hi," Marcus said.

"Hi. I was starting to get worried. Did you get lost?"

"No."

Moving aside to let him in, she held out her hand for his leather bomber jacket. "Oh." He took her hand and pulled her to him, planted a light kiss on her lips, then released her almost immediately.

"Something smells good," he said.

"Dinner."

Marcus flashed her a smile. "Yeah, that smells good, too."

She used the walk over to the closet to collect herself. Is it too warm in here? Maybe I should open another window. "Everything's done. Ready to eat?"

Roxanne flicked the light switch off so they could dine by candlelight. She served a tossed spinach salad lightly covered with homemade vinaigrette dressing to start. The main course was grilled herbed salmon steaks, baked potatoes, and asparagus almondine with a chilled bottle of white zinfandel.

Roxanne knew she was a good cook, but she was always nervous when someone ate her cooking for the first time. She felt herself relax when Marcus ate everything placed before him, including two helpings of the bananas Foster she'd made for dessert.

After dinner, they kicked off their shoes and sat on the couch. Marcus commandeered the remote and flipped from channel to channel. "Man," he said as he changed channels for the umpteenth time, "I've been working so much, I haven't watched TV in ages. This is great!"

Wow, he was easy. A home-cooked meal, a nineteen-inch color TV, and cable was all it took. "I'm sharing my most prized possession with you. I'm glad to see that you're so appreciative," Roxanne said.

"I am," he assured her as he tuned into *SportsCenter* on ESPN.

"I'm serious," she said. "Cable is my big luxury. My mother didn't get a color television until I was almost finished with college. She kept saying there was nothing wrong with the black-and-white we had. Can you believe that?"

"Sounds like a practical woman to me."

"A chronically broke woman is more like it." It wasn't that her mother didn't work. Dot Miller had always had a job, but there were many days when they had been one step away from welfare. She was always looking—no, hoping—for some man to come along and rescue her from a life of waitressing and convenience store drudgery.

Roxanne had learned from her mother that white knights were in short supply. She didn't plan on relying on anybody but herself for financial stability. Still, men were kind of nice to have around. Most of them could reach things in high places, and her bed was a warmer, more comfy place to be when it had a man in it. And she was all for comfort.

As if it was the most natural thing in the world, Marcus put Roxanne's feet in his lap and began massaging them. "Your feet are so tiny," he said. While he rubbed and kneaded them, he thanked her for the meal. "I haven't felt this relaxed in a long time." Roxanne was glad one of them was relaxed. She hoped he didn't notice her leg trembling.

Eventually, the stroking and low drone of the TV got to her. Roxanne started to drift off.

"I wanted to thank you properly for dinner," Marcus said.

"You already did," Roxanne murmured.

"Not the way I want to." Marcus bent his head and pressed his lips against hers. She stared at him in sleepy surprise. Then he lifted her onto his lap.

Roxanne was wide awake now. Instinctively, she leaned closer to him, putting her arms around his neck and opening her mouth to deepen the kiss.

Their tongues did a wonderful little dance that seemed to go on forever. Soon their ragged breathing had drowned out the sounds coming from the television.

They shifted positions, and Roxanne lay on her back as Marcus kissed her neck and then began to tease her earlobe by flicking it with his tongue. He was driving her crazy. She wriggled in his arms in an attempt to escape his wicked tongue. Her hands roamed over his back, down to his butt, and back again. Somewhere in the dim recesses of her mind, she thought, We have on way too many clothes.

Marcus' mouth was now at her cleavage. The barrier of her blouse caused him to pause for a moment. Roxanne, disoriented and confused by the sudden removal of his tantalizing lips, opened her eyes to find him staring down at her. She had wanted Marcus from the moment she'd laid eyes on him. She had no intention of playing coy now that she had him. In response to his unspoken question, she breathed, "Yes."

Marcus stood up with Roxanne still in his arms. She clung to his neck and pressed her face against his chest as he carried her to the bedroom. She'd never been literally swept off her feet. It made her feel very vulnerable, yet protected.

She didn't have much furniture in the bedroom, but it had the one thing they needed—a bed.

After he lowered her onto it, Roxanne felt awkward for the first time since they'd started kissing. She bent her head and began to fumble with the top button of her blouse. Then Marcus' hand rested on hers to still it. "No. Let me," he said.

He gently pushed her back onto the bed and slowly started to unbutton. His hands were steady and sure. His eyes tracked her every expression and every sound. Roxanne couldn't contain the moan that escaped her when his fingers paused to explore her before moving on.

Roxanne felt her blouse pull free from the waistband of her pants, and Marcus tossed it to the floor. Then he unzipped her pants and slowly eased them down over her thighs, past her calves, and with one final tug they were gone.

All that remained were her matching panties and bra. Lying on the bed, Roxanne silently thanked Cynthia for that Victoria's Secret gift certificate.

Then she gasped. Oh, Lord, the man was sucking her toes! A rush of heat invaded her midsection. Marcus left a trail of kisses as he slowly worked his way up the length of her body. When he kissed the inside of one of her thighs, she almost leapt off the bed. His lips paused when he reached the patch of cloth above her thighs, then he began rubbing his face from side to side, pulling the edges of her panties with his teeth. Roxanne could feel the heat of his breath through the sheer material. She groaned. If he didn't stop teasing her soon, she was gonna yank the panties off herself!

Mercifully, he continued his journey upward. His lips skimmed over her stomach and the curve of her waist, finally reaching her breasts. He unsnapped her bra, pushed her breasts together to form one soft mountain, and then buried his face in them. Marcus inhaled, and when he came up for air, he murmured, "You have the most beautiful breasts I've ever seen. And they're so soft. You're so soft."

He used one hand to push her panties down. Once they reached her ankles, Roxanne kicked them off. She felt cool air on her skin when Marcus stood up to remove his clothes. He quickly discarded his sweater, jeans, and socks. As he stood there in his nakedness, Roxanne realized that he hadn't been wearing any underwear.

She wasn't a religious person, but even in the darkness of the room it was clear that he had a body that inspired worship. His silhouette suggested a flat stomach and a well-developed upper body—not too bulky, not too thin. His butt seemed to be tight and round. But the only way Roxanne could be certain was to examine it for herself . . . and she would, too. Just as soon as he got his fine self over here.

She opened the drawer of the bedside table. Then she turned to face him, holding a condom out in invitation.

He joined her on the bed, his body covering hers. He kissed her on the lips as his hands sought the place where the panties had been. She lifted her hips to help him find what he was searching for. Her hands kneaded his backside. Just as she'd suspected, he was rock-solid and warm to the touch. Roxanne pressed her lips to his furry chest. She breathed in the smell of Egoïste and sighed as she traced lazy circles around his nipple with her tongue and felt it harden. Her hands roamed until they found, then stroked the length of him. Ah, his nipple wasn't the only thing that was hard. . . .

The shrill ring of the phone shook Roxanne out of the sleep of the dead. Her hand fumbled around for the phone. The receiver clattered over the edge of the table. Roxanne opened one eye and pulled it back up by the cord.

"Hello," she mumbled.

"Well, hello, Miss Thang," Cynthia's cheery voice said. "What are you doing still in bed at two o'clock on a Saturday afternoon, may I ask? Normally, you're up at the crack of dawn."

"I'm tired. I had Marcus for dinner last night." Too late, Roxanne realized her mistake.

"Did you now?" Cynthia drawled softly. "And did he taste good?"

Roxanne blushed. Cynthia was all ladylike most of the time, and then she'd turn around and be downright vulgar when you least expected it. "Cyn, you've got a filthy mind."

"So are you saying you didn't do the nasty last night?" When Roxanne didn't respond, Cynthia crowed, "I knew it! I knew it! Well, looks like he wore you out. Wait a minute, is he still there?"

"No, he needed to get to the office." When Marcus had left at daybreak, Roxanne could only stumble after him like some punch-drunk boxer. She kissed him good-bye at the door and dragged her aching body back to bed to rest the sore muscles that until last night, she hadn't used in a while.

"Well, I'll let you get your much-needed rest. All I gotta say is congratulations and I hope you used a condom."

Roxanne put the phone back on the cradle and turned on her side, hugging the pillow. She knew she wouldn't have to tell Monique or Gayle about Marcus. Her business would be all over the street by the time she woke up.

Chapter

17

Dead leaves crunched under her feet as Gayle moved over to the desk. She frowned at the dejected-looking fern that hung from the side wall. The thing had the nerve to be dying even though she watered it faithfully.

She looked around her little cubicle. Nothing set it apart from any other office on the floor, and Gayle was beginning to hate it. It was too small and there was no door. She didn't even have a watchdog secretary to intercede on her behalf and get rid of unwanted visitors. Anybody could just drop by unannounced.

That's exactly what Reggie had been doing. The first time he'd shown up was the Monday after their failed date. He had stopped by to ask how her mother was feeling. Barely looking at him, Gayle had said, "She's better, thanks," then kept shuffling the papers on her desk until he finally took the hint and said he had to get back to work.

He went away that day, but it seemed like every time she looked up, there he was, leaning in the doorway. He continued to invite her to lunch, but Gayle always found some excuse. She was busy; she had a lunch meeting; she'd brought her lunch. . . .

She couldn't figure out what he wanted. Was he just a friendly person in general, or was he really interested in her? His persistence made her extremely nervous.

She'd never had anyone pursue her before—if that's what

he was doing. Hell, she didn't even know what to call it. Try not to think about it, she told herself. You'll only drive yourself crazy if you do. Gayle focused on her work. It was the only sensible thing to do.

A little later, a shadow appeared at the doorway. When the shadow didn't move or speak, Gayle looked up. She wasn't surprised to see Reggie standing there. But her eyes opened wide when she caught sight of the huge picnic basket he was holding. He placed it on the chair across from her desk. Without saying a word, humming all the while, he began clearing a space on Gayle's desk, putting papers and folders in two neat piles.

Gayle's mouth hung open when he reached into the basket and shook out a red-and-white-checked tablecloth and placed it on her desk.

He had on a suit for once, instead of his normal Dockers and a tie. Reggie took the blue jacket off and hung it on the back of one of the chairs.

"Reggie, what are you doing?" she asked.

"I'm having lunch with you. Since you're always too busy to go to lunch, I thought I'd bring lunch to you."

"But—"

"No buts. I came up here early to make sure I caught you before you went to lunch. And if you brought your lunch, save it for later. I'm sure what I have is much more appetizing." He set two wineglasses down on the desk.

She immediately started to protest. "Reggie, are you crazy? There's no way I'm drinking in the middle of a workday!"

He flashed a smile. "Relax. It's nonalcoholic. I just thought drinking from wineglasses would be a lot more fun than having Cokes from a can."

He placed various containers and foil-wrapped packages on the desk. "OK, we got cheese and crackers. We've got roasted chicken or ham sandwiches. If you don't want meat, there's some spinach quiche." When she didn't say anything, he went on. "Let's see, we got some potato salad. No picnic would be complete without it. And last but not least, we got dessert. Take your pick, fresh fruit or chocolate cake." He took out two plates, two napkins, and an assortment of plastic utensils. Gayle was expecting him to pull a white rabbit out of the basket any minute.

She was speechless. Nobody had ever done anything like this for her. "Reggie, this is really sweet. You really didn't have to do this. . . ."

"Oh, but that's where you're wrong. I did have to do this. We've barely said two words to each other in months. And every time I try to talk to you, you're busy. So I decided to take matters into my own hands."

"I'm sorry," she said. The words of apology sounded feeble even to her own ears.

"I don't know what happened. We were just getting to know one another, then, boom, you disappeared." He had put the picnic basket on the floor and was now sitting across from her. He poured the sparkling cider into the glasses and handed Gayle one. His eyes never wavering from hers, he raised his glass. "Let's drink to new beginnings." He lightly touched his glass to Gayle's.

She took a tentative sip. The cider was sweet with a carbonated kick to it. She took a larger sip. It did wonders for her tongue and throat, which had both gone dry.

"Well, Madame, or is it Mademoiselle, what will you be having?" Reggie said in his best impersonation of a French waiter.

Gayle hesitated. She was tongue-tied. All of a sudden, every little decision took great thought. Besides, she'd lost her appetite. She always did when she was nervous.

She didn't want to not eat because then she'd hurt his feelings—even more than she already had. She considered her options. She didn't want the quiche. Suppose she got spinach stuck in her teeth? And she didn't think she could get through a whole piece of chicken. She picked up a ham sandwich. That should be safe enough. Maybe she wouldn't choke if she took small bites. She scooped out a little potato salad and put it on her plate.

Reggie watched her as she took a bite of the sandwich. After she was done chewing, because he seemed to be expecting some kind of response, she said, "Tastes great."

Satisfied, Reggie gave a broad smile and helped himself to the chicken and potato salad.

The situation had a surreal quality about it. Here they were in her tacky little office having a picnic while computer keyboards clicked and phones rang all around them. Reggie ate his food in silence, which made her even more nervous. He was supposed to be rattling on like he usually did.

She couldn't take it. "So . . . did you make this all yourself?" she asked.

"Yep."

For some reason, that made her feel horrible. "You shouldn't have gone to so much trouble. I have to take you out to lunch one—"

Reggie held up a hand to stop her. "Gayle," he said, "I was just kidding. I bought it at the grocery store last night. You're way too serious. And even if I had slaved all day over a hot stove, I wouldn't expect you to pay me back. You don't owe me anything. I just like your company."

"Oh." She felt silly. To cover her embarrassment, she took another bite of her sandwich. This was a lot better than the can of split pea soup she had been planning to have for lunch.

"So, are you gonna tell me what I did that's made you avoid me like the plague?"

Gayle looked up in surprise. He thought *he'd* done something? Now she really felt bad. Then she saw the teasing look in his eyes.

"Was it my breath?" he asked. "I'll buy Certs. Was it my deodorant?" He pretended to sniff his armpits.

He really *was* cute. Especially if he could laugh at himself. Gayle wished she could do the same. A tiny smile tugged at the corner of her mouth.

Encouraged, Reggie continued. "I know. It's because I'm an accountant. You think I'm a nerd, don't you?"

Gayle's smile grew even wider.

"Aha! That's it! You think I'm a dweeb." He hung his head in shame and said, "OK, I admit that I used to wear a pocket protector with six pens sticking out, and I had tape around the handles of my glasses to hold them together. . . ." He raised his head. "But I've changed. I'm hip now. I wear contacts. I tell you, I'm cool!" Raising his voice imploringly, "You gotta believe me. I'm a new man since I joined AA— Accountants Anonymous."

Gayle couldn't help laughing. He started laughing, too. They caught each other's eye, then laughed some more.

Gayle quickly looked through the open doorway then lowered her voice. Everybody is probably wondering what is going on in here. Great, now I'll be this week's gossip.

When she looked back at Reggie, he was still smiling. She smiled back, and for once tried not to care what other people were thinking. She was having fun.

Suddenly, she was hungry. She reached for the chocolate cake. "Reggie, you are absolutely crazy."

"If wanting to see you smile is crazy, then crazy I am." His tone was suddenly very serious.

Surprised, she looked at him. He didn't blink.

"That's right. I'm crazy about your smile. I missed it. I'm glad to see it back."

He was making her nervous again. She wished he would stop looking at her like that. How dare he look so calm when she was a wreck inside? She put the fork full of cake she'd been about to devour back on the plate.

"I hadn't realized I had lost my smile," she said.

"Maybe you haven't lost it altogether. But it was lost to me, because I have rarely had the opportunity to see it lately."

She didn't know what to say to that. "Well, I'm sorry you were deprived." She placed a finger to each of her cheeks to artificially dimple them and then gave him a big exaggerated smile. "Here's my biggest and bestest smile."

"Beautiful," he said softly. "Beautiful bone structure and beautiful eyes—warm, liquid, and mysterious. I sometimes wonder what they see, what they're thinking."

When he placed a warm hand against her cheek, Gayle froze. He couldn't have shocked her more if he'd zapped her with a cattle prod. She hoped to God he didn't notice the tension his touch caused. But how could he not notice? Gayle knew her surprise . . . and fear must be reflected in her eyes. And her back was as stiff as a foot soldier's in the presence of a four-star general.

Her efforts to lighten things up hadn't worked at all. If possible, Reggie was even more intense than he had been a few minutes earlier. He slowly withdrew his hand but continued to stare into her eyes, as if searching for something.

"I'm going to miss that face—"

"What?" she said, confused. Why was he going to miss her face?

"One of the reasons that I had to have lunch with you today is that I'll be working at the Chicago office starting next week. And I couldn't leave without spending some time with you."

Gayle felt her body go hot, then cold. How could he do this to her? Why hadn't he said he was transferring in the first place? Why come in here and give her all this attention, only to take off? What was the point?

"Gayle? Gayle, did you hear me?" he asked. "I'm going to be doing a training rotation in the Chicago office."

"Training rotation?" she repeated. She didn't understand.

"Yeah. I'll be there for a few months, then I'll be back in July." He looked at her uncertainly. "Are you OK? You disappeared again for a minute."

He picked up her wineglass and sniffed the liquid in it. "If I didn't know this was nonalcoholic, I'd swear you'd been hitting the bottle," he teased.

Gayle gave him a weak smile. Her mind was still in a whirl. He was only going for a few months, then he would be back. She'd thought . . . forget what she'd thought.

"I wasn't told until four days ago that I'd have to go there. Since I'll be away for a while, I wanted to say good-bye before I left. And lately it seems like you never have any time, so—"

"Well, I'm glad you stopped by. I'm sorry if you felt I was avoiding you. Just know that it had nothing to do with anything you said or did." No, I'm the one with the problem, she thought.

He was looking at her like he expected her to elaborate.

What was she supposed to say? My father's a drunk, my mother's sick, and I'm too scared of men to let one get close to me? "Well, I'm sure everyone around here will miss you," she said. That was as close to the truth as she dared get.

Reggie had started clearing away what was left of their lunch. He paused. "I don't care about everyone. But I do hope that *you* will miss me."

It was a question. He waited for an answer. Tell him you will, a little voice was shouting. But I'm scared, another voice was shouting even louder. The scared voice won out. "We'll *all* miss you," she repeated.

She saw his shoulders slump. He looked away from her and concentrated on stuffing things back into the picnic basket. When he was done, he picked up the basket. Holding it at his side, he said, "I know I'll miss you. Who knows, maybe one day the feeling will be mutual. Only time will tell. See you in July." He turned and left.

"Reggie, I will miss you," she said softly. But she knew he was probably halfway down the hall. Gayle began to slowly bang her head on her desk, saying over and over, "Stupid, stupid, stupid."

Chapter
18

Cynthia was surprised by the number of personal ads placed in such a small paper. It made her feel better. At least she wasn't the only one searching for that perfect someone. At first she couldn't make heads or tails of all the abbreviations used: SWM, DHF, GM. But she eventually got the hang of it.

She quickly developed a sense of what she was and was not interested in. Anything that referred to casual sex or superficial physical characteristics had to go. Ads that asked for photos or that read something like "handsome hunk looking for open-minded beer babe for love in the afternoon" or "busy executive looking for travel companion, no strings attached" or "swinging couple looking for third member for a ménage à trois" were the first to be axed, which meant a lot of ads were crossed off the list. Some were scary to think about. Like the person who was looking for an SWF with silver hair in her sixties who wore dentures and liked waterskiing.

After about three weeks, Cynthia felt like giving up because she rarely saw any ad that said "BM," and if it did, he was usually looking for anything but a "BF." Then one day she finally saw something that got her attention:

32 yr old professional BM seeks 25–35 yr old educated BF who loves jazz, intelligent conversation, old movies, and God. Seeking a friendship and possible committed relationship. Only the mature woman need reply.

Cynthia read the ad over and over. She couldn't believe it. Somebody out there was looking for her! Except for the old movies, but heck, all she needed to do was watch American Movie Classics on cable for a few weeks and she'd be set. Best of all, he didn't mention any craziness like Frederick's of Hollywood lingerie, or swimming naked at midnight. *And* he was religious.

Her mother would love that!

It took her a week to get up the courage to respond to the ad. She left a message at the voice-mail number listed with the ad, and a couple of days later David called.

His voice, deep and sexy, made her toes curl. God, he could have been a DJ on some late night show that only played songs for lovers. And she loved the way he paused between sentences as if giving thought and care to each word.

Although his law practice was in Daytona Beach, David had advertised in the Tampa paper because he came there a lot for business. He had never been married and had no children. Cynthia gave a silent prayer of thanks for that. The last thing she needed was baggage from a previous relationship.

They talked for about a half hour the first time. When Cynthia got off the phone, her eyes were shining with excitement. She did a little jig around her bedroom. "This is looking good, girl," she said to her four walls. "He doesn't sound ignorant. He ain't got no kids. He didn't just talk about himself. He asked about my job and my family but wasn't so nosy that he needed to know all my business." Not that she had a lot of business to tell.

Unlike some men who ask for a woman's number and then never call or call six months later and try to start from where they'd left off, David called back a few days later. This conversation went as smoothly as the first. They talked about their common interest in jazz. They both liked Charlie "Bird" Parker. Neither considered Quincy Jones true jazz. And he didn't freak out when she criticized his favorite, Miles Davis, for being an egotistical womanizer.

All he said was, "Yeah, maybe so. But Miles can play. I love Miles the musician, not necessarily the person."

Cynthia decided she could live with that.

She flirted with him big-time. And she liked that he kept it clean; no signs that he was looking to jump her bones at the first opportunity. Whether or not this respectful boy-next-door image was true remained to be seen, but she appreciated the fact that he had the good grace to act like a gentleman.

Finally came the big question. David said, in that thrilling voice of his, "When can we meet? I'd like to put a face to the wonderful person I'm getting to know over the phone. It seems like you and I have a lot in common."

Cynthia acted cool and calm, but if he'd been in her apartment he would have seen her jumping up and down in the middle of her bedroom, pumping her fist in a silent Yes! Yes!

David suggested they meet in some neutral public place where she didn't have to worry about being attacked or kidnapped by some unknown man.

How perceptive of him to realize that thoughts like that *did* cross women's minds. I think I'm going to like this guy. She replied, "Who knows? Maybe I'll kidnap you."

With a laugh David asked, "But is it really kidnapping if the victim is willing?"

"I guess I'll find out on Saturday night," Cynthia said.

Orlando was halfway between Tampa and Daytona, so they decided to meet at a jazz supper club near Epcot Center that they both had been to before.

After Cynthia hung up the phone, she slumped to the floor. She thought to herself, If talking to him on the phone leaves me this weak in the knees, I don't know if I can handle seeing the man in the flesh.

What would people think if they knew what she was up to? Her mother would be appalled. This was not the proper way to meet a young man. But good old Roxanne would urge her on. "Go for it, girl!" she'd say. Gayle, on the other hand, would be cautious. Cynthia could just hear her mothering tone. "I can't believe you answered a personal ad! Be careful. You don't know nothing about that man. Don't let him get you nowhere by yourself!"

A potential lecture from Gayle was enough to persuade her

to hold on to her secret just a little longer, even though it was killing her to do it. There'd been too many false alarms in the past. She would call them all excited about some man, and then she'd feel like a fool when nothing came of it.

No, just this once I'll wait and see how things turn out before I open my big mouth.

She and David had set up the date on Wednesday, and by Friday her nerves were shot to hell. Lisa, her secretary, was on the brink of strangling her. All day, Cynthia kept misplacing files, and she waited until the last minute to give her notes for a press release. As a result, Lisa had to stop working on another project, and they both ended up working late to get it out on time.

In the middle of all this craziness, David called to ask how they would be able to recognize each other, since they'd never met before. This little detail had slipped her mind. He described himself as being around six feet tall, with a fade haircut, and said he'd be wearing a gray suit.

Cynthia had no idea what she'd be wearing but said she shouldn't be too hard to spot. She'd be the light-skinned woman with blue eyes and shoulder-length reddish brown hair. He seemed surprised by the blue eyes part but recovered nicely and said he'd meet her at around eight o'clock the next night.

She was relieved when Saturday finally came because at least she didn't have to deal with anyone and could just plan for the night ahead.

Never an early riser if she didn't have to be, Cynthia was busy tearing apart her closet searching for the perfect outfit to wear at eight o'clock on Saturday morning. By noon she was sitting in the middle of the floor surrounded by mounds of clothes. All rejects.

After turning her closets upside down, Cynthia decided on a simple black dress. Black was always a safe bet. The Norma Kamali was one of her favorites. It was lined linen and short-sleeved, had a rounded neckline, flared at the hips, and stopped just above the knees. Now, here was a designer smart enough to know that not all women looked like twigs. Her double strand of pearls and pearl earrings would go with the dress just fine.

Cynthia started some long-overdue household chores to make the day go faster. She did three loads of laundry, vacuumed the entire apartment, and soaked and scrubbed all of her china. The next time she looked at the clock, it was six o'clock. She'd have to hustle if she didn't want to be late. She took a quick shower, then applied her favorite fragrance in layers, just like her mother had taught her. Using the powder, lotion, and perfume versions of White Linen would give the scent lasting power.

Her turned-under flip required only a few flicks of the curling iron. She slipped on the dress and put a robe over it as she put on her makeup. With the ease of an expert, she applied foundation, lipstick, blush, teal eyeliner, and a little gray-blue eye shadow to bring out the color of her eyes. As a final touch, she added the necklace and earrings. She stood back and surveyed her reflection.

"Damn, I look good."

Cynthia was on the road by seven o'clock. She took I-75 South to I-4 East. It was a seventy-mile drive to Orlando, and as the scenery sped by, she felt calm. She had never had a problem talking to anybody, and she already knew what David's interests were. They would share a meal and listen to some jazz. It was about time she had some fun.

She arrived only fifteen minutes late, which wasn't too bad. The restaurant smelled of tangy Cajun spices. Her stomach growled in response, reminding her that all she'd eaten all day was a bagel.

She was supposed to meet David at the bar, which was to the left of the entrance. It was partially hidden by huge potted plants along the wooden railing that separated the bar from the dining area.

The bar was on a raised platform. As Cynthia walked around its perimeter, only her head could be seen over the plants. She strained her eyes trying to catch a glimpse of David before he spotted her.

A man wearing a gray suit and a black turtleneck was sitting on a bar stool facing the dining area. He had one elbow resting on the counter. Even from her partially blocked view through the foliage, Cynthia liked the way the formfitting material stretched across his chest. He had a well-defined body but a so-so face, and the ears were kind of big. As she rounded the corner, he spotted Cynthia and gave her a big smile that totally transformed him. He had two adorable dimples that more than made up for his goofy-looking ears.

She smiled at him and waved. By the eager way he stood up to greet her, she could tell that he liked what he saw.

When Cynthia reached the top of the small set of stairs and stood in full view, though, his smile faltered. He hesitated for a moment, then walked over to her and extended his hand.

She took a deep breath and willed herself to relax.

He asked her if she'd care for a drink, but his voice lacked the warmth that she'd initially seen in his eyes. Cynthia swallowed and her heart sank. Something was wrong.

Cynthia, she told herself, don't jump to conclusions. Maybe he saw something going on behind you, and that caused the change of expression.

She shook his hand and apologized for being late. They had a drink at the bar, and he asked her how the drive to the restaurant had been.

Sipping her wine, Cynthia felt herself start to relax. Everything was fine. Maybe that fleeting look of disappointment she'd seen in his face had been her imagination.

Soon, the waitress told them that their table was ready. They followed her over to a table near the front. The view of the quartet was excellent. They sat for a while in silence, letting the sounds of the sensuous alto sax float over them.

The waitress came back to take their order. "Would you care for an appetizer?" she asked.

David's eyes raked over Cynthia, and without even bothering to consult her, he said, "No, I don't think so. We'll just be ordering dinner."

Great, thought Cynthia, my perfect man is turning out to be a cheapskate. Even though she was ravenous, she just smiled and said, "That's OK with me. I'm ready to order. Are you?"

David said, "I'm not sure. I was thinking of the jambalaya or the fried catfish."

Cynthia knew exactly what she wanted. She'd been craving it ever since they had decided to come to this place. She said, "Well, I'm going to get the blackened Cajun steak."

David looked up from his menu. "Are you sure you want that? I thought you might like some type of light salad. The seafood Caesar's pretty good."

"Oh, that sounds delicious," Cynthia lied.

David's approving smile returned.

Cynthia didn't dare look at the waitress. Even though he hadn't said anything outright rude like "You're too damn fat to be eating a steak," she felt like a child who had been disciplined in front of her friends.

By the time the food was served, she had lost her appetite entirely. She didn't feel comfortable eating in front of David. All he talked about while they were waiting for the meal was how important he felt diet and exercise were and how some of his married male friends were really turned off by their wives, who had grown fat and lazy after they had gotten a ring on their finger.

If that was supposed to be a hint, Cynthia took it. David didn't seem to notice that she just picked at her salad.

In between talking about the evils of being overweight, there were long silences where they both focused on the music. The sax had gone from sexy to sad. Or was it just her?

David talked about his job some and commented on the music a few times. But Cynthia couldn't think of a single thing to chat about to save her life. His politeness was killing her. The minute he had started talking about his dislike of overweight people, she knew the date was over. The flirtatious woman he'd spoken to on the phone had vanished.

The Norma Kamali dress that she had thought was so chic, so flattering, now felt like a sackcloth. No matter how prettily she wrapped the package, in the end she was still just a pig-in-a-blanket.

After his attempts to make conversation went nowhere, David gave up. An uncomfortable silence settled over the table.

Cynthia felt nothing but relief when the waitress came to clear their table. This time she said no to dessert before David got a chance to do it for her.

When the band took a break around ten o'clock, David hinted that he had to be up early the next morning. On a Sunday, Cynthia thought, yeah, right. Aloud, she said, "Me, too. I have to go to church."

They parted with a handshake, and David didn't insult her by claiming he'd call her soon. Even in her depressed mood, Cynthia could appreciate that. He was basically a decent man. He just didn't want her.

She cried so hard on the drive home that she had to pull over to the side of the road a couple of times. She cried all day Sunday. By Monday morning she'd cried herself out.

The same day, she called Weight Watchers. Making the most of what she had just wasn't going to cut it. If she hadn't known that before, she knew it now, and all it had taken was one disappointed look from a man she didn't even know.

Chapter

19

Gayle covered her mouth with her hands as another series of coughs from deep within her chest seized her. Her eyes were watery and she looked like she hadn't slept in a couple of days.

April 15 was right around the corner, and Monique had asked Gayle to do her income tax return because she couldn't find a tax preparer at this late date. Crunching numbers aggravated Monique, so when she did her own taxes she tended to be careless with her math or forget to fill out a required schedule. When she'd made a desperate call to Gayle earlier in the week, Gayle had sounded like her normal self. Now she could barely speak.

Monique said, "Gayle, I never would have asked you to come to Cleveland if I'd known you were sick. Why didn't you say something?"

"I'm fine—" Gayle sneezed into a balled-up wad of facial tissues. "I just have a little cold."

"Sounds more like walking pneumonia to me. Have you seen a doctor?"

Gayle shook her head. "I'm fine," she repeated. Monique was stalling. Gayle couldn't understand why she was so intimidated by a simple tax form. "Where's your W-2?"

Monique rooted through a pile of papers she'd dumped on the dining room table. She looked annoyed. Gayle coughed, trying to clear the phlegm from her throat. "You know,

Monique, this wouldn't be so traumatic if you would just organize things a bit during the year."

Monique silently handed her the W-2, which had been stuck to the bottom of her coffee cup.

Gayle looked at the W-2 and scribbled something on a yellow legal pad. "Now, I need all the records of interest income you earned this year." Monique again delved into the pile. She handed Gayle the statements from her savings and money market accounts.

After glancing at them, Gayle said, "You made over four hundred dollars in interest."

"So?"

"So you're going to have to complete Part One of Schedule B. And if you have received any taxable stock dividends, you may have to complete Part Two of Schedule B."

Monique ground out her cigarette. As far she was concerned, Gayle had ceased speaking English. "I'm ready for a glass of wine. Can I get you anything?"

Another cough. "Tea with lemon would be nice. But I can get it myself."

Gayle started to rise, but Monique pushed her back down in her seat. "Don't move. I'll get it. It's the least I can do."

Rubbing her eyes, Gayle began putting the various pieces of paper into categories. She was never going to get anything done if she had to wait for Monique to search through the pile every time she needed something. Once she had sorted things out, she went back to work. She looked over the 1099-DIVs from several mutual funds and called out, "Pretty impressive, Monique. You might not be raking in the dough over at the prosecutor's office, but you have quite the portfolio going."

Monique returned with Gayle's tea, a bottle of wine, and a wineglass. She handed Gayle the mug. "Don't be impressed with me. You can thank my parents for that. They keep giving me stocks and bonds as gifts. The Washington-Edwards are practical folk, if not too personal, huh?"

Maybe so, Gayle thought, but Monique should be a little more grateful. Some parents could only dream about giving their kids a financial leg up. She certainly wouldn't turn *her* nose up at a mutual fund.

"I just try to put fifty or a hundred dollars in each one of them here and there," Monique said.

"Well, it's nice of your parents to help you out." Gayle punched a few numbers on her calculator, then wrote the sum on the appropriate line on the tax return. She turned to Monique's records of gifts to charity, the biggest pile she'd made. Gayle wasn't surprised. For some reason, Monique put up this tough-girl front, but Gayle knew her. The long list of charitable contributions showed a softer side of her that Gayle long knew existed.

A thin stream of smoke wafted past her, and Gayle rubbed her nose. Her throat, her entire face really, hurt. The cigarette smoke wasn't helping. She turned to Monique, who was resting her arms on the table and mixing up the piles Gayle had so carefully sorted. "Monique, don't you have anything else you could be doing?"

Monique immediately removed her elbows from the piles of papers. *That was Gayle, always hinting, never quite asking, even when she had every right to.* Monique stood up, taking the wine bottle and glass with her. "I take it I'm bothering you. I guess I could go wash my hair. My scalp is itching like crazy."

Good, thought Gayle. It took Monique's thick hair forever to dry. Maybe then she could get some work done. "Well, don't let me keep you," Gayle said.

Monique dried her hair in her room with the door closed. Gayle was doing her a huge favor, so she didn't want to get in her way. Anybody else would have said no at such short notice. But she'd make it up to her. Tonight she was going to treat Gayle to an expensive meal, then try and get her to have a little fun. Maybe they would go club-hopping in the Flats.

Monique loved sampling the cluster of nightclubs and bars that had sprung up along Cleveland's revamped waterfront. And if Gayle was feeling up to it, tomorrow they might go to the Rock and Roll Hall of Fame. Monique hadn't been there yet, but everything she'd heard about the place had sounded interesting. This was not the same city that had been the butt of late night talk show hosts years and years ago. Back then, crazy things had happened, like the Cuyahoga River catching on fire because it was so polluted. Or when a young and inexperienced mayor let the city go into default. Despite its rebirth, Cleveland still had to live down a bad rap.

She dropped the last curler into the hatbox she kept them in. *I'll wait until we get ready to leave for dinner before I comb my hair out.* Deciding she'd kept out of Gayle's way long enough, Monique went to see how she was progressing.

In the living room, Monique found that her tax documents were neatly stacked on the table—except for the tax form itself, which was trapped beneath Gayle's arms and the weight of her head.

Gayle was fast asleep.

Monique felt a pang of guilt. *Shit! She's exhausted. I should have made her lie down and done it myself. So what if I added something wrong? It wouldn't be the first time.*

Monique tiptoed into the kitchen and put what was left of the wine back into the refrigerator.

"Monique, is that you?"

Damn! She hadn't wanted to wake her up. *You're batting a thousand tonight, Monique.* "Yeah, Gayle. I'll be right out."

Gayle's arms were stretched above her head when Monique turned the corner. Gayle was looking worse, not better, after her nap.

Half apologetically, Gayle said, "I guess I dozed off."

Dozing? Is that what it was? "Gayle, every other week something is wrong with you. Today it's a cold; last week it was lower-back pain." Monique knew she was treading on dangerous ground, but it had to be said. "Then you had that mysterious ringing in your ears. It doesn't take a rocket scientist to figure out it's stress. You're working too hard. You're trying too hard to take care of your family. Gayle, everybody in that house is old enough to be taking care of themselves."

Gayle's answer was on a different track. "Work is crazy right now. We have a big audit coming up. It's this random thing. Of all the departments to choose from, why did my department have to be picked?" Monique looked skeptical as she went on. "Plus, my mother needs me. She just hasn't been herself since the stroke. She's so frail and her energy is low."

Monique knew better than to suggest that nothing was wrong with Mrs. Blackman that forcing her to take care of herself a bit wouldn't cure. "OK, Gayle, how is your mother going to be able to rely on you if you don't take of yourself?"

The very idea of not being there when her mother needed her scared Gayle. "But I'm fine," she said without much conviction.

"Yeah, right. That's why you slept twelve hours straight yesterday. Do you even remember getting ready for bed last night?"

Gayle thought for a moment but drew a blank. The last thing she remembered about yesterday was hearing Monique talking on the extension in the bedroom. She stared helplessly at her friend.

"Uh-huh, I thought as much. You didn't get ready for bed. You passed out from fatigue. I just threw a blanket over you, and you didn't budge until late this morning. Gayle, you've got to get some rest."

Gayle knew Monique was right. She was so tired her bones hurt. But she couldn't just take off work. "Monique, you know I can't leave the office in the lurch at this time of year. I'll have to wait until the summer."

This wasn't even about the office, and Gayle knew it.

"I have an offer you can't refuse. Remember how Angie's wedding was supposed to be this big reunion for us?"

Gayle nodded.

"But instead it turned out to be a big pain in the butt and we didn't really get to spend any time together. I think we should do a real reunion this summer. The four of us should just take off—go to Club Med or Alaska. I don't care."

Gayle laughed. "I ain't got no Club Med money, and Roxanne ain't got no money, period."

"I don't care. You're stressed. If I don't make definite plans, my mother will start making some for me." Gloria was expecting her to vacation on Martha's Vineyard with the rest of the family on Memorial Day weekend and her father's side of the family had a reunion in August. New Orleans in August was not her idea of a fun time.

She had to get Gayle to agree to a vacation somewhere. Monique wanted to be able to say that a few of her days off had been spent doing something she enjoyed. "Roxanne probably needs to come up for air. From what I heard, her and that Marcus have been going at it like rabbits. And Cynthia . . . well, Cyn will be game for anything as long as there's shopping and men available. And not necessarily in that order."

Monique certainly had their number, but Gayle still wasn't sure that going away was such a good idea. Her mother was looking tired all the time, and then her father was constantly over at the house upsetting her. "But, Monique—" She stopped short, jarred by another coughing spasm.

When she was done, Monique said, "I rest my case. Stop fighting me. You know you need some time off. During that last coughing spell, I thought you were going to hack up a lung."

There was no point arguing with Monique. Once she got an idea in her head, she was like a dog with a bone. "OK, you win," Gayle said. "See what Cyn and Roxanne say, and try to find someplace that's not too expensive."

"In the meantime, I want you to come up to Cleveland at least one weekend out of the month until this trip happens—"

"But—"

"No buts. Summer's not here yet, and if I don't make you take a break every once in a while, you might be dead by summer. I'll talk to Roxanne and Cyn, but be assured, we are going to have this reunion even if I have to pay for it myself."

At this Gayle grinned. She waited a beat before giving the punch line: "You sure are generous for someone who owes the IRS eight hundred and thirty-one dollars."

Chapter

20

Gayle compared the two computer printouts for the third time, then nibbled on the eraser of her pencil. Why weren't the numbers coming out right? What had happened to the other three hundred and fifty thousand dollars in the Hudson account?

The pencil was now clenched between her teeth. The one thing she liked about her job as client services manager was that most of her work was done during business hours. But this time somebody had screwed up and she had to fix it. Why did she always get stuck straightening out other people's messes? This is *not* how she'd planned to spend her Sunday afternoon.

The papers slipped out of her hands when the phone rang. "Hello."

"Hey, girl, what's up?" Roxanne said.

"Work."

"On a Sunday? You're starting to sound like Marcus."

Gayle dropped an Earl Grey tea bag into the mug of hot water that was sitting on the desk in her bedroom. She had this lingering cold that wouldn't go away. Roxanne didn't sound like her usual upbeat self, either. "Trouble in paradise?"

"That's just it. I'm not sure." Roxanne turned the television off and moved over to the couch and made herself more comfortable. It was obvious Gayle was busy, but she really needed to talk to somebody. "It seems like all I ever do is go to Marcus' apartment and watch TV while he works. And when he's done working, which could be anywhere from three to five hours later, he's horny."

"He's horny? I wish I had that problem," Gayle said.

"Don't get me wrong, the sex is incredible, but even that gets tired after a while when that's all there is to the relationship." She and Marcus had settled into a pattern. He'd call her on Friday afternoon and ask her to go for a walk after work, and they would end up at his place.

"The only things Marcus does on a regular basis are take walks, go to the gym, and talk about work. And given the sorry state of my bank account, you know I can't talk finance with him."

Gayle laughed.

"And the one time I went to the gym with him, he almost killed me. It was almost a week before I could walk without pain." She wasn't out of shape, either, but they had worked out for almost three hours. Marcus expected her to keep pace with a program that included weight training and running up all twenty floors in his building.

Even taking a walk with him was exhausting. Roxanne liked a nice stroll as much as the next person, but Marcus' idea of a walk was having her trek from downtown to Cambridge in the freezing cold.

"Gayle, stop laughing," she said.

"Sorry." But she couldn't help it. What Roxanne was saying was serious, but how she was saying it was cracking her up. An image of Roxanne—with her short little legs—trying to keep pace with an ex-basketball player as he sprinted up a flight of stairs was hysterical.

"You should be," Roxanne said. "I have a real problem. Marcus and I have never gone to a movie or a concert together. I can count on one hand the number of times we've gone out for a meal. He's never expressed any interest in meeting any of my friends. And as far as I know, he doesn't have any friends—at least not in Boston. Last week one of his old basketball teammates was in town, and I had to practically force him to meet the guy for dinner." It had really hurt her feelings when Marcus hadn't invited her to come along. After all, it *was* her idea.

"I talked to Monique, and she told me to dump him. You know Monique—if at first you don't succeed, fuck it."

"Is that what you want?" Gayle asked as she scooped up the papers off the floor where they had fallen.

"Well, Cyn said I should be patient. That Marcus was trying to build his career, and he'd appreciate me more for being supportive rather than demanding."

"Yes, that sounds like Cyn. But you still didn't answer my question. What do you want?" Gayle said.

"I want to spend more time with Marcus. He's busy, though, and I don't want to be pushy."

Gayle said, "Roxanne, please, you're the most laid-back person I know. Monique might be pushy, but you? Never."

A nervous habit of hers, Roxanne twirled the ends of her dreadlocks. "Gayle, what do you think about this? A couple of weeks ago, I spent the night at Marcus' apartment. The next day we got up and had breakfast, and when I said I needed to head home, he didn't offer to drive me, even though it was freezing outside."

Gayle said slowly, "Well, that does seem kind of wrong."

Roxanne had to smile. Gayle was a sweetie . . . and tactful. When she had told Monique the same story, her instant response was, "He's an asshole. Dump him. And while you're at it, try to figure out what your problem is for putting up with his shit."

That was easier said than done. Roxanne couldn't just turn off her feelings like Monique could. She didn't run hot and cold like that. Somehow, talking to Monique never made her feel any better. Cynthia and Gayle must have been out that day.

"I know he was wrong. But I don't want to drive him away," Roxanne whined.

Gayle took a sip of tea. It had grown cold. "Well, Roxanne, since everybody else is dispensing free advice, here's mine. Talk to him. Tell him how you feel. He isn't a mind reader. How is he supposed to know that stuff is bothering you?"

"Yeah. Yeah, that sounds like a good idea," Roxanne said. She was too ashamed to admit that she'd already tried to talk to Marcus—more than once. But whenever she hinted or tried to teasingly let him know that she wasn't happy, the conversation just didn't go anywhere from there. Maybe she needed to be more direct.

"Really, Gayle, thanks for the advice," Roxanne said. "I'm going to call Marcus as soon as we get off the phone." That issue covered, she switched gears. "Here, I've been just talking about myself and my problems. What's going on with you? You sound congested or something."

"Huh?" Gayle was flipping through her quarterly report. "I'm fine. Don't worry about me. Just got a lot of work to do. I'll dominate the conversation next time."

"OK." But Roxanne knew she wouldn't. Gayle hated talking about herself. "I'll talk to you soon."

"Bye."

Roxanne took a deep breath. No time like the present, she told herself, and auto-dialed Marcus.

"Hello." Just one word and Roxanne got hot all over.

"Hi, Marcus." She cleared her throat and started again. "Uh, Marcus, I . . . was wondering, if . . . if I could come over tonight?"

"What's the matter, baby? Feeling kind of lonely?"

"Well, I always miss you."

A husky laugh. "Damn, baby, is it twitching that bad? What are you wearing? Is this a bootie call?"

"No, no. But I was hoping we could get out. Maybe go to a movie or something."

"Sorry, no can do. I got too much work."

"Well, how about we get together on Tuesday or Wednesday? There's an Annie Leibovitz exhibit at the Institute of Contemporary Art, and it's easier to get in during the week." Roxanne crossed her fingers and closed her eyes. *Maybe just this once we can do something besides bump and grind.*

"Annie who?" he asked.

"Annie Leibovitz. She's a photographer. Takes a lot of celebrity photos." Roxanne inspected nonexistent dirt under her fingernails. Maybe Marcus wasn't into art. She'd never asked him. She wasn't really sure what Marcus' interests were besides work and sex.

"Roxanne, you know what your problem is?" She sat up straight. She didn't know she had a problem. "You have too much time on your hands."

"Marcus, what are you talking about? I teach all day. And then I volunteer at the Rape Crisis Center. There's my tutoring and Project Literacy. I'm plenty busy."

"Yeah, there's all that stuff. But how is that going to help *you*? If it's not going to further your career, why bother?"

Roxanne was baffled. Did he not understand the concept of volunteerism?

Marcus continued, "You really need to have a five-year plan. I got one, and it includes having a woman who has her own vision. On your salary, you'll be paying back student loans until the day you die. Have you thought about going back to school?"

"No." Roxanne was lost. What did her career have to do with anything?

Marcus said excitedly, "Don't you see? That would be perfect. If you were back in grad school. Like maybe Harvard Business School. You'd be striving toward a real goal. Something that could get you ahead in life."

Oh, that's what this was all about. Roxanne had heard enough. "Wait! Wait! Why are we talking about the 'B' School? Marcus, I feel like we're having two different conversations. You're talking about finding me a new career when all I wanted was to get together for an art exhibit this week."

"And I told you, I can't go." His voice was several degrees cooler than it had been moments ago. "Look, Roxanne. I got a ton to do tonight. See you on Friday?"

Marcus must be tired, she thought. Why else would he be acting like this? Roxanne hesitated for only a moment, then gave in. "OK."

Chapter

21

Transfixed by her image in the health club's floor-to-ceiling mirror, Cynthia absently pedaled the stationary bike. She had dropped two dress sizes, and she barely recognized herself anymore. Even her breathing seemed lighter. Her body was happy not carrying all that fat around anymore. Cynthia smiled at her new and improved self. All the exercise and hard work was starting to pay off.

A man momentarily passed in front of her, both blocking her view of herself and capturing her attention. Cynthia hadn't seen too many brothers in this place. Her eyes followed him as he picked up a clean towel from a nearby rack. Hmm, he looked like he had a nice rack, too, from the way that muscle shirt was clinging to him. He turned around, and Cynthia looked away before he could catch her checking him out.

He was coming her way. Just as he prepared to get on the exercise bike next to hers, Cynthia nonchalantly pushed her *Cosmo* magazine to the edge of the plastic holder until it fell.

The guy leaned down to pick it up, as she had hoped he would. When he bent over, she got a spectacular view of muscular legs encased in a pair of tight-fitting black bike shorts.

He handed her the magazine and climbed on his bike. With a big smile, she thanked him. Cynthia hoped she wasn't sweating too much. It was hard to exercise and look cute at the same time. She could feel a trickle of sweat running down her face but didn't dare wipe it away and risk smearing makeup everywhere.

He said, "Is what your magazine says true?"

"I beg your pardon?" He pointed at the title on the open page of her magazine. It was an article about where to meet men. Cynthia couldn't even pretend that she hadn't read it, because she'd drawn little red stars next to the places that seemed most promising. Cynthia mumbled something about borrowing the magazine from a friend and started pedaling even faster.

He laughed.

Cynthia watched him out of the corner of her eye. He was extremely dark, and his nose was more angular than broad. It flared at the nostrils. Her inspection drifted a little lower. His lips were full. If those lips kissed you, you'd know it. His hair was cut short and was receding a little. She spotted a gray strand here and there, and guessed that he was between thirty-five and forty years old. He looked very fit. It was obvious he worked hard to keep in shape.

He interrupted her covert inspection of him. "Can I borrow your magazine, since you don't appear to be reading it?"

Cynthia blushed. She'd been caught again. She hadn't turned the page in the last five minutes.

"Why do you want it? It's a women's magazine."

"If I want to understand how women think, I need to read what they are reading," he said.

She closed the magazine and gave it to him. She noticed that he immediately turned to the article about where to meet men. How strange. Maybe he was gay.

He ignored her. Every so often he'd murmur "Uh-huh" or give a little grunt that was difficult to interpret.

When Cynthia's ten remaining minutes on the bike were up, she got off and stood next to him. He seemed unaware of her presence. "Uh, I'm just about done . . . if you're finished with my magazine? I mean, my friend's magazine. . . ."

At first she thought he hadn't heard her. He kept on pedaling with the magazine still in his hand. She was about to ask for it again when he looked up at her and said, "Oh, sure. . . . I'm done." With a flick of the wrist, he closed it and handed it to her. "It was very illuminating."

"How's that?"

"Well, now I know where I'm supposed to hang out in order to run across all those women who might want to meet me."

Cynthia rolled her eyes. He certainly had an inflated opinion of himself. She practically snatched the magazine out of his hand, picked up her towel, which was still on the handle of the other exercise bike, and headed toward the door.

Just as she reached the doorway, she heard somebody call her name. She turned around, and it was him.

He said, "Oh, by the way, Cynthia, I just wanted to thank you again for loaning me your magazine."

She looked at him in confusion. How did he know her name? He pointed at the magazine. Oh, no, the label on the front cover of the magazine! It had her name and address on it as bold as day.

Her face was bright red as she hurried out of the gym. His laughter followed her down the hallway as she fled to the safety of the women's locker room.

While she showered, she mulled over her encounter with whatshisname. So much for getting his attention without being obvious about it. How humiliating, outsmarted by a man!

Whatever possessed me to put little stars by those pickup places? Now he probably thinks I'm totally desperate—which is true. But I don't need him knowing that. I'm obviously losing my touch.

She consoled herself with the usual excuses. He wasn't all that cute anyway. This is a big place, and I'll probably never see him again.

Cynthia decided to stop by the club's juice bar after her shower. She'd met a few people at the club, and hanging out at the bar gave her a chance to chat. She paid for her drink and found a small table in the center of the room. She took a sip of her lemon-flavored seltzer water. As she always did after a workout, she took a couple of laxatives and a water pill out of her gym bag, then swallowed them down. It was important to keep her system unclogged. Every little bit helped.

Frowning, she watched other people laughing, talking, and slurping down the high-caloric fruit drinks. Didn't they know the juice bar was just a ploy by the health club owners to keep themselves in business? No way was she going to undo all her hard work by drinking fruit juice.

It was a slow night, she noticed. She didn't see any familiar faces.

Just then a voice from behind her said, "Hello, Cindy. We meet again."

Cynthia looked over her shoulder, and there was whatshisname, dressed in cutoff blue jeans and a white polo shirt. He had a drink in his hand, and sat down uninvited.

She gave him a cool nod. "Hi. I don't know your name, but mine is Cynthia, not Cindy."

He didn't seem the least bit put off. He held out his hand. "My name's Anthony."

She shook his hand. It was big, warm, and dry. His handshake was firm. "I know your name is Cynthia, but you look like a Cindy to me."

Now, what the hell did that mean?

"Cynthia seems so formal. Cindy, on the other hand, sounds youthful, easygoing, fun, and friendly . . . you definitely seem more like a Cindy to me. So which is it, Cynthia or Cindy?" he asked with a little smile.

How was she supposed to answer that? If she said Cynthia, then she was stuck up. If she said Cindy, it would mean agreeing with him, and he was already smug enough. She took another sip of her water. "Actually, to strangers it's Ms. Johnson."

"Touché. Well, Ms. Johnson, it's a pleasure to meet you. I just started a trial membership at this club. But if all the patrons are as attractive as you, I think I'm going to be here for a while."

Was he flirting? Cynthia batted her eyes and leaned closer to him until their shoulders almost touched. "Well, it looks like you've been working out somewhere already."

He shrugged. "I try to run and play tennis regularly."

"Looks like it's paid off," Cynthia said. "So, what made you decide to join a health club?"

He gave her a devilish smile. "I read in *Cosmo* that it's a great place to meet women."

"Oh really?" she drawled. "Far be it for me to disagree with the experts at *Cosmo*. What else did they have to say?"

They spent the next hour casually flirting. It was fun.

Reluctant though she was to end the conversation, it was getting late. He walked her to her car. Cynthia shook his hand again, then got into the car. She rolled down the window and said, "Maybe I'll see you here next time."

"Maybe."

Cynthia threw her purse on the bed. God, it had been a long workday. And the grapevine had been busy. A major layoff was pending, and everybody, both anxious employees and reporters looking for a scoop, was coming to her for information. Playing ignorant, which was what she had to do until the layoff was officially announced, was hard work. After answering one phone message after the other, Cynthia had thought she'd never get out of the office.

She looked at her watch. If she'd known what kind of day it would turn out to be, she would have packed some gym clothes and taken them to work with her. Now she'd really have to hustle to get to the gym before it closed. She was feeling tense enough without heaping some guilt on top of it because she'd been too lazy to exercise. Lately, she'd noticed that she just didn't feel right, couldn't just let it go, if she skipped a workout. But guilt was good. It would keep her committed to losing the weight.

The doorbell rang as Cynthia began to take off her work clothes. She quickly threw a robe over the slip she was wearing and went to answer it.

A delivery boy stood there with a flower box in his hand. With a delighted smile, Cynthia took the box from him. She loved getting gifts. In her excitement, she closed the door in his face.

The last person to send her anything had been her father

on her birthday. But it couldn't be him. Her birthday was months away. She lifted the top and pulled apart the tissue paper. Inside were a dozen long-stemmed pink roses. They were beautiful, but this was quite the mystery. She hadn't gotten a promotion or graduated from anything recently. What was the occasion?

She felt around the inside of the box, searching for a card. There wasn't one. Maybe Gayle or Monique was trying to be nice. They knew she'd been kind of stressed out at work lately. It couldn't have been Roxanne, she thought. She never had any money. She shook her head. It was unlikely that any of her friends had sent the flowers. She'd be seeing all of them in a few months anyway, since they'd decided that Tampa was the perfect place for a reunion.

No one else came to mind and she didn't have any more time to speculate. Cynthia needed to hurry over to the club if she was going to get in a workout tonight. She was already running late. She found a crystal vase under the sink, half filled it with water, and put the roses in it. They smelled wonderful. She put the vase in the center of the dining room table. That would have to do for now until she found a better place for them.

Tonight's workout would have to be short. It was late and she was more tired than usual. As long as she got at least twenty minutes of some kind of aerobic exercise, she'd be happy. She'd lost forty pounds, and she was not about to back-slide now.

Once at the club, she did some stretching exercises before heading for the treadmill. She alternated between jogging for three minutes and walking for three. She was huffing and puffing when she heard, "Hi, Cindy. Looks like you're working hard."

Anthony was standing in front of the treadmill, looking as fresh as a daisy. He had a white towel around his neck, and this time the bike shorts were electric blue. Cynthia could feel the sweat emanating from her scalp, and her wet blouse was sticking to her back. This just was not her day. "Is that another way of saying I look whipped?" she asked.

"Whipped isn't exactly the word I'd use," he said. He rubbed his chin and eyed her thoughtfully. "No, alive and vibrant sounds more like it. Your eyes are bright. Your cheeks are flushed. . . . No, they're rosy. Yeah, that's it, a pink rose blush. . . ."

Rosy? She gave him a surprised look. "You?" He was smiling. She stopped the machine and got off.

She was a little breathless. "Did you send me the roses?"

He nodded. "You can thank *Cosmo* for that. Your address was on the front cover, remember?"

Chapter

22

Marcus was supposed to come over to her place to watch the Knicks and Celtics. Game time came and went and still no Marcus. Where the hell was he? When Roxanne finished off a party-sized bag of potato chips all by herself, she decided it was time to call him.

"Oh, I forgot," he said. No explanations. No remorse.

Roxanne didn't hear from him for the rest of the weekend. He went to Atlanta on the following Monday. She didn't hear from him while he was there, either.

He finally called late Friday night. "Hey, baby."

Roxanne wasn't feeling particularly like his baby. If she was, it was time for someone to report him for child neglect. "Hi, Marcus," she said without much enthusiasm. "How was your trip?"

"It was good, especially since I got back a day earlier than I had expected to."

"But you were supposed to get back today."

"I know, but I came back yesterday."

"Really?" And he hadn't bothered to call.

"Have you ever been to Bob the Chef's?

Roxanne perked up a bit at the mention of the soul food restaurant. She'd never been there, but she'd heard the food was good. And she'd love to go with Marcus. "No. I haven't been there."

"Well, you should go," Marcus said. "I went there last

night. Had me some collard greens, fried pork chops, candied sweet potatoes, and corn bread. Then I went over to the Harbor Hangout." That was a white club that catered to the black crowd on Thursday nights.

Roxanne's blood began to boil. It wasn't that she was dying to go to Bob the Chef's, and certainly not to the Harbor Hangout, which she boycotted on principle. She thought it was insulting that Thursday night had been designated "black night." Like black people didn't have to work on Fridays.

Here was a man who claimed he never had any free time, but when he did get some, he chose to spend it without her. While he went on and on about what a great time he'd had last night, it dawned on her that Marcus hadn't set foot in her apartment since that night he'd come over for dinner; the first night they'd made love. Roxanne was always going to his place because it was more convenient—*for him.*

She didn't say anything for the longest time. He didn't even notice!

The next words out of his mouth were, "Do you want to go to dinner tomorrow?"

So surprised that he was offering to do something other than have sex, Roxanne found herself agreeing. Even though she was still upset with him, a part of her didn't want to believe that Marcus could really be as big a jerk as he seemed to be.

The next day, though, Marcus didn't call to finalize the dinner plans. Roxanne called him and asked what had happened. He said laughingly, "Oops, I forgot. Guess you'll have to take a rain check."

Doesn't he notice that I'm not laughing right along with him?

They tentatively planned to meet at his apartment the next afternoon. Roxanne was hoping to have a serious talk with him then. His inconsiderate behavior had to stop.

Roxanne didn't sleep very well that night, but she was wide awake by seven the next morning.

To kill time, she decided to do the Freedom Trail, a three-mile walking tour of all the historic sites of Boston. At Park Street, she started following the red line on the sidewalk that marked the trail. She got as far as the Paul Revere House in the North End before she got tired of it. The temperature was only in the upper forties and it was windy, not exactly walking weather.

She backtracked to Faneuil Hall and had lunch at one of the restaurants in the food court there. The clam chowder thawed her out a little. She headed over to the Filene's at Downtown Crossing, passing roasted-peanut vendors, flower vendors, and street performers on her way.

Once in the department store, she wandered aimlessly down the rows of expensive perfumes, creams, and lotions. At one point a saleslady jumped in front of her and sprayed a mist of Obsession in her direction. "Buy a purchase worth thirty dollars or more and get a free gift," she'd said with a bright-red-lipstick smile. She handed Roxanne a little beige card that reeked of the scent and moved on to the next unsuspecting shopper.

As Roxanne neared the escalators, she thought about going to Filene's Basement. It was actually a separate store on the two lower levels that sold quality clothing at markdown prices. But the place was usually a zoo. And she wasn't really in the mood to be stepped on by bargain-shoppers arguing over who had reached for the green silk blouse first.

She decided instead to call Marcus from one of the pay phones located next to the ladies' room on the fourth floor. "What are you doing?" she asked.

"Working." *Why was she not surprised?*

"I'm downtown. Is it OK if I come over in about"—she looked at her watch—"twenty minutes?"

"That's fine. I'll be working at home all afternoon."

Roxanne hung up and spent a few minutes looking in the designer fashions department. Whenever she saw anything that caught her eye, she'd take a peek at the price tag. It was depressing to know that out there somewhere were people who could really afford a dress that cost seven hundred dollars. She barely had that much in her savings account.

Ten minutes later, she headed for Marcus' place. As she walked past the office buildings at Government Center, she tried to recall the points she wanted to make when she talked to Marcus. She always felt better if her thoughts were organized. Sort of like a lesson plan.

He lived in a downtown high-rise near the financial district. Besides being close to work, Marcus wanted to live somewhere he was able to network with potential clients. A lot of the doctors who worked at Mass General lived in his apartment complex.

Marcus paid a hefty twelve hundred a month for the privilege of sharing the same elevator with his wealthy and influential neighbors. No wonder his apartment was virtually empty. Come to think of it, she realized, he had never gotten around to buying the perfect bed and couch he'd been searching for on their first date. He had two chairs, a table for his computer, a mattress and box spring on the living room floor, an expensive stereo system, and a TV that he never used. And his bedroom was totally empty. Marcus claimed that most of his stuff was still in storage in New York because he just hadn't had time to arrange for it to be shipped.

When she got to Marcus' building, the concierge rang him. There was no answer. "That's weird. He's expecting me." Roxanne figured he must be in the bathroom or had stepped out for a minute, so she sat down on a cushioned bench directly across from the elevator.

She sat for a while, then had the concierge ring him again. Still no answer. The man gave her a pitying look as she sat back down. For the better part of an hour, she tried to look inconspicuous when people entering and leaving the building gave her curious glances. Finally, she gave the concierge a message for Marcus and left.

She felt extremely stupid as she slid her monthly pass through the turnstile at the subway stop. She felt even worse when Marcus didn't call for hours after she got home. She ate dinner, washed her hair, and watched a rerun of *Murder, She Wrote*. Through it all, the red light of her answering machine stared back at her unblinking.

Finally, she called him. He had the nerve to pick up on the first ring. "Marcus?"

Marcus said, "Oh, hi, Roxanne, what's up?"

I just know this Negro is not acting all surprised to hear from me. "What's up is that I came to your apartment today and you were nowhere to be found," Roxanne said.

"Oh, I had to go to the office to copy some stuff onto a floppy disk," he said as if that explained everything.

"Marcus, you knew I was coming over. I sat in the lobby like an idiot for almost an hour. You could have waited for me to get there before leaving or at the very least left a message with the concierge. And I don't suppose you got the message I left?"

She didn't wait for his answer. "I shouldn't have to call you to find out what happened. In the past week alone, you've *forgotten* to show up three times, and each time you act like it's no big deal that I'm sitting around waiting for you. And then there's Thursday. You get a free day and you'd rather spend it by yourself than with me. And you had the nerve to tell me what a good time you had! I thought we were in a relationship."

"Why are you tripping?" he said, so sincerely Roxanne almost fell off the couch. Then he said, "Look, Roxanne, we're not in a relationship. We're just friends."

A pain shot through her chest. *What is he talking about?* He knew that she didn't just sleep around. She had been really up-front about that. Roxanne expelled a breath before she spoke. "Marcus, you're constantly saying that I'm your best friend here in Boston, but friends don't treat each other the way you treat me."

"Roxanne, when I first met you, I thought, *Here's a real hard-core homegirl.* But I see you just can't take it. Where I come from, you have to be able to accept that friends will not always be there."

A hard-core homegirl? What was that? Either you treated people with respect or you didn't. And he had the nerve to accuse *her* of tripping.

Take the high road, Roxanne, she told herself. "There's a difference between not always being there and never being there. I don't think it's a sign of weakness that I get upset when a friend blows me off. Not showing up whenever you feel like it is just plain selfish."

He gave a little laugh and said in this seductive, knowing tone, "Now, baby, you know the last thing I am is selfish."

Roxanne mimicked putting a gun to her head and pulling the trigger. She took her glasses off and rubbed a weary hand over her face. He just didn't get it. "Marcus, I'm talking about *outside* the bedroom. I guess we have a different definition of friendship. Maybe you can tell me what yours is?"

When he realized that she wasn't going to let him play it off, he got defensive. "Look, Roxanne, I have lots of female friends."

This was the first she'd heard about his female friends.

"A: There's this girl I used to date when I was at the University of Michigan. We've been there for each other through thick and thin. B: There's my ex-fiancée."

Now, this one Roxanne had heard about. This was the broad who'd cheated on him but had refused to give back his six-thousand-dollar ring, which he was still paying for. This is the same woman who was wearing his ring on her right hand and her new fiancé's on her left. But she was still on the list. Cool.

"C: There's my friend Rita in Memphis. Now, Rita's a real homegirl. She's from the 'hood, but she's on the fast track. She owns her own home, has a black-on-black BMW and an unbelievable portfolio for someone her age."

Bully for Rita! You've described her financial situation. But how about her personality?

Marcus wasn't done yet. "D: There is you; and E: I met this fine woman at the Harbor Hangout the other night! She had a body on her!"

The pain in her chest grew more intense. Thank God he couldn't see the effect his words were having on her.

". . . nothing is going to develop with the woman from the club. She isn't educated." Was it her imagination, or did he sound disappointed?

"Let me get this straight. You got about five female *friends*, and I'm number four on the list—or was it letter D? I forget."

Marcus started laughing. "Now, you know I didn't mean it like that, Roxanne. It's not like there's a particular order."

She was momentarily speechless. Didn't he know that being part of a list was insulting enough, especially when she didn't even know there was a list. "Marcus, I'm glad you can laugh, because I don't find this funny at all," Roxanne said. "And you can take D off the list."

Still trying to act like it was a joke, he said, "Aw, Roxanne, don't be like that."

"Let me ask you this: If you could have someone with the body of the Harbor Hangout woman and the ambition of the homegirl with the BMW or the kind of friendship I offer, who would you be interested in?"

He didn't even have to think about it. "The ambitious homegirl."

Roxanne tried to keep her voice light. "I'm glad we had this little talk. It's always good to know where things stand."

Marcus was completely oblivious. "So, we can still be friends?"

This doesn't really hurt, she told her heart. "Yeah, sure, Marcus, we can still be friends. But I meant what I said about being taken off the list."

"Now see, that's what I like about you, Roxanne," he said. "A lot of women would still be tripping hard . . . and over nothing."

Roxanne held back a sigh. *Nothing* just about summed it up.

PART THREE

Stop the Madness

Chapter

23

The Florida sunshine filtered through the patio doors, casting its light on Gayle's closest friends in the world. Her almond-shaped eyes were more than a little unfocused as they slowly scanned the restaurant—tropical plants, an array of delectable foods to choose from, and a good-looking West Indian waiter hovering attentively in the background. Cynthia had picked a great place for brunch, and on a Saturday, too!

Just the thought of being out of Columbus for four whole days made her smile. Except for a few visits to Monique's place in Cleveland, she hadn't been away from home in months. With so many people looking for jobs, she had yet to figure out why they were short-staffed at the bank and why all the extra work seemed to end up in her lap. And she never knew what little domestic drama she'd walk into when she got home every night. Lately, her mother and Buddy seemed to be going at it like cats and dogs. And every time she crossed the threshold, there was Daddy, grinning and giving orders like he owned the place. Yes, it was definitely time for a break.

Gayle swallowed more of her mimosa. The tang of the orange juice mixed with champagne made her mouth water and her stomach warm. So what if she had drunk more this morning than she had all year long? Hell, she was on vacation, and she was determined to live a little.

Cynthia leaned forward to show Monique her silk-wrapped

fingernails. A pair of Ray Bans were perched atop her reddish brown locks. A low-cut powder blue silk blouse that matched the blue of her eyes and a string of faux pearls drew attention to her nonexistent cleavage. Flat-chested or not, Cynthia was looking good, Gayle silently observed. She'd lost almost fifty pounds in the last year.

Cynthia said, "Girl, I just had to do something about these nubs. I can't be doing a presentation and having my hands look like I been scrubbing toilets all day. Image is everything, you know. And I had to get rid of that hair weave.

"Don't you know, I was in a meeting with the senior VP of my division when he picked something off the floor and, looking all confused, held it out to me. Girl, that man had a clump of my store-bought hair in his hand!"

Monique ran her well-manicured nails through her own naturally long, wavy black hair. "Please tell me you're lying!"

"If I'm lying, I'm flying."

"What did you do?"

Cynthia's Southern drawl was even more pronounced than usual, causing Gayle to smile. "Child, I said, just as cool as you please, I am so sorry, Mr. Ross, I have a little Pekingese and she's been shedding all over the place. Before he had a chance to think, I snatched my hair right out of his hands, threw it in my appointment book. So those Korean women can keep their hair because I can't be having people at the office tracking me down by following the hair trail."

This had them all howling. Roxanne took off her round wire-rimmed glasses to wipe the tears from her eyes. "Girl, don't make me laugh like that. You gonna make me pee on myself." She patted her little explosion of dreadlocks. "Don't expect me to feel sorry for you, either, because if you accepted your natural African beauty, you wouldn't have to worry about your fake hair falling out all over the place."

Monique laughed. "This from the woman who wore a JheriCurl for three years."

"Yeah, but I was young and naive. Then one night, when I was sick to death of dealing with my hair, I gathered up everything—the blow-dryer, hot curlers, hair grease, activator, mousse. I marched down the hall to the trash compactor and let her rip. The grinding sound that followed was music to my ears and freedom for my tortured hair.

"The next day I went to a barber. I told him, Don't stop cutting till you see my native Africa."

Her friends burst into laughter. Gayle said, "Amen, speak the truth, Reverend Miller!"

"Nowadays, it's just wash and wear. And let me tell you, I been feeling better ever since. So, my sistas, I pray you don't have to sink to the same depths of despair I did before you too see the light."

A plain white headband pulled Monique's hair away from her face. Her café-au-lait skin had been lightly kissed by the summer sun. She reached into her leather Coach purse and pulled out a pack of Virginia Slims and a lighter. She took in Roxanne's Afro-centric hair and clothes: the orange, yellow, and red kente cloth sundress clinging to chocolate-colored curves.

It was easy for Roxanne to preach about getting in touch with our roots. As a public school teacher, she didn't have to deal with conservative yuppie assholes. In fact, it was probably an asset to dress ethnic. And Gayle might be amening now, but there was no way she was going to show up at the bank dressed like a member of a reggae band to talk with clients about managing their portfolios.

Monique exhaled and watched the white-gray smoke drift across the table.

Cynthia immediately began waving her hands back and forth in front of her face. This was soon followed by little choking noises, as if she couldn't catch her breath, and she kept flashing distressed glances at Monique the whole time.

Monique's eyes narrowed, then she blew a puff of smoke in Cynthia's direction. Let her choke. Maybe she'd come back in another life as someone with enough guts to ask for what she wanted.

Roxanne said, "Hey, girl, why don't you put that cancer stick out? Can't you see I'm trying to eat? That secondary smoke is killing me."

"Trying to educate those juvenile delinquents is going to kill you long before my cigarette smoke will."

Roxanne wasn't going to stand for that. "Hey, most of my kids are great. I don't see my job as any more or less dangerous than yours. You're the one who works with criminals every day."

"Yeah, but criminals have to walk through metal detectors and there are armed officers on the premises. Didn't I hear something about a race riot at one of the schools in Boston this spring? Why you ever decided to move to that racist place is beyond me."

"As far as Boston being racist goes, this is America. Show me a place that isn't racist and I'll show you a Michael Jackson without plastic surgery—"

Gayle banged her champagne glass on the table. "Hey," she said, her voice slurred, "are we on vacation or what? I don't want to hear this crap. I didn't come to Tampa to talk 'bout racism and riots. Let's drink a toast, goddammit!"

Champagne splashed her fingers as she raised her glass. "Here's to us. What social isolation and lack of sex in a rural Minnesota college town has brought together, let no man pull us under!"

The other three women looked first at her and then at one another.

"Let no man pull us under?" Monique said. "Gayle, your ass is drunk."

"No, not drunk. I am happy! Happy! Happy! Happy! I am thirsty, too. Oh, *garçon* . . ." snapping her fingers for the waiter.

The waiter's white tuxedo jacket matched his startlingly white teeth. Both were an attractive contrast to his dark brown skin. With a lilting accent and an indulgent smile, he asked, "Is there something I can do for you ladies?"

Gayle's alcohol-soaked eyes examined him from head to toe like she was looking over a tasty treat. "Well, I don't know about them, but I could use a good—"

A hand suddenly clamped over her mouth.

Monique said, "What my friend was about to say is that she

could use a big, cold glass of water. In fact, we probably all need refills."

The waiter nodded and slipped away.

Monique removed her hand and wagged a finger at Gayle. "OK, slut puppy. I don't even want to know what you were going to say to that poor man. You lush!"

When the waiter refilled their glasses, Cynthia thanked him several times.

After he left, Gayle asked, "So how come Cynthia gets to bat her big blue eyes at him and I'm shushed for opening my mouth?"

"Hey," Cynthia said, "I was just being polite and showing my good upbringing. You, on the other hand, looked like you were about to offer him your drawers . . . with you still in 'em."

Gayle didn't see what was so damn funny. Now Monique was talking, and . . . what was Monique saying? She saw her mouth moving, but no sound was coming out. A flash of light-headedness shot through her. She felt sick to her stomach . . . and why did Monique have that weird expression on her face . . . ?

Gayle pitched forward, and her head hit the table with a thud that rattled the silverware. Startled, Cynthia jumped back from the table, managing to overturn her champagne glass in the process. The pale gold liquid spread across the linen tablecloth and slowly dripped onto the carpet. To her horror, she saw that one side of Gayle's face was submerged in the syrup from her French toast.

The restaurant became unnaturally quiet as all heads turned to observe the commotion. A man who Roxanne suspected was the manager was headed their way. He couldn't have been more than thirty, but male pattern baldness had already set in. He gave reassuring smiles and nods to the other patrons as he crossed the room.

The smile disappeared from his face when he stopped in front of their table. He looked like he'd sniffed something and found it quite funky. "Is there a problem, ladies? Is your friend sick?"

They stared at him blankly. Gayle was usually the one who bailed them out of trouble. Finally, Monique spoke up. "We're really sorry. My friend is . . . I mean, she has . . . narcolepsy. You know, those sleeping spells. If you could just tell us where the bathroom is, we'll splash some water on her face and she should be just fine."

His expression pained, he told them that bathrooms were located to the right of the entrance in the hotel lobby. Cynthia and Monique got up. Supporting Gayle on each side, they slowly moved toward the door. Suddenly, Gayle's head rose and she mumbled something about wanting her Caribbean cupcake. Monique answered by pushing Gayle's syrupy head away from her new shorts suit.

The manager cleared his throat. "Who is going to take care of the bill?"

Very unhappy, Roxanne turned to follow him.

Cynthia couldn't get across the room fast enough. This was really great. Everybody else would fly back home in a few days, but she still had to live and work in Tampa. It didn't help that Monique was walking in slow motion. Just keep looking down, look at the floor, she told herself.

Seconds later, she gave a strangled cry. She'd suddenly realized that champagne had splashed all over her new hundred-and-fifty-dollar sling-back Ferragamos. Did champagne leave a stain? she wondered. She hoped not, or else Gayle was going to be in big trouble when she finally sobered up. What in the world had gotten into that girl anyway? Cynthia couldn't remember ever seeing Gayle tipsy, let alone stone-cold drunk.

When they entered the ladies' room, they were greeted by soft piped-in classical music and the scent of cinnamon-and-spice potpourri. A well-preserved blonde was touching up her makeup at the brown-and-beige marbled counters. Even though she was holding a compact in her hand, she made no secret of watching their every move. They managed to lower Gayle onto a couch.

Monique shook Gayle by the shoulders. "Gayle, do you hear me, girl? Wake up!" When Gayle didn't respond, she turned to Cynthia for help, but she'd wandered off. Monique's head whipped to the right and she spied her standing next to the blonde. Cyn was holding her shoes up to the mirror's lights. What the hell was she doing that for?

Gayle muttered something incomprehensible, then slumped sideways, bringing her face into contact with the soft leather of the couch. Monique grasped her shoulders and set her upright again. Streaks of syrup and food crumbs had attached themselves to the couch. "Cyn, do you think you could make yourself useful by wetting some towels?"

After putting her shoes on the makeup counter with great care, Cynthia grabbed a handful of paper towels and wet them. Clicking her tongue, she began carefully wiping away the sticky mess on the couch.

Monique stared at her. Un-fucking-believable! Here sat Gayle unconscious, legs spread apart, syrup clotting in her hair, and Cynthia was cleaning the damn sofa.

She snatched the towels out of Cynthia's hands and ordered her to get more. Monique used the other side of the damp towels to wipe Gayle's face. As she cleaned the even-toned, dark brown skin, she listened to Gayle's incoherent murmurings.

How many times through the years had the positions been reversed? Gayle had put up with a lot of shit from them: man problems, family problems, work problems. . . . They could always count on Gayle. Now it was their turn to take care of her.

Gayle opened her eyes. "Monique, I love you," she proclaimed.

Monique had to smile. "Gayle, you are an idiot." Actually, she was glad Gayle had gotten drunk. She certainly had reason to. That bank was draining her dry. And her mother wouldn't lift a finger to take care of herself. She was glad she hadn't let Gayle back out of this trip like she'd been trying to.

The woman at the mirror gave them a disgusted look. Monique returned the look, and the woman turned away.

Cynthia came over with more towels and water in a small paper cup. The two of them worked in unison. Cynthia daubed at Gayle's hair while Monique scrubbed her face. At length, they surveyed their handiwork and agreed that Gayle looked as good as she could given the circumstances. Monique said, "OK, Gayle. On your feet. Stand up!"

Gayle's head lolled from side to side. "Ouch!" Her eyes flew open. "Somebody pinched me."

Monique and Cynthia pulled her by the arms, trying to make her stand up.

"OK. OK. I'm up. Stop yanking me around," she complained.

"Good," Monique said. "Now, do you think you can walk?"

Gayle didn't answer. A woman with dilated pupils and matted hair stared back at her from the mirror. When she recognized her own reflection, she let out a small scream that caused her to stagger forward.

Clutching at the air, her fingers closed around something soft and padded. Then she gazed into the eyes of a woman who had a thick streak of blood running from her chin to her cheek. Gayle backed away and let out another scream. She also let out the contents of her heaving stomach.

Roxanne's face burned as she hurried across the carpeted floor. Why did these things always happen to her? Naturally, as the poorest among them, she would get stuck with the check. And to have her credit card declined because she was one dollar over her limit was the ultimate humiliation. One lousy dollar! This was not what happened in those commercials. In the TV ads, the customer service rep bent over backward to help the person out.

And that little twerp was smirking the whole time. To think he had actually suggested she ask one of her friends to pay the bill. And die of embarrassment? Roxanne didn't think so. Thank God she had enough money on her to pay the tip in cash and put the rest on her Visa.

Will I ever be debt-free in this lifetime? she asked herself.

Roxanne was about to open the bathroom door when a middle-aged blonde with lipstick smeared all over her face slammed into her. The woman didn't break stride as she stalked off toward the restaurant.

Roxanne yelled after her, "I guess 'Excuse me' ain't in your vocabulary!"

She stopped dead in her tracks at the sight of Monique and Cynthia on their hands and knees scrubbing the carpet in the bathroom. Gayle was nowhere to be seen, but an awful retching noise was coming from one of the stalls.

Cynthia reached into one of her skirt pockets and tossed her keys to Roxanne, who in a reflexive gesture caught them. "Quick. Go get the car and bring it around front."

This was not the time to ask questions. Roxanne did a quick about-face and headed for the parking lot.

As she pulled up to the entrance of the hotel in Cynthia's lavender Toyota Camry, her three friends emerged through the automatic glass doors. Monique practically threw Gayle into the backseat before scrambling in after her. A barefoot Cynthia, shoes in hand, exchanged places with Roxanne in the driver's seat. She placed the Ray Bans on the tip of her nose and peeled rubber as she pulled away.

Roxanne turned around to look at the damage. Gayle's head was resting on Monique's lap. She didn't think it possible, but Gayle actually looked pale. Monique was trying to remove strands of Gayle's hair that were sticking to her hands. All in all, it was a pretty pitiful sight.

"Well, is anyone going to tell me why we had to leave the restaurant like fugitives from justice?" Roxanne asked.

Monique spoke from the backseat. "Did you see a blond woman running out of the bathroom?"

"Yeah, I couldn't miss her. That rude witch almost ran me down!"

"Well, our friend Gayle almost puked all over her. So the woman started ranting and raving about how this used to be a nice place until they started letting in anybody off the street. That's when Gayle grabbed her hair and asked if it was true that plastic-surgery scars could be hidden at the hairline. I thought her eyes were gonna pop right out of her head. My girl started screaming that she'd been assaulted. When she went running off, we didn't know if it was to get security or what. Cyn thought it was best if we fled the scene, so to speak, rather than risk, and I quote, 'dying of embarrassment.' "

Cynthia added, "I'm gonna kill Gayle when she finally sobers up. I'm too through with her. She knows she can't drink. Y'all know she can't drink. Y'all shouldn't have let her drink."

"Excuse me," Roxanne said, "but do I look like the booze patrol? I was eating my eggs Benedict and minding my own business, thank you very much! I didn't see you counting her drinks, either. I guess you were too busy admiring your new fingernails."

Gayle stirred against Monique's thigh. Monique said, "Hey, y'all be quiet. I'm trying to hear what Gayle is saying. She might need to throw up again."

Cynthia flashed a look at the backseat. "What! She ain't throwing up in here. I'm pulling over." But when she looked in the rearview mirror, she saw a long line of cars to her right. There was no way she could switch to the outside lane.

"What did you say, Gayle? I can't hear you," Monique said, an edge of panic in her voice.

Lifting her head, Gayle said, "That place sure had a nice bathroom."

Chapter
24

Roxanne was settled in one of Cynthia's white wicker chairs. She glanced over at Gayle, who had promptly passed out again the minute they entered the apartment. Gayle couldn't possibly be comfortable on the overstuffed pink and turquoise love seat. Not with her head hanging halfway off the cushion. Roxanne had opted for the chair simply because she couldn't find a spot in Cynthia's "Pastel Palace" where the edge of a decorative pillow didn't jab her in the butt.

A pink, red, and white silk floral arrangement was set on the square glass table in the center of the room. A large framed portrait photo of Cynthia in an off-the-shoulder dusky rose evening gown dominated one wall. Roxanne stood up and walked past a state-of-the-art entertainment center. She stopped in front of a set of sliding glass doors leading to a wooden patio that looked out over the complex's kidney-shaped pool.

Sighing, Roxanne couldn't help comparing it to her own drab one-bedroom in Boston.

Monique came into the room. Lighting a cigarette, she lifted the numerous fashion magazines that covered the coffee table. "Damn that Cynthia! Just because she stopped smoking doesn't mean she has to be inconsiderate of those of us who still do. Have you seen an ashtray around here?"

"Here, use this." Roxanne handed her a ceramic coaster

from a stack of them on the entertainment center. "I was just thinking about how unfair life is."

"And this is news to you?" Monique sat down in the chair Roxanne had vacated. "Put some music on. How about Sadé?"

"Uh-uh, too depressing. I'm depressed enough."

"About what?"

Roxanne waved her hands around the room. "About this. . . . This apartment is great. It's clean, quiet, and color-coordinated—if you like pastel. Meanwhile, I live in the slums."

"I thought you lived in a transitional neighborhood."

"Yeah, but what is it transitioning into? My poor grand-mother almost had a heart attack when she visited a few months ago. Right in the middle of *Wheel of Fortune*, a mouse ran across her foot." Grandma Reynolds had let out such a terrified scream that one of her usually uncaring neigh-bors had actually knocked on her door to see if everything was OK.

Monique laughed. "I'm sure this wasn't the first time your grandmother has seen a rodent in the house."

Leave it to Monique to remind her of her poverty-stricken childhood. "Maybe so, but it was still embarrassing. Here I am, this professional person, two college degrees, and I got rats and roaches. Life just ain't fair."

"If you hate it so much, why don't you move?"

"All I can afford is something equally bad or worse."

Monique ground out her cigarette and propped her legs on the table. "Sounds to me like you need a better paying job."

Roxanne sighed. "Monique, I'm a newly hired public school teacher. There are no pay raises in my immediate future. You just don't understand what it's like to not live the way you want to."

"It's not like I'm raking in the dough, you know."

Monique had conveniently forgotten about those fat checks her parents regularly sent her from Texas. "Talking to you is *not* making me feel any better. I'm going to see what Cyn is up to."

"Hey, Cynthia," Roxanne called out as she headed for the master bedroom. "How much rent you paying for this joint?"

When she entered the bedroom, though, there was no sign of Cynthia.

Like the living room, pink was the reigning color. A down comforter with a lush peonies and roses design was bunched at the end of the bed. It had a matching pillow sham and bed ruffle. Somehow, a few pillows had wedged themselves between the railings of the white headboard.

An assortment of costume jewelry covered every inch of the dresser. Some of the drawers were half open with clothes hanging out. Tossed carelessly on a chair in a corner were the blue blouse and white skirt that Cynthia had worn to brunch. Both closets were open and overflowing. The left closet contained blouses and pants, and the right one held dresses and skirts. Roxanne smiled at Cynthia's halfhearted attempt at organization. There were just as many clothes piled on the floor as there were on hangers, the price tag still on some of them.

Even as a college student, Cynthia had always been a last-minute person. But Roxanne gave her credit, Cyn had it down to an art. If she had a class at eight, she'd roll out of bed at seven-thirty, wash her face, slap on some makeup, work miracles with the curling iron, and be headed out the door by seven fifty-five.

She'd been like that with class assignments, too. She'd pull an all-nighter, arrive at the end of class with the term paper in hand, oozing Southern charm. She'd get an A. Roxanne, on the other hand, would study like crazy yet still end up with a B plus. In public relations, Cyn had found a career that paid her well for utilizing her skills as an extraordinary bullshitter. Some people just had it like that, had that ability to get by on charm and personality.

Roxanne sighed. There was something awfully familiar about standing in a room littered with Cynthia's possessions and feeling sorry for herself.

She heard water running in the adjacent bathroom. The door was slightly ajar, so she pushed it wide open. "Hey, Cyn, what are you doing in here?"

Cynthia, wearing only matching fuchsia panties and a bra, was hunched over the sink. At the sound of Roxanne's voice, she jumped. "You scared me!"

Roxanne took in Cynthia's flushed face and bloodshot eyes. "Whew! It smells pretty raw in here. I thought Gayle was the sick one."

"I think I ate too much at brunch, so my stomach's kind of out of whack."

Roxanne was mystified. "I don't see how fruit salad, plain toast, and juice could upset your stomach," she said. "That's all you ate."

"Well, it did. Not all of us have cast-iron stomachs like you. If you hadn't brought your nosy self in here, my bodily functions wouldn't be offending you."

Not deterred, Roxanne walked farther into the room. She touched and sniffed the various perfumes on a silver tray on the counter. She picked up the Oscar de la Renta and sprayed it into the air. "Honey, it should be offending you, too."

"Hey!" Cynthia said, trying to take the bottle from Roxanne. "Gimme that. Do you know how much that stuff costs?"

Roxanne hurried to the other side of the room, putting the bottle behind her back. "Yeah. It's expensive! But I'm using it for a worthy cause—preventing us from being overcome by toxic fumes." She held the perfume up and released another spurt of mist.

With a strangled cry, Cynthia snatched the bottle out of her hands and placed it with the others. She rearranged the bottles on the tray.

Roxanne leaned against the door, arms folded across her chest, to survey the scene.

The bathroom was just as cluttered as the bedroom. There were cotton balls, Q-Tips, cleansing bars, moisturizers, and makeup remover strewn all over the place. Roxanne crossed to the sink. She twisted up one of the lipstick tubes, put a dash of it on the back of her hand, shook her head, and put the top back on. She repeated this with another one, a Christian Dior called Verona, Verona. It was a creamy orange color.

"Cynthia, why don't you have some stuff black people could wear? Some reds, plums, burgundies . . . ? What's with all the peach and coral?"

Cynthia took the lipstick out of her hands. "Do you see a sign that says 'Avon Lady'? Excuse me for not having a makeup supply to fit all the beauty needs of my friends. Actually, in your case nobody has a supply that vast." Pointing at Roxanne with the lipstick, she added, "Why are you in here, anyhow? Are you a voyeur? Are you lesbo? Don't you have anybody else to bug?"

Roxanne gave her a scornful look. "Even if I were lesbo, as you so politically incorrectly put it, I wouldn't be interested in your scrawny butt. I do have a question, though. Why are you walking around in nothing but your drawers in the middle of the day?"

"I am going to work out. I had to pick y'all up at the airport yesterday, so I didn't get a chance to exercise. Now I'm feeling like a fat pig. Look at how my stomach is sticking out."

Roxanne dutifully focused her attention on Cynthia's midriff. She didn't see a thing except the outline of her ribs sticking out above a concave stomach. She estimated the padded bra to be a 34A cup. Roxanne shook her head ruefully. She might be short, but at least she had boobs and hips. She couldn't have gotten one breast in that bra even if she had sewn the two cups together.

"All I see are skin and bones. I don't think one day without exercise is gonna kill you," she said.

"Maybe so, but I am not taking any chances. You can talk because you've always been able to eat like a pig without gaining an ounce. All I have to do is look at food and my thighs start to expand."

"It's just hard to believe that this is the same woman who almost didn't graduate from college because she refused to take any PE requirements until her last semester senior year. Has your body been taken over by a fitness-crazed alien?"

"No, I've just become more conscious of taking care of my

body in my old age. You might want to work on trimming that bubble butt of yours."

Roxanne patted her firm, round backside. "Jealousy will get you nowhere. Men love this butt. I can't help it if you're flat as a board coming and going."

"If you say so. I'm going to work out in the other room." Cynthia had turned the spare bedroom into her own fitness center, complete with StairMaster, treadmill, stationary bike, and rowing machine.

"Well, I'll let you get to it," Roxanne said on her way out.

When she was gone, Cynthia closed and locked the bathroom door, then opened the cabinet under the sink. She felt around until her hand closed over what she was looking for. She shook out ten laxatives, popped them in her mouth, and washed them down with water. She put the rest of the pills back behind the cleaning supplies. As she straightened up, she felt herself relaxing. Just a little exercise and she'd be back on schedule, back to normal.

Chapter

25

Gayle's head pounded as if someone with a large cast-iron skillet were steadily banging against the side of it. She groaned and pressed two fingers to her throbbing temples. When she couldn't free her fingers from her hair, her eyes popped open in confusion. She tugged at the tenacious strands.

Roxanne and Monique doubled over with laughter. "That one was priceless! Quick! Snap the picture, Roxanne."

"Please, be quiet," Gayle begged, her voice croaking. "That racket is killing me." *Couldn't they see her obvious distress?* "Hey," she said, interrupting their laughter. "Would one of you get me some water?"

"Roxanne and I are busy. The kitchen's right over there. A little exercise might do you some good," Monique said.

Gayle gave Monique the evil eye and slowly raised the middle finger of her left hand.

Such outright hostility was so unlike Gayle, Roxanne took pity on her and went to get the water.

Unperturbed, Monique beamed at her, then picked up the photos, which had scattered on the couch. Gayle leaned forward a bit to sneak a peek, but just at that moment her view was blocked by Roxanne, who had returned with a glass of ice water.

Monique said, "Gayle, you don't look so good."

Gayle reached for the glass of water and gulped half of it down. It felt good sliding over parched lips and down her throat. Her vocal cords now lubricated, she responded. "Is that surprising?"

"No, no. I mean you really don't look too good," Monique said, flashing Polaroids of Gayle passed out on the couch like a winning poker hand.

She cheerfully described each one. "That's Gayle sleeping with her mouth open. Is that a little drool I see on the corner of the towel? That's Gayle's undies showing as she tossed and turned on the couch. What's this one? Oh, that's Gayle waking up looking bug-eyed, dazed, and confused. . . ."

"That's cold, y'all. I can't believe you're getting your kicks by watching me suffer," Gayle said indignantly. "OK, you've had your fun. Now hand them over so I can rip them up and flush them down the toilet where they belong."

Monique clutched the pictures to her breast. "Think again, my sister. These pictures are evidence."

"Evidence?"

"The next time you open your saintly little mouth to lecture us about the evils of drugs and alcohol, I'll just whip out my evidence of the day that little halo of yours crashed and burned!"

Gayle shook her head. "Oh, go ahead and keep your evidence. How can you compare my one little slipup to y'all's lifetime of questionable behavior?"

Monique just laughed.

As Gayle's stomach churned and bubbled, she wondered how her father could endure this on a regular basis. She could count on one hand the number of times she'd been drunk—and she remembered none of them fondly. Some people might think getting drunk was hilarious, but she didn't. She couldn't. Not after seeing firsthand what it could lead to—a lack of control, total disrespect for yourself and other people. An image of stepping in to receive a blow meant for her mother flashed in her mind, reminding her all too well that violence was also sometimes a result of overindulging.

Why had she listened to Monique when she insisted she have that third mimosa? Monique, who drank like a fish. . . . Gayle stopped. She could only blame herself. She never should have had anything to drink when she was overtired and sleep-deprived. The alcohol had gone right to her head. But in one way, it was OK—she'd had her fill of liquor for the weekend. "Why didn't Cynthia join in on your sick fun?" she asked them.

"Oh, she's in the other room doing her Jane Fonda impersonation," Roxanne said. "But we'll make sure to show her the results of our photo session."

Gayle heaved herself off the couch and announced to the room at large that she was going to take a shower. Roxanne and Monique were so busy congratulating themselves for being clever, they barely noticed her leaving the room.

As Gayle walked unsteadily down the hall, she heard the rhythmic squeaking of pedals. Curious, she poked her head in the doorway.

Cynthia was marching to the beat of whatever she was listening to on her Walkman, which was attached to her shiny turquoise spandex bodysuit. A pink headband kept the sweat out of her eyes, but dark stains were visible underneath her armpits, between her breasts, and at her crotch.

Up and down. Up and down. Just looking at her was making Gayle tired and a little light-headed. She silently withdrew and headed for the shower.

Cynthia had pretended not to notice Gayle. Her knees ached and the back of her thighs were burning, but she didn't stop her relentless pace. She still had about five minutes left. She'd become so accustomed to this routine that she could accurately estimate when the workout would be over just by feeling the adjustments the machine made.

At last, she slowed her pace, happy in the knowledge that she'd made it through once again. She stood still and the pedals slowly de-elevated. Before getting off, Cynthia grabbed a towel and gave her face and neck a thorough rub.

She sat on the edge of her newly assembled treadmill to give her heart a chance to slow down. She had doubled her aerobic exercise for today by doing both the stationary bike and the stair-stepper. Served her right for missing her workout last night.

But that tense, anxious feeling had gone away. Looking at all that food at brunch had made her physically ill. And Roxanne had sat there shoveling it in without a care in the world.

Maybe I should do another ten minutes on the stepper. That champagne was loaded with calories.

It was great to have all of her friends around, but if they were going to be gorging themselves like this for the next few days, she didn't know how she would survive. Cynthia was kind of thankful Gayle had passed out when she did. Before that, she couldn't stop thinking about when she'd get an opportunity to excuse herself and stick her head in the nearest toilet.

It was bad enough that she had to wait until she got home, and she'd almost died when Roxanne came bursting into the bathroom. It was only sheer luck that Roxanne hadn't caught her puking her brains out. She couldn't believe she'd forgotten to lock the door.

But the toilet had been calling to her. She couldn't wait another minute. She didn't even have to stick her finger down her throat anymore. Just thinking about how fat and disgusting she would become if she let the food stay in her stomach was enough to make her throw up.

She picked up two twelve-pound dumbbells from a metal rack. Standing in front of the mirrored wall, she began her muscle-toning exercises. She looked at the loose flesh on the back of her arms and on her inner thighs with loathing. She had lost weight so fast that the excess skin had yet to firm up.

She started doing lunges. Even though it hurt like hell, she made sure that her back knee touched the ground, because it stretched out the muscles of the thigh even farther. And she needed all the help she could get.

She thought back to the previous night when she'd met her friends at the airport. Even though they tried not to make a big deal of it, they had been impressed by how great she looked. She suspected that Gayle was maybe even a little jealous.

She began three sets of biceps curls.

"A pretty face but . . ." was the story of her life. People always used to give her backhanded compliments. "Cynthia, you would be so pretty if you just lost some weight." Now that Cynthia had shed all those pounds and gotten rid of the only barrier between her and true happiness, she never wanted to hear the words "You've got such a pretty face, but . . ." again.

She pulled off the headband. Her hair was damp, but silky, smooth. Good thing she'd gotten that touch-up last week, before her hair reverted back to a kinky bush. Why couldn't she have wavy hair like Monique? *She* never had to worry about her hair snapping the teeth of combs.

Cynthia started doing arm raises, holding the weights out to her side. She frowned at her pale skin. She would never understand why some of the darker sisters used fade creams to lighten their beautiful brown skin.

She let her arms drop.

For years she had avoided sports like the plague, but now she had finally seen the light. Now that Anthony was in her life, she had no intention of messing up a good thing. A few aching muscles were well worth what she was getting in return.

Cynthia completed her final set of shoulder shrugs, using the weights for resistance. She put the barbells back on the rack and went to take a shower.

Chapter

26

Click.

The screen faded to black.

Roxanne whirled around in surprise. When she saw the remote in Monique's hand, she cried, "Turn it back on! It was really interesting."

"Puh-leez! It was bullshit. And we ain't watching it."

Gayle sighed. As a chronically dateless woman, she had been kind of interested in what a group of black men had to say on the subject of what they look for in a woman. But if Monique didn't like something, she expected everybody else to feel the same way.

"If you don't want to watch it, there are other rooms in this apartment you can go to," Roxanne said. "Besides, maybe Gayle wants to watch it, too."

Gayle didn't want to get involved in Roxanne and Monique's bickering. "My name is Bennett. And I ain't in it."

"You ain't in what?" Cynthia asked as she walked into the room. She had changed into a white tank top and a pair of pink shorts.

Gayle stared at her. She couldn't get over how small she was. "Monique and Roxanne are arguing over a TV show, and they want me to take sides, which I refuse to do."

"What show is it?" Cynthia asked, reaching for a straw basket underneath the glass table. She sat on the couch with Monique and began rummaging through the basket. It contained an assortment of nail polish, cuticle remover, files, and clippers. She took out a cotton ball, soaked it in polish remover, and began wiping off the chipped coral pink polish on her toenails.

"Some show about what black men find attractive in women."

"It sucks!" Monique said. "They lie like dogs."

Roxanne said, "See, that's the problem with black women today. We don't listen enough to what black men have to say."

Monique made an annoyed face. "Yeah, if they were saying something worthwhile, I'd be the first to listen. But if they're gonna talk bullshit about being attracted to women's auras, I don't want to hear it. What the fuck is an aura?"

Cynthia said, working on her rounded toenails, "I agree with Roxanne. The best way to defeat the enemy is to know the enemy."

"Sounds to me like you're outvoted, Monique," Roxanne crowed. "Turn it back on."

Monique pressed the little red on button. The picture cleared just in time to show the credits rolling. A soulful R&B soundtrack signaled the end of the show.

Roxanne glared at Monique. "Damn! You made me miss it."

Monique did not try to hide a triumphant grin. "No great loss, if you ask me. You don't need to watch a TV show to find out what men are looking for. Everybody in this room is probably an expert on the subject. Especially you, Roxanne."

"Yeah, Roxanne," Gayle teased, "who is it this month?"

This was an old joke dating back to college. There might have been a time when she had a steady stream of dates, but living in Boston had quickly turned that around, as well they knew.

"Listening to y'all talk, you'd think my love life rated right up there with Madonna or some other tramp," Roxanne said.

Cynthia asked, "What's going on with you and Marcus?"

"Not a thing since I found out I had to stand in line to get his attention."

"Have you heard from him since then?" Gayle asked.

"Last time I talked to him, he asked me for the number of one of the women who had been sitting at our table that night we first met."

"Oh no, he didn't!" Monique said.

"Oh yes, he did!"

Cynthia, who was now fanning her newly polished toenails with a magazine, paused to ask, "So, what did you say?"

Roxanne shrugged. "I didn't even want to get into it with him. I told him I couldn't believe he was calling to ask me for some other woman's number. I didn't even know her number. And I told him even if I did, why would I hook him up with anyone after the way he treated me?"

"Way to go, girl," Monique said.

"Then he was like, I guess I caught you at a bad time. I'll call back when you're in a better mood."

Gayle just shook her head. Nobody could be that insensitive and dense.

"Damn, he really has a lot of nerve," Cynthia said.

"Either nerves or shit for brains," Monique said. "Roxanne, you're way too nice. The reason he keeps on calling is because you let him believe that he hasn't hurt you. Honey, it's practically guaranteed that every time he calls, he'll say something asinine."

Roxanne didn't respond. Monique was always pushing for confrontation, as if that were the only way to settle things. Yes, it hurt, but Marcus hadn't done any lasting damage. He had disappointed her, but she'd live and she didn't need to get her blood pressure up because some man wasn't what she wanted him to be.

Cynthia said, "Monique, not all of us use the drop-kick method."

"Who did I drop-kick?" Monique asked.

"The doctor."

Monique rolled her eyes. "Winston? I did not drop-kick him. Winston was a loser." Cynthia had been visiting her in Cleveland last year and was the one who'd brought Winston to her attention when they'd been at a reggae club down in the Flats.

"A loser?" Cynthia said, arching an eyebrow. She looked at Gayle and Roxanne for support. "Homeboy has an M.D. and a Ph.D.! Once he finishes his residency, he's gonna be bringing home the bacon."

Monique's answering look said that she was not impressed by Winston's financial potential. "On our first date, Winston takes me to a movie about dancing transvestites in New York. He didn't consult me about the choice. He wanted to go to a five-thirty show so that we could still get in at the matinee price. Over dinner—at Denny's—he proceeds to tell me he was twenty-five years old when he lost his virginity, then he wants to know how old I was when I lost mine. I almost choked on my cheeseburger. I told him my virginity, or lack thereof, wasn't something I discussed."

She gave the others a slanted look. She had their rapt attention. "He then goes on to say that everyone he dates has the potential to be his wife, as if this was some great honor. According to him, sex is the most important foundation for a relationship, and he likes to know if he's sexually compatible with a woman before putting in the time to develop a friendship. I'm like, Hmm, that's an interesting philosophy. Then I offer to split the check—"

"What!" Cynthia cried. "Never, ever offer to pay for the meal. According to Emily Post, it robs a man of his manhood and dignity."

Gayle laughed. Cynthia was the only person she knew who actually owned a book on etiquette.

Monique said, "We'll get to his manhood in a minute, but as far as the check was concerned, he had no trouble giving up his dignity. He nicely let me pay for my meal. Not split the check, mind you, but pay exactly what I owed—because I had ordered more than he did.

"The next time we talk, he tells me about how he used to drive a pickup truck but had to get rid of it because the people he dated never seemed interested in a second date."

"Did he ever consider that it might not be the truck?" Gayle said.

Monique smiled. "I guess not. Because he decided to buy

a Porsche instead. Anyway, after discussing his sexual escapades for a while, he said that he really wanted to spend a relaxing evening with me. . . ."

"And you said no," Gayle said.

"I wish I could tell you that I did, but I can't. It probably had something to do with my mother asking me earlier that same day if I was a lesbian."

Everybody in unison shouted, "She asked what!"

"Oh, my God!" Cynthia cried. "I can't believe she said that."

"That's 'cause you don't know my mother. Anyway, he said he wanted to do something special for me and offered to make dinner, then take in a movie."

Cynthia clapped her hands together. "Oh-oh. He wanted the bootie."

Gayle looked enviously at Cynthia's new pedicure and then at her own unadorned fingernails. Holding her hands out palm side down, she asked Cynthia to do her nails.

"I swear, Gayle," Cynthia said, "what do you do when I'm not around?" Gayle was forever asking someone to do her nails or hair or just about anything related to personal grooming short of giving her a bath. She began sorting through the nail colors in her basket. She picked up a shade of pink, looked at Gayle's deep brown hue, then put it down. "I don't know if I have any polish that would suit your . . . shall we say, distinctive coloring."

"I'm sure you have something. Ain't you got any reds in there?"

Cynthia shook a bottle of ruby red nail enamel. "Monique, switch seats with Gayle so I can do her nails." Gayle took Monique's place on the couch. She sat with one leg curled underneath her bottom, the other on the floor.

As Cynthia filed and shaped the nail of her thumb, Gayle asked, "Are you gonna give me a pedicure, too?"

Cynthia looked down at Gayle's one exposed foot. Years of wearing tight-fitting high-heeled shoes had left their mark; corns and calluses dotted just about every toe. The nails were hard and dark. "Gayle, I love ya like a sister, but honey, you need a podiatrist, not a pedicure. Ain't no amount of polish gonna help those babies."

She took in Monique's pained expression and arms folded across her chest. "Oh, stop pouting," Cynthia said. "We're still listening. Go ahead."

Monique decided that was enough of an apology and went on. "Winston lives in Shaker Heights, which is a very ritzy suburb, but his place was teeny-tiny." Personally, Monique thought he would have been better off living within the Cleveland city limits and getting more bang for his bucks. "For appetizers he passed around some celery and carrot sticks with some store-bought dip. And, I kid you not, I had eaten two lousy carrot sticks when he said to me, 'Wow, you're really wolfing those down.' So I'm like, OK, no more pigging out for me.

"The 'special meal' he had fixed turned out to be a tossed salad, and the main dish was white rice with chopped chicken bits in it. And the minute I was done, he snatched my plate off the table and put it in the sink. I guess having seconds was not an option. So I'm sitting there, my stomach still growling, consoling myself by saying, Well, at least we're going to a movie. But check this out. After dinner he says he has several videotapes and I can pick the one I want to see."

Being constantly broke herself, Roxanne felt a pang of sympathy for him. "But Monique, wasn't he just a resident? He probably didn't have a whole lot of money."

Cynthia said, "I don't care. There's a difference between asking someone out for dinner and a movie versus dinner and a *video*. Besides, he couldn't have been too broke if he had money for a Porsche and an apartment in a high-rent district."

Monique fingered the plastic wrapping of her cigarette carton, debating whether to take one out. "Anyway, his television just happened to be in his bedroom. We go in there and he brings out these movies he's pirated from cable. Most of them were Eddie Murphy and Spike Lee movies I'd already seen. The rest were soft porn.

"So there we were, watching *Basic Instinct*. . . . He's on the bed and I'm in this chair next to the bed, bored out of my mind. He leans toward me and says, 'I knew you were special from the start.' Apparently, he could tell I was intelligent just by looking at me because, get this, I had the right hair and the right height. He stopped just short of saying I had the right skin tone. But I knew he was thinking it, because he went on to tell me that most of his friends were white and that he generally dated white women. . . ."

Cynthia's brush paused in midair. Roxanne and Gayle both held their breath. Monique's feelings about interracial dating were well known.

Gayle finally said, "Just one question. Is this man still alive?"

"Yeah, he's alive," Monique said indifferently. "If you call self-loathing and hatred of your race being alive. He told me that black people have always given him a hard time and how black women have never really thought he was attractive, etc. . . . And how whites were the only ones who seemed to accept him, blah, blah, blah. . . .

"My stomach is turning over listening to this. I mean, this brother is so dark, not even his teeth are white, and he's talking about why white people are better than black people. When I stood up to leave, he tries to kiss me . . . on the lips! I turned my face to the side and felt this dribble on my cheek. Girl, that's all it took for me to break out of whatever trance I'd been in. I jumped away from him, rubbed his slobber off my cheek, and told him, 'I am not attracted to you at all.' "

Roxanne said, "Monique, you could have at least let him down gently."

"He's lucky I didn't cuss his ass out, considering that, according to him, my best qualities were my physical similarities to white women. Anyway, I'm not a total bitch. I told him that I wasn't really looking for a relationship at the moment."

"Honey, you ain't looking for a relationship, period," Cynthia said.

"Don't you know, that man called me three weeks later with an attitude. He was like, I haven't heard from you and I'm wondering what the deal is. He pissed me off. So I was like, What deal? What part of 'I ain't interested' didn't you understand? So then he says, 'Well, I know what you said, but I was just calling to make sure you meant it.' Talk about a lost soul."

Roxanne shook her head. "Monique, you're a real Evilina."

Her sympathy for the pitiful little piece of a man didn't surprise Monique. "Not at all," she said. "He brought this on himself. Some people just can't take a hint. . . . Don't you know, he wanted to know *why* I wasn't interested. So I told him.

"I said, First of all, I can't deal with somebody, especially a black somebody, that didn't like black people. Secondly, it's an insult to be liked for things that I have absolutely no control over and that say nothing about me as a person. And it seemed a little backward to me that sex should come *before* developing a friendship. I finished by saying that he seemed to attribute his success and failures to the wrong things, and he might want to think about reexamining his values, because they were weak."

Gayle said, "I hope he had some privacy when he picked his face off the floor after you were done stomping on it. What else did you say to him?"

"Nothing. But the last thing he said to me was that I was probably right, and that he had just had his first therapy session the day before."

Roxanne's eyes widened. "What! Damn, Monique, you dogged the man so bad he had to seek professional help."

Monique said, "Don't go blaming me. He was a head case before I met him. So if a little bit of rejection pushed him to get his shit together, I'm glad."

At that moment, Cynthia splashed red polish on Gayle's skin near the cuticles. She set the bottle down in disgust and began dabbing at the smear with a cotton ball soaked in remover. "What a cheapskate! You didn't want him anyhow . . . that penny-pinching bastard would probably have you eating macaroni and cheese three times a week," she said. "I'm sorry I ever pointed him out to you."

"Not as sorry as I am," Monique said, rising to pull out the damp towel that Gayle had been drying her hair with. She draped it over the arm of the chair.

Gayle held her nails out to inspect them, and Monique agreed with her that Cyn had done an excellent job. *She*, on the other hand, had no patience for primping. A coat of clear polish was as far as she was willing to go.

She took a drag from her cigarette. "Gayle, how's your love life?"

Gayle turned her head to the left and then to the right, as if searching for the person Monique was talking to. Unable to locate this unseen person, she pointed to herself. "I know you ain't talking to me. What's a love life?" Her expression was solemn as she added, "You know I suffer from a chronic illness that makes dating nearly impossible."

Not wanting her friends to see the laughter lurking in her eyes, Gayle kept them downcast. "The official diagnosis is pal-on-a-pedestal syndrome—POPS."

She paused to let that sink in. "It's an illness that afflicts many black women. Some of the more common symptoms are: having at least one male friend who complains to you constantly about the lack of quality black women out there, despite the fact that he knows you spend most weekends sitting at home watching reruns; having at least one male friend who seeks you out on a regular basis for honesty, emotional support, and intelligent conversation, but chooses to date women who provide none of the above; and having at least one male friend who feels quite comfortable discussing his numerous relationships—in more detail than you would ever want to hear—but acts jealous at any hint that you might be in a romantic relationship yourself."

"So, you got POPS?" Monique said. "OK, what has Kenny done now?" Gayle had finally gotten over that ridiculous crush on Kenny, but she couldn't seem to let go of her role as his unpaid psychotherapist.

"Same old, same old," Gayle said. "He called me the other day complaining about being broke."

"Who isn't?" Roxanne lamented.

Monique said, "Isn't he a big-time corporate attorney down in Dallas?"

"Yeah, but you know he's got child support payments." Kenny had met a girl the summer after he got out of college and she ended up pregnant. So he did the honorable and increasingly rare thing and married her. But with the stress of law school and the fact that he never loved her in the first place, they were separated by the time the little boy was a toddler.

"Oh, yeah," Monique said, "I forgot he had a kid."

"Two kids," Gayle corrected.

"Two!" Cynthia exclaimed, "Ain't the brother ever heard of a condom?"

"Well, the second one came along when they got back together for a hot minute to try and work things out."

"How in the hell did old girl *accidentally* come up pregnant when things were already shaky?" Cynthia said.

"It takes two to tango," Monique said. *When would men stop thinking with their little head and start thinking with the big one?*

Gayle said, "When he started his job, she must have figured they'd hit the big time, because she went hog wild spending money. He finally realized that it would be cheaper to get rid of her. Now the woman uses the kids to weasel money out of him at every opportunity."

"Sounds like Kenny has three kids, not just two," Monique observed. "Still, he's got to be making between fifty and sixty thousand a year. Even with child support, he shouldn't be that broke."

Gayle felt kind of disloyal telling all his business, but it wasn't like any of them would be running into Kenny anytime soon. "Well, you see, he has this new girlfriend."

"Oh really?" Cynthia said, leaning closer to Gayle. "Tell us more."

"I think he met her on a business trip. She lives in New York, so it's been kind of a long-distance thing, but that's gonna change soon. She's supposed to be moving to Texas as soon as she's allowed to leave the state—"

Monique's lawyer's antennae perked up. "Whoa! Run that last part by me again," she said. "Why can't she leave New York? Is she on parole or something?"

"No. But she's in the middle of a nasty custody battle, and her husband or ex-husband, I'm not sure which it is, doesn't want her taking their daughter out of the state—"

"Then how the hell is she moving to Texas, and what's that got to do with Kenny being broke?" Monique said.

Gayle shrugged. "I don't know, but one of the reasons Kenny doesn't have any money is that he's been flying to New York to visit her, and he's been paying for her to come to Houston. . . ."

"You seem to know an awful lot about how Kenny spends his money," Monique said. "What's up with that?"

"Well . . . if you must know, Kenny borrowed two hundred dollars from me to pay for her plane ticket once—"

"Why didn't she pay for her own ticket? Don't tell me, girlfriend is unemployed!" Roxanne said.

"No, she works for Macy's doing something. Anyway, she tried to buy a ticket, but she had maxed out her credit cards . . . so she asked Kenny to get a ticket for her and—"

Cynthia burst out laughing. "That declined-credit-card bit is the oldest trick in the book."

Remembering her earlier embarrassment at the restaurant, Roxanne wasn't so sure about that. Sometimes you really didn't have any money. "Cynthia, you're so damned suspicious. Maybe she really didn't have enough to cover the ticket."

"Wait, y'all, we're getting sidetracked here," Monique said. "So, how did *you* end up paying for the ticket?"

"I didn't pay for the whole thing, only part of it," Gayle said. "I guess Kenny overextended himself during Christmas, you know, with the kids and everything. Plus, he went to New York for two weeks around that time, too. He bought her a set of Louis Vuitton luggage, since that's what she asked for—" When she saw the incredulous looks on her friends' faces, she added a trifle defensively, "It's not like he's not going to pay me back."

Monique said, "Sounds to me like Kenny's money is going

to be tied up for quite a while. So, where is Miss Thang gonna live once she gets to Texas?"

"Well, Kenny said they just bought a house. . . ."

"What! How long have they known each other?" Cynthia asked.

"Since about Thanksgiving, I think," Gayle said.

Cynthia said, "Let me see if I got this straight. He met homegirl less than a year ago. Her divorce isn't even final yet. But nevertheless, he's been jetting to New York, where, I presume, he pays for everything. He buys her expensive gifts, then he borrows money from you. And to top it off, he's buying her a house?" She shook her head. "If I'd known old Kenny was this generous and this dumb, I would have given him a little bit while he was still in the wilds of Minnesota."

"Cynthia, you are a mercenary little something," Roxanne said.

"So, what's the deal with the house?" Monique asked Gayle.

"According to Kenny, the house is in her name, but he made the initial down payment and is having repairs done to it before they move in. That's where all his money is going right now."

Monique smacked a hand against her forehead. "His name ain't on nothing, but he's paying for everything?"

"Yep."

"Is he out of his fucking mind? I can't believe somebody gave him a law degree. If he manages his cases like he manages his life, I feel sorry for his clients," Monique said. "Un-fucking-believable! If she gets pissed at him down the line, his ass will be out on the street. My God, did he sleep through Contracts when he was in law school?"

Gayle's reaction had been the same. But love must be deaf as well as blind because Kenny hadn't paid her any attention. No one ever listened to her—not Kenny, not her other friends, and certainly not her own family. It was enough to make a person want to scream, but no one would probably notice that, either.

"Kenny's just plain stupid," Gayle said. "Get this. He's walking around blind as a bat right now because he lost his glasses and he can't afford to buy another pair. He can buy a house for his woman, but he can't buy a pair of glasses for himself!"

"All I can say is that girlfriend must be whipping it on him in bed 'cause he seems like a man in a daze," Roxanne said. "Now why can't I find me a man like that?"

"Well, I don't know what Kenny's problem is, but it really ain't none of my business. I gave him my opinion, but he chose to ignore it," Gayle said.

In Cynthia's opinion, Kenny had made it Gayle's business when he started borrowing money from her. The man really ought to have more pride about himself. "Just try not to be as stupid as he is," she advised. "Don't be loaning him money to support his sex addiction. 'Cause as the song says, what has he done for you lately?"

Monique looked hard at Gayle and said, "You know, I hear this pal-on-a-pedestal thing is curable. All you gotta do is cut loose men who drain you emotionally, and in this case financially, while lavishing all their attention and money on some undeserving skeezer."

"Yeah, c'mon, Gayle," Cynthia said, "there have got to be some available men in Columbus. Shit, you work in a bank. There ought to be plenty of men there."

"Yeah, middle-aged white men. And believe me, they ain't interested in me, and vice versa."

"I might believe you, Gayle, if hadn't heard you calling out in your sleep for someone named Reggie," Roxanne said. "So 'fess up and tell us about the man of your dreams."

Gayle groaned and hid her face in her hands. She couldn't believe she'd been talking in her sleep. She prayed to God she hadn't said anything too stupid or X-rated. She renewed her vow to stay away from alcohol for the rest of the trip.

When she removed her hands, three pairs of eyes were looking at her expectantly. "It's no big mystery. Reggie is a guy who works in the bank. Cyn and Monique already know about him. One night we're supposed to go to dinner. I canceled because my mother was sick. End of story."

"That's it?" Roxanne said.

"That's it." Gayle's voice discouraged further discussion of the subject.

The truth was, Gayle didn't know what was wrong with her. Reggie had been very understanding, but she had treated him like a leper. Now he was gone.

Three months was a long time. Anything could happen. Reggie could have met some wonderful, normal-acting woman in Chicago. She'd had her chance and she blew it. Nothing for her to do but put it behind her and move on.

She said, "Reggie is doing a training program in Chicago. For all I know, he could be engaged by now."

"Do you have to be so pessimistic, Gayle?" Roxanne asked. "Haven't you ever heard that absence makes the heart grow fonder?"

"Yeah, but I also heard, out of sight, out of mind."

"Why do I even try?" Roxanne said glumly. "Cyn, tell us about your man since you're the only one who has one."

Cynthia thought they'd never get around to her. She eagerly described her relationship with Anthony. He was the best thing that had happened to her. "There is never a dull minute with Anthony. Like that time he just dropped by and asked me to pack my bags. Next thing I know, I'm spending Memorial Day weekend in the Bahamas. We had a wonderful time. I told y'all about how he sent me roses the day after I met him."

Monique lit another cigarette. "So he's romantic, he's spontaneous. . . . Anything else about this paragon of virtue we haven't heard?" Her tone was sarcastic, but she was happy for Cynthia. No point in them all being miserable.

"I forgot generous," Cynthia said. "He bought me all the exercise equipment in the spare room."

Gayle was immediately suspicious. "Cynthia Johnson, did you ask that man to buy you a home gym?"

Cynthia tried to look insulted. "My mother didn't raise no beggar. Is it my fault if I mentioned in passing that it would be much more convenient and less expensive to work out at home and he takes it upon himself to buy me a bunch of exercise equipment?"

Gayle was speechless. She wouldn't dream of hinting at a present so some man would go out and buy it. Must be nice to have no shame.

"Oh!" Cynthia exclaimed. "Did I show you what he just bought me last week?" Before they could answer, she jumped up and ran off in the direction of the bedroom.

"Maybe it's an engagement ring," Roxanne suggested.

Monique sighed. "Get real. Cyn couldn't have kept an engagement ring a secret for five minutes, let alone an entire week. If she'd gotten a ring, this whole trip would have revolved around picking out bridesmaids' dresses."

Cynthia came bounding back into the room. She stuck her wrist out for the benefit of the three spectators. On it was a gorgeous diamond tennis bracelet. Monique whistled through her teeth. "Umm, that's pretty impressive, Cynthia. What did you say this guy does for a living?"

"He has his own public relations firm."

Roxanne couldn't hide her envy. "So I suppose if you get laid off, he could offer you a job, too."

Cynthia smiled. "You know, I never thought of that, but thanks for the tip."

Gayle said, "Well, obviously this guy likes you a lot if he's going to spend this kind of money on you. When do we get to meet him?"

Cynthia's smile faded. "He's not here this week. He had to go out of town on business."

"And you just expect us to take your word for it that Mr. Wonderful exists," Monique teased. "I submit to you," she said, glancing at Gayle and Roxanne, "that this gentleman does not in fact exist, but is simply a figment of this poor desperate woman's overactive imagination."

In reply, Cynthia dragged a heavy photo album with a floral design on its cover from underneath the coffee table. She flipped through several pages until she found what she was looking for. "There you go. Pictures of our trip to the Bahamas."

The other three women crowded around the table to have a look. On the first page were pictures of Cynthia in the hotel lobby surrounded by luggage. Monique wondered why on earth she needed two large suitcases and an overnight bag for a weekend trip, but didn't ask. On the next page was a picture of a decent-looking black man whose cutoff shorts showcased a pair of muscular legs.

"Is that him?" Roxanne asked.

"Yes, that's my honeybunny," Cynthia said proudly.

"Nice legs," Gayle observed.

"Why am I not surprised that you went and found yourself a deep, dark Kunta Kinte brother," Monique said, referring to the main character in Alex Haley's *Roots*. It was a long-standing joke that Cynthia didn't date anyone lighter than the color of Hershey's Kisses.

Cynthia turned to the next plastic-covered page. "That's us on a booze cruise."

There were two pictures of Cynthia with her arms around Anthony's waist. She had an expression on her face that they had all seen plenty of times. She was plastered. It was difficult to tell if she was holding on to him out of affection or because she couldn't stand on her own two legs.

"I can see you were getting your money's worth," Gayle said.

"Given that you're still recovering from a hangover yourself, I suggest you keep quiet, Miss Gayle," Cynthia said. "I was having a good time. Something you would know nothing about. Besides, I really don't drink much anymore, in case you hadn't noticed."

"I'm never gonna live this weekend down," Gayle muttered.

"I've seen enough," Roxanne said. "I'm filled with envy. I'm depressed. Gimme something to eat. It's the only thing that eases my depression."

"That's what you say about your loneliness, and your anxiety, and your happiness. . . ." Cynthia said. "But I'll stop torturing you with tales of my wonderful love life. I'm going to stop by the grocery store to get some salad fixings for me, but I can pick up pizza, Chinese, or Mexican food for y'all."

"Pizza sounds good," Monique said. Roxanne nodded in agreement.

Gayle's stomach had been settling down, but at the mention of food it started to churn again. "Bring me back a can of chicken broth, some crackers, and some ginger ale. Maybe they'll settle my stomach," she said.

Cynthia grabbed her car keys and purse from the dining room table. "OK, I'm all set. Anybody want to ride with me?" she asked.

"I will," Roxanne volunteered.

"Given that Gayle isn't feeling well, I thought we'd stay home tonight. I was thinking about getting some videos. Any suggestions?" Cynthia asked.

"Ooh . . . I know. Why don't we do a Denzel Washington/ Wesley Snipes film festival?" Roxanne said. "And if we get *Mo' Better Blues*, we can get two for the price of one!"

"Sounds good to me," Gayle said.

Roxanne was still rattling off movies as Cynthia pushed her out the door. "And Denzel is fine with his hair shaved off in *Glory*. He looked so noble, so dignified. . . ."

Monique shook her head. Roxanne was a glutton for punishment. After Marcus, she thought Roxanne would have had enough of bald men.

Chapter

27

Gayle stretched out alongside Roxanne on the blanket. She was glad they had persuaded Cynthia to drive them to Clearwater for a day at the beach. Even though the edges of crushed seashells poked her back through the blanket, she didn't mind. It felt good just to relax and not worry about anything. She'd called her mother yesterday and she was doing fine. Aunt Ruby was going to take her to church, and her father hadn't been around in over a week.

Damn, she'd forgotten to ask about Buddy. She guessed everything was OK or her mother would have said something. Gayle was going to have a long talk with that boy real soon. The friends he'd been hanging out with lately weren't about nothing. It didn't help that her mother was so lenient with him. . . .

Gayle could feel herself tensing up. *Stop it!* She turned her face toward the sun instead. "What did Cynthia do with the tanning lotion?"

Roxanne laughed. "As dark as you are, what do you need suntan lotion for?"

"I still tan, you know. But I want some 'cause I like the coconutty smell."

Roxanne brushed off the sand that was clinging to her legs and feet. "I'm hungry. When are those two gonna get back?"

Not particularly sun lovers, Monique and Cynthia had eagerly volunteered to pick up lunch. "They've only been gone fifteen minutes. If you're that hungry, why don't you try to catch you a fish with your teeth?"

"If they don't get back soon, I may just have to do that," said Roxanne. She glanced over at Gayle. Her legs were ashy and streaked with salt and sand. Her hair was a mess. "Gayle, you look like something the cat dragged in."

Gayle touched her hair. It had dried into salt-encrusted clumps. "Instead of talking about it, why don't you comb some of these kinks out?"

Sighing, Roxanne took the comb and brush Gayle had conveniently placed right in her bag. She ordered Gayle to turn around, then knelt behind her as Gayle sat cross-legged on the blanket.

Gayle had no sooner picked up Roxanne's discarded romance novel than she cried, "Ouch! That hurt!"

"Ain't my fault you got nappy hair," Roxanne said.

"It ain't nappy. I put a relaxer in it."

"When? Last Christmas?" Roxanne asked. She could see an inch or so of coarse hair at the roots. "You need to put some conditioner or something on it."

"Just comb the tangles out. I'm going to have to wash the salt out when we get home, anyway."

Like a stern mother, Roxanne jerked Gayle's head back. "You're gonna have to sit up straight if you want me to do anything with this mess."

"Oww. . . . If you wanted me to sit up, all you had to do was say so. You didn't have to try to break my neck."

"Hey, lady, why you combing her hair?" The question came from a little girl who couldn't have been more than five years old. Her brown cheeks were chubby, and her lips were stained red from something she had eaten or drunk. She was wearing a white-and-red-polka-dot two-piece. Her hair was parted down the middle to create two braids that had barrettes on the ends, one red and one white. Standing next to her, sucking her thumb, was another little girl, who resembled her in every way except that her swimsuit was a white and blue polka-dot.

"Why you combing her hair?" she repeated.

"Because she doesn't know how to comb it herself," Roxanne replied as she started to part Gayle's hair down the middle.

The two girls stared at Roxanne as if they'd never heard anything so strange. The white and blue polka dots spoke up. "But . . . my mama says big girls can comb they hair all by they self." Pointing at Gayle, "She a real big girl."

"Yeah," her sister added. "My mama says, we can comb our hair by ourself when we get dis many years old." She held up all ten fingers. "I'm four and a half. How are old are you?" she asked Gayle.

"I'm more than ten years old, and . . ." she said, correcting Roxanne, "I do know how to comb my hair. I was just tired today, so my friend combed it for me."

Roxanne smiled at the two girls. "My name is Roxanne, and this is my friend Gayle. What's your name?"

The girl in red was obviously the more outgoing one. She introduced the both of them. "My name is Bobbie and this is Robbie. I'm four and a half years old, too," she added proudly.

Roxanne loved children, and these two were adorable. She extended her hand. "Well, pleased to meet you, Robbie and Bobbie." She shook hands with both of them.

Robbie, whose thumb went right back in her mouth, stared down at Gayle, who was trying to appear fascinated by the romance of Prince Rafael and Princess Katherine. It wasn't that she didn't like kids, but she was better with kids she had regular contact with.

"I don't know how to read," Robbie said, as if answering a question that had been posed.

Gayle sighed and closed the book. "That's OK. You'll learn how to read in a few years, when you're a little older."

Robbie was still eyeing the book. "Will you read me the story?" she asked.

The child's request caught Gayle off guard. She could just hear the child asking, What's a lusty wench? What's a throbbing manhood? "Uh, this book is for grown-ups," Gayle explained.

"Why?"

"Why? Uh, it uses a lot of big words and that sometimes . . . confuses kids." *Yeah, that sounded good.* "Little kids have to start with little words 'cause it's easier." She gave Robbie a covert glance. *Was she buying any of this?*

The little girl had sat down and was playing with sand that had collected on the blanket. "I can say my ABCs," Robbie said. "A, B, C, D, LMNOP."

"It's A, B, C, D, QRSTZ," contradicted Bobbie. "You don't know your ABCs."

"Yes, I do!" Robbie screamed.

"No, you don't!"

Roxanne smoothly interjected, "You're both partly right. You both got the first part right." She then correctly recited the alphabet song.

Gayle could tell by the respectful silence that followed that Frick and Frack were impressed. As long as neither one of them was wrong and the other right, peace would prevail. "Does your mama know where you are?" she asked.

When Bobbie stared at the ground, Roxanne stood up in alarm and started looking around.

Gayle asked, "Do you remember where your mother was sitting?"

"Over dere," Robbie said, vaguely pointing to the right. Roxanne put up her hands to shield her eyes and looked in that direction. People had set up camp in about a dozen or so spots. Maybe she could just walk with the girls in that direction until they stumbled across their mother.

"We was wid our daddy," Bobbie said. "He was 'posed to build sand stuff wid us, but he went swimming. He was gone a long time. . . ." *And you decided to wander off,* Roxanne deduced. *Mom probably thinks they're under the watchful eye of Dad, and Dad must be out of his mind to leave two toddlers unsupervised at the ocean.*

"Robbie . . . Bobbie . . ." came a call over the sound of lapping waves. Roxanne spotted a woman approaching them from the opposite end of the beach. There was a note of panic in her voice. Lines of worry marred her exceptionally pretty face: creamy brown skin and no blemishes to speak of. She looked to be in her late twenties or early thirties. She was wearing white shorts and a tank top.

"Mama!" Robbie ran over to her. The woman bent at the waist and hugged her hard for a brief moment.

"Where have you girls been?" she cried, her voice laced with anger and relief. "Your father and I have been searching everywhere for you."

"We was talking to Roxanne and Gayle," Bobbie explained matter-of-factly.

Roxanne spoke first. "Hi, Mrs. . . ."

"Traci," the woman said. "Thanks so much for finding the girls."

"Well, actually, they found us. They just walked up to us," Gayle said. Obviously, these two hadn't been given the childhood lecture on not talking to strangers.

Traci stood between her two daughters, holding their hands. "I have to get back. My husband is still out looking for them. I told him to meet me back at the blanket in five minutes if he couldn't find them. Thanks again for looking after them."

She started walking in the direction in which Robbie had pointed earlier, but Bobbie stopped and turned back. "Roxanne, will you come build sand stuff wid us?"

Her mother said, "Bobbie, these ladies have already spent plenty of time with you. Stop bugging them."

"It was no problem," Roxanne assured her. "Your girls are really sweet. We're waiting on our friends to come back with our lunch. If you're still here after we've eaten, I'll come over and build stuff in the sand," she promised.

"Yay!" Bobbie cheered.

Traci gave Roxanne another smile. "You really don't have to do that," she said. "But we should still be around until about six. I have to get back, or my husband's going to think I'm missing, too." She hurried away with both girls firmly in tow.

Roxanne resumed her place on the blanket. With a sigh, she said, "Weren't they precious?"

"Precious? I guess that's one way to describe them. Scary

would be another. Did you see the look on their mother's face? I thought the woman was going to have a coronary." Shielding her eyes from the sun, Gayle took in Roxanne's wistful expression. She was going to make an excellent mother someday.

"Yeah, having kids is a big responsibility, but most of them do make it to adulthood. Look at us, we made it."

"Just barely," Gayle muttered under her breath. Child or adult, life had treated her about the same. Responsibility was nothing new.

Roxanne hugged herself tightly and smiled, "I don't care. I want to have a whole basketball team. I'll be the coach."

Gayle found herself smiling in return. "Five kids? Don't you think you'd better get started? Your biological clock has probably gone from ticking to booming by now."

"I know, but I gotta find the right man first. From the looks of things, Cyn's got a jump on the rest of us. You know, being all in love and everything."

From the way Cyn had gone on about Anthony last night, she did have it bad, but Gayle couldn't see her chasing around after a house full of kids. Knowing Cyn, she'd hire a nanny to do the dirty work. Gayle picked up the comb Roxanne had discarded. "You may be right, but if you want some practice at being a mommy, you can start combing my hair—like you promised."

Roxanne snatched the comb. So much for trying to distract Gayle. She was like Monique in that respect: neither one of them would let you forget anything.

Chapter
28

Irritated by the weight of her hair on the back of her neck, Monique adjusted the band that was holding her ponytail in place. "I hope you two appreciate all the trouble we went through to feed you."

Roxanne took out a package of cold cuts, wheat bread, apples and pears, tortilla chips, a head of lettuce, plastic silverware, and several slices of cheesecake. There was a huge bottle of Evian water, cans of Coke, and a six-pack. Roxanne started to make herself a ham and cheese sandwich. "Where's the Miracle Whip?" she asked.

"Ungrateful as usual, I see," Monique said. She handed Roxanne a small jar of mayo that had rolled behind her.

"What was so hard about getting some food?" Gayle asked.

Monique said, "First, we needed to find a gas station because Cynthia was riding around with the fuel light on."

"We had a quarter of a tank left," Cynthia said sharply.

Monique was about to reply when, to her amazement, Cynthia tore off her bread crusts and put exactly five lettuce leaves between the two slices. Next, she took a knife and divided the sandwich into four small squares.

"Yeah," Monique said, recovering. "I heard you tell Gayle the same thing this morning when we were driving from Tampa."

"I know my car. We still had plenty of gas."

"Ninety-degree weather is not the time to put it to the test."

"We found a gas station. All's well that ends well, OK?" Cynthia retorted. "It's not like we were in the middle of nowhere. Clearwater is still civilization."

As Cyn bit into one of her lettuce sandwiches, Monique was surprised she didn't bite her fingers, the darn thing was so small. Next, Cynthia opened her purse and took out a small plain yogurt and began peeling away its tinfoil covering.

Monique asked, "Is that all you're having—a lettuce sandwich and some plain yogurt?"

"You don't hear me saying nothing about all that salt you're ingesting," Cynthia said, pointing at the handful of tortilla chips Monique was holding. "So don't worry about what I eat."

Gayle looked from one to the other. Had something happened on the way to the store? Monique was just being Monique, but Cyn was sounding downright pissed off. Changing the subject, she said brightly, "Roxanne and I rescued two little girls while you were gone."

Cynthia's eyes flew toward the shoreline. "Oh, no. Were they drowning?"

"Well, it was nothing as dramatic as all that," Gayle said. "They were lost."

"You should have seen them," Roxanne said. "They were so cute. Twin girls about four years old."

When Cynthia heard about how they had come to be lost, she said, "Any husband of mine who left my kids to fend for themselves while he went swimming would catch hell. What was the man thinking?"

"Well, in my family, both the kids and the father would have been in trouble. My daddy for leaving us alone, and us for wandering off," Gayle said. "My mama didn't play. If we didn't mind, she'd have us cut a switch from one of the bushes in the front yard to whip our behinds with."

"I'm not hitting my kids. That's child abuse," Cynthia said. "You would think black folks got enough beatings during slavery to put us off it for generations to come. My parents never laid a finger on me, and I turned out all right."

"That's a matter of opinion," Monique said dryly. "Who's ready for cake?" At her prompting, Gayle and Roxanne each took a slice of plastic-wrapped cheesecake.

Cynthia shook her head. "No, thanks. I'll have a pear," she said. Monique had to be joking, she thought. That cake had more calories than she consumed in an entire day.

"Cyn, I gotta tell you, you have more self-discipline than I had ever thought possible," Gayle said as she licked her fingers. "I can remember a time when you almost physically attacked somebody over a piece of cake."

Rolling her eyes, Cynthia said, "Child, please, don't remind me of that wedding from hell."

Monique snapped the top off a bottle of sunscreen and began rubbing it all over her arms. "Was Angie's mother a bitch or what!"

"Like hell on wheels with an automatic transmission," Cynthia agreed.

"I'm tellin y'all right now, don't ask me to be in your wedding if you are going to pick a hideous bridesmaid's dress," Gayle said.

Monique began to gather up empty wrappers and soda cans, using one of the crumpled grocery bags as a trash can. "The bridesmaids always get stuck in taffeta, ruffles, and bows from hell. By comparison, the bride can't help but look good."

"All of you will be in my wedding," Cynthia said in a matter-of-fact voice. "And I will be looking better than you . . . not because you'll have on ugly dresses, but because I am naturally more stunning."

Monique's lip curled. "You must have put a little something in that bottled water. You seem to be suffering from delusions of adequacy."

Roxanne said, "Don't you think you should concentrate on finding the right man first?"

"Who says I haven't?" Cynthia smoothly countered.

"Well, I heard that!" Gayle said. "Cynthia, child, I'm scared of you."

"And I won't be like Angie. You *will* get thank-you notes and wedding pictures. And you *will* hear from me again," Cynthia assured them. She draped her arms around Gayle and Roxanne, who were sitting on either side of her. "Unlike Angie, you are my true friends, not just bodies recruited to convince people I have friends." She smiled at them. "You're like sisters."

"Aren't we getting a little sentimental?" Monique said, having settled into a beach chair.

Her friends shared a knowing smile. Monique hated displays of affection. As if on cue, they all rushed over, knocking Monique from her chair as they covered her with hugs and kisses.

Monique tried to push them away. "Yuck, get away from me." She picked up her overturned chair, then smoothed her T-shirt before sitting down again. "People are going to think we're too weird."

Gayle teased, "Since when did you start caring about what people think?"

"Since I had three crazy women slobbering all over me in public." She stood up abruptly. "I think I'm going to go wash off your grubby paw prints," she said. She quickly marched off, sidestepping the bodies sprawled near her chair.

Cynthia offered to go with her, then turned back. "Gayle, aren't you coming?" Gayle always had to go to the bathroom.

Gayle shook her head no.

Roxanne announced, "I'm going to find those two little girls we were telling you about." Neither Cynthia nor Monique gave any sign of having heard her. "Look for us when you get back. We'll be with a set of twins."

Roxanne picked up Cynthia's boom box and the bags. "Help me with this," she said to Gayle, who was opening the romance novel again.

Gayle pretended to be reading. "Help you with what?"

"I don't want to leave our valuables here while we are playing with the kids."

"We?" Now Gayle looked at her. "I never promised to play with the little brats. You did."

"Come on, Gayle, it'll be fun. And you saw them, they're very well behaved."

"Count me out."

"OK," Roxanne said casually, "but don't expect me to touch that nappy head of yours for the rest of the trip."

"What?" Gayle sighed, then closed the book. "All right. . . . Where do we find the little darlings?"

Laden down with their wallets and the rest of their things, the two set out in the direction in which the girls and their mother had gone earlier. They skirted around the hordes of oil-covered sunbathers. Gayle had never seen so many semi-naked people in her life. Some were stretched out with arms at their sides, faces turned toward the sun. Others lay on their stomachs, giving their glistening backs an equal chance to get some color. A few bold individuals had taken off their bikini tops so they wouldn't have tan lines. Gayle just hoped they didn't turn over in their sleep or else everybody on the beach would have a show.

Gayle smiled at all the white people trying so earnestly to get some color, undeterred by the threat of sunburn or skin cancer. *They knew good and darn well none of them wanted to be brown, at least not permanently.*

Gayle wrapped her arms around her knees and watched as Roxanne and the girls splashed around in the shallow water. Roxanne's ability to quickly gain the trust of kids probably made her an excellent teacher, but Gayle couldn't imagine having Roxanne's job. It was hard enough for the average parent to deal with one or two adolescents, but to have thirty or forty of them at the same time would work Gayle's last nerve. . . .

"Are those two women over there your friends?" Traci asked.

Monique had an annoyed look on her face and seemed to be hobbling a little. And where had Cynthia gotten that big floppy straw hat from? Gayle stood up. "Hey, Cynthia, over here!"

Cynthia waved back and started walking toward them.

Gayle made introductions, and more space was cleared on the blanket. Monique immediately took off her shoe and turned it upside down. A couple of small pebbles fell out.

"Sorry about that," she apologized as she brushed them off the blanket, "but these stupid rocks and shells keep finding their way into my shoe."

Traci opened a large plastic cooler. "Would you like something to drink?" she asked. They all declined, and Traci took out a diet soda.

Cynthia noticed the long and slender line of her neck as Traci tilted the can to her lips. Why the hell was *she* drinking diet soda? The woman did not have the figure of someone who had squeezed out two children. Cynthia gave Traci a disarming smile when she noticed her staring. "I was just admiring your wedding ring," she lied.

"Actually, it's new. Our tenth wedding anniversary was last month, and my husband took us all to Puerto Rico. One night when the two of us were out to dinner, he gave me this ring," she said.

"That's so sweet," Gayle said.

"You know what he said?" Traci asked, her voice becoming softer. "He said this ring was to make up for the fact that he'd only been able to get me an inexpensive one when we got engaged eleven years ago. You see, he was just starting his business, and money was really tight at the time."

"Sounds like your husband is a romantic guy," Cynthia said.

"He is," Traci confirmed. "He's a real sweetheart."

Cynthia eyed the pear-shaped diamond, nestled in an antique setting with an inset of smaller diamonds, one last time. It had probably cost a small fortune. Someday she wanted to have exactly what Traci had. A great husband, a couple of kids, a nice body, and enough money to buy the things she wanted.

Monique tapped Gayle on the shoulder and whispered, "So, where are Roxanne and the two *adorable* kids she was raving about?"

"Over there playing in the water."

Rising to her feet, Monique announced, "I'm going to go see what Roxanne is up to. And maybe I'll even get my feet wet. That'll make my trip to the beach official."

As she neared the water's edge, she called, "Hey, Roxanne! What in the world are you doing?"

Rivulets of water ran from Roxanne's hair until they disappeared at the edges of her swimsuit. "We're playing Sharks and Minnows. As the shark, my job is to capture the minnows as they try to swim by. If I catch a minnow, it becomes a shark, too, but of course you had to screw that up by distracting me."

One little girl openly stared at Monique. "I'm Bobbie. Who are you? Are you Ree-Ree's friend?"

"Ree-Ree?"

"That's me," Roxanne said. "Bobbie thought I should have a nickname."

"Yeah," Bobbie said. "Robbie is for Robin, Bobbie is for Roberta, and Ree-Ree is for Roxanne. What's your nickname?" she asked.

"I don't have one," Monique replied, "but my name is Monique."

"Everybody's got a nickname," Robbie insisted.

Not in the Washington-Edwards clan, Monique wanted to tell her. Names were passed down from generation to generation. Shortening them would defeat the purpose of honoring long-dead ancestors. At least, that's what her mother had told her.

Roxanne quickly apologized. "She's another boring adult, no sense of humor. . . . Watch," she said. She bent down and splashed a huge swat of water in Monique's face.

Monique sputtered, then glared at Roxanne.

"See what I mean?" Roxanne said to the twins, who were giggling at the sight of water running down Monique's face. "No sense of humor at all."

"You wanna play the game wid us?" Bobbie asked.

"Why not?" Monique agreed. She was already soaked anyhow.

"Monique is a lawyer," Roxanne said. "I think she'd be a *really* good shark."

Monique lunged after Roxanne, crying, "I'll show you how a big shark eats a little shark. . . ."

Traci said, "I'm looking forward to returning to teaching once the girls are in school full-time. I know that doesn't sound like much of a change, because I'll still be around kids all day, but once I'm back at school there will be other teachers and parents to interact with."

Cynthia tried to hide a smirk. *So, the woman didn't have it all. She was starving for adult conversation.*

Traci continued, "I don't think I could stand another year of soap operas and talk shows."

Gayle's eyes immediately lit up, and Cynthia groaned. Gayle, who generally was level-headed, was addicted to the soaps. Her in-depth analysis of each character's flawed decision-making was a source of amusement among her friends. Cynthia, on the other hand, could take or leave soap operas. She had enough problems of her own to deal with without having to worry about fictional characters'.

Traci and Gayle chattered happily, moving from the dastardly doings in Genoa City to those in Oakdale. Finally, Cynthia decided it was time to switch the subject. "I can't believe they're still in the water," she said, watching the group of four frolic in the shallow waves.

Traci said, "We have a swimming pool at home, and my two are in there constantly. So this is nothing."

Their own pool? Cynthia could feel her jealousy resurfacing.

Traci said, "My husband was thinking ahead. He bought the lots on both sides of our house so that we could add things as we became able to afford them. A pool was one of those add-ons."

"Your husband sounds like a smart guy," Gayle said. "It's really nice to hear about a marriage where the couple actually works together to achieve goals."

"Don't get me wrong. We don't have this perfect marriage," Traci said. "My husband and I have our little run-ins just like everybody else. But overall, I'd recommend marriage to anyone."

I'd recommend marriage to anyone, Cynthia mimicked in her head. She rhythmically rubbed a hand across her chin. Something about Traci reminded her of her mother. Maybe it was the way she didn't seem to have to work very hard to get what she wanted. Everything was just so, so perfect.

Getting to her feet, she abruptly announced, "I'm going to go see what the rest of the gang is up to."

As Cynthia walked slowly toward the water, she felt a wave of exhaustion. And it was harder than usual to ignore the rumblings of her stomach. She told herself, You are not hungry. You just ate. That noise is just the food settling down. It will go away.

Still, she sank to her knees on the sand. She needed to rest a minute. While in this kneeling position, she remembered that she'd left her hat on the blanket. It would have to wait, she just couldn't deal with the Happy Little Homemaker right now.

Because her head was bowed, she didn't see Monique walk over to her. "Hey, Cyn," Monique said. "Wake up. You can't be snoozing out here in this heat."

Cynthia slowly opened her eyes. Monique was soaking wet and had a huge smile on her face. "What are you so happy about?" she asked. "I thought you hated the beach."

"Like you're always telling me, it's a woman's prerogative to change her mind. I figured, if you can't beat 'em, you might as well join 'em."

She found Monique's good humor irritating. "Would you get Roxanne? I'm tired and ready to go."

Monique gave Cynthia a probing look. "Are you sick or something?"

"Yeah, I'm sick of being here. I'll get Gayle," she said, leaping to her feet too fast. She felt a little dizzy. "Tell Roxanne to make it quick."

Cynthia rejoined Gayle and Traci, only to discover that they were still talking about Traci's husband and the joys of married life. Traci smiled when she saw her standing there. Unclenching her jaw, Cynthia returned the smile.

"Back so soon?" Traci said.

Cynthia stooped to pick up her hat. "Yeah, I think I had a little too much sun. So we're going to take off pretty soon."

"You do look pretty wiped out," Gayle agreed. "Why don't you sit down until Roxanne and Monique get here?"

Cynthia silently complied with this suggestion. She put the hat on her head, not only as protection from the sun but to form a little barrier between herself and Gayle's worried eyes.

"Do you have a headache?" Traci asked. "I think I have some aspirin somewhere." She opened a duffel bag and took out a small bottle.

"Do you have any water?" she asked. Traci told her there was a bottle of water in the cooler behind her and some little plastic cups right next to it.

Gayle said, "Traci, thanks for getting me caught up on my soaps."

"Please, you're the one doing me a favor. It was nice to have adult company for a change. I only wish you could have met my husband. I don't know where he's gotten to. This must be the day for missing persons in this family."

"I wish I'd met him, too," Gayle said, then laughed. "You know what? All this time you've been saying my husband this or my husband that. You never did say what his name is."

"I didn't?" Traci seemed surprised by her oversight. "Well, it's Anthony."

Anthony? Cynthia's hand shook as she poured the water. It was a pretty common name.

"Really?" Gayle cried. "Cynthia's boyfriend's name is Anthony, too."

The aspirin all but forgotten, Cynthia heard her heart starting to pound in her ears. She lifted her head slightly, and out of the corner of her eye she could see Roxanne and Monique and the kids walking toward them.

Suddenly, Robbie yelled, "Daddy!" then took off running, followed by Bobbie.

"So, their long-lost father finally decided to put in an appearance," Roxanne said.

From a distance, the man was about average height and had dark brown skin. Monique strained to see his face. There was something about him that looked familiar. But how could that be? Maybe she'd seen him earlier in the day. He was wearing a pair of cutoffs and no shirt.

"Nice legs," Roxanne whistled appreciatively.

A feeling of dread invaded the pit of Monique's stomach. She quickened her pace. "Hurry up, Roxanne," Monique said, grabbing her friend's arm and practically dragging her across the sand.

Traci said in surprise, "Your boyfriend's name is Anthony, too? How funny!"

Cynthia leaned on the cooler for support.

"Mama!" came Robbie's excited cry. "Daddy's back!" The girls scrambled over to the blanket.

Gayle looked up to greet the man she'd been hearing so much about. And her mouth almost fell open. He was the man from Cynthia's vacation pictures!

Traci stood up and put her arms around her husband. "Honey, I want you to meet Gayle. She's one of the people who found Bobbie and Robbie, and . . ." She paused, waiting for Cynthia to turn around.

Cynthia's hand was shaking so badly she dropped the plastic cup. The water was quickly absorbed by the hot, greedy sand. She somehow found the strength to turn around, but she couldn't lift her head, or her eyes, which remained hidden beneath the brim of her hat.

Traci said, ". . . this is Cynthia."

Her husband said not a word.

Gayle watched as Traci frowned, her pretty brow wrinkled, confused by her husband's lack of response. Then she looked from Cynthia's ashen face to her husband's stunned one. Comprehension hit, and her arms fell away from him.

"Pleased to meet you," Gayle babbled into the silence, words tumbling over one another. "I'm sorry, but we've got to . . . got to leave."

She looked around for Roxanne and Monique. They were racing toward her. *Thank God.* She helped Cynthia, who still had not spoken, to her feet.

Hot and out of breath by the time she reached the silent group, Monique wasted no time talking. She quickly gathered up their belongings and ushered her friends away. Braving a glance over her shoulder, Traci's stricken face was the last thing she saw, her wounded eyes following them as they hurried off.

Chapter

29

Once inside the city limits, Monique asked, "Cyn, what's our exit?"

Silence.

"Cyn?" Monique repeated, her voice tinged with impatience.

After another brief pause, Cynthia said, "Get off at Armenia."

Roxanne felt herself relax a bit. Although Cynthia's directions were limited to only a few words, at least she'd said something. She hadn't spoken at all on the ride home. Hadn't even protested when Monique asked for her car keys.

Within minutes, Monique turned into the entrance of Cynthia's apartment complex. The guard at the gate, recognizing Cynthia's car, waved them through.

Monique pulled up to Cynthia's building. "Why don't we unload this stuff first and then I'll park the car?"

As Roxanne stepped outside, she was reminded again of the heat. It was not quite as bad as it had been earlier in the day, but it was still muggy. Several of Cyn's neighbors were lounging around the pool.

Roxanne walked to the rear of the car and found that, like everything else belonging to Cynthia, the trunk was a mess. They had thrown the aluminum chairs over the spare tire and a shiny red toolbox that look like it had never been opened. Their canvas bags were wedged between two brown cardboard boxes that were bulging with manila folders. Monique took out the two bags, the sand-encrusted blanket, and a couple of damp towels. She handed everything to Roxanne except the blanket, which she tucked under her arm, and then closed the trunk.

After Gayle and Cynthia were out of earshot, Monique said, "Can you believe this shit?" She gave the blanket a vigorous shake. Roxanne moved off a couple of paces to avoid being hit by flying sand. "That little fucker was married! The minute I saw him, I knew that I'd seen him somewhere before. Then you said something about his legs and it clicked." She shook her head. "Man, he really played Cyn for a fool. And what a way to find out."

The bags were weighing Roxanne down, and she said, "I'm sure we'll be talking about this for the rest of the day. So, ain't no point in me standing here straining my back. I'll see you upstairs." She turned around at the foot of the stairs. "Do you want me to take the blanket?"

"No, I got it. I'm going to park and then I'll be right up. Gayle and Cynthia are probably waiting for us. I think I have the key to the apartment," she said, holding up the ring of keys.

Roxanne found, though, that Gayle and Cynthia were already in the apartment. She walked in through the open door. The contrast between the sweltering heat outside and the chilly air of Cynthia's place caused goose pimples to rise on her arms and neck.

She dropped the bags on the nearest couch and looked around.

The door to Cynthia's room was closed, and Gayle was nowhere in sight. She stood in the middle of the floor, staring at the closed door at the end of the hall. She began playing with one of her dreadlocks. Should she go in there? But she didn't know what to say to Cynthia. *I'm sorry your dream man turned out to be married with children. Better luck next time?*

Moments later, Gayle came out of the guest bathroom. "Where's Cynthia?" Roxanne asked.

"She went into her room," Gayle said. "I think she locked the door."

"Did she say anything?"

"No. She just went into her room and closed the door," Gayle said. "I think somebody ought to go in and talk to her."

Roxanne nodded and gave Gayle a hopeful look.

Gayle said, "Why you looking at me?"

"C'mon, Gayle. It's either you or me. Monique is definitely not the one to do it—"

"Monique's definitely not the one to do what?" Monique said as she entered the apartment. "And why y'all wasting Cyn's electricity?" She pushed the door shut and came into the room. "So, what am I not qualified to do?"

Gayle and Roxanne looked at each other, then Roxanne spoke up. "You're not the best one to talk to Cynthia."

Monique bristled. "And why not? In case you forgot, communicating is what I do on a daily basis."

"You badger and browbeat people for a living," Roxanne corrected.

"Now is not the time for a debate," Gayle pleaded, jerking her head toward the closed bedroom door. "We need to figure out how we can help Cyn."

Roxanne nodded in agreement, feeling a little ashamed of herself. Arguing with Monique was just a way to stall. She didn't know what to say or how Cyn might react. What if she said the wrong thing? Then what?

She'd never had to deal with a situation like this. Then she reminded herself that this wasn't some stranger but one of her best friends. No matter how awkward or embarrassing this was for her, Cynthia had to be feeling ten times worse. "All right, I'll talk to her," Roxanne said.

"Good," said Gayle.

Roxanne could hear the relief in her voice and realized they all relied on Gayle too much in a crisis. But it just seemed like Gayle could handle things. Now it was her turn.

She tapped softly on Cynthia's door. There was no response. Roxanne glanced back at Gayle and Monique, who were standing a ways down the hall near the kitchen. Gayle gestured for her to knock again. This time Roxanne knocked a little harder. "Cynthia," she called.

Still no answer.

What if Cyn had done something crazy, like taken an overdose of pills or slit her wrists? Those pink Lady Bic shavers in her bathroom might look innocent, but they still had razor blades in them.

She tried turning the knob. It was unlocked.

Roxanne poked her head in. No gruesome scene greeted her. Cynthia had stripped down to her underwear and was lying on the unmade bed. The floral comforter lay at the foot of the bed.

Roxanne came into the room and shut the door behind her. Cynthia was on her stomach with her face toward the wall and away from the door. Roxanne touched her shoulder. Her skin was cold and clammy. "Cynthia," she said, sitting down on the bed, "are you OK?"

Silence.

"I know you're upset, but I wish you'd say something 'cause I'm really worried about you."

Without turning her head, Cynthia said, "I'm not OK. But I don't want to talk about it. All right?"

"I feel really bad . . . about everything," Roxanne said. "Tell me what I can do to help. It's not like you to be this quiet. I wish you would scream, cry, or rant and rave, like you usually do." She paused. "We'll slash his tires, we'll break his windshield . . . whatever you want."

Roxanne was encouraged by the soft chuckle that came from the bed. At least Cyn hadn't lost her vindictive streak. Plotting revenge had been a favorite tactic for her and Monique. Not that they ever followed through on their schemes. Well, almost never. There was that time they had trashed Garland's dorm room with sixteen rolls of crumpled toilet paper to relay their feeling that he was a big asshole.

Cynthia slowly rolled over to face her. "But the best thing you could do for me right now is leave me alone. I'll be all right. I just have a lot to think about."

Roxanne turned on the lamp next to the bed. This was the

most Cynthia had said since leaving the beach. Seeing Cynthia's sallow complexion and listlessness made her question whether further discussion was the best thing. "I'll drop it for now, but," she warned, "I'm not leaving the state of Florida with you looking this pitiful." She picked up the comforter from the foot of the bed and put it over Cynthia. "Here, cover yourself up. You're like a block of ice. I'm gonna turn down the air-conditioning." She put out the light and moved to the door. She turned to look back at Cynthia, who seemed engulfed by the queen-size bed. "You look worn out, so I'll let you get some rest, but"—she mock-quoted Arnold Schwarzenegger's line from *The Terminator*—"I'll be back."

Cynthia frowned at the weak impersonation.

Roxanne said, "Get some sleep, and in the meantime I'll see what Old Mother Hubbard has in her cupboard. I know that lettuce sandwich you had for lunch has to have worn off by now." She shut the door behind her. She half expected Gayle and Monique to be listening at the keyhole. But they weren't.

Left in the cold darkness of her room, Cynthia pulled the covers tightly around her. She welcomed the black solitude.

She was exhausted. Talking to Roxanne, the ride home, any little movement, took tremendous effort. It took all she had to keep from falling apart. And she couldn't get the image of Anthony standing on the beach in his wife's arms out of her head. Along with that image came the humiliation, over and over again.

Thank God for Gayle. Without her, she would probably still be standing there steeped in shame and mortification. And, oh God, the look in Traci's eyes. As long as she lived, she'd never forget the devastation she'd seen there. The devastation she had caused. Why hadn't the ground just opened up and swallowed her? That's all she'd wanted at the time. Instead, Gayle had whisked her away.

On the car ride home, she'd been close to the brink. If they'd asked her anything about her relationship with Anthony, she would have been reduced to a crying, pathetic mess. Even with her eyes closed, she still saw Traci's stunned expression and disbelieving eyes.

Cynthia shivered despite being enveloped by the heavy comforter. Her teeth chattered. Roxanne could adjust the thermostat all she wanted. Cynthia knew that the coldness she was feeling had nothing to do with the air-conditioning. It was coming from deep within her.

Her chest hurt. The sensation was more one of pressure than of pain. But Cynthia didn't want to feel anything. She desperately wanted to rush into the bathroom and vomit until the blessed numbness and emptiness that followed came. But she couldn't. She didn't even have the energy to lift her head off the pillow.

Her weakness made her want to cry. Through it all, she hadn't cried. And even now the tears wouldn't come. The ball of pain in the pit of her stomach had moved past her chest, upward to her throat, where it sat in a gigantic, unmoving lump.

Then, unexpectedly, her chest heaved, mimicking the violent movements of vomiting, but, unlike the latter, brought her no relief. Cynthia stuffed the corner of the comforter in her mouth, her eyes riveted on the small beam of light under the door. *Had they heard her?* She didn't want them to see her like this. It was bad enough knowing that they were undoubtedly sitting in her living room talking about her right now. . . .

"Girl, all I can say is that Cynthia is a better woman than me," Monique declared. " 'Cause homeboy's ass would have been kicked before I left that beach."

They were sitting at Cynthia's dining room table. The silk-flower arrangement had been pushed aside so they all had a clear view of one another.

Roxanne took a sip of water from the glass she was holding. "Give her a break, Monique. It probably shocked the hell out of her to find out he even had a wife. And what was she supposed to say with the man's kids standing right there?"

She set the glass back on the table. "She still looks like she's in a state of shock."

"I know what you mean," Gayle said. "If it had been me dithering like an idiot when he strolled over with those kids, I would have been speechless, too. I really feel sorry for his wife and kids. I just *do not* understand men. Traci is a nice woman, good-looking, educated, a dedicated and patient mother. From everything she said, they seemed like the perfect family. Why on earth would he cheat on her? Monique, you didn't hear how she was going on about him. That woman worships the ground he walks on."

"Make that past tense . . . she worshipped," Monique said. "What I wouldn't give to be a fly on the wall in that house tonight."

Roxanne didn't share Monique's morbid curiosity or desire for revenge. She thought it was a sad situation for everybody concerned, especially the twins. Today's events could change their lives forever. One day they have a happy home; the next day they're just another casualty of divorce. It could turn out awful.

Gayle said softly, "Hey, are you OK?"

"What?" Roxanne replied, embarrassed. She quickly blinked her eyes to clear away any telltale tears. "Oh . . . I just think it's so sad, especially for the kids."

Monique said, "Roxanne, I don't know how you manage to get through life being so emotional. It's one thing to sympathize, but crying about it isn't gonna fix anything."

Before the squabbling could start again, Gayle said, "Y'all, what are we gonna do about Cynthia?"

"What do you mean? If she doesn't want to talk about it, there's not a lot we can do," Monique said matter-of-factly.

"She's going to have to talk about it sometime," Gayle said. "We'll be here for two more days, and we can't just pretend nothing happened. Maybe we should just go home a day early," she suggested. "That way she won't feel like she has to entertain us when she has other things on her mind."

Monique liked that idea. "You know, we bought those cheapo tickets. It'll probably cost us to make changes, but I can check it out with the airline. Does anybody know where Cynthia keeps her yellow pages?" She got up from the table to search for it.

"I don't know," Roxanne mumbled. "I feel like we're abandoning her if we just up and leave. I know I wouldn't want to be left alone at a time like this."

Seeing Roxanne's doubtful expression, Gayle said, "It's not a done deal yet. We're just checking things out, in case we decide to go that route."

Monique came back into the room. "I couldn't find the phone book. It must be in Cynthia's room."

Gayle said, "Roxanne thinks we should stick around to give Cyn some moral support."

Monique's scowl showed what she thought of that idea. "Kind of hard to support somebody who's holed up in her room," she observed. "I'm going to look at my plane ticket, maybe there is a 1-800 number on it. If not, I'll call Information." She went in search of her purse.

The other two women resumed their conversation.

"I say we follow Cynthia's lead," Gayle said. "If she wants us to stay, we'll stay. If not, then we're outta here."

"I don't think Cynthia even knows what she wants right now. You should have seen her. She looked like a little kid. All of her normal spunk was gone."

Roxanne couldn't remember the last time she had been in a room with Cyn for more than two seconds before she'd launch into some animated conversation, her drawl conspiratorial and slightly apologetic as she gossiped about this person or that. Here was a perfect opportunity to get their attention, and she had nothing to say. Her silence was spooky.

"It's only gonna cost us twenty-five dollars extra if we leave tomorrow at one-fifteen instead of Tuesday morning," Monique announced as she walked back into the room.

"That's not too bad," Gayle said. "Roxanne, maybe you should check on other flights, too."

Roxanne stood up. She surveyed the discarded clothes, purses, and beach paraphernalia. "Maybe later. First I'm going to go wash some of this sand off me. Then we'd better straighten this place up. Cynthia will have a fit if she sees sand and our junk all over her precious pink sofas."

"Forget about her stupid sofas," Monique said, scratching the side of her leg. "I'm more concerned about these sand mites or whatever they're called that seem to have hitched a ride on my legs."

Roxanne regarded the little red welts developing where Monique had raked her leg with her nails. "Well, stop scratching like a mangy dog and go take a shower. You keep clawing yourself, you're just gonna end up infecting the bites."

"Thanks for the advice," Monique said, "but I'd watch the name-calling if I were you. . . ." As she passed by Roxanne, she tweaked one of her dreadlocks. "With this hair, you're about the mangiest thing I've seen so far today."

"Hey," Roxanne said, trying to grab Monique's hand. But given her superior height, Monique was able to keep Roxanne at arm's length while still holding on to the twisted lock of hair. At last, Roxanne stood still. Struggling only resulted in her hair being yanked harder and her scalp hurting even more.

"It would be interesting to see whether I could use this rope to spin you like a top, but—" Monique sighed, regretfully— "my hot shower is calling." She let go of Roxanne's hair and started walking down the hall. "I'm taking the guest bathroom. It's cleaner than Cynthia's. You can use hers. You're used to her clutter."

Roxanne rubbed her tender scalp. "Your sensitivity to my needs is underwhelming," she said.

Gayle waved a hand in mock disgust. "Whenever you get together, you and Monique act like two little kids. I just hope the level of immaturity shown by you two isn't representative of the rest of the nation's educators and lawyers."

"Aw, hush up," Roxanne muttered. "I'm on vacation. Can't I get a break from all that doing-the-right-thing crap a couple of days out of the year?"

"Uh-huh," Gayle said absently as she picked up the blanket from one of the sofas. She opened a white shuttered closet next to the kitchen which hid Cynthia's small washer-and-dryer unit. She peered inside the washer. "I hope this thing is big enough," she said as she stuffed the blanket in it. "The drum is awfully small." She poured a capful of liquid detergent on the load and closed the door.

"Since you're doing the cleaning, I'll do the cooking," Roxanne promised. "After I take my shower, I'll get dressed and go buy groceries."

In the guest bedroom, Roxanne shed her swimsuit, and thinking of a great idea, she walked across the hall to the bathroom. The heat from the shower had made the room warm and steamy. She could barely make out Monique's silhouette behind the curtain.

She walked over to the toilet and flushed.

"Oww!" came Monique's cry from behind the curtain.

Roxanne grinned. Flushing had caused a change in water temperature, just as she had hoped.

"I was just scalded in here!" Monique yelled. "Who in the hell flushed the toilet?" She poked her head out the curtain but couldn't see the guilty party because a wall separated the toilet and sink area from the shower. "I know it was you, Roxanne. You little runt," she said through her teeth.

When there was no answer, she yanked the curtain shut again.

Roxanne was seated on the toilet, doubling over with silent laughter. A couple of minutes passed, then she tentatively poked her head around the corner. From the movements behind the curtain, she could tell Monique had resumed showering. Roxanne stealthily positioned herself in front of the curtain, then pulled it back.

The sudden gust of cold air caused Monique, who was shampooing her hair, to gasp in surprise. The bottle of shampoo she was holding fell from her grasp and landed on one of her toes. "Ow, ow!" she cried, hopping around on one foot.

Roxanne laughed, holding her aching side with one hand and pointing at Monique with the other.

Monique braced herself against the tiled wall of the shower and rubbed her injured foot. She glared at Roxanne. "I swear to God, Roxanne, I'm gonna kick your ass when I get out of this tub. I could have broken my toe."

Through her laughter Roxanne said, "Please, that little-bitty travel-sized plastic bottle ain't gonna do no damage to those Bozo the Clown feet."

"Yeah, we'll see what kind of damage these Bozo feet do to your munchkin-sized rump when I kick you in it."

Roxanne reached for a towel and shook her head. Airily, she said, "When will you big people realize that if you use your size to overpower little people to win the battle, we little people have to resort to superior intellect and guerrilla tactics in order to win the war?"

Gayle was on her way to throw some stuff in the spare room when her attention was drawn to voices coming from the open bathroom door. She stopped short at the sight of the two naked women, one wet and one dry, facing off totally unaware of her presence. Monique in all her long-legged glory, soapy hair dripping, was leaning against the wall. Roxanne was standing with her legs apart and one hand on her hip, giving Gayle a full view of her brown butt. In Roxanne's other hand was a yellow-and-white-striped towel.

Gayle stared for a moment, then went about her business. She didn't *even* want to know what they were doing. There must be something in the air or the water in Tampa. Everybody had gone crazy.

Chapter

30

Gayle unfastened the top button of her jeans and rubbed her full stomach. She relaxed against the sofa behind her. The glass coffee table in the living room had been cleared, and a couple of the beach towels substituted for a tablecloth.

There hadn't been much dinner conversation because taking the edge off their hunger had been their sole priority. As usual, Roxanne had outdone herself, but the truth was Gayle was so hungry that a meal made in an Easy Bake oven would have tasted like haute cuisine to her.

Monique flicked her cigarette on the side of her empty plate, and as she did so, a few ashes fell on the terry-cloth towel. She rubbed them in, which only caused a grayish smudge to appear. She shrugged and put the cigarette to her lips again.

Roxanne said, pointing at the smudge and talking as if Monique weren't in the room, "Completely lazy and disrespectful. Just ruining people's property and hard work."

"She can make all the mess she wants. I know I ain't washing no more clothes on this vacation," Gayle firmly stated. "And somebody better clean up this mess before Cyn sees it."

"Yeah, well, the cleanliness fetish seems to stop at the bedroom door, because it's a jungle in there," Monique said. "And there's so much fungus growing on the tile in her bathroom, you could conduct biology experiments."

Gayle shook her head slowly. "I can't believe you're gonna

sit right here in her living room and bad-mouth her like that."

"I ain't bad-mouthing her. I'm just telling the truth. At heart Cynthia is a down-and-out slob. If you want to meet the real Cyn, go into her bedroom."

Maybe so. But Gayle still thought it was wrong to talk about a friend in her own home.

"I don't know why the two of you are looking at me like I'm Attila the Hun or something," Monique said. "I ain't saying nothing that I haven't already said to Cyn's face."

"And just what have you said to my face?"

The trio looked up to find Cynthia staring at them with red-rimmed eyes. She looked almost as white as the silk robe she was wearing.

"It's alive!" Monique joked.

"That's debatable." Cynthia grabbed the arm of one of the wicker chairs for support, then slowly eased herself into it, tucking her legs beneath her.

Gayle was glad Cynthia sat down before she fell down. She was moving like an old lady. Gayle said, "I thought you would sleep through the night."

"Who could sleep with all the yapping going on in here?"

"Sorry," Gayle apologized. "I didn't know we were that loud."

Cynthia said quickly, "No, I'm just being a grouch. Y'all didn't wake me up. I think it was the smell of food cooking."

Roxanne got up from the table. "You must be starving! What do you want? We had chicken and rice."

Cynthia closed her eyes. The sleeve of the robe, which was a couple of sizes too big, flapped back and forth as she waved a hand in dismissal. "I really couldn't eat anything right now. I might as well wait till tomorrow morning."

Gayle could see blue veins running across Cynthia's closed eyelids. "C'mon, Cyn, you gotta eat something. It's been hours since you had that sandwich."

"Yeah, girl. You look like death warmed over," Monique said.

Roxanne said, "We were just about to have dessert. So while

we're eating that, why don't I warm you up a can of tomato soup?"

Cynthia didn't argue, and Roxanne headed for the kitchen. The whir of the electric can opener could be heard, followed by the metallic click of the top being sucked onto the magnet.

A few minutes later, Roxanne came back into the room with a steaming bowl of soup on a plate and a serving of rice on the side. She tapped Cynthia's shoulder. "Cyn, here's your soup."

She heard Cynthia's stomach rumble noisily and laughed. "I thought you said you weren't hungry. Seems your stomach disagrees."

Cynthia held her hand out for the plate. "Thanks. I guess I am a little hungry." She sat up straight in the chair and balanced the plate on her lap.

"I'll be right back with brownies and ice cream," Roxanne said to Gayle and Monique.

Cynthia quickly polished off the soup and was finishing up the rice when Roxanne returned. She noticed the empty bowl and smiled in satisfaction. "See? I knew you were hungry."

Gayle studied Cynthia, trying to understand why her face had turned red all of a sudden. So what if she cleaned her plate? There was no shame in having a good appetite. Maybe she was just thinking about Anthony again.

"Come and sit with us," Roxanne said, clearing a space on the floor.

Cynthia stared for a long time at the half-gallon carton of ice cream and tin of brownies in the center of the table. "I'm comfortable right where I am."

Monique said, "Roxanne, don't beg her to sit with us. We were having a nice little conversation before she so rudely interrupted us."

Cynthia said, "I heard my name mentioned. . . . I suppose y'all were talking about me and Anthony?"

"Well, actually, we were talking about your lousy housekeeping habits, but since you brought it up, we would like to know what the hell happened this afternoon," Monique said with her usual bluntness.

Cynthia let out a deep sigh. "I don't even know where to start," she said.

Gayle said in a gentle voice, "It must have blown your mind to find out he had a wife and two kids."

"Not really," Cynthia said, so softly no one heard her.

"Men make me sick sometimes. They can be such dogs. Did I tell you about the guy who propositioned me while I was at a party at his house? His wife was in the same room. Talk about lack of respect!" Monique said. "Then there was this one cop named Fred, who . . ."

Though the glass patio doors, Cynthia stared out into the inky darkness that covered the city. Her head ached. *Why is Monique talking about all this? Can't she see that I don't care about her stupid stories?* She shifted her gaze from the window to Monique. *What was she talking about?* she asked herself wearily. *Why was Monique always talking? This isn't about her. It's about me.*

". . . So, the moral of the story is, even the best of us can be fooled. You can only operate on the information you've been given. So don't feel bad, girl."

So far Cynthia hadn't heard anything that remotely resembled what had been going on between her and Anthony. She put her plate and bowl on the floor next to the chair. "I knew he was married," she said as she straightened up.

In the deathly quiet that followed, Cynthia wasn't sure she'd actually said it aloud. Just to be sure, she said it again. "I knew he was married and stayed with him anyway." Nervously, she raised her eyes to gauge her friends' reaction.

Roxanne was the first one to speak. "So, what happened? He must have tricked you," she said, her eyes seeking confirmation.

Of course, there couldn't be any other rational explanation, Cynthia thought, bowing her head. It was so like Roxanne to unquestioningly believe in the innocence of her friends. Cynthia appreciated being given the benefit of the doubt. She only wished she deserved it. "No, he told me the first time we went out that he was married. We hadn't even kissed, much less slept together."

"What!" Monique cried, having finally found her voice. "You knew and you just put up with it? What the hell is wrong with you?"

"You're a grown woman, Cyn. You don't have to explain or justify anything to us," Gayle said.

Cynthia gave a little sigh. She was so tired. "I know, I don't *have* to tell you anything. But I think y'all deserve to hear the truth. . . . Then . . . I just want to forget today ever happened."

She coughed a few times to clear her throat. "Like I told you before, Anthony sent me those beautiful roses, and the next time I saw him, he invited me to dinner."

He had taken her to a really elegant, expensive restaurant overlooking the bay. It was small and they had a great view from their table. "I felt beautiful for the first time in God knows when. It was the first time I'd been out with anyone since losing the weight. I was wearing a regular-size dress instead of those tents I used to wear." The compliments had been flying left and right.

"I was on cloud nine." A sad smile flickered across her face. "Have you ever had someone touch you and . . . it's like . . . a shock of electricity?"

Only Roxanne nodded her head.

"He held my hand and I'm hot all over . . . and he tells me that I should know he was married. . . . I couldn't breathe. . . . I . . . I felt like crying. . . . I couldn't believe it. . . . Yet another good one slipping through my fingers—"

A sound of disgust came from Monique. "I wouldn't have been worrying about this joker getting away! I'd have wanted to know why the hell he'd asked me out in the first place."

Cynthia shrank back into the chair and hugged herself to ward off Monique's disapproval. "Do you think that I didn't ask him? He told me that just because he was married didn't mean he didn't enjoy being around other women. He didn't see why he shouldn't socialize with other women who shared interests with him that his wife didn't."

"Socialize?" Monique scoffed. "Gimme a break."

"Monique, maybe I'm not explaining this well. . . ." Cynthia forced herself to meet Monique's eyes. "He left it all up to me."

Monique drummed her fingers on the arm of the couch. "Why didn't you just get up, walk out the door, and hail the first cab you saw?"

Cynthia bit her lip, tasted blood, and quickly licked it away. "Because I couldn't . . . I didn't have the strength . . . and I realize now that I probably just didn't want to."

Her voice rose. "I was tired . . . tired of shopping around, tired of sticking my neck out and getting it chopped off," she said, remembering the personals-ad fiasco. "I had a man in front of me who had exactly what I was looking for. He was reasonably attractive, extremely attentive, financially secure, intelligent and charming and—"

"And married!" Monique reminded her.

"And what about me? I'm no spring chicken," Cynthia said, turning to Roxanne and Gayle. "I'm knocking the hell out of thirty, and what do I have to show for it? Ain't nothing going on for me but the rent and bills and loneliness!" She waved her hands, gesturing to the apartment. "All the promotions and nice furniture in the world cannot compensate for the lack of a man's touch, or someone telling you the sound of your voice made his day.

"I was tired of trying to strike up a conversation with some unsuspecting man in the produce department; tired of going to church hoping to meet a 'nice' man when every other sister there was down on her knees praying in earnest for the same thing; tired of reading *Vogue, Cosmo,* and *Essence* to uncover the flaws *in me* that were keeping me from getting a man. And I was tired of spending my weekends going shopping and to the movies with girlfriends."

Her hands moved restlessly in her lap.

Why are they all looking at me like I've lost my mind? They've been begging me to talk all day. And now that I am, nobody wants to hear it. Nobody understands.

Cynthia could feel a knot forming in the pit of her stomach, but she pressed on. "We're told to get our education, get a job, and settle down. But how are we supposed to do that?

Men aren't interested in marriage. Nowadays men can get as much sex as they like with no strings attached. I'm living proof of that," she said with a bitter laugh. "Why buy the cow when you can get the milk for free?"

"Cyn, not all men are looking for sex. Some men want commitment, too."

Cynthia raised an eyebrow. Gayle didn't know what the hell she was talking about. Commitment-seeking men had gone the way of the dinosaur—they were extinct! "When a man finally does settle down, do you think he wants someone our age?" Cynthia asked. "Hell, no. He wants an eighteen- or twenty-year-old with a firm butt and a mind he can control."

"But, Cyn—" Gayle began.

Cynthia said, "Save it, Gayle, I don't want to hear it. Think about last night. Just between the three of you there are enough horror stories to fill a book."

How could Gayle of all people sit here and defend men to me? She couldn't draw a man with a Magic Marker!

She rubbed her eyes tiredly. In a small voice she said, "I must have been out of my mind. But how could I not fall for Anthony? He was wonderful to me. He treated me like a queen." Cynthia looked at them for some glimmer of understanding. "I thought I was in control, but I was like a love-starved puppy . . . I needed the attention. I needed somebody to acknowledge that I was a woman, not just some machine that went to work, then came back to this empty apartment.

"Y'all remember what it was like when we were in college? Four years of invisibility. What the hell were we thinking of, sending ourselves into social exile like that? But then again, I wonder if being in Minnesota was the real problem, 'cause I see sisters who went to Spelman, Howard, Tuskegee . . . and they ain't got nobody, either.

"I know I can take care of myself. But it's nice to have someone else do it once in a while. I don't mean to set the feminist movement back. But I'm sorry. I *like* being catered to." Her voice grew soft again. "I want somebody to lean on."

Cynthia caught Monique rolling her eyes and looking at the other two as if to say, Can you believe this shit?

Monique asked, "Where were his wife and two kids while he was giving you a shoulder to lean on?"

Cynthia teared up as guilt and shame flooded her once again. Her voice was husky when she answered. "He didn't say much about them and I didn't ask. He was with me so much of the time, I could almost pretend that they didn't exist." That delusion had come crashing down this afternoon. "Honestly," Cynthia said, "I didn't even know his wife's name. I didn't want to know."

Gayle asked, "But how was he able to have so much free time? His poor wife . . . didn't suspect a thing."

Sensing Gayle's obvious sympathy for Traci, Cynthia felt another stab of guilt. "He has a condo downtown to avoid the commute. He stayed there a lot."

"See, that was homegirl's first mistake—there wouldn't have been no separate residences," Monique said. "Where he goes, I go, and vice versa."

Gayle disagreed. "If someone wants to fool around, they will, whether you're in the next town or the next room. You can't control another person. If you don't believe me, just ask my mother about my father."

Cynthia had tried not to notice that he chose restaurants in out-of-the-way places or tables in secluded corners. She convinced herself that he did this because he wanted her all to himself. Or that those weekend trips to Miami or the Keys were due to his spontaneous, romantic nature alone and not because he was trying to avoid people who might know that he was married.

"I guess I was hoping he'd realize what a prize I was and divorce her. But I couldn't bring the subject up. . . . I didn't want to risk spoiling things. . . ." Cynthia's voice trailed off.

Gayle said, "Cyn, I'm sorry things turned out like this."

No one else had anything to add. Cynthia stared at the blue-lit seconds flashing on the VCR clock. It was a little after midnight. Never before had there been such a prolonged silence between them.

Finally, Roxanne said, "Cynthia, you look so pitiful sitting there in that big old robe. I've been wanting to give you a hug all day." She moved toward Cynthia, her arm brushing against the container of ice cream.

Cynthia leaned forward to accept Roxanne's embrace. It wasn't until she felt Roxanne's arms around her that she realized how badly she needed human contact. She had thought she'd wanted to be alone in her misery, but now she held on tight as Roxanne gave her back comforting, gentle rubs.

Gayle half crawled over to Cynthia's chair and held out her arms in silent invitation. Cynthia leaned forward to hug her, too. "I'm sorry you had such a rough time," Gayle said.

"Me, too," Cynthia said. She gave a little sniff and wiped away a solitary tear.

Roxanne perched on the arm of Cynthia's chair, and Gayle leaned on her knees. Monique remained seated on the couch.

"Aren't you gonna join this hug-fest, love-in thing we got going?" Gayle asked with a smile.

Monique did not return her smile. "You know I ain't the hugging kind."

If Monique had something on her mind, good or bad, it was bound to come out sooner or later. Cynthia wanted to hear it now instead of later because a delayed reaction would only give Monique more time to sharpen her tongue. "Monique, it's obvious you have something to say. I wish you'd just say it and be done with it."

"Cyn, I'm sorry you had such a rough day. I'm sorry you got dogged . . ." Monique said.

Cynthia breathed a little easier. That wasn't so bad, she thought. Monique was actually being kind of nice.

". . . but I cannot *believe* you let that man buy you," Monique finished.

Cynthia trembled, hoping Roxanne and Gayle couldn't feel the vibrations. A part of her felt she deserved this. Gayle and Roxanne had been way too easy on her. Her selfishness shouldn't go unpunished. Monique would see to that.

"I can't believe you'd sell yourself for a couple of weekend trips, some sports equipment, and a free meal every now and then—"

Roxanne interrupted her. "Monique, don't nobody want

to hear this. Cyn's already upset enough without you making it worse. So just shut up, OK?"

"I wasn't gonna say anything. *She* asked me," Monique reminded her. "I'm just trying to be honest," she said, looking directly at Cynthia. "I'm truly sorry the whole situation blew up in your face like this. A lot of shit happens in this life that we have no control over—somebody dies, we get laid off from a job. Then again, there's a whole lot of shit that's avoidable. And you may not want to hear this, but fooling around with a married man falls into the avoidable-situations category."

Monique's voice rose. "I've been lied to and I don't like it. For one thing, it makes you look bad, and for another thing, it makes me feel stupid. If we're supposed to be friends, I just don't understand why you didn't confide in us from the start."

Cynthia put her head in her hands and began crying. "I don't know," she repeated over and over again. "I—I was scared."

"Scared of what?" Monique cried. "Scared we might warn you that you were headed for disaster and heartache?"

Cynthia's sobs grew louder.

Roxanne jumped to her feet and stood in front of Monique, physically shielding Cynthia from the verbal attack. "Shut the hell up, goddammit!"

Monique's eyes widened in surprise.

Roxanne stood with hands on hips, breathing fire with every word. "I know you're a lawyer, but who made you judge and jury, too? Besides which, she is not on trial. She made a mistake, for God's sake! People make mistakes," Roxanne said. "Of course, the great Monique never makes any mistakes—"

"Roxanne—" Monique began.

Roxanne held up a hand. "No, let me finish. It's time for you to hear some of that same honesty you're so famous for. Well, let me tell you, it's easy not to make a mistake when you're too cowardly to take any risks at all!"

Monique's quick intake of breath coincided with Cynthia's. Then Cynthia's face crumpled and she began crying again. "This is all my fault," she said. "This was supposed to be a vacation. Now, thanks to me, everybody is at each other's throat."

Gayle squeezed her hand and told her that wasn't true, but Cynthia knew better.

Monique ignored her tears and focused exclusively on Roxanne. "I don't know what you're talking about, but I suggest you give it a rest."

"Not yet," Roxanne said, not intimidated by the threat in Monique's voice. "Monique, what risk have you ever taken in your life?"

Monique sat stony-faced.

"You've spent your whole life *not* trying too hard just in case you might fail. You're so scared of not living up to your family's inflated expectations—all those fourth-generation college grads and pillars of the community—you've always taken the easiest route available.

"Lack of money and options are why I was stuck in Minnesota, but what about you? Did you even *attempt* to get into an Ivy League school or a historically black college—I'm sure either would have done your family proud.

"And being a lawyer is pretty prestigious for most folks, but a lowly prosecutor must be way down on the totem pole for the Edwards of Houston. And why are you still in Cleveland? I don't think it's because you're in love with the place."

Monique's eyes were almost slits.

"Cat got your tongue?" Roxanne taunted. "Monique, every single decision you've made in your life was done out of cowardice. So what if Cyn made a mistake. So what if I've made mistakes," she challenged. "How do you ever truly learn or live without taking any chances?"

Monique stood up, towering over Roxanne, who instinctively took a step backward.

Cynthia's stomach lurched. *Please, please don't let this get out of hand. I don't know if I can ever forgive myself.*

Monique put her hands together. Clap. Clap. Clap. "Bravo!

But if that little performance was supposed to make me hang my head in shame, forget it. I suppose you think you read me, but you don't know shit about what goes on inside my head. And if I ever need to have it examined, I'll get a professional to do it, thank you.

"Now, if you'll get out of my way, I'm going to go outside and have me a smoke. Maybe you can analyze that, too, while I'm gone." She stepped around Roxanne, grabbed her cigarettes and lighter off the table, then went out the front door.

Instinctively, Cynthia winced, anticipating a loud slam that never came.

Chapter
31

At first there was only a hazy blur, something moving around off in the distance.

Roxanne rubbed an impatient finger across one eyelid, thinking maybe she had forgotten to put in her contacts. It wouldn't have been the first time. The ridge of the clear plastic moved around in her eye. It was in there, but not doing her much good.

When she tried to push herself upright to get a better look, her hands encountered a soft, slippery material. Puzzled, Roxanne looked down to find that she was lying in an enormous bed that was covered with emerald-colored satin sheets. One leg from the knee down was exposed. Its walnut brown sheen contrasted with the shimmering fabric.

Where the hell was she? With some trepidation she peeked under the sheet. "Oh, my God! I'm butt-naked!"

Her eyes darted from side to side. The room wasn't dark, but she still felt like she couldn't see. Everything except the bed and the figure slowly approaching her seemed to be engulfed in a sea of whiteness. And how strange . . . the bed was bathed in bright light, but there were no lamps. There wasn't a light switch on the wall, either.

Slowly, her eyes traveled upward. Cut into the high ceiling was a huge skylight overlooking the bed. Through eyes partially shielded by her fingers, she could see a few wispy clouds in a pale blue sky.

This is too weird, she thought.

She again glanced at the figure, whose brownish color set it apart from the complete whiteness of the room. It was getting closer and closer . . . the amorphous blob gradually began to take the shape of a man. . . .

Instinctively, Roxanne clutched the covers tightly around her, torn between curiosity and fear.

The man was kind of tall . . . kind of dark . . . and oddly familiar. . . . There was something about the way he was walking; he held himself proud, erect, and confident. . . .

Roxanne's eyes opened even wider. Her mouth formed a little O of surprise. No. . . . It couldn't be. . . . But then . . . Oh yes, it was. . . .

. . . Denzel!

Her earlier fears vanished. She sat entranced as Denzel Washington, one of America's most gifted actors and certainly the country's finest-looking one, drew even closer to her.

He was dressed only in a skimpy white apron with a heart strategically located at the spot where his thighs met, and held two glasses of champagne in his hands. A big sexy grin and a knowing look in his eyes had her practically panting.

The brass headboard felt cold against her overheated flesh. But she didn't mind. She needed something to cool her off— *like maybe a glacier!*

He stopped at the side of the bed and gazed down at her with desire in his eyes which was as naked as the woman before him. He didn't say a word and neither did Roxanne. Denzel put one of the champagne glasses on the nightstand. Then he used his free hand to pull on the ankle of her exposed leg until once again she was lying flat on her back.

Her eyes filled with gleeful anticipation. *Hot damn! What's next?*

His smile was enigmatic as he slowly pulled back the covers, completely revealing her nakedness. He calmly took a sip of his champagne. Roxanne, on the other hand, almost stopped breathing when he sat next to her and slowly began to pour little droplets of the golden liquid down the little hollow in her throat, across her bare breasts, down her stomach, and below. Then he put the half-empty glass on the nightstand and began to trace the trail of the liquid with his lips.

It was official. Roxanne was on fire!

She started to moan . . . really loudly. So loud she surprised herself. Then, without warning, Denzel started to fade away. The close-cropped head bending over her so lovingly began to just disappear.

"Come back, Denzel," she cried. "Don't leave me like this." She stretched out her arms to pull him close. But they encircled the empty air. His beautiful image had melted away to nothingness.

But in her ears she could still hear the moaning . . . strangled and fretful sounds . . . and they were not coming from her!

Roxanne jerked awake. In the darkness, her eyes immediately fixed on the light from the digital alarm clock. It was 3:47—A.M.

Why was the alarm clock so far away? It was supposed to be right next to the bed.

Her eyes slowly adjusted to the dark as they scanned the room. *What on earth? The place was a mess: mounds of clothes all over the place; drawers open left and right.*

This was not like her at all. . . . And the layout of the room . . . It wasn't right. For one thing, the place was too big. . . .

Roxanne rolled over and immediately felt a soft lump underneath the covers. That's all wrong, too, she thought. There shouldn't be anyone in my bed.

Then she remembered . . . the argument with Monique. Cynthia had been upset. So she had offered to keep her company. *I must have drifted off.*

The bed creaked slightly as Cynthia tossed and turned beside her.

She must be having a nightmare, Roxanne thought.

"Cyn," she whispered, not wanting to wake up the others. "Wake up." When Cynthia didn't respond, Roxanne gave her shoulders a little shake.

She let go in surprise. Cynthia's skin was ice-cold.

She pulled the metal string on the reading lamp near the bed. In the bright glow of the light, Cynthia's face was chalk white. Roxanne shook Cynthia more roughly and called her name, no longer caring if she disturbed Monique and Gayle.

"Wake up!" she said over and over again. She was trying to stay calm, but touching Cynthia's damp, cold skin was unnerving her.

After what seemed like ages, Cynthia's eyes finally fluttered open. But Roxanne didn't have time to feel relieved. One look at Cynthia's glazed-over eyes made her mouth go dry with fear.

The room was suddenly flooded with light. Roxanne spun around.

Monique leaned on the doorframe with one hand still on the light switch. She was wearing a faded Case Western Reserve T-shirt, and her hair, a tangled mass of curls, partially covered one eye. Her voice was still husky with sleep. "What's the matter?"

"Monique, help me," Roxanne said. "There is something wrong with Cynthia."

Hearing the urgency in Roxanne's voice, Monique pushed the hair out of her eyes. "What is it?" she asked as she hurried over to the bed.

"I don't know. I heard her moaning in her sleep. I thought she was having a nightmare. But she won't wake up. And feel her. She's ice-cold."

Indeed, Cynthia was cold to the touch, and Monique could see blue veins standing out beneath the almost translucent skin of her closed eyelids. "Maybe she has one of those twenty-four-hour viruses. She's been looking sickly all day."

"Oh . . ." Cynthia moaned. But her eyes remained closed.

Monique attempted to wake her up. Unlike Roxanne, she didn't try gentle whispers. Her voice was loud and commanding. "Wake up, Cynthia," she repeated several times. But other than an occasional moan, Cynthia was unresponsive.

Gayle came into the room, and Roxanne quickly told her what was going on.

Gayle changed places with Monique. She called Cynthia's name.

To Roxanne's surprise, Cynthia immediately opened her eyes. "Gayle. . . . Gayle," Cynthia said.

"Yes?" Gayle said.

"Tell Roxanne I didn't feed those fucking fish my reefer. I wouldn't waste good weed on no fish. I just forgot . . ." Roxanne stared into the eyes of a crazy woman. "I forgot to change the goddamn water. . . ."

Roxanne exchanged a troubled look with Gayle and Monique.

Cynthia's voice grew louder. ". . . goddamn clear water. Fuckers live in the ocean. God don't change the water. And that don't seem to bother 'em. . . ."

"Cyn, hush," Gayle said, trying to calm her down. Cynthia kept on talking, but her voice grew softer. "Didn't mean to kill them . . ." she said.

Gayle stood up. "We need to get her to a hospital," she said.

Roxanne sat on the bed with Cynthia while Monique called for help. She could hear Gayle moving around in the other room, putting something on.

Roxanne called out to Gayle, "Look for Cynthia's purse and see if her health insurance card is in it. And bring me some shoes."

When Gayle came back into the room, she dropped a small overnight bag and Roxanne's shoes by the bed.

Cynthia had fallen asleep with her robe on, so they didn't bother getting her dressed. Gayle slipped a pair of white cotton socks on Cynthia's feet and stuck a few toiletries, the most important of which was Cyn's makeup, in a plastic shopping bag. She knew Cyn would have a fit if she woke up in a hospital room and had to face the world without it.

The paramedics arrived, and scowling, Monique led them into the bedroom. Despite the official-looking uniforms with the orange crosses on them, the two women didn't look old enough to know a thing about medicine.

The pasty-faced little redhead fired a series of questions at them while the other one, a slightly built black woman, checked Cynthia's vital signs. "What's the problem? How long has she been out? What did she eat today? Is she on any medication?" Her hair was parted down the middle and bound by rubber bands to create two carrot-colored ponytails that bobbed as she talked.

Monique's scowl deepened. *How could they possibly take someone who looked like Pippi Longstocking seriously?*

Roxanne answered as best she could. "We don't know . . . but we can't get her to wake up. She opened her eyes for a while, but when she talked, she didn't make any sense. . . ."

The way the girl was cracking that gum was grating on Monique's nerves. "Look, we don't know what's wrong with her. That's why we called you. . . ."

The redhead said, "Look, miss, we're just trying to do our job. . . ."

Her coworker, who had been shining a small light in Cynthia's eyes, interrupted them. "Sarah, we gotta move her. Her BPs real low and her heartbeat is irregular."

Moving rapidly in unison, they put her on a stretcher and covered Cynthia with a dark blanket, then tightened two black straps to keep her in place. With cool efficiency, they lifted her up and took her outside.

As they rounded the corner of the second-floor landing, the side of the stretcher bumped against the wall. "Watch it," Monique warned. "That's not a piece of wood you're carrying." The paramedics kept moving.

Gayle and Roxanne brought up the rear of the little procession.

The whirling light from the ambulance cast restless shadows across the apartment-complex walls.

After Cynthia had been installed in the ambulance, Monique started to climb into it. But Sarah, the redhead, stopped her.

"Where do you think you're going?" she asked.

"I'm riding with my friend," Monique said.

"I'm sorry, but you can't do that. It's against the rules."

"Get out of my way," Monique said, trying to brush past the woman.

The smaller woman stood her ground. Her pale green eyes

said, I've seen a lot tougher than you, so I'm not impressed. "Look, miss, you've been watching too much TV. This is not *Rescue 911*. You can't come, and that's final."

"But—" Monique couldn't believe she'd been told off twice in one night.

"But nothing," the paramedic said in a voice that brooked no argument. "Don't be a jerk! Do you want your friend to die while you stand here arguing?" She climbed inside the ambulance and slammed the doors shut in Monique's face.

Gayle tugged on her arm. "She's right, Monique. We can meet them at the hospital."

"Huh?" Monique was still staring at the lights of the ambulance as it sped away. She couldn't believe they'd slammed the door in her face. *That was fucked up!*

Gayle pulled her arm again to get her attention. "I said the other woman gave Roxanne directions, so we can meet them there. Let's go."

Chapter

32

Gayle tried to take shallow breaths. That universal hospital smell of medicine and strong antiseptic cleaning solution always made her a little nauseous, and her shoulder was starting to go numb. Roxanne's head had been resting on it for the past twenty minutes. Gayle tried to gently move her shoulder around to get the circulation going again, but the weight of Roxanne's head pinned her back against the wall.

She was exhausted but she couldn't sleep. She envied Roxanne and the other occupants in the waiting area. One woman had pulled two aqua-colored chairs together to create a makeshift bed. She had curled into a ball on her side and was fast asleep. Gayle watched in fascination as a gray-haired older man fought valiantly against sleep. Every few minutes or so, the guy would start to nod off; then his head would jerk up and his eyes would fly open. He reminded her of a crazy cartoon character who tries to use toothpicks to prop his eyes open. But eventually his eyelids would become so heavy that the toothpicks would break in half and his eyes would snap open like a shutter on a window.

A barefoot woman in a housecoat and curlers stared fixedly at the television set in an effort to keep awake. Gayle had tried that, but somehow watching the Health Channel while sitting in a hospital emergency room did nothing to reduce her anxiety. She was able to sit through the story on good

cholesterol and bad cholesterol, but when they started showing an open-heart surgery, she'd seen enough.

The glare and hum of the fluorescent lights were starting
to get to her, not to mention the ugly decor. Hospitals must
get a whopping discount for buying furniture in colors that
no one else, except maybe a clown, would touch, like neon
green, aqua, and sunrise yellow.

Gayle rubbed her gritty eyes. When she moved her hands
away, she saw a police officer inserting coins into one of the
vending machines down the hall. He had a blue cap perched
on his gray curls. Standing next to him was a young black
woman wearing only a thin hospital gown and a pair of hand-
cuffs. Gayle wondered if she was on her way to or from a lo-
cal jail. She hoped the girl had something on underneath that
thing. Why did they design hospital gowns so all your stuff
flapped in the wind every time you turned around?

Just as the pair began to move off, Monique came in, blocking her view. Gayle started in surprise, inadvertently jarring
Roxanne awake.

"What . . . whatsa matter, Mama?" Roxanne sputtered.

"Roxanne, we're still at the hospital," Gayle reminded her.

Roxanne rubbed her eyes. "Oh," she said. Then she searched
Monique's face for some clue as to Cynthia's condition. "Did
you talk to Cyn?" she asked.

Monique speared Roxanne with a hostile glance before directing her comments to Gayle. *Does she really think I've forgotten all the shit she said to me tonight?* "No. Believe it or
not, it took this long just to get her paperwork squared away."
She sat down in a row of plastic chairs across from them.

"Somebody dumped this crack head at the entrance and
then took off. Needless to say, it took forever for the receptionist to get all of the necessary information out of him."

"When do you think we'll hear something?" Roxanne
asked, no longer leaning against Gayle's shoulder.

Monique shrugged. "Gayle, are there any good magazines
around here?" Not waiting for an answer, she picked up a
discarded newspaper from a nearby chair.

Roxanne sighed and rested her head on her hand. "So it's gonna be like that?" she said.

Not looking up from her paper, Monique said, "Like what?"

Gayle started in alarm when Roxanne leaned forward and snatched the paper out of Monique's hand. "If you're still mad about what I said, then why don't you just say that and stop acting childish."

"Oh, so now I'm gutless *and* childish?" Monique said.

Gayle glanced around nervously. The woman who had been watching TV was now listening with interest to their conversation. "Come on, ya'll, can't this wait until tomorrow?"

"It is tomorrow," Monique reminded her. "And no, it can't wait."

Roxanne nodded her head in agreement. "Talk away. I've already said what I had to say."

Monique's hand balled into a fist. "Yeah, but who are you to read me? You've met my family . . . what? A couple of times? Who are you to tell me that I'm not living up to their expectations or up to my potential?"

"Please, y'all, keep your voices down," Gayle pleaded. "People are trying to sleep."

In a gesture meant to calm her, Roxanne patted Gayle on the knee, then said, "Monique, I really don't care whether you drive a garbage truck or sell shoes at Payless. What you do with your life is not the point. What pisses me off is how quick you are to criticize how other people are living their lives."

"Are you sitting there telling me that you're OK with Cyn chasing after some married man?" Monique hissed.

Roxanne shook her head. "Not at all. I was just as shocked as you and thought what she did was dumb. But there is a time and place for everything. What Cyn needed tonight was support, and what did she get from you? A swift kick when she was already down. And I wasn't having it."

She wasn't having it? Undoubtedly, the shock showed on her face, but Monique couldn't help it. Roxanne had never spoken to her like this. At the same time, though, she was almost afraid to say anything back. Anything she said would just make her look like she was in the wrong. Monique rolled her head around, trying to ease some of the tension that clung to her neck and shoulders.

How was she supposed to react? Cynthia could be shallow, but Monique had truly thought she had sense enough and pride enough not to put herself in such a no-win situation. She and Cynthia had both been brought up to believe that finding a suitable husband and career, which if you were lucky were one and the same thing, and engaging in activities that reflected the real or imagined status of their families were the primary reasons for being. That's why she felt close to Cyn in ways she could never be with Gayle or Roxanne.

Monique admired Cynthia's dogged determination to obtain happiness—even if personally, she thought that trying to achieve it through a man and money wasn't the way to go. Monique loved Cyn's fighting spirit. The path toward a goal was sometimes roundabout and downright confusing to those around her, but Cyn usually got what she wanted. Underneath all the makeup, fake nails, and fluff was a very strong and determined individual.

To see her give up hope and become some married man's plaything, to sell out on her dreams, was hard to accept. It was something Monique had never thought she'd do. But whose problem was it?

"OK, so maybe I was a little out of line for getting on Cynthia's case," she conceded finally. "But can't you see that I said what I did because I was worried about her?"

"Maybe so, but all I heard was anger and criticism, and I'm sure that's what Cyn heard, too. Monique, we can't make people do what we think is best for them through sheer force of our personality . . . no matter how concerned or worried we are." She added more quietly, "I thought you of all people would know that."

Monique looked at her for a moment, then closed her eyes. Slowly, her fingers uncurled and she let her clenched teeth relax. How sobering to realize that after all these years, she really was her mother's daughter.

When she opened her eyes again, a line from the hymn "Amazing Grace" flashed in her mind: "Was blind, but now I see."

Monique was quiet for so long, Roxanne thought she was giving her the silent treatment. Monique could shut completely down when she felt like it. So it came as a surprise when after a while, Monique said, without any of her usual belligerence, "Maybe you're right, Roxanne. Maybe there are a lot of things I should know about myself . . . and other people that I don't."

Their stunned expressions were worth the beating her pride took to admit she was wrong. That was as close to an apology as Roxanne was going to get.

Monique flashed them a smile and opened her purse. After searching through it, she patted the pockets of her pants. "Shit!" she exclaimed, waking up the gray-haired man, who had finally lost his fight against sleep.

He shot straight up and looked around wildly. He gave them a dirty look.

"Sorry," Gayle said.

Monique said, "I really need a cigarette." She looked around hoping to find someone she could bum a cigarette from, but everyone was asleep except for the woman who was again watching TV and she said she didn't smoke. Monique's eyes lit up when she spied the vending machines in the hallway behind her. She opened her purse again and took out her wallet. She unzipped the change section and turned it upside down. A quarter and a dime rolled out.

"Shit!" she said again. Gayle ventured a glance at the old man, but he'd already fallen asleep again.

"Empty your pockets, girls," Monique ordered. "If I don't get a cigarette soon, I'm gonna have a nicotine fit. And trust me, it won't be pretty."

Between the two of them, Gayle and Roxanne quickly scraped together another two dollars and ten cents.

As she handed over the money, Roxanne asked again about Cynthia.

"The lady at admissions said she'd send someone over here as soon as she could, but she didn't have any info on Cyn herself," Monique said, her feet already pointed in the direction of the vending machines.

Gayle could feel herself zoning out. She stared unseeingly at the sign posted on the wall directly in front of her. It took a while before its message penetrated her brain.

The sign said THIS IS A SMOKE-FREE ENVIRONMENT. NO SMOKING ON HOSPITAL PREMISES. Gayle got the feeling Monique was going to be sorely disappointed when she reached her destination.

The sun was starting to rise when the doctor finally found time to speak to them. Gayle woke up Roxanne again and went outside to find Monique. She had managed to procure cigarettes from somewhere and had been disappearing every fifteen minutes to have a smoke.

Once they were all together, the doctor led them through a set of double doors. They passed a series of curtained-off treatment areas. In one room, a young boy was having a plaster cast put on his leg. In another, two doctors conferred about a case. Many of the curtains were drawn, so Gayle couldn't tell if they were occupied or not. She keep expecting to see Cynthia, but she wasn't anywhere.

He ushered them into a small conference room that was next door to the ER radiology lab. They all took a seat and looked at him with varying degrees of anxiety. He was in his late twenties, and a day's growth of dark beard covered his face. His short-cropped wiry hair was standing on end. He stroked his chin several times, either out of habit or because the stubble was scratchy.

That his green surgery scrubs were immaculate somehow made Gayle feel better. Sitting in the waiting room for hours had given her plenty of time to imagine all kinds of horrific things happening to Cyn behind those double doors.

He clasped his hands together and rested them on the ta-

ble. "I'm Dr. Burns, one of the residents on staff. You can call
me Rudy. Normally, we don't release information to non-
relatives, but Sheila, our admissions clerk, told me you guys
have been waiting up most of the night. So first let me say
that her prognosis is good."

"Thank God," Gayle breathed.

"However, she is a very sick woman. It's a good thing you
brought her in when you did—"

Monique interrupted. "What does 'very sick' mean? What's
wrong with her? And where is she?"

He held up a hand. "Whoa! I was just getting to that," he
said. "Right now we are responding to her hypothermia—"

"Her hypo-what?" Roxanne asked.

"Hypothermia means that her body temperature is lower
than it should be. When she got here, it was thirty-five degrees centigrade instead of thirty-seven degrees. That may
not seem like much of a difference, but believe me, thirty-five
degrees is pretty low. Did any of you notice that her hands or
feet were icy to the touch?"

Roxanne nodded her head vigorously. "Yes, when I tried to
shake her awake, she was freezing!"

"When hypothermia sets in, the body tries to keep its core—
the heart, lungs, et cetera—warm by clamping down on heat
to the extremities. Thus, the cold hands and feet," the doctor
explained.

Gayle couldn't understand how this could have happened.
She could see it if they'd been stranded in a blizzard, but it
had been unbearably hot all weekend. "But . . . but it's so hot
outside. . . ."

"Hypothermia isn't always brought on by exposure to the
elements," he explained. "In Ms. Johnson's case, her system
was already out of whack in a lot of ways."

"But how? This is the healthiest she's ever been," Gayle said.

The doctor shook his head. "Well, I'm afraid I can't agree
with that. Not given the condition she's in right now. She's also
suffering from dehydration and has a potassium deficiency,
which may have been brought on by the hypothermia."

Monique gave the other two an accusing look. "I told them

it was too hot to be sitting in the sun today. But no, they just had to go to the beach."

"Is dehydration a big problem?" Gayle asked.

"It can be. When I examined her, Ms. Johnson was show-ing signs of muscle weakness, abdominal distension, drowsi-ness, mental confusion, and an irregular heartbeat."

Mental confusion? Irregular heartbeat? None of this sounded good to Roxanne.

"Are you sure she's out of danger?" she asked. "Everything you've said so far sounds pretty serious."

Dr. Burns corrected her. "I didn't say she was out of dan-ger. I said her prognosis was good. She's responding well to the treatment she's been given so far."

"But I still don't understand what brought this on," Gayle said.

"We're trying to figure that one out ourselves. Ms. Johnson is semiconscious, very groggy. So she hasn't really been able to tell us much. Maybe you ladies can fill in some of the miss-ing pieces of the puzzle. Is she currently using any drugs or medication?"

"Illegal drugs? No way!" Monique rushed to Cynthia's de-fense. "She rarely drinks alcohol anymore. The Pill is the only prescription drug I know for a fact she takes."

"Have there been any recent changes in her diet, weight, or level of fitness?"

"That's what I was trying to tell you before," Gayle said. "Cynthia has worked really hard in the past year to get in shape. She's lost a ton of weight. I mean, she used to refuse to exercise at all. Now she's bought her own exercise equipment plus joined a gym. She's eating better . . . eating less. Doing everything right."

Dr. Burns took a pen out of his shirt pocket and scribbled some notes on the paper attached to a wooden clipboard. "Has your friend ever made herself throw up or abused laxatives?"

Gayle stared at him openmouthed. What was he getting at? Cyn had never done anything crazy like that.

Roxanne looked just as confused but said slowly, "Well . . . I've never actually seen her throwing up . . . but yesterday I walked in on her in the bathroom and it smelled awful. She told me that her stomach was upset. . . . We'd gone out for a brunch . . . but . . . she didn't really eat anything."

"That's right. She's been eating salads, lettuce sandwiches, and drinking water the whole time we've been here," Monique said. "So, Doc, what do you think is going on?"

Rudy Burns clicked his pen, then scratched his wavy hair with its tip. "Well, I won't know for sure until I talk with Ms. Johnson directly, but if she is starving herself, vomiting, or abusing laxatives, that kind of behavior could put her at risk for kidney or heart failure. Losing a lot of weight in such a short period of time puts a tremendous strain on the body. And if she was exercising and eating like you describe, it's not surprising that she wound up sick."

Gayle had been very frightened for Cynthia, not knowing what was wrong. But she hadn't expected anything like this. Now it was all starting to make sense. They had all joked about the lack of food in the house but hadn't thought anything of it. Cyn had never been big on cooking. Gayle thought she'd kept the fridge empty to resist the temptation to snack.

"Are you saying that she has an eating disorder? Some kind of psychological problem?" Monique asked.

"It is one possibility. We'll do a more thorough assessment later in the day, when she's more alert."

Gayle's stomach turned as she remembered the fat-burning exercise book she'd sent Cynthia for her birthday. She had wanted to encourage her to keep up the good work. *Maybe Cynthia wouldn't be in this mess if I hadn't constantly praised her for losing more and more weight.*

Roxanne's mind was in a whirl. *Was is it possible that Cynthia had a problem with food?* As someone who loved to eat, she could not imagine or comprehend what Cynthia had done to herself. To her, food was life-sustaining, not some enemy that you had to get rid of. How could Cynthia not know that?

Monique said, "When can we see her?"

"She's still here in the ER, but we're going to be moving

her to one of the wards fairly soon," the doctor said. "I'll let you peek in on her. But don't expect her to hold a conversation. She's still very weak."

They silently followed him back to the treatment area. Instead of going back through the curtained-off area, he stopped in front of a door near an X-ray room.

"Before you go in there, don't get too freaked out by all the tubes and wires. It looks a lot more ominous than it really is. OK?"

They all nodded.

Although he'd warned them, it was still a shock to see Cynthia lying so pale in the narrow hospital bed, surrounded by monitors and other medical hardware. Sitting next to the bed was the blond nurse Monique had seen earlier at the admissions desk. She gave a slight smile of recognition when she saw Monique.

However, Monique couldn't return the smile. All of a sudden, her palms were sweating, and her heart began to race. She'd been so busy completing paperwork and asking questions, she'd totally forgotten about her aversion to sickrooms and hospitals. Now the reality of it was starting to sink in. Even though the room was a lot bigger than the ones they had passed before, with all the equipment, plus five people squeezed in around the bed, it felt small and claustrophobic. She felt like she couldn't breathe and quickly took a couple of big gulps of air, hoping no one would notice.

Roxanne stared at the IV as it slowly dripped the nourishment Cyn had so foolishly deprived herself of directly into her veins. She was unable to hold back a sob. Gayle quickly put an arm around her.

The hushed voice the doctor used was probably meant to be soothing, but instead had the effect of reinforcing the seriousness of the situation. "We treated the hypothermia first since it was the most immediate threat," he explained. "The hypokalemic IV we've started is heated warmer than the body temperature. . . ." He paused when he saw their blank expressions. "Hypokalemic means the IV solution is slowly replacing the potassium and magnesium in her system that had been lost. When we drew blood, we discovered that not only are her electrolytes a mess, but her blood-sugar level is low. So the IV has a glucose solution in it as well."

Roxanne was only half listening to him. Her attention had been captured by the frightening picture of Cynthia's unmoving body. The doctor walked over to the door and held it open, a signal that it was time for them to leave.

Once out in the hall, he said, "I suggest you all go home, get a few hours of sleep, and then come back this afternoon."

"Is she going to be OK?" Gayle asked. "She didn't even know we were there. I couldn't even tell if she was breathing."

He patted her shoulder reassuringly. A gesture oddly old-fashioned coming from such a young man. "Trust me, she was just sleeping. Her body's been through a lot. Why don't you come back after you've gotten some rest? She'll probably be awake by then."

None of them wanted to leave, but they were dead on their feet. After a moment or so, the doctor announced that he had to go.

"Will you be the doctor on this case?" Monique asked.

"Probably not. I only work in ER. But rest assured the physician assigned to her will be fully briefed on her condition. Excuse me, ladies, I've really got to run," he said, turning away.

He started walking down the hall, his strides brisk. Probably dashing off to the next emergency, Gayle thought. Instead, he stopped in front of one of the vending machines across from the waiting room and leaned over to retrieve something, and when he straightened up, he had a small paper coffee cup in his hand. As he took a sip, he ran the other hand through his hair, shut his eyes, and leaned against the wall for a moment.

He looks whipped, Gayle thought. She had heard about interns and residents pulling forty-eight- or sometimes seventy-two-hour shifts. It made her appreciate his going out of his way to put their minds at ease. She wished they had thanked him. A lot of the doctors she'd dealt with after her mother's stroke had been arrogant and impatient and seemed to resent any extra second spent answering questions.

He moved away from the wall and disappeared around a corner.

It struck Gayle as sadly ironic that Rudy Burns was just what Cynthia claimed she needed: a good-looking, obviously sensitive black man with the right initials behind his name. What a shame she wasn't in any condition to take full advantage of the fact.

Chapter

33

Monique hesitated, causing Gayle and Roxanne, who were following close behind, to bump into each other. "Are you sure this is the right room?" she asked. "There's nobody in here."

Roxanne eyed the empty bed. "I'm pretty sure the receptionist said Room 326."

A rustling sound came from behind the curtain that divided the room in half. In a surprisingly strong voice Cynthia called out, "I'm over here, y'all."

Monique's footsteps faltered for a second time. Someone was behind the curtain talking to Cynthia. Reluctant to walk in on some gross medical procedure, she asked, "Is it OK if we come in?"

"Yeah."

Roxanne drew the curtain back. Cynthia was propped up in bed. She still looked really fragile and tired around the eyes, but she'd gotten back some of her color and was wide awake.

A lock of dark brown hair covered one of the nurse's green eyes as he fiddled with the controls on Cynthia's IV. He was wearing a standard nurse's uniform—a white tunic and white pants. But this was no typical nurse. His five o'clock shadow looked deliberately cultivated, and his bulging biceps and forearms were covered with a fine dusting of brown hair.

Stepping forward, Gayle gave Cynthia a slight hug and pressed her cheek briefly against her friend's. As she straightened up, she said in a fierce whisper, "Don't ever scare us like that again."

Roxanne handed Cynthia a bunch of daisies wrapped in plastic. "I wanted to get some pink roses or something pink," she apologized. "Monday . . ." She couldn't believe it was Monday already. The time kept shifting from slow motion to fast forward. "Monday . . . must be a busy florist's day around here," Roxanne said.

"Thanks," Cynthia said, placing the flowers on the nightstand. "I'll have to put those in something. I just feel bad that ya'll had to spend your vacation at a hospital." Fear lurked in her eyes as she looked in Monique's general direction. "Go ahead. Let me have it. I know you're probably itching to."

"Wrong, as usual," Monique said. "Listen up, because you may never hear this again. . . . I'm just glad to hear the sound of your voice. Last time I saw you, you looked like you were knocking on death's door. And as for telling you off . . . I—I was out of line last night. The only thing I'm itching to do is tell you how relieved I am that you're OK."

Tears welled up in Cynthia's eyes. Monique's apology moved her more than a typical tongue-lashing from her ever could. "I'm so, so sorry, ya'll. . . ." Her voice cracked.

Gayle stilled Cynthia's hand, which was clawing nervously at the covers. "Cynthia, we're here to make sure you're all right, not make you cry."

"Listen to her, Miss Johnson," the nurse said. "Getting emotional is not good for your blood pressure. Your visitors will have to leave if having them here makes you agitated. As it is, I have to change this darn IV."

Monique flinched as he slowly withdrew the IV needle from Cynthia's arm. A track of red needle marks dotted her otherwise pale skin. *She looks like a junkie, for chrissake.*

The nurse began vigorously rubbing Cynthia's hand between his. "My hand was starting to get all cold and numb," she explained, temporarily distracted from her earlier distress. "My buddy Ricky here is going to fix me right up." She smiled at the man, but her "buddy" was all business.

"I'm gonna try sticking one of the veins on the top part of your hand," he said.

When Monique saw the silver flash of the needle, a spot on the floor suddenly became ultrafascinating and in need of her complete attention.

"There," Ricky said after he finished taping the needle in place. "Hopefully, your circulation will be better now. Just buzz me if it starts to feel numb again."

He gave them another warning before he left the room. "Remember, don't upset her or ya'll will have to go."

"Charming fellow," Monique remarked. "And what a bedside manner. No patient wants to hear 'I'm gonna stick you.' "

"He may be a little low on personality, but did you see those arms?" Roxanne gushed. "And that tight little rear. Polyester nurse's pants never looked so good, huh, Cyn?" She winked at her friend.

Cynthia's mouth twisted and she gave a little shrug. "You're asking the wrong person, girlfriend. After yesterday, I'm through with men."

They all stared, afraid this meant she was not only physically ill but suicidal. To break the tension, Cynthia gave a rueful smile. "OK, OK. So maybe I'm just through with them until I'm back on my feet, or until I find one that ain't a dog or married, whichever comes first."

Roxanne laughed in relief. "Now that's more like the Cynthia we all know and love."

Cynthia laughed briefly before her face clouded over. "You all are being extremely nice to me, and I just want you to know how sorry I am for putting you through all of this—"

Gayle said, "Enough with the apologies. People get sick." She hesitated, then asked, "What did the doctor say about your condition?"

"I don't remember much about the brother. I was so out of it when he was talking to me. But the other guy—Dr. Cohen, I think that's his name—he said I was dehydrated, had low blood sugar, and a lot of stuff starting with 'hypo' or 'hyper' . . . nothing too serious," she assured them. Cynthia caught the looks the other three exchanged. "What?" she asked. "Why y'all looking at me like that?"

Monique said, "Last night you were practically comatose. Now you're claiming it was nothing serious?"

"That was last night. Look at me now. I'm ten times better already," Cynthia argued.

Gayle noticed the high color in her face and hastened to calm her. "Cyn, while it's true you look a whole lot better than you did last night, you didn't get sick out of the blue."

Cynthia gave her a questioning look.

Gayle said, "Last night the doctor told us that you got sick because you might be abusing your body. . . ."

"Yeah, right. Like what? Hitting myself with a hammer or beating my head against a wall?" Cynthia scoffed.

Monique said, "No, more like starving yourself, exercising like crazy, and popping laxatives."

The hot color had spread to Cynthia's neck. "What?" she spluttered. Her hands frantically smoothed a fold in the sheet.

Gayle sat next to her on the bed. "Look, Cyn, we don't want to upset you. But the doctor told us you probably have an eating disorder."

Cynthia closed her eyes and shook her head. "No . . . no, I don't."

Gayle put a hand on Cynthia's shoulder. "Cyn," she gently commanded, "open your eyes." After an agonizing pause, Cynthia's pupils stared out at the small group gathered around her bed. "I know it's hard to admit it and it was stupid of us not to figure it out sooner, but you have a problem. You've been eating like a bird and obsessing about how fat you look ever since we got here."

"That's right," Roxanne echoed. "And after I spoke with the doctor this morning, I got to thinking about when I walked in on you in the bathroom the other day. So I checked out your medicine cabinet and bathroom cupboards. . . ."

Cynthia's hands clutched the edge of the sheet. Roxanne thought she might pull it over her head to hide under. "Cyn, there is only one reason I can think of why you would have a lifetime supply of Ex-Lax, water pills, and syrup of ipecac stashed in your bathroom."

"I can't believe you snooped around my house," Cynthia whispered.

Roxanne said, "I can't believe I had to. Call me nosy if you want, but I needed to know what the hell was going on."

Cynthia sighed and let go of the sheet. "I still don't think I have an eating disorder. Maybe I did go a bit overboard with my dieting," she conceded.

Gayle frowned and took one of Cynthia's hands, forcing her to look at her. "Cyn, that's an understatement and you know it. Dieting isn't supposed to jeopardize your health."

Cyn interrupted her, "I know, Gayle, but I just wanted to stay thin and pretty."

Roxanne sighed. She just could not relate. "Cyn, any man who cares about you should be interested primarily in what you've got going on inside. Outside beauty is something you have limited control over. Besides, there are plenty of fat women that's got a man. And plenty of skinny ones that don't, Monique being a prime example."

Monique let that one pass in the interest of presenting a united front.

"Look at the kind of pressure you put on yourself, trying to live up to somebody else's stupid idea of beauty. You literally made yourself sick," Gayle said. "Besides which, whether you believe it or not, you're already beautiful."

Of course, Cynthia didn't really believe Gayle. Friends *had* to say stuff like that. "I appreciate the concern, and I'm really going to try hard to get back on track."

"How do you plan on doing that?" Roxanne asked.

Cynthia's eyes darted around the room like a trapped animal's. "You know when I said I'd be back to normal in a couple of days?" They all nodded. "Well, I lied. The doctor told me that they have an eating-disorders unit here. He wants me to stay there for a minimum of two weeks. It seems he doesn't trust me to feed myself if left to my own devices. Can you believe that?" she asked indignantly.

Without hesitation they all answered: "Yes."

Gayle went on, "That sounds like a sensible idea to me. You are way too thin. You need to learn how to eat like a normal person again."

"But I can't stay here for two weeks," Cynthia whined. "How will I explain it to the people at work? And then there's my mother . . . she calls me practically every day. She would flip out if she couldn't get a hold of me for two whole weeks!"

"Hey, slow down," Gayle said. "You don't have to tell the whole office your business, but I'm sure something can be worked out. Tell them you're suffering from exhaustion."

"That'll look really good come promotion time. Cynthia Johnson? Wasn't she the one too exhausted to work last summer?"

"It sounds a hell of a lot better than: Cynthia Johnson? Wasn't she the one who died of starvation last summer?" Monique shot back.

"And as far as your mother is concerned, don't you think you ought to call your parents?" Gayle said.

Cynthia shot straight up in the bed, almost tipping over the pole that held the dangling IV bag. Just as quickly, she collapsed back against the pillow. "Are you out of your friggin' mind?" she cried. "I don't want my parents to know anything."

"All right. All right. Keep your drawers on. It was just a suggestion," Monique said. "Stop yelling or RoboNurse will throw us out."

Cynthia squeezed Gayle's hand, trying to win her over. "I really do feel better. I'm gonna talk to that silly old doctor. With a couple days' rest, I'll be raring to go."

"Cyn, now who's the one being silly?" Monique lectured. "Why don't you just do what the doctor says so you can really get better?" Her eyes moved around the sterile room, and her lips curled with distaste. "I really don't want to see the inside of another hospital room because you didn't take care of yourself and ended up having a relapse."

"Yeah," Roxanne said, "you need to do whatever it takes to get better."

"Hah!" Cynthia snorted. "I don't see how anybody can get well in this place. They've been poking and prodding me since I got here. Every time I fall asleep, somebody comes waking me up. Miss Johnson, we need to take your temperature. Miss Johnson, we need to draw some blood. . . ."

Roxanne laughed.

"It's not funny," Cynthia said. "I'm telling you, if I'm here another twenty-four hours, I won't have a drop of blood left. They're like . . . like . . . bloodsucking vampires."

"Cyn, you just sound scared to me," Gayle said. "Just do what the doctors tell you. Believe me, it's for the best. And though it may seem like we're giving you a hard time, you do have all of our support."

Cynthia felt a little ashamed. Gayle was right. She knew they'd be there for her no matter what, even if Monique did take this tough-love stuff too far.

A thought suddenly occurred to her. "What time is it?" she asked, knowing that it had to be early evening. "What are ya'll still doing here? Weren't you supposed to be leaving today?"

"No, but don't worry," Gayle said. "Monique and I changed our reservations. We're leaving around three o'clock tomorrow afternoon instead of in the morning."

Cynthia groaned and covered her face with her hands. "I still feel bad about this."

"Well, don't," Gayle said. "We wanted to be here. With you."

Roxanne added, "And I decided to stay for a while longer. I didn't know about the whole eating-disorders-unit thing, but I was going to stick around anyhow to keep you company while you were recuperating."

"I can't let you do that!" Cynthia cried.

Roxanne said, "Why not? I'm a teacher, remember? I have

the summer off. I've been doing mostly volunteer work, but nothing so vital they can't get somebody else to do it for a couple of days."

"But still . . ."

"But nothing. They say charity starts at home. And you're like family to me. So you come first."

Picking up the little box of tissues next to her bed, Cynthia said, "You're gonna make me cry."

Ricky the nurse came back into the room. He eyed them suspiciously, making sure they had done no harm to his patient. "I need to check your blood pressure," he said to Cynthia as he reached for the equipment on the wall next to the bed.

He placed his stethoscope on the pulse at the crook in her arm and pumped a small oblong plastic ball. "Still kind of low," he murmured to himself. He jotted something down on his clipboard and left them without a backward glance.

Cynthia had a thoughtful look on her face. "You know, Roxanne, you were right."

"About what?"

"His butt, of course. It's tight and round enough to bounce a quarter off."

They all burst out laughing.

Cynthia was the first to pull herself together. "Anybody got a mirror?" she asked.

Monique gave her a small compact. Cynthia looked at her reflection and groaned. "I look like hell," she said. She daubed powder on her forehead, chin, and cheeks and began rubbing them in with the pad. "Monique, what else you got in that bag?" she asked.

Monique reached in and came out with a lipstick and blush. "It's darker than the stuff you use, more of a violet than a pink," she warned, handing them over.

Cynthia stopped her primping long enough to grab the rest of the makeup. "Beggars can't be choosers," she said. "Why didn't ya'll tell me I look like crap?"

Gayle shrugged her shoulders. "Well, it didn't seem like the most sensitive—"

"Sensitive!" Cynthia said. "You wouldn't have been hurting my feelings one bit. I *want* to know when I look like a refugee from a Halloween party."

She put the cap back on the lipstick and gazed in the small mirror again. The foundation was a little dark for her, but otherwise she didn't look too bad. "That'll do for now," she announced. "Not wearing makeup is like leaving the house with no clothes on. And what if that cutie from the emergency room stops by? Then where will I be?" She smoothed her hair. "I'm glad I had my relaxer touched up. Nappy hair *and* no makeup is more than any woman should have to bear."

Gayle smiled. Hearing Cynthia philosophize about makeup was funny and disturbing at the same time. "I'm really sorry," she apologized. "I packed a bag with your makeup, a couple of gowns, and some underwear, but I keep leaving it in the car."

"Honey, next time don't forget. I bet this hospital is crawling with eligible men."

"I thought you'd sworn off men," Roxanne teased.

"I have, I have," Cynthia said. "But you never know. . . . Maybe the right one can make me change my mind. Besides, can't I look good just for myself?"

Doubt lingered in her friends' eyes despite her cheerful words. Cynthia prayed that she would be able to live up to them. She didn't want to disappoint herself or her friends again. She was confident that this whole dieting thing was just a temporary setback. One day she would look back on it and laugh. She deserved to be happy and she would be. The challenge was figuring out how to do that without half killing herself in the process. Obviously, starving herself was not the answer. But no matter, next time she'd get it right.

"Cyn, I think we should take off," Gayle said. "You seem a little tired."

She smiled. Gayle was always the perceptive one. "You're right, I do feel a little sleepy. I assume I'll see ya'll before you leave?"

"Of course."

After they left, Cynthia rolled over onto her side, staring at the flowers Roxanne had given her. She'd agreed only with Gayle because she wanted some time alone. Actually, she didn't feel tired at all but knew she needed to get some rest. She had the feeling that she would need all her strength in the coming weeks. Finding happiness was turning out to be a lot of hard work.

PART FOUR

Shifting Gears

Chapter
34

After sitting on the runway inhaling stale, uncirculated air for a good hour and a half while a steady deluge of heavy rain pelted the plane, Monique didn't know whether to be relieved or scared when the pilot's voice crackled over the loudspeaker, announcing that they had been cleared for takeoff and that he planned to fly above the storm. With the bluish black sky periodically discharging thundering booms and flashes of lightning, Monique had thought the flight would be canceled.

Despite the pilot's promise to bypass the storm, there wasn't an air pocket the plane didn't hit. Monique could feel a headache coming on and searched her briefcase for the bottle of aspirin she always kept on hand. She located the pills but realized that she'd have to wait until the flight attendant came along with some water before she took them. Massaging her temples, she tried to focus on the papers spread all over her tray table.

The flight was full, and booking at the last minute meant she and Gayle had to accept whatever seats they could get. If their seats had been any farther to the rear, they would have been out of the plane altogether.

The drone of the jet's engine reverberated through the plastic paneling behind their seats. Monique's ears were clogged and she couldn't even hear herself think. She tried yawning, hoping her ears would pop.

The bobbing up and down didn't seem to bother Gayle, who had curled up on her side with a paperback and fallen asleep with her face pressed against the tiny window of the plane. Monique let her sleep. It wasn't like she was missing out on anything. Gayle was probably exhausted. Monique knew she herself was. Last night they had gotten to bed at a reasonable hour for the first time since arriving in Tampa, but lack of sleep and dealing with all the drama of the past few days had finally caught up with Gayle.

Well, at least somebody is getting some shut-eye, Monique thought as she nudged Gayle, whose feet were practically on her lap.

Monique glared at the bony, pinched-face woman sitting to her right. But the woman was too busy using a saliva-moistened finger to turn the pages of a dog-eared copy of a book entitled *Fighting Back with Assertiveness* to notice Monique's hostility. From time to time she nodded her scraggly permed head as she read.

Thanks to her, Monique had been relegated to the middle seat, which she hated. With her long legs, she always felt cramped in the narrowly spaced rows of movie theaters and planes. So whenever possible, she opted for an aisle seat. That way she didn't end up feeling like a pretzel.

She had tried to persuade the old biddy next to her to change to either the window or the middle seat, but nothing doing.

"I need to be close to the bathroom," the woman had claimed, her pop-bottle glasses giving her an owlish look.

Monique had tried to reason with her, explaining that the bathroom was right behind them and that she would be more than happy to get out of her way if she had to go. All she wanted was a little leg room. But the woman was determined to stand her ground. She had even waved her boarding pass under Monique's nose like a red flag. The aisle seat rightfully belonged to her, and she wasn't about to give it up.

When people around them started craning their necks to see what was going on, Gayle had begged her to take a seat before the flight attendants came over and kicked them both off the plane.

Monique was dying to stretch out her legs, but she couldn't because her overnight bag and Gayle's purse were stuffed under the seat in front of her. To add insult to injury, the FASTEN YOUR SEAT BELT sign had been lit during the entire bumpy flight. So all the other woman's fuss about going to the bathroom was for nothing.

She shifted uncomfortably in her seat. It seemed like forever since her last cigarette. Monique sighed. There was no way she was going to get anything done. She gathered up her papers, then tapped them until all the edges were aligned, locked the tray table into place, then crammed the papers into her briefcase.

She closed her eyes, hoping that by some miracle she might doze off. If she was sleeping, maybe she wouldn't be conscious of how confined she felt. But in a matter of minutes, the clattering of metal and talking arose in the nearby galley, disturbing the darkness behind her eyelids.

A gray metal cart was wheeled past her. The flight crew was making its way down the aisle to dispense airline "snacks." For those people who weren't already airsick, Monique was pretty sure the snacks would soon have them feeling that way.

Gayle didn't budge when a tanned male flight attendant came by and asked, "What would y'all like to drink, ma'am?"

Monique poked her in the ribs.

Instantly awake, Gayle sat up and turned toward her. "What?"

"What do you want to drink?"

"Drink?" In an automatic gesture Gayle unlocked her tray table. "Orange juice is fine."

Monique eagerly accepted a can of apple juice to wash the aspirin down.

After the flight attendant moved on, Gayle said, having sat up fully, "Cyn looked much better this morning, don't you think?"

"That's 'cause she had her war paint on." This time when they had stopped by the hospital to say good-bye, Gayle had remembered to bring Cynthia's makeup. Monique had laughed at the way Cyn had pounced on it like a dog on a juicy bone.

"No, it wasn't just the makeup. It seemed like she'd perked up some. She was laughing and smiling the whole time. She didn't even mention Anthony. It was almost like . . . none of this ever happened."

"Is that surprising? Everything about this weekend shows how vast Cyn's capacity for denial is."

"Well, thank God Cyn finally came to her senses and agreed to the eating-disorders program. And I'm so glad she let us call her parents to tell them what was going on."

"Frankly, I was going to call them whether she agreed or not. Roxanne can't stay down in Florida forever, you know."

Actually, Gayle had suspected that Monique was going to take matters into her own hands, which was precisely why she felt it was so important for Cyn to make the decision herself. She had wanted to avoid yet another argument before they left.

Monique couldn't get over how messed up Cynthia's life had become, all because she wanted a man. In Cynthia's mind, not having a man was tantamount to not having air to breathe. "I just don't understand why Cyn was acting so desperate—starving herself, sleeping with a married man. I've had boyfriends, and I've been alone—and the funny thing is the world kept spinning around in either case."

"I don't really understand it, either." Gayle set her plastic cup on the tray. "But I do know that there is a difference between being alone and being lonely. And being lonely ain't no fun at all. Loneliness is a powerful, scary thing. Maybe Cyn gave in to it. Maybe she let her loneliness take control to the point where she forgot who she was or what she wanted. . . . Maybe she was just trying to find some happiness."

Monique heard the conviction in Gayle's voice. Here was a woman who knew what she was talking about.

Happiness? Monique wasn't sure if she was happy or not. She'd never really thought about it. She'd made a life for herself in Cleveland. No, she didn't have the greatest job in the world, but it was challenging and it kept her busy. She had a few people she could hang out with—when she was in the mood. She didn't have to deal with her family on a daily basis and could pay her bills. What was there to be unhappy about?

She said to Gayle, "How do you know if you're happy?"

Gayle smiled, "Monique, you ask that question like I'm really supposed to know the answer."

Gayle was right. They were always turning to her for answers, but this time she was just curious. "I know it's only your personal opinion, but I really want to know what you think."

Gayle's fingers played with the rim of her cup, her brows furrowed in concentration. At last she looked at Monique. "I think happiness is feeling like nothing important is missing or broken in your life. Or even if it is, happiness means having faith that you can get what's missing or at the very least fix those broken parts."

"Hmm, that's an interesting definition," Monique said. "So, are you happy?"

"No. . . . No, I'm not," Gayle said quietly and with certainty.

Monique was surprised and then not surprised. If nothing else, Gayle was honest. But she didn't like the thought of Gayle being unhappy in any way. If anybody deserved to be happy, it was her.

As a flight attendant walked by their row, the woman sitting next to her asked, "Is it OK for me to go to the ladies' room?"

The attendant flashed her a smile. "Yes, ma'am. The sign is turned off."

After they both left, Monique turned her attention back to Gayle. "So, what are the missing parts for you? What do you need to be happy?"

Gayle smiled at her but looked sad nonetheless. It was impossible to answer a question like that. She tried not to think about what she needed. What would be the point? Unlike her friends, she couldn't just up and leave, move to another place, start life over from scratch. Cyn had even resorted to leading a double life. She'd gone to Tampa and reinvented herself. But Gayle couldn't do that. She wouldn't do that. There were other people to consider. Her mother was sick, and she depended on her. *If my mama's happy, then I'll be happy,* she told herself.

"We weren't talking about me, Monique. We're talking about you. What's missing for you?"

Monique marveled at Gayle's ability to evade questions she'd rather not answer. But she knew better than to push her, because as accommodating as Gayle was when it came to helping others, she was a very private person. She rarely shared her feelings and problems even with her closest friends.

"What is missing for me?" Monique thought about that for a moment. "Not much. . . . I miss Tyson sometimes, though."

"Why?"

"Because I love Tyson more than I do some members of my immediate family."

"Is that a bad thing?"

"That's just it. I don't know. I love him like an old pair of shoes. Being with Tyson is comfortable, relaxed. He is a good fit. And, of course, my parents absolutely adore him," she added, sounding disgusted.

"So, the man gets along with your family. You're going to hold that against him?"

Monique thought for a moment or so about her last conversation with Tyson in Cleveland. "Tyson is really a wonderful guy. He's been my best friend all of my life. He knows me better than anyone. He took me seriously when the rest of my family, except maybe my father, thought my life was a big joke. I don't know if you would call it happiness, but I just felt better whenever he was around."

Monique sighed. It was hard to explain. Her parents loved Tyson for the wrong reasons—his family background, his career, his social status. They—well, not they, to be fair—her mother kept pushing him at her. She hated being pushed.

"When we were engaged, sometimes I would look at Tyson and this picture of us turning into my parents keep popping into my head and it scared the hell out of me." After a pause, she said, "Doesn't that sound crazy?" Gayle didn't answer.

There was no need. Monique was simply sorting out her feelings aloud. "To tell you the truth, I'm not really sure why I broke up with Tyson."

"Maybe you were so busy running away from home, you didn't think about where you were running to and what else or who else you might be leaving behind."

As usual, Gayle had hit it right on the money. Monique could feel it in her very soul. "When did you get so smart?" she asked in awe.

Gayle shrugged. She wasn't so smart.

"When I went away to college, we agreed to date other people. I never did . . . not that I had much choice." There were no men in Minnesota, especially no black men. And as far as Monique was concerned, dating white men wasn't even an option. Her father would have had a heart attack if she'd come home with a white man.

"You know how little we had to choose from at school. But Tyson dated. He went out with cheerleaders and little sisters from his fraternity. And, Gayle, honest to God, I was never jealous. Just kind of curious about the kind of woman Tyson would be attracted to. Would a woman who is supposedly in love react that way?"

"A woman who was very sure of how her man felt about her might."

But where was the mystery in knowing exactly how the other person felt? Monique didn't want just compatibility. Where was the fire and the passion?

Monique slowly shook her head. "I still don't know what I want. But I miss him a lot. I just don't want to hurt him again. I don't think he would forgive me this time."

"Then don't let your mouth write any checks that your heart can't cash," Gayle advised.

"What?"

"Don't make any promises you can't keep. Take it slow. Besides which, what makes you think Tyson will let you rush back into his life? He's been hurt before. He's probably going to be a lot more cautious with you the second time around.

He might just make you prove your love. Make you do some work."

Gayle was right. Maybe she had been too young to commit to someone for the rest of her life. She hadn't been certain there wasn't anyone better suited out there for her. How could she know, when her parents had so skillfully limited her exposure to only the "right" people? But that was then and this was now. For years she'd been out in the world, and the pickings were slim. "What if Tyson isn't even interested? What if he thinks I'm the biggest bitch to walk the face of the earth?"

One emotion after another flitted across Monique's face, and Gayle felt sorry for her. Vulnerability was a new feeling for her. "Come on, Monique. I don't care how pushy your mother is. If Tyson hated you that much, he never would have come to Cleveland at all. Maybe he really wanted to spend time with you. Maybe he misses you, too."

Monique wished she had the answers to those questions. And for the first time in her life, the thought of *not* trying to find answers scared her more than ignorance.

"Are you finished, ma'am?"

Monique looked up to find a flight attendant's hand poised over her half-empty cup of apple juice.

"What?"

"Are you done?" the woman repeated. "I need to collect this because we'll be landing soon."

"Oh . . . yeah, take it," Monique said, handing over the plastic cup. She put the tray up. Glancing over Gayle's shoulders, through the breaks in the clouds, she could see little patches of green landscape. Thank God. The hellacious ordeal was almost over.

She leaned back in her seat, thinking once again of Tyson. She never wanted to feel responsible for causing someone so much heartache. She was just grateful that Tyson was still even speaking to her after the way she had hurt him. Monique tried to hold on to one hopeful thought. Tyson had forgiven her long before her mother had.

She couldn't help wondering if in her quest for something

great she had lost something that was really good. But she'd taken the easy way out so many other times. Monique wanted to have at least one dream that she wasn't afraid to go after.

She fastened her seat belt as the grinding of the landing gear signaled that they were making their final descent.

Calling Tyson would be her first order of business when she got home.

Chapter

35

Although it was nine o'clock at night, it was still light out. A group of young kids were playing a game of kickball in the street. As Monique's car eased toward them, they scampered over to the sidewalk. The moment it passed, the kids ran back into the street and resumed play. She pulled into the driveway, then switched off the ignition.

The sudden lack of motion woke Gayle up. She started in confusion but relaxed once she saw familiar surroundings. She gave a big openmouthed yawn as she stretched her arms as high as the low car ceiling would allow.

Boy, I must have been really tired, Gayle thought. She remembered going to long-term airport parking to pick up Monique's car. But she didn't remember getting on the highway. She was glad to be home. Poor Monique, though, still had a two-hour drive ahead of her.

"Do you want to stay over?" Gayle asked. "You could get up an hour or so earlier tomorrow and drive up then."

Monique shook her head. She was tired, but more than anything, she wanted to wake up in her own bed. After this so-called vacation, she'd had enough of staying over at other people's houses for a while. Besides, if she stayed in Columbus overnight, she and Gayle would probably spend the night talking, and she'd end up even more exhausted tomorrow than if she drove home right now.

"I need to get back," Monique said. "I was supposed to be at work this afternoon, and my boss is pissed off already. I don't want to take any chances on being late tomorrow. Besides, traffic will be lighter at this time of night as opposed to tomorrow morning."

"You're sure?"

"I'm sure," Monique said.

Gayle stepped out of the car, then reached in to unlock the rear door on the passenger side. She struggled to drag her suitcase through the door. The angle wasn't right.

"Do you need any help?" Monique asked.

"Naw, I got it." Gayle gave the suitcase another tug and it popped out. She used her hip to bump the door shut. She stopped to double-check that both doors on her side were locked before walking around to Monique's side of the car.

She leaned toward the window. "It's been a crazy weekend, huh?"

Monique shrugged. "No crazier than a day in court."

"Well, I can't argue with that. But you look a little tired to me. Drive carefully."

Monique started the car. "OK."

As she straightened up, Gayle said, "And call me when you get home."

"OK, Mom," Monique said. She quickly began backing out the driveway before Gayle could think of additional instructions to give her. Monique smiled when the word "smart-ass" reached her ears. She tossed Gayle a saucy wave and disappeared down the street.

Watching her go, Gayle adjusted the strap of her overnight bag and then felt around in her purse for her keys. Monique thought she was invincible, but anybody could have an accident on the way home, including her. For some reason, she had never grasped the concept that people might actually worry about her.

Gayle pushed the door open with her shoulder. Tired and distracted, she was in the middle of the living room when she became of aware of the stench of her father's cheap cigars. She dropped her bags on the floor and silently mouthed the words "Oh, no."

She didn't allow herself the luxury of hoping that maybe he had come and gone already because voices could clearly be heard coming from the kitchen. If she was real quiet, maybe she could tiptoe upstairs and they wouldn't even know she was in the house. She picked up her bags again and went over to the staircase. Even though the wooden stairs were carpeted, Gayle prayed they wouldn't creak and give her away. She was about midway up the stairs when her mother's voice called out, "Gayle, is that you?"

Gayle stopped in her tracks. *How did she know I was here? I haven't made a sound.* When her mother didn't call out again, Gayle continued to tiptoe up the stairs. She was on the top step when her mother's voice came from directly below her.

"Oh, it is you," Barbara said. "I thought I heard somebody pull into the driveway."

Gayle's head whipped around. Her mother stood at the bottom of the stairwell looking up at her. She was wearing a pastel housecoat, with a thin yellow cotton nightgown underneath and faded yellow Isotoner slippers. She had both hands on her hips.

"Didn't you hear me calling you?" she asked.

"I . . . I . . ."

"I . . . I . . . nothing," her mother teased. "When you didn't answer, I had to come and investigate. I thought I had me a prowler up in here."

Gayle had to smile. What was her skinny old mother gonna do if it had been a prowler?

"Don't stand there grinning like a nut. Put your stuff down and come on in the kitchen and say hi to your daddy. We wanna hear all about your vacation." Her mother turned away before she could see Gayle's smile vanish.

Funny how Daddy didn't come running to investigate. Instead, he left it to his sickly wife to rid the house of intruders. How typical! And she really didn't want to "say hi" to him.

She just wanted to know why he was here and when he was leaving.

In uncharacteristic fashion, Gayle threw her bags in a heap on the bed. She glanced at her answering machine. Great, she'd forgotten to turn it on before she left for vacation. She pushed the on switch and a small red light appeared.

She shrugged. What difference did it make? She probably hadn't gotten any calls anyhow. She had just spent the weekend with the three people most likely to call. And if there was a crisis at work, too darn bad. Somebody else would have to deal with it for a change.

Her bad mood did not improve when she walked into the kitchen and saw her father finishing off a beer. Another can was positioned nearby, ready to be popped open as soon as he was done with the first.

Gayle frowned. *Two-fisted drinking, how lovely.*

"Hi, Daddy," she said, her voice devoid of emotion.

"Hey, Black Beauty. What's shaking?" he said, reaching for his second beer.

Gayle sat down in the nearest chair and rested her elbows on the table. "Not much. Just tired." For her mother's sake, she wanted to be pleasant, but the sight of him drinking bugged the hell out of her. Gayle closed her eyes. Maybe he'd be gone when she opened them again.

Everything seemed calm and homey right now, but she knew from past experience that it wouldn't last, especially if her father was sitting here drinking when supposedly he had quit.

"You so tired you can't give your old mama a hug?" her mother said.

Gayle opened her eyes and turned toward her mother, who was sitting right next to her. She held out her arms. "You hug me. I'm too tired to get up."

Her mother leaned over and wrapped her arms around her daughter. "You a spoiled old something, ain't ya?"

Gayle smiled at her teasing. Normally, she loved it when her mother was in an affectionate mood, but this time she stiffened. Combined with her mother's usually comforting smells was something else.

Her mother chattered on, unmindful of Gayle's sudden stillness. "So tell us about your trip," she murmured against Gayle's cheek. Her breath was warm against Gayle's face.

There it was again. That smell. Gayle wrinkled her nose, then pulled away from her mother. She quickly scanned the table, then frowned at her mother. She couldn't believe what she was seeing.

Her mother looked back at her in confusion. "Gayle, what's . . ."

Gayle's eyes were locked on the can of Rolling Rock next to her mother's right hand. "Mama," she said in a shocked whisper, "I can't believe you're drinking beer."

Barbara blushed and then looked away. "Now, Gayle, it's only one little beer."

"But what about your medication? Don't you know you're not supposed to mix alcohol and prescription drugs?"

"Aw, Gayle," her father said, "one little beer ain't gonna hurt her."

"Daddy, I'm not talking to you," she snapped. "Just because you drink like a fish and haven't keeled over—yet—don't mean you got to be pushing alcohol on my mother."

"Gayle . . ." her mother pleaded.

Gayle was trying to understand what was going on. "Mama, I can't believe you. Why are you risking your health like this?"

"Really, Gayle," her mother said, "it's only one beer. I just opened it. And I barely took a sip, I swear."

Gayle picked up the can. It was almost full. "I'm throwing this out."

She walked toward the sink, but quick as lightning, her father was standing in front of her. He held out his hand for the can. "Gayle, what's wrong with you, girl? Don't be throwing no whole can of beer away."

She was so mad at him, she was tempted to throw the beer in his face. "Daddy, get out of my way. If you want to be a drunk, then go ahead, but don't you dare bring liquor into this house and give it to my mother."

"Gayle," her mother pleaded, "he didn't pour it down my throat. He asked me if I'd have a beer with him and I said yes."

Had her mother completely lost her mind?

She withered a little under Gayle's look but remained insistent. "Honey, I don't even want the beer anymore. Why don't you give it to your father? It's his beer, he paid for it."

Gayle still held the can away from her father's outstretched hand. They were the same height and were practically standing toe-to-toe. She'd never been this close to giving in to the urge to slap him. She wanted to slap him so hard his teeth rattled around in his head.

"Yeah, it's my hard-earned money that paid for it. And what me or yo' mama do ain't none of yo' business in the first place. We grown," her father said.

"I thought you stopped drinking. I thought you had cleaned up your act, started going to AA meetings every day. I leave for a few days and come back to find you downing beers like there's no tomorrow. It's fine if you want to kill yourself, 'cause, frankly, I don't care!" she screamed at him. "But I'm not gonna let you kill my mama, too."

"Don't raise your voice at me," her father warned. "I'm still the daddy here and you the child."

Gayle had heard that tone many times before. Her father wasn't drunk, but he had just enough alcohol in his system to give him the excuse he needed to take a swing at her. "Fine, fine. Here." She thrust the beer at him, splashing it down the front of his shirt. "Drink to your heart's content. Or until your liver rots, whichever comes first."

A prolonged argument avoided, Barbara Blackman visibly relaxed. Gayle rejected the gratitude she saw in her mother's eyes. Her father sat back down at the table, took a big swig out of his wife's can, and set it on the table with a satisfied bang.

Gayle remained standing, regarding him with distaste. "I've

seen you drinking out of three different beer cans in the last three minutes," she remarked. Her father said nothing. "You don't need to be drinking anyway, since you have to drive home."

"Don't worry about me getting home," her father said with a smile.

"I ain't worried about you. I'm thinking about all the innocent people you might hurt while you're drinking and driving."

"Well, don't worry about them neither. 'Cause I won't be driving nowhere tonight."

"What?" Gayle said. Her father just gave her another smug smile. She turned to her mother. "What is he talking about?"

Her mother twisted her wedding band a couple of times, then looked away. "I told your daddy he could move back in."

"What!"

Her mother took in Gayle's dazed expression before speaking again. "I told your daddy he could come back home."

"When? I just called on Sunday, and you said everything was fine."

"Everything was fine."

"But . . . you hadn't even seen him in a week!"

"I know, I know," her mother said, nodding her head. "This may seem sudden to you, but I've been thinking about it for a long time. And even though Willie hadn't been over in a while, we were still talking on the phone almost every day."

Gayle had no idea.

"Then while you were in Florida, I got to thinking . . . and I realized how much I miss him."

Gayle silently berated herself. *I should never have gone on that trip. I just gave Daddy the perfect opportunity to ease back in here.*

"Miss him how, Mama?" Gayle asked, talking about her father as if he weren't in the room. "Think about all the reasons that you asked him to leave in the first place—have you seen any improvement in any of them? He certainly hasn't stopped drinking. In fact, now he's got you drinking, too. And does he spend any time with Buddy? Does he take you places or fix this place up or run errands or do anything that you said was making you unhappy before?"

From the far end of the table, her father started to make a blustery protest in his own defense, but Gayle quelled him with a look.

"Gayle, baby, he *is* drinking less. He just had a couple of beers last night and a couple tonight. And Buddy is practically a grown man now. He's too old to be hanging around with his daddy anymore. And . . . and we need each other."

Did Mama have any idea how lame she sounded?

Gayle shook her head. It's so sad. Mama needs Daddy like she needs a hole in the head. He needs her a hell of a lot more than she needs him. She's just lonely because all she ever does is sit in this empty house. I should have made her do something with her time. She's probably scared that she's getting old and won't be able to find anybody better. But this is crazy.

Her mother's eyes begged for understanding. But Gayle just couldn't give it. Letting her father move back in was a mistake, and she couldn't pretend otherwise.

Her father, by this point, had lost interest in the conversation. Gayle wasn't going to let him talk. So he turned on the small black-and-white TV on the kitchen counter. A *Bonanza* rerun bloomed on the screen.

Gayle left the sink and moved to her mother's side. "Mama, I don't know what you want me to say. I don't think this is a good idea. And I really don't want him living here."

Her mother's face crumbled a little, and she stared at the plain gold band on her left hand for a long time. At last, she looked up and reached over to touch her daughter's hand. In a quiet voice she said, "Gayle, I'm sorry you feel that way. But the last time I looked at the deed to this house, it had Barbara Blackman on it, not Gayle Blackman."

A sharp pain shot through Gayle's chest. She pulled her shaking arm out of her mother's loose grasp. Her eyes filled up.

After all I've done for Mama, it's come down to this? Has she forgotten that I'm the one who took care of her when she was sick? Daddy didn't even want to come to the hospital because he hated being around sick people. I'm the one who drove her all over town to see doctors and visit friends. After letting—no, begging—me to take care of all of her responsibilities for years, *now* Mama decides to pull rank.

The walls were closing in around her. She needed to get out of here before she said something she would probably regret. "I guess that says it all then." She practically ran from the room. For the second time that night, she ignored the sound of her mother calling her name.

Her father chuckled at something on the show. "That Hop Sing is something else," she heard him say as she started up the stairs.

Her mother followed Gayle to her room. "Gayle, I'm sorry I upset you. Baby, you got to let me explain. I been with your father most of my life. I—"

"Mama, I'm tired. I know you want me to say everything is OK and be supportive, but I can't. I love both of you. But I've seen how crazy things can be when the two of you live under the same roof. Daddy has a serious drinking problem and he needs help. Letting him come back while he's still drinking is sending the wrong message."

"But, Gigi," her mother said, using her childhood nickname, "he is doing so much better right now. And he'll keep going to AA meetings, even if I have to drag him there myself."

The bright hope shining in her mother's eyes scared her. Who was Mama trying to convince, me or herself? She's living in a fantasy world. Her mother was scared to drive herself anywhere, let alone anybody else.

But Gayle didn't bother mentioning this. It was clear her mama had made up her mind.

The words of wisdom she'd shared with her friends just a few short days ago came back to haunt her: "You cannot control another person." That was the reality whether it was a cheating husband or an emotionally dependent mother.

Her mother had spoken the truth earlier. It was her house and her life. And that was the bottom line. She could have anybody she wanted living in it, and there wasn't a thing Gayle could do about it.

Gayle began undressing while her mother talked. She took an oversized T-shirt from the dresser drawer, slipped it over her head, then pushed all her bags onto the floor and climbed into bed. She rested her back against the headboard and sat facing her mother, who was sitting at the foot of the bed. She continued to listen but didn't respond to her mother's happy predictions for the future.

After a while Barbara realized that she was having a one-sided conversation. Gayle's eyes were closed. Her clasped hands rested on her lap on top of the covers.

"Gayle, are you asleep?"

"No."

Silence.

"I guess you're tired then?"

"Uh-huh."

"Maybe we can finish our talk tomorrow. I'll let you get some sleep."

"OK."

Gayle heard her mother flick the light switch on her way out the door. She gave an inward sigh and burrowed more deeply under the covers.

"Gayle?"

"Huh?"

"I almost forgot to mention it . . . but could you talk to your brother tomorrow?"

Gayle opened her eyes. The light from the hallway illuminated her mother's thin silhouette in the doorway. "About what?"

"Lately, he's been talking about not going to college in the fall. Says he's producing some rap group. Could you talk some sense into that crazy boy? You the only one anybody around here listens to."

The irony of that last statement did not escape Gayle.

"OK, Mama," she said wearily, then rolled over onto her side, curled in the fetal position. She would have promised anything to get her mother out of the room. She couldn't deal with another crisis right now.

Chapter

36

In a heavy Eastern European accent the cabbie thanked Roxanne for his tip before pulling away. The twenty-dollar ride from Logan Airport had probably blown her budget for the month, but Roxanne didn't care. She'd been gone for a long, trying week, and she wanted to get home.

Normally, Cyn could be a lot of fun, but there was only so much she could do from a hospital bed. Then Cyn's parents had arrived.

Mrs. Johnson hadn't cried. She didn't seem sad or angry, either, just determined. All she said in her soft voice was, "Honey, we're going to fix this, right?" As far as Roxanne could tell, it hadn't really been a question. So of course Cyn could only nod her head in agreement.

With her perky hats and soft pastels, Mrs. Johnson looked like a dainty flower compared to her husband, who was at least a foot taller than her. But he seemed to have a harder time dealing with Cyn's illness. When he'd seen Cyn for the first time, he'd sat on the edge of the bed and started crying like a baby. Then Cyn started crying, and before long Roxanne teared up, too, and then the nurse came in and kicked them all out.

After that Mrs. Johnson took control. Having been a fashion writer for years, she knew a lot about eating disorders. She asked the doctors a million and one questions about the specifics of the program, including family involvement in treatment and what care was available once Cynthia left the hospital.

Then Mrs. Johnson decided that Cyn's hospital room needed to be cheerier and insisted Roxanne help her bring in some personal things from Cynthia's apartment like family pictures, more flowers, and a few colorful pillows for Cyn's room. Besides having nowhere to put the stuff, Roxanne had thought it was probably against hospital policy. But nobody said anything. Roxanne could see where Cyn got her ability to sweet-talk people from. Mrs. Johnson was a pro. She was one of those Southern steel magnolias. Always smiling, soft-spoken and gracious, and always getting her way.

One day they had gone to a mall in search of fabric because Mrs. Johnson had decided to make some new curtains and clean up Cynthia's apartment to surprise her when she came home. During the trip there, Mrs. Johnson had confided that she felt stupid for not figuring out much earlier that Cynthia had a problem. "Now, I could stand here feeling guilty about that. But what good would it do? Guilt is only useful when it spurs you to do something constructive."

And constructive she was. She was the one who tactfully fielded calls from Cyn's friends. And Roxanne hadn't eaten so well in years. Mrs. Johnson's fried chicken gave her grand-ma's some competition. Cyn might not regain any weight anytime soon, but Roxanne would have if she hadn't backed away from Mrs. Johnson's Southern cooking.

But it was really Mr. Johnson's guilt and need for Roxanne to rehash every single detail of the weekend that made her realize it was time to go home. Cyn wasn't talking, especially about the whole Anthony fiasco, and she had sworn Roxanne to secrecy. Cynthia even left a message on Anthony's machine at work asking him not to call because her parents were in town.

But it was hard to come up with creative lies about what they'd been doing all weekend and whether there was anything happening in Cynthia's life that might have upset her. The Johnsons were really nice people, and Roxanne had never been a good liar. So she decided to leave before she caught herself up in a lie she couldn't get out of.

She didn't feel too guilty about leaving, though. If the amount of hovering and pillow-fluffing was anything to go by, Cyn was in good hands.

Roxanne hefted her duffel bag on her shoulder and walked around several large plastic bags of trash that someone had thoughtlessly left on the narrow patch of stony dirt in front of her apartment building. No wonder the grass wouldn't grow. Would it really have been too much trouble to walk a few more feet to the Dumpster in the alley?

Stepping out of the early evening sunlight into the gloomy foyer of her building, Roxanne stopped to extract her mail from the much dented and often vandalized mailboxes. After quickly surveying a week's worth of envelopes, Roxanne expressed regret that the vandals hadn't seen fit to steal some of her bills.

"As-salaam alaykum, Roxanne," a male voice called out in greeting.

"Alaykum salaam," Roxanne automatically replied. She wasn't sure which of her African neighbors she'd said hello to because when she looked up, she saw only the back of the man's head as he slipped out the door.

Having exhausted her Arabic vocabulary, Roxanne proceeded up a short flight of stairs to the first-floor landing. As she turned to climb the next set of stairs, something large and furry streaked by her. Roxanne moved out of its path and looked up at the single bulb that flickered hypnotically but provided very little light. Roxanne was tempted to put it out of its misery. *But no, that was what the management company was paying that lazy-ass Bob to do.*

She continued up the stairs, careful to keep away from the grime that might be waiting for an opportunity to jump off the dingy walls and onto her clean clothes.

After setting her bags down in the middle of the living room floor, Roxanne walked over to the windows and pulled up the miniblinds. She actually smiled at the familiar sight of the ashy gray bricks of the apartment across the alley from hers.

"Hello, alley," she said after opening the windows to let in some air.

She kicked her sandals off. The hardwood floor was warm under her feet, not freezing like it was in the winter. Still, she really did need to invest in a couple of rugs.

Rubbing her stomach, Roxanne padded over to the refrigerator. She opened the door and gazed at its empty interior. Nothing. Even Cyn had bottled water and a couple of frozen dinners. Roxanne had eaten all the perishable stuff before she left for vacation. *How could I have forgotten that? Maybe there are some crackers in the cabinet.*

Roxanne turned on the kitchen light. There was movement by the sink. She took an aluminum can out of the cabinet. "Hello, cockroaches," she said, blasting the scuttling bugs with spray. "Did you miss me? Looks like we're all starving tonight."

Not waiting for a reply, she went back into the living room and picked up her suitcases. After taking them into the bedroom, she began listening to her messages as she unpacked.

"Hello, Roxanne, this is Leslie. Call me as soon as you get back. We're having problems recruiting tutors for the second half of the summer program."

"Hi, Roxanne." Surprised to hear Marcus' voice, Roxanne turned to stare at the machine. "I hadn't heard from you in a while. Just called to talk."

Roxanne threw some clothes in the laundry basket. She could not imagine what they had to talk about. The next message came on.

"Hello, Roxanne. This is Cindy Tavis. Janice Coleman gave me your number. She said you'd be the perfect person to co-ordinate our next Dollars for Scholars fund-raiser. She said you did a wonderful job with the ABC program last winter. Please call me at your earliest convenience."

Roxanne picked up a notepad from the nightstand to write the woman's number down. She also made a note to call Janice and ask her to stop volunteering her for stuff.

The machine beeped again. After a long pause, she heard, "Hello? Hello? Oh, Roxie, I thought it was really you. I hate talking to these darn machines. . . . Oh, Roxie . . . it's me, your granny. . . ."

Roxanne smiled as she pulled the zipper around the suitcase to close it. *Who else would it be?*

"I didn't want nothing. I done told you about going out of town without leaving me a number where I can reach you. Call your old granny when you get back. I love you. Bye."

"Hi, Roxanne. It's Marcus again. Call me."

There were a few more messages. Roxanne took the suitcase to the hallway closet when the tape started to rewind. She didn't know what Marcus was calling her for, but she hoped he wasn't holding his breath waiting for her to call back.

The unpacking is done. Guess I better call Grandma, and prepare to be blessed out for disappearing for a week.

Just as she was about to pick up the phone, it rang.

"Hello?"

"Hi, Roxanne." Marcus' voice came over the line. "Where have you been?"

He really was something else. Calling her out of the blue and wanting to know her business. "Vacation."

"Oh, really? Great . . . great."

Roxanne waited.

"It's been a long time. . . . I was wondering if we could get together. . . ."

Surprised, Roxanne sat on the bed. *Was this, to use Marcus' own words, a bootie call?* "For what?" she asked, not masking her wariness.

Marcus laughed. "I know what you're thinking, and believe me, it's not like that."

Then what was it like? "Marcus, I just walked in the door. I'm hungry and I'm tired. I'm not up for visiting anybody—"

"Who said anything about *you* visiting anybody? I'll come over there."

Her eyes widened. During the entire time she and Marcus had gone out, he'd only been to her place once. And that was only to get a free meal and a little nookie, she reminded herself. "Marcus, what is this all about?"

"I just really want to talk to you. And you don't even have to lift a finger. I'll even bring the food. How about pizza?"

He was going way too fast for her. "But—"

"Forget it, Roxanne. I'm not taking no for an answer. I'll see you in . . . let's say, an hour to an hour and a half?"

He hung up before she could answer.

A bouquet of red roses lay on top of the pizza box Marcus was carrying. In his left hand was a bottle of wine. "Hi, Roxanne," he said. "Grab the flowers, they're for you."

Roxanne took the flowers. She was trying to stay calm, but Marcus looked damned good in his white polo shirt and olive green walking shorts. Khaki never looked so good.

He set the box on the table and turned to face her. "I missed you," he said, then leaned forward and kissed her on the lips.

She forced herself not to melt against him. She'd forgotten how soft Marcus' lips were. And damn her legs for going rubbery at the slightest bit of contact. He'd barely touched her, for God's sake. She was weak-minded and her body was a traitor.

She stepped away from him. "Thanks for the flowers. What's the occasion?"

"Nothing. I've been thinking a lot about some of the things you said about friendship . . . you know . . . when you told me off last spring."

Marcus sat down on the couch. Or, more precisely, he sprawled all over the thing, his hands hanging loosely between his wide-open legs.

"Oh," Roxanne said, turning away before her imagination started to run wild. She used to fit between those legs like a hand in a glove. She cleared her suddenly dry throat.

"I'm—I'm going to find a vase for these," she said, clutching the roses as if they could provide protection against her raging hormones. "We probably should eat the pizza before it gets cold. Why don't you sit at the table? I'll bring some glasses and plates."

They didn't talk much at first. Then Marcus smiled at her

as he picked up his third slice of pizza. Teeth straight and gleaming white, he could have been a poster boy for the American Dental Association. Better yet, that smile should have been illegal. It was a lethal weapon.

"It's so good to see you, Roxanne."

"Thanks." She took a sip of wine. No point in flattering his ego, it was always good to *see* him. A faint five o'clock shadow covered his light brown skin, making him appear even more dangerous and sexy than usual, if that were possible. Slender yet strong fingers lightly held the pizza, just as they had held her trembling body more times than she cared to remember. Yes, it was definitely good to see him.

"Like I said before, I've been thinking about you a lot lately."

"Good thoughts, I hope."

His smile appeared again. Slow and slightly amused. "Very good. I've been thinking about what you said about friendship and how there needs to be give-and-take. And how friends should follow through on promises. . . ."

Roxanne couldn't believe what she was hearing. Marcus had actually listened to something she'd said. What month was it? July? It had taken him long enough, but maybe there was hope for him after all. If Marcus was being sincere, maybe there was hope for *them*.

"It may not have seemed like it at the time, but what you said had a big impact on me."

Maybe Marcus had turned over a new leaf. She'd always felt he had a lot of potential. He just needed to learn how to treat people. Not be so selfish. Maybe there was some truth to the idea that men matured more slowly than women.

Roxanne picked up her glass. More wine was needed. "Really?"

"Yes, and you will be happy to hear that I haven't hurt anybody—at least I don't think I have since you told me about myself."

Roxanne didn't know what to say exactly. It would have been nice if he'd had this attitude a long time ago, say, when he was dating her. "I didn't exactly tell you about yourself. I was just tired and angry because you were taking me for granted."

Marcus took her hand in his. "I know and I'm sorry. Do you forgive me?"

Roxanne reached for the wine again. How could she not forgive him when he looked at her like that? His eyes still had the power to mesmerize her, and obviously he was sorry about what he'd done. "It's OK, Marcus. Lucky for you, I'm not one to hold a grudge."

He breathed a sigh. "You don't know how happy it makes me to hear you say that. Roxanne, you really do have the biggest heart of anyone I've ever known. That's why I can't wait to tell you my good news."

"Good news? I'm all ears for some good news. Wait until you hear about my miserable vacation—"

"Yeah. Yeah, but my news first."

Roxanne smiled. She wasn't bothered by the interruption. She could tell him about Tampa later. He really seemed excited about something. She couldn't resist this boyish side of him. He looked ready to burst if he didn't tell her his big news. "So, what's up?"

He took a deep breath. "Well, a lot has happened since the last time I talked to you. . . ."

She nodded for him to continue, all the while admiring the way the taut muscles in his thigh rippled as he crossed one leg over the other. "Like what? Why are you stopping now? Don't keep me in suspense," Roxanne said. But she was guessing that all the neglect she had put up with had finally paid off, and he'd gotten that promotion he'd been hoping for.

"I met this wonderful woman."

"What?"

"I met this wonderful woman. Her name is Kelly O'Brien."

"What?" She could not be hearing him right. Marcus hadn't come all the way over here to talk to her about some woman he was dating.

Now that he'd finally given her the news, Marcus chattered on like a dam that had broken and the words came flooding out like a long-pent-up river. He was oblivious to Roxanne's disbelieving expression. "Her name is Kelly O'Brien. I met her at one of the shops in Faneuil Hall."

When she was able to utter something besides an idiotic "What?" Roxanne said, "I see. So tell me all about her."

"Well, I met Kelly about a month ago. I was looking for some new silk ties, and Kelly came over to help me."

"So she works at the store . . . the store where you met?"

Marcus nodded enthusiastically. "Uh-huh. She's a salesgirl there. I never met anyone like her."

"Really?" Roxanne dropped the slice of pizza. It missed her plate and landed on the table. She left it there as she wiped the grease from her hands with a paper napkin. *So Kelly didn't own the store? Hell, she didn't even manage it. What had happened to having an advanced degree? Where was Kelly's five-year plan?*

Marcus' eyes were shining. Roxanne had never seen him this animated outside the bedroom. "Roxanne, you don't know how great it feels to finally tell somebody about Kelly."

"I can see that." She got a smile in return. That's when Roxanne realized the man couldn't pick up on sarcasm even if it jumped up and bit him on the butt. "So, just why *haven't* you told anyone else?"

It was Marcus' turn to lift his wineglass to his lips. He set the glass back down, then looked at Roxanne uncertainly. "Well, uh, see . . . I was just getting to that part. . . ."

Roxanne waited patiently for him to continue.

"Uh, Kelly is white. Actually, she's Irish . . . from Ireland. . . ."

A lifted eyebrow was her only response. At this point nothing Marcus could have said would have surprised her. Before, she hadn't been black enough for him. Hadn't been street enough, not down enough to hang with Mr. Inner City Life himself. But Kelly O'Brien from Ireland was.

"Really? And?"

"And, well, I've been dying to talk to somebody about Kelly. My family probably could care less. I only speak to them a couple of times a year, anyway. But my boys . . . how can I explain it to my fellas? Roxanne, this is love. They're going to crack on me . . . they wouldn't understand."

"And you wanted to tell me first because you knew I would understand?"

Marcus nodded. "Roxanne, I really want you to meet her. She's pretty, sweet, the nicest—"

Roxanne pushed away from the table, snatching the flowers out of the vase on her way up. Then she grabbed the pizza box, walked over to the front door, and opened it. "Get out," she said, surprised her voice was so calm.

"What?" he said in confusion.

"Get out."

He walked toward her. "Roxanne, I can't believe you're acting like this."

"I know, I'm probably tripping again, huh?" She threw the flowers out into the hall. If he didn't get to stepping a little quicker, Marcus would be next.

"I can't believe you're freaking out because I'm dating a white woman."

It was almost laughable. Roxanne only hoped she didn't look as crazy as she felt. She thrust the half-empty box at him. "You think it's because she's white?"

Marcus gave her an uncomprehending stare. "What else is there? She's white and you can't deal with it."

Roxanne did laugh then. "Marcus, her being white is like the straw that broke the camel's back. You say you came over here in search of some understanding? See, that was your first mistake. I understand you only too well. The problem is, you never took the time to understand me—or yourself, for that matter. Now get out of my apartment and do yourself and me a favor. Don't call me anymore. And if you see me on the street, turn and look the other way. That's what I plan on doing if I see you."

He jumped out of the way just in time to keep the door from hitting him.

Roxanne plopped down on the sofa and twisted her braids. She stared first at the aging building across from hers, then up at the intricate patterns the peeling paint and brown water stains made on the ceiling. Eventually, her breathing returned to normal.

She didn't have a fancy apartment or a high-powered career. She wasn't white, not that she wanted to be, and Lord knows when she'd *ever* meet a decent man. But she had something infinitely more precious—Roxanne had peace of mind.

Sighing, she closed her eyes. It was good to be home.

Chapter
37

The week had come and gone so quickly, it was Monday again and Gayle still hadn't caught her breath. The tension in her parents' house was starting to get to her, and it didn't help that Buddy had told her to stay out of his business when she'd tried to talk to him about his plans for the future.

Despite the mental and physical weariness she'd been feeling the night before, Gayle woke up almost an hour before the alarm was due to go off. She didn't feel tempted to turn back over and go to sleep. In fact, she was looking forward to going to work. Anything was better than enduring her mother's false cheerfulness and her father's undisguised glee over being back in the house in spite of Gayle's disapproval.

Gayle swung her legs over the edge of the bed. She took a quick shower and hurried out of the house before anyone else got up. She still wasn't in a talking mood where they were concerned.

When she got off the elevator at work, as familiar as she was with the floor layout, she was a little disoriented. She had done a lot of running around before she got to work, and maybe she was more tired than she had thought. Come to think of it, she'd been bone-tired ever since she got back home. Maybe it was time to start taking multivitamins or some kind of pick-me-up.

Gayle made her way past the rows and rows of desks, her heels clicking on the tiled walkway. The place was deserted, but she didn't mind. She was glad. She had been out of the office for three days last week, and she had a lot of unfinished business to attend to this morning.

Once she reached the tiny cubicle, she put the bags she'd been carrying on a nearby chair. She looked at the desk, which was littered with papers and computer printouts. The place was a mess. She began stacking everything into little neat piles on the right-hand side of the desk. They could be sorted out later on. All she needed now was some elbow room. It was so cramped in here.

Gayle walked over to the little mirror that was attached to the wall near the entrance to the cubicle. She had felt like a change today. Her hair was parted on the left side, curled slightly under with bangs in front. Gayle ruffled the bangs. They gave her a softer, younger look, she thought.

For the first time in God knows how long, she'd worn a dress instead of a suit to work. The short-sleeved, formfitting linen dress was yellow, with a modest V neckline, but plunged so low in the back that she had to wear a strapless bra. Gayle gave her hemline a self-conscious little tug.

She spoke to her reflection. "Come on, Gayle, it's not like you have on a micromini. The dress stops a couple of inches above the knee, but it's still professional-looking." She wondered what kind of reaction she'd get to the sunburst yellow color instead of her usual blue or black.

Satisfied that she looked presentable, Gayle turned away from the mirror. Her eyes quickly scanned the room, searching for something to do. She had all this time before the day officially began but didn't know what to do with herself. She frowned at the stack of papers on the desk.

Then she remembered the two bags she'd left on the chair when she'd come in. Might as well organize and unpack stuff, she thought, reaching into the bags.

That task took less than a minute. Gayle sat down behind the desk again and carefully folded each bag along the creases. She stuck them both underneath the desk when she was done.

Gayle drummed her fingers on the desk. She checked her

watch. Seven thirty-five. *Time was going mighty slow this morning.* She reshuffled the papers on the desk and sorted them into new piles.

She just couldn't get going. Her stomach gurgled loudly. Gayle rubbed a hand across it. She'd run out of the house so fast this morning, there'd been no time for her usual breakfast of coffee and cereal.

Bored, Gayle stared straight ahead, listening for some indication that other people were starting to arrive at work. Several minutes went by without the ping of the elevator stopping on her floor. Her eyes strayed to her unopened briefcase, then lit up. Gayle quickly clicked open its gold locks and took out her *Wall Street Journal.* No wonder she couldn't get into a groove. She wasn't following her daily routine. Time to see what was going on in the world of high finance.

Gayle took the clear plastic wrapper off and unfolded the paper. She checked out the front page to get a synopsis of the news and financial briefs. She quickly scanned the article titles, then went back to one of them to read it more thoroughly.

The yen was strong against the dollar. And the Japanese were dragging their feet about reducing trade restrictions on U.S. imports. She moved on to the Op-Ed section.

Gayle smiled to herself. Nothing had changed on that front. They were still ripping the Democrats' budget proposals to shreds. . . .

Engrossed in her reading, Gayle soon tuned out the telltale signs that the workday was slowly beginning. In the background, morning greetings were called out and the low humming and clicking of computer keyboards could be heard as people filtered in.

Gayle's face was hidden behind the paper as she held it up to see what had happened Friday on the stock exchange.

"Gayle?" an uncertain voice asked, causing her to jump in her seat and drop the paper onto the desk.

Reggie's lanky frame filled the doorway. He did a double take.

"Hey, Reggie. Welcome back," she said shyly. She

hastily gathered up the newspaper sections to cover her embarrassment.

He walked into the office, a quizzical smile on his face. He looked at the woman seated behind *his* desk and the little piles of food arranged so neatly on it. "Should I go back out and come in again?" he asked. "I must have gotten off on the wrong floor."

He turned around, but Gayle called him back. "Stop being silly, Reggie. You know you have the right office. I just wanted to surprise you."

"Wow . . ." he said, looking at the small feast that was taking up a substantial portion of his desk. There were croissants, and three kinds of muffins, a couple of apple fritters, and two large cups of coffee, and some juice bottles. "Wow . . ." he repeated. He shook his head and looked at Gayle for some kind of explanation.

"Wow? Is that all you can say?" she asked.

"No, I'm just bowled over. How did you know?"

Now it was Gayle's turn to look confused. "How did I know what?"

"How did you know it was my birthday? Who told you?"

His birthday? Oh, God. "Well, umm . . . I, umm . . . your birthday?" she stammered.

Reggie was smiling at her.

"What were you saying?" he prompted.

"Oh . . . your birthday. See, I, umm . . ."

Somewhere between being yelled at by her brother, emptying the overflowing ashtrays her father had left on the sink, and climbing into the shower this morning, Gayle had decided that she needed to start living *her* life, not other people's.

While she showered, she kept telling herself that she really needed to make some changes in her life. Then she remembered Reggie was coming back from his assignment in Chicago.

She was determined to do something to let the man know that she was interested. An anxiety-laced funk had enveloped her as she loaded all the stuff into the grocery cart this morning. But by the time she got to the bus stop, she had her speech all prepared. She knew exactly how she would explain being in his office. She would be cool, calm, and sexy. She had practiced it over and over in her head on the bus ride to work. Now he had gone and confused her. . . .

Seeing her dismayed expression, Reggie laughed. "Relax, Gayle. It's not my birthday. I'm just teasing you."

"Huh? Oh." Now she felt even sillier.

He sat down in the chair next to the desk. Picking up a spinach and cheese croissant, he offered it to Gayle, who was still trying to remember her speech. She absently shook her head. He put the croissant down on a napkin and regarded her with curious eyes. "So tell me, to what do I owe this very pleasant surprise?"

Gayle licked her lips nervously. "Well, I wanted to pay you back for the lunch you brought to my office that day. . . ." *Why is he looking at me like that? Like he's hanging on my every word?* She blinked. He was still staring. He had a bad habit of doing that.

"Uh-huh. That's nice, but you really didn't have to pay me back—"

Gayle jumped in, apologetic. "I know it's not as fancy as the picnic lunch you treated me to. I mean . . . I've been crazy busy since I got back from vacation last week, and I didn't have time to really plan and . . ."

"And now I'm *really* touched," he said. "Do you mean to tell me that despite your busy schedule, your top priority was making sure I got a decent breakfast?"

"I guess. . . ."

"If I didn't know better," he said speculatively, "I'd think you missed me or something." He paused, waiting for her to respond.

Gayle took a deep breath. *OK, Gayle, don't blow it this time. Just say it!*

She opened her mouth. "And I guess you'd be right. I did miss you . . . like . . . like . . . peanut butter misses jelly!"

Reggie pretended to fall out of his chair.

Gayle gave a little laugh. She had surprised herself, too. *How about that? Kind of corny, but still a bona fide flirtatious remark.*

He picked up a piece of paper off the desk and handed it to her. "I don't believe my ears. I want this in writing, because it may be the only proof I'll ever have that you really said what I thought you said."

Gayle stared at him and the piece of paper, then made a decision. She grabbed a pen from the desk and the paper from his hand and wrote, "I, Gayle Blackman, missed Reggie while he was away. I'm very happy he's back." She signed and dated it with a flourish and gave it back to him.

"Wow . . ." he said, staring at the slip of paper for a moment. "I'm speechless." He folded the paper with great care and put it in his jacket pocket. "Can we eat now?"

Before Reggie picked up the croissant, Gayle placed a hand over his. She'd gone this far, she might as well go for broke. "This breakfast feast comes with a small price," she said.

A roguish smile lit up Reggie's face. "You want a sexual favor?"

Gayle blushed, then smiled. "Not exactly. I—I was wondering if you'd be interested in going apartment hunting with me," she said shyly.

"Sure you don't want a sexual favor?" he asked hopefully.

Gayle rolled her eyes at him and shook her head.

"Apartment hunting sounds good." Then he added with a lecherous grin and suggestive eyes, "Who knows what that might lead to?"

Gayle met this proposition with what she hoped was an interested but not too inviting smile.

For once Reggie had run out of things to say. He silently offered her half of his croissant, and this time she accepted it.